An Enemy of My Enemy

To: Phyllis ———

For all the memories
And the good Times.
We were part of
the class of '58.
None better!
Best Wishes
↓
Good Luck
[signature]

# An Enemy of My Enemy

Robert L. Jones

greatunpublished.com
Title No. 580
2001

An Enemy of My Enemy

# TABLE OF CONTENTS

# PROLOGUE

## THE EYE OF THE STORM

*It had been nearly nine years since President George W. Bush*
declared the end of the Gulf War with the pronouncement "Kuwait
is liberated. Iraq's army is defeated. Our military objectives are met.
Kuwait is once more in the Hands of Kuwaitis, in control of their
own destiny . . . " Saddam Hussein had subsequently expelled the
United Nations weapons inspectors from Iraq. United States Air
Force pilots were still patrolling the skies over Iraq to enforce the
no fly zones in the north and the south. However, it was no longer
newsworthy. The longest running production since "Hello Dolly"
appeared to have played itself out. One could scan the newspapers
and TV in vain, but couldn't catch so much as a passing mention
of the scourge known as Saddam Hussein, an individual who had
monopolized the time and attention of the President and his
Administration for longer than most people could remember. But,
it wasn't just the result of a long admiring public losing interest in
the person that they had long ago loved to hate. He was now small
peanuts, having been relegated to a bit player, upstaged by a new kid
on the block–Serbian leader Slobodan Milosevic. There was a new
bully in town who almost overnight had stolen the show and the
focus of the world's attention, and in so doing, had muscled Saddam
out of the minds and hearts of the American public. A Satan, that

some claimed was even more evil, more menacing, and a greater threat to world peace than Saddam had ever been.

In an effort to stop Milosevic's ethnic cleansing of Albanians in Kosova, the President had made a political end run around the U.N. in support of NATO air strikes on Serbia. As "Operation Allied Force" thundered on week after week, with no end in sight, political leaders continued to insist that this war was a necessary evil to prevent an even greater conflict which could threaten the peace of the European continent. NATO aircraft had flown more than 400 sorties a day, reigning bombs on everything that even remotely resembled a military target. There were no body counts as there were in Viet Nam under General Westmoreland. However, each day NATO briefers, playing to a sympathetic public, went on national T.V. to describe a long list of targets that had been struck the previous day.

While it was readily apparent that the unrelenting bombing campaign was achieving its goal of destroying much of the logistics infrastructure of Serbia, at least one downside of the "parallel warfare" strategy had been exposed. Many of the people that we were there to save had long sense departed, creating one continuous line of refugees fleeing the country with their homes in ruin. The flood of refugees, associated humanitarian crises, and suffering was unparalleled in this part of the world since the dark days of WW II. Hundreds of thousands of people around the globe were planted in front of their televisions, eyes riveted on the screen as they watched this greatest of human tragedies play itself out in the living room of their homes. Finally, and mercifully, the 18-month war ended when Serbian leader President Slobodan Milosevic, cried "uncle," accepting a U.N. backed plan to halt 78 days of NATO bombing. Left in the wake of the war was human disaster, destruction, and economic ruin far beyond anyone's worst nightmare. Acting on good faith and principles supported by the highest of moral standards, the U.S. ended up trapped in a true "Catch 22" situation, whereby we literally had to "destroy the village to save the village."

Well, that's show business. One day you're flying high and the next, you're just a mere footnote in the annals of history. There were some who were now sarcastically suggesting that the U. S. had finally discovered a way to free the planet from the scourge of Saddam—simply ignore him and he would seemingly go away. In a world where everything is not black and white, the importance of many matters is determined relative to what else happens to be going on at the time. Had the reason that Saddam held center stage for so long and been the cause of so much concern on the part of the Administration, been at least partly attributed to the fact that it had been a slow news day. Was the "Wag the Dog" theory alive and well after all? Had Saddam been a convenient whipping boy-the best available opportunity to divert the American's public's attention away from sultry domestic issues? Had the new war in the Balkans with all its attendant publicity been all that had been missing to convince the American public that Saddam was no longer the menace to world peace that he had been for the past decade? Had the last installment played itself out and the final curtain come down on the Saddam Show?

*This book is dedicated to my wife, Carmelita.*

# CHAPTER ONE

# IN FOR A NICKEL, IN FOR A DIME

*Donovan awakes with a start, bathed in sweat and his heart* pounding wildly. He is curled up in a fetal position, trembling with fear. It was always the same recurring nightmare, even down to the minute detail. He appears to be in a small room at the bottom of a shaft far beneath the surface of the earth. He strains his eyes attempting to penetrate a cloud of smoke which fills the room. Suddenly, the haze lifts revealing a large poster depicting Saddam Hussein with a broad smile on his face, bearing the inscription "Donovan's Tomb." He began each day with it clearly etched in his mind, the defining roar of aircraft engines and the pungent odor of jet fuel. As the dream closed, questions always remained. Where was he and what was he doing there? With military service in Vietnam and the Gulf War, his days as a gladiator were over. But perhaps even more disturbing, was the obvious. Finding himself in a hostile environment that was clearly life threatening, why hadn't he made an effort to escape?

Stumbling the few steps from his bed to the bathroom, Donovan splashes cold water on his face in a futile effort to return himself to the present. Over the running water in the basin, he hears a vehicle approach in the driveway, car doors closing, and soon thereafter, door chimes. The sound of a man's voice and muffled conversation follow. Emerging from the bathroom, Donovan meets his wife at the top of the stairs gasping between breaths, that an individual with an impressive looking badge is asking for him. He descends the steps with trepidation wondering who this visitor is and what has brought him to his door on this particular day. His mind and heart are in a footrace, both stampeding along at a mile a minute.

One glimpse of the short, stocky-built man on the porch and Donovan has the sudden sinking feeling that a messenger from hell is about to serve his death warrant. His complexion appears as if he has been in a gravel fight, and his deep sunken eyes resemble two cigarette burns in a Georgia State road map. Dressed as though he just stepped out of an Army surplus store, the telltale sign of a sidearm protrudes beneath his khaki bush jacket.

The visitor flashes a badge identifying himself as Agent Blue of the CIA. Donovan ushers him into the family room and motions for him to take a seat on the couch. After a few minutes of the customary small talk about the weather and the beauty of the countryside, a bomb detonates beneath Donovan's chair.

"You've just won the lottery," Agent Blue declares with a disarming smile, "a once in a lifetime opportunity. First prize is an all expense-paid trip to Baghdad, Iraq, as an uninvited guest of Saddam Hussein. You have been selected as the primary operative in a covert operation to neutralize some dirty weapons he has developed, capable of being delivered on targets in Israel, Saudi Arabia, and Turkey."

The force of the blast caves in Donovan's diaphragm, causing him to gasp for each breath of air, leaving only an unintelligible stutter for speech. Staring into the "Fright-Night" face of Agent Blue in complete bewilderment, he is hoping to pick up some small sign that will betray his candor and reveal that this is all somehow, just someone's idea of a bad joke. A not too shabby day has suddenly deteriorated into a train wreck. He cannot believe what he is hearing, praying desperately that it is a case of mistaken identity. Blue had obviously intended to have this conversation with someone else, but had misread his map and arrived at his door instead. Surely, this will all be straightened out in a short time, and he can go about picking up the shattered pieces of his life that are strewn around the room. Responding to the ashen look of horror on his face and apparent loss for words, Blue volunteers, "What can I say, Mr. Donovan? In this business, everything is not as it appears to be."

"Why me?," Donovan sputters with exasperation. "I don't want any part of this. I have a family and I'm retired."

"Nice try, but let's not pretend we're fooling each other. That response doesn't square with everything we know about you. I've got your complete dossier here. Someone went to a lot of time and effort to put all this together. You don't think that I just happened to be in the neighborhood and stopped in to say hello, do you? Having done some work for us before, you know how thorough we are.

"Would you like to hear the short version? You've been an executive, so for your sake, we'll refer to it as the executive summary. The objective statement on your officer brief from your military personnel files stated that you only wanted to be considered for the most difficult and challenging missions, and that you were a standing volunteer for worldwide assignment at any time. You spent a total of three and a-half years in Southeast Asia during the Viet Nam War. In 1965, you were assigned to a USAF fighter wing which flew combat missions over North Viet Nam. Later in the war, you served as a Military Advisor to Viet Nam, Cambodia, Laos, and Thailand. After the war, you spent three years with the Presidential Wing at Andrews Air Force Base, and then a year as a Squadron Commander in a fighter wing at Kunsan, Korea. You completed your career as a Military Planner at the Pentagon. You are a graduate of the Industrial College of the Armed Forces, and the Air War College. In addition, you have an M.S. degree from the Air Force Institute of Technology where you were a distinguished graduate. You were awarded numerous military decorations during your military service, including the Bronze Star with 'V' for valor, the Vietnam Service Medal with three oak leaf clusters, the Republic of Vietnam Gallantry Cross with Palm, the Republic of Vietnam Campaign Medal, and the Purple Heart. Your commanding officers considered you to be completely dependable, highly motivated, a risk taker, fanatically patriotic, and possessing a passion for success that won't allow you to fail.

"You retired from the USAF to accept employment with a defense contractor in the Middle East. With a temporary lull in world wars and boredom setting in from flying a desk in the world's largest office building at the Pentagon, you were off once again in search of excitement. However, even with your nose for high adventure, I doubt you had any idea that the vast deserts of the Middle East can sometimes conceal a swamp loaded with gators, which is desperately in need of being drained. Your job was to train and assist the Royal Saudi Armed Forces in the operation and maintenance of their latest high-tech weapon systems acquired from the U.S. However, unknown to you or anyone else at that time, you were preparing them for the vital role they would play in the Gulf War. Defying your corporate CEO's direction to evacuate during Saddam's daily Scud attacks on the capital city of Riyadh, you and your staff stayed on through the end of the war to the delight of your Saudi counterparts, and to the dismay of your corporate headquarters back in Washington, D.C. Thirteen years after your arrival, you packed your bags and headed back to the U.S. At that time, you were quoted as saying, 'I feel like I am leaving home, rather than returning home.'

"On the personal side, you haven't been as successful. Your military career and extended time in the Middle East apparently took quite a toll on your family life. You are on your third marriage. Along the way, you managed to have three children, two boys and a girl, none of whom you spent much time with during their formative years. However, it appears that you have been working hard the last few years in an effort to make it up to them. Were the personal sacrifices worth all the fame and glory? In my own case, I would have to say that they weren't. But then, I expect that the two of us have a good deal in common. I am a career 'company' man, much as you were a 'military' man. Our job was to take orders from our superiors, and without question execute them to the best of our ability. They owned our body, mind, and soul 24 hours a day, seven days a week. Our personal needs were always secondary to those of our country, and no sacrifice is ever considered too great when answering your country's call. Right, Donovan?

"To cut to the chase, you are our man. In addition to the qualities that your commanding officers and corporate superiors saw in you, from everything we know, you also possess the one trait that may perhaps be the most important of all. It appears that you would be a very tough nut to crack if you were captured. The assignment we have in mind for you will require the utmost secrecy. In a 'worst case' scenario of mission failure, no one must ever find out that the U.S. Government was behind all of this. Our involvement must not be exposed, at all costs. It was just a bunch of rogues, paramilitary types out there playing Cowboy and Indian with the financial backing of some extremist patriotic groups operating outside the legal limits permitted by the U.S. Government. Should you be captured or killed, the U.S. Government will disavow any knowledge of your activities. As they say, Donovan, 'Success has a thousand fathers, but failure is an orphan.' Do you get my drift?"

"You've got the wrong man," Donovan states positively, wiping the perspiration from his brow. "I'm just an ordinary citizen living a simple life."

"On the contrary," Blue retorts sharply, "we know who you are and what you are. You are anything, but an ordinary citizen, and the life that you've led has been anything, but simple. You've been leading two lives, one is the truth and the other is a lie. The truth is that you are one of us and not one of them."

"I'm not that way anymore. I've changed," Donovan offers with quiet introspection. "I'm a family man with family responsibilities."

"You apparently have temporarily fooled your neighbors and many other people in this community, Donovan. On the outside, you may appear to be just an average citizen. However, underneath that outer facade, you can't change the spots that are indelibly burned in your soul and on your conscience. They are just as distinctive as if they had been placed there by a white hot branding iron during Spring roundup. Yes, peel back that thin layer of exterior veneer, and any resemblance to your 'ordinary' citizen quickly evaporates like the dew on a rose petal at high noon—once again, exposing the prickly thorns of the rose bush for the whole world to see."

"Get someone else," Donovan pleads, his skin suddenly cold and clammy, and his knuckles whitening as his grip tightens on the armrest of his chair. "There must be plenty of people out there who are as well or better qualified to do this job."

"You are much too modest, but I guess that comes with the new suit of clothes and the new you. You didn't just make the short list. You are the short list. Consequently, you're in very select company as it turns out—your own. The fact of the matter is, no one else possesses all the unique qualifications for this job that you do. And, before you ask how we happen to be able to make such a matter of fact statement as that, let me quickly explain how we came to that conclusion. To eliminate the human element and take as much subjectivity out of the decision-making process as possible, we called on your old friends in the 'Checkmate' office in the Pentagon to assist us. They put together a computer model and we developed an extensive list of qualifications desired in what we would consider to be the profile of the 'perfect' candidate. Using this laundry list as our criteria, we fed information into our data base from the personnel files of hundreds of candidates who possessed many of the desired qualifications. The computer algorithm did the rest. It plugged, chugged, and spit out a list of our candidates, ranked in percentile order, based on how well their total personal profile matched the desired criteria in our ideal candidate. Believe it or not, your name came out on top of the list with a computer assigned rating of 99 percentile. As a matter of fact, it wasn't even close. The candidate ranked number two was several points off your rating. Tie breakers weren't required. However, you also win that category hands down. In addition to the 13 years you spent in the Middle East with your understanding of Arab culture and language ability, you are the only candidate with feet on the ground experience in Baghdad. Do you recall a little job you did for us in Iraq in 1989?" Blue asks in an inquisitive tone.

"Isn't it wonderful what modern computers can do in the hands of trained operational research analysts with a little information provided by 'Big Brother' from government files? I'm sure you would want to be one of the first to congratulate us on our creative genius and ingenuity.

"I may have been at the wrong place at the wrong time on a few occasions in the past, but I am no hero. I was just doing my job," Donovan affirms, swallowing hard.

"Ah, yes, it's the old line that all heroes utter, only slightly masked with their best efforts at extreme modesty, 'I was just doing my job,'" mimics Blue. "I would have been disappointed if you hadn't brought it up. You get a couple of extra points for effort. However, after a careful review and study of your past, I have come to the conclusion that all those remarkable successes achieved under difficult and challenging circumstances, many times in a high-risk environment, were not just coincidental. I don't have the complete answer, and I doubt that you do either. Perhaps, you have been leading a charmed life, or your guardian angel has been putting in a lot of overtime. You have achieved levels of success where most ordinary mortals would have been swallowed up by the beast of adversity at the very first bend in the road. Somehow, you always managed to work your way through the pot holes and land mines without so much as breaking a sweat. You, Donovan, most definitely have the 'right stuff.'

"It appears that in spite of our kind offer to make you a national hero, you may require further convincing. At this point, why don't we just think of it as a clear case of reciprocity. You scratch our back and we'll scratch yours. You perform the requested service for us, and we'll reciprocate by promising you the full protection of the U.S. Government. For starters, no future IRS audits, no more probing of your past by the FBI, and no more questioning by Department of Justice personnel. That's one heck of a deal, wouldn't you say? When you stop and consider it, you'll find that we've just made you an offer you can't refuse. Just think of it as 'the last of the one time good deals.' Well, what do you say? Let's hear from you."

Donovan straightens himself from his slouched position in his chair, and fixes his antagonist with a steely glare. "What can I say, Blue? I guess I'm overwhelmed by the receipt of so much good news all in one day. You seem to be the Tooth Fairy, Easter Bunny, and Santa Claus, all wrapped up into one big package of pure joy, with a little ecstasy thrown in for good measure. It's kind of hard to imagine, such a plethora of attention and special treatment showered on a poor country boy from Oregon. This must be my lucky day, and I'm not even carrying a rabbit's foot, horseshoe, or a four leaf clover. However, in spite of your most generous offer, I must respectfully decline on the basis that I am not completely insane. Perhaps, I'm somewhat mentally and emotionally disadvantaged, but I still can tell the good guys from the bad guys, even in my worse nightmare—which I believe just occurred. I can't thank you enough for stopping by. It really made my day. Now, if you will excuse me, I need to get on with my life, or at least what's left of it at this point."

Agent Blue is relentless in pursuit of his prey, keeping him between his cross hairs at all times. He systematically covers the required turf, slowly narrowing the playing field and tightening the noose on his mark. "Cut me some slack and give us a little credit, Donovan. We've done our homework. Do you think I came all the way down here to the big dance to waltz around the room a few times with you, only to be stood up at the door and return home alone? And to think, I could have saved that fifty cents I spent at the flower shop on this boutonniere selected especially for this occasion. Apparently, in spite of my personal charm and best efforts to get you to accept Uncle Sam's marriage proposal, you seem to be harboring some residual doubts. However, in this case, there's no chance of our getting left at the altar. We're kind of like that splinter in your finger. At first it's just an annoyance. However, after awhile it may fester and bring you pain. In the meantime, it's always there reminding you of its presence.

"You appear to be a good person, and I hate to give good people bad news," Blue offers, doing his best to appear sincere. "I've been as forthcoming as I can. I'm here because we need your help. And the fact of the matter is, you're going to help us whether you want to or not. When all is said and done at the end of the day, we are convinced that you will see it our way. This might be a good time to start thinking about where you would like to spend your honeymoon."

"What is it about the word 'no' that you don't understand? You've misjudged me. I may be a patriot, but I'm no fool," Donovan exclaims, his voice rising in inflection as his temper flares.

"It was once suggested that you refused evacuation from the Middle East during the Gulf War because of peer pressure. Was that the real reason you put on your 'game' face? Were you trying to conceal a yellow streak that you were afraid would be exposed to your peers, and didn't want to be the first one to blink?"

Blue's remarks cut to the quick like a straight razor to the juggler, eliciting the hoped for response from Donovan. He bolts from his chair as if he has been shot out of a cannon by P.T. Barnum. Leaping over the coffee table that separated them, his hands grasp the agent's throat in a death grip. Donovan's wife hearing the sound of furniture and bodies crashing to the floor, runs screaming into the room. She is just in time to witness what her husband experiences- cold steal against the side of his neck, and the sound of a gun being cocked as the hammer retracts on a Colt 45 revolver.

"Hold it, right there! I'm just the messenger," Blue exclaims in a raspy whisper, gasping for breath through a collapsed wind pipe. "If you happen to get lucky and slip past me, they'll just send someone else in my place. Chances are, they won't be as patient and understanding as I've been. While having the life's breath squeezed out of me is not exactly my idea of a good time, I did witness some of the passion that we've heard so much about. If I were to press charges, they wouldn't have to dust my throat for fingerprints," Blue muses, massaging his throat with the fingers of his left hand. "Perhaps there is a bit of fire still burning in the old belly. Despite the picture you attempt to portray as a senile old artifact gathering dust in a museum, the embers haven't been completely extinguished, have they? You still seem to be driven. But, what is the driver? Is it fear of failure, not living up to expectations, or letting people down? Is it the ghost of Christmas past still lurking about, waiting for the opportune time to tell the world where all the skeletons are buried?"

Donovan makes no effort to respond. This is his worst

nightmare come true and there doesn't seem to be any end to it. He pushes back into his overstuffed chair as far as possible, hoping somehow he will just sink out of sight and disappear.

"You are a hard man to figure," Blue states, shaking his head from side to side. "In reading through your file, I was struck by the fact that you seem to be an enigma. Some portray you as warm, outgoing, and fun loving, with a great sense of humor. On the other hand, others picture you as cold and calculating, unrelentingly driven, undistracted by concerns or fears that would thwart most mortals. Which is the real Donovan? What is it that makes you tick? Obviously, by what I've just witnessed, you've still got a lot of emotion bottled up inside. Perhaps you would feel better if you unburdened yourself.

"Let's start with your trip into Phnom Penh, Cambodia, during the war. Who, What, When, Where, and Why?"

"I was assigned to the Military Assistance Advisory Group in Bangkok, Thailand, during the war in South East Asia. The majority of my time was spent working with the Royal Thai Air Force. However, I also supported an Equipment Delivery Team that was providing assistance to the U.S. war effort in the capital city of Phnom Penh, Cambodia. The Cambodian Air Force, like the Thai and Laotian Air Forces, was using outdated military equipment that had been acquired from the U.S. Government through the Grant Aid Program. The Equipment Delivery Team was reviewing aircraft mission support requirements to determine if all the necessary support equipment was on-hand to ensure the Royal Khmer Air Force could be as effective as possible in defending their homeland at this critical juncture in the war effort. It was my understanding that as a result of a treaty in effect, a maximum of 100 active duty U.S. military personnel could be in Cambodia at any one time. This restriction necessitated, on many occasions, someone having to depart the country before another individual could go in, even for a short-term temporary visit. In addition, it required the extensive use of, and dependence upon, civilian contractors to provide essential logistics services to the Royal Khmer Air Force. As such, civilian contractors became an essential and important element of support in the U.S. war efforts in both Cambodia and Laos.

Donovan continues, anxious to escape from the present by losing himself in the past. In between words, he draws deep breaths in an effort to calm himself. "On the occasion in question, the war effort was not going well in Cambodia. The Royal Khmer Air Force was doing its best, however, complaints had been voiced regarding shortfalls in logistics support that were impacting aircraft readiness. Each aircraft that was out of commission for spares or maintenance for even a short period of time, severely hampered the war effort. Therefore, it became necessary for someone to fly into the major air base located in the capital city of Phnom Penh and evaluate the effectiveness of the logistics support being provided by the contractor. I was chosen for that assignment. However, in spite of the U.S. assistance, the effort was doomed to failure. In January 1975, the Chinese-backed revolutionaries, known as the Khmer Rouge, launched a major offensive against the Government of Cambodia. They overran the capital city of Phnom Penh in April of 1975, and established their own Communist government to control the country."

"Well, thank you for the history lesson," Blue replies with a yawn. "However, according to the report that I have, it appears that you omitted a few critical details regarding that mission. Was it not true that you traveled and performed the evaluation in civilian clothes? Was it not also true that you were asked to leave your military identification behind in Bangkok while you were in Cambodia? And, furthermore, was it not true that as your aircraft was cleared for landing in Phnom Penh, the airfield came under mortar attack, and your first order of business was to beat a hasty retreat to the nearest underground shelter?"

"Yes, you are correct on all of the above. However, I was in no more danger than anyone else working the Cambodian war effort at the time."

"So you say. I guess the fact that you and I are here today having this conversation is an indication that you survived the dangers of that occasion. Once again, you must have been living right. However, did you ever stop to think of the consequences of your being killed or taken prisoner while in Cambodia? You were wearing civilian clothes with no military identification, in what appeared to be an obvious effort to skirt the restriction on the 100 active duty military head count that was in effect at the time."

"Quite frankly, I was too busy doing my job and concerned about the success of our war effort at the time to give it any serious thought. It was a job that needed doing, and I was the best qualified person to do it." Blue has cleverly spun the web and Donovan has unwittingly become entrapped in it, playing right into his hands.

"Well, well, I couldn't have said it better, myself. I see that we're making some progress, and you're starting to come around to my point of view. Now, what about this newspaper article in the Washington Post during the Gulf War? What was going on here?"

"I assume that you are talking about the article that appeared on the front page of the Business Section on August 23, 1990."

"You assumed correctly. Now, how about the what and why-fors of that little escapade?"

While by this time, it was intuitively obvious to even the most casual observer that Blue already had all the answers, Donovan continued to oblige. Perhaps by talking, he could prolong the conversation and postpone the inevitable conclusion that was sure to follow. "In the news article you referenced, the CEO of the company that I worked for expressed concern for the safety of his employees and their dependents living in Riyadh, Saudi Arabia. The situation in the Persian Gulf was growing more ominous each day. He wanted to get the women and children out immediately, and was close to a decision to evacuate the employees. However, in his words, 'the employees were being difficult.' He related a telephone conversation that we had earlier that day. During that call, I informed him that the employees stationed there, many of whom were retired military people, didn't want to leave and didn't want their families to leave. I also told him that if he tried to send the dependents out, we would resign. Two aircraft manufacturers with employees working in the region had already evacuated their employees. One of them pulled out one of its new planes, blackened out the name of the airline that was to buy the aircraft, and flew it to Saudi Arabia to pick up their employees. They offered extra seats to us, but we refused evacuation. Later in the same article, he explained that we had told him we did not feel threatened, particularly in the face of the growing U.S. military buildup. In addition, many of us who served in Viet Nam, also argued that it would send the wrong signal if we were to leave. It would look like we were walking out on an ally, as well as deserting our client, the Royal Saudi Air Force."

"It sounds as if you took the Gulf War personally."

"You're darn right. It was personal! How could it be otherwise?" Donovan snapped, his tone of voice dripping with righteous indignation and his eyebrows flaring. "My home and my family had been threatened. No one can take that lightly."

"Please describe what it meant to you."

Leaping to his feet with hands on hips in defiance, Donovan closes the distance between he and his adversary, delivering an "in your face" response laced with emotion. "When President Bush said, 'This will not be another Viet Nam,' it was like I had my life handed back to me. I had been stripped of my pride and dignity in Southeast Asia. Now, I had the opportunity to earn it back. Not have it given back to me, but to demonstrate that it shouldn't have been taken away in the first place. We only pass this way once, and no one wants to go out a loser. By staying in Saudi Arabia throughout the war, I was finally able to get that monkey, or rather that 800-pound gorilla of SEA off my back. I had come to think that I would take the memory of that bitter defeat to my grave. However, as fate was to have it, I was given a chance for redemption. I had truly been in the right place at the right time. I had an opportunity to participate in and contribute to a successful war effort. The victory and sense of accomplishment that accompanied it went a long way in replacing the personal feelings of discouragement and disillusionment from the failed effort in SEA. While the regret remains over the outcome in SEA, I was finally able to make peace with my conscience, and exorcize my personal ghost of Viet Nam."

As Donovan completes his soliloquy and reclaims his chair, Blue decides that he has heard enough. He is convinced beyond a shadow of a doubt that he indeed has his man. It is time to bring this conversation to closure.

"All right, I think I have a better idea of what makes you tick, and perhaps you feel better having unburdened yourself. Now, here's the deal. As I'm sure we both understand, you're in this whether you want to be or not. You've heard the old saying, 'In for a nickel, in for a dime.' It's in your best interest to declare yourself in the game early on so that you can at least cut the cards before they're dealt. A select group of personnel is being assembled at the Pentagon even as we speak to review an operational plan to neutralize the threat of Saddam's best kept secret. If you sign on now, we will extend you an invitation to sit in on this phase of the operation. As the primary operative, charged with the responsibility for carrying it out, you might be interested in how it all got put together. And, as an added bonus, if you agree to participate with the proper attitude, you might even be allowed to voice your opinion on some of the planning details. Why don't we just think of it as a spontaneous revival of latent patriotism?"

The pounding in Donovan's head drowns out the words. Any attempt to escape the grasp of the tentacles that entangled him, would be an exercise in futility.

Agent Blue's mouth widens in a fiendish smile, and his dark eyes penetrate Donovan's with satanic intensity. "It's your life, Donovan. Please give it some serious consideration. You have two choices as I see it. Option one has you coming on board up-front and being a full participant in the planning phase. In option two, you sit on the sidelines and pout, and we fill you in on the mission details after the fact. Then, you can live, or die as the case may be, with the results. I know! It's crooked. But at the moment, it's the only game in town. It's your call. What's your pleasure?"

# CHAPTER TWO

## OBSTACLE OR OPPORTUNITY

*Mitch Richman smiles as he pores over the file marked "For* the eyes of the National Security Advisor only." Placing his feet on his desk, he tips back in his chair. Mitch rarely allowed himself a moment of self-indulgence. However, he had certainly earned it and it was well deserved. All the hard work and personal sacrifice had paid off. The melodic strains of Neil Diamond softly singing "Sweet Caroline" on his CD player, said it all. "Good times never seemed so good."

It was late, O' dark thirty in civil service time. Everyone else in the office had long since departed. Rush hour would be slowing if not snarling the traffic on the Key Bridge between Rosslyn and Georgetown. The marrieds would be on their commute home to their families, and the singles to Georgetown to meet their friends for a drink, or perhaps try their success at picking up someone. Who knows, maybe tonight, they would get lucky. It was a beautiful Fall evening which meant that the TGIF crowds partying in the singles bars would soon be overflowing onto the sidewalks, and then into the street celebrating the end of another week in the Nation's Capital.

Mitch was an imposing physical presence. He stood six-foot two with sandy hair and blue eyes. The NSA kept himself in shape working out at an athletic club several times a week. He had learned long ago that the pressure and stress of working in the NSA took its toll, physically, mentally, and emotionally. Physical exercise was his one outlet and allowed him to maintain some semblance of a balance in his life. Each day, Mitch found time to squeeze in a three-mile run, followed by a tossed salad, and a glass of juice for dinner. He could still turn some heads, and had been mentioned in several of the tabloids for sale at the check-out lines in grocery stores to be among the top ten eligible bachelors. He was flattered by the attention. What man wouldn't be? However, the reference to "eligible" was somewhat misleading. Mitch was completely focused on his professional career, and at least for the time being, there would be no distractions, including pretty ladies.

There was a time when social life and dating were high on Mitch's list of priorities. However, those days had long since passed. This job had greatly altered his lifestyle. Still a bachelor, the NSA was tied closer to his desk than most fathers were to their wives and kids. During the day, he did the people things, attending meetings and listening to briefings. After the people went home, he did the paper things, remaining in his office as long as necessary to completely clean out his in-basket. Each new day could then begin with a clean slate. It had been a long day and an even longer week. However, as Mitch glanced around the room, he felt a renewed surge of energy and enthusiasm. Whoever said that "power is the ultimate aphrodisiac," had been absolutely right. As he surveyed the trappings of his office, his chest swelled with pride. Everywhere he looked were reminders of the past, jogging his memory as to where he had been at the time, and what he had accomplished. It was his version of an athlete's trophy case. "Who'd ever thunk it," Mitch muttered aloud to himself–"from humble beginnings to the office of the NSA of the most powerful nation on the face of the planet?"

Mitch Richman had done well in high school, but had gone through on cruise control, operating well below his potential. Following graduation, he joined the USAF, after an Air Force recruiter had extolled the educational opportunities available. Mitch attended night school in the Service, and after completion of his four-year enlistment, had saved enough to go full time and finish his bachelor's degree. But this time, he was a serious student, fully aware of the benefits of a higher education. Three years older, with his new found maturity and the personal discipline ingrained in him from military service, he went through the remainder of his undergraduate education like Sherman through Atlanta. Mitch graduated magna cum laude with a B.A. in Political Science at the top of his class at the University of California at Berkeley. He received a generous scholarship for his achievement and went on to Georgetown in Washington, D.C. where he received his Master's in International Relations. It was there working on his graduate degree that he fell in love with the city of Washington, or perhaps what it represented. The seat of government of the United States, make it the seat of power of the free world. Mitch vowed that he would return someday, and make his presence known in the city by the Potomac.

Mitch was offered a job out of Georgetown with Ross Perot at EDS. Working hard within the system, he was soon recognized as someone who had greater things in store for him. After successfully completing his apprenticeship, he was promoted as a member of the elite "Salvage Crew." This select group of individuals was assigned to manage programs that had gone south. The job had a short term objective—do everything within your power with all the resources of EDS behind you to cut corporate losses. After visiting with the client and completing the initial damage assessment, the squeeze was on. Mitch attempted to wring every last drop of everything there was to wring out of everything and everybody, including the employees, the client, the budget, and any other resources available. It was a great training environment, but came at a high price. Mitch worked in a pressure cooker. From the time he walked in the door in the morning until he staggered out late at night, he was wound up like the propeller on a toy airplane and spinning like a top. The NSA could now empathize with the basic lightbulb that you screwed in the socket, tripped the switch, and allowed to burn nonstop 24 hours a day, 7 days a week.

It was while Mitch was working a particularly difficult program glitch involving a client at the Pentagon, that he came to the attention of a high-level government official. Mitch was a fast study, always seeming to know which buttons to push and when. In addition, his energy, prowess at problem solving, and never say die attitude, were just the qualities desired in a staffer working in the office of the National Security Advisor. Back home in Washington, D.C. where he had dreamed of returning, Mitch wasn't about to blow this opportunity. He threw himself into his new job like never before. Frequently working around the clock, he spent more nights on the couch in the office than he did in his bed at home.

In any large agency, one of the primary keys to success is quickly gaining an understanding of both the formal and informal workings of the organization, and who the major players are that control those processes. The big picture was fairly straightforward. The National Security Council was a U.S. federal executive council established in 1947, to coordinate the defense and foreign policy of the U.S. Its members are the President, Vice President, and Secretaries of State and Defense. Their statutory advisors are the Chairman of the Joint Chiefs of Staff and the Director of the Central Intelligence Agency. The National Security Advisor, who is the assistant to the President for national security affairs, heads the council's staff. It would take Mitch a little longer to ferret out all the intricacies of the organization. However, there was one aspect of the office that jumped right out at him. In any organization, access symbolizes power. The NSA was the only person in the White House who had direct access to the President without going through the Chief of Staff. There was no question in Mitch's mind that someday, he was going to be sitting at that desk, answering the phone, "Office of the National Security Advisor."

It wasn't long before the big break Mitch had been praying for came along, catapulting him into the national limelight, and establishing him as an authority in Middle East affairs. He had achieved considerable recognition as the architect of the blue print for peace negotiations in the Middle East between Israel and the

Palestinian Liberation Organization. This proposed land-for-peace treaty, would guarantee the future security of Israel in exchange for a pullback in the Golan Heights, captured during the 1967 Mideast War. It had been a complex negotiation. Key issues included borders, water, security arrangements, and normalization of relations. He had produced an eight-page document, summarizing points of accord and discord, which became the basis for an eventual "core agreement." The next step had been to offer "bridging proposals" designed to close the gap where the two sides were in disagreement. They served as a point of departure for the negotiating parties, cutting through many of the normal preliminary hang-ups that keep negotiations from getting off the ground, including political posturing, and important considerations such as the shape of the conference table.

When the National Security Advisor submitted his resignation due to failing health and a desire to spend more time with his family, President Maxwell asked Mitch to replace him. His appointment was quickly confirmed by the Senate. Having briefed many members of congressional committees, they were aware of the successes he had achieved, and the President's trust and confidence in him.

Mitch attributed much of his political success to the fact that he was a consensus builder and a gate keeper. He used the missionary approach of "building on common ground." You don't go out to convert the world to your religion by pointing out and debating the differences in your beliefs. That was a non-starter, and about as effective as poking a sharp stick in your eye. You first attempted to accentuate the positive, by establishing a dialogue based on shared values. There are certain basic givens that all humanity embraces regardless of skin color, language, heritage, or religion. The same principles applied to the political process in consensus building. However, there was one big difference—compromise with a capital "C." It is a rare occasion when you get everything you go after in a negotiated settlement. Most successful political agreements or arrangements are based on the principle of "win-win." Each individual in the negotiation has to be willing to take something off the table for themselves and leave something for the other party. And, most importantly, they have to be convinced they have done the very best they could for themselves and their constituency. As an architect of foreign policy, Mitch had to bring the parties to the negotiation along one step at a time, ensuring that they were comfortable with each small bit of progress. Once one issue was resolved, it was time to move on to tackle the next stumbling block. Success depended upon meticulous attention to details, ensuring that all the "t"s were crossed and all the "i"s dotted. It was excruciatingly slow and demanded incredible patience, tolerance, and understanding. In some negotiations, it seemed that every detail under discussion resulted in a crisis. He likened the process to taking a hill in combat, where progress is sometimes measured in inches.

Mitch was a man of many talents. However, perhaps his greatest gift was the ability to quickly take the measure of a man, size him up, identify his weaknesses, and discover his soft underbelly—that which would make his knees buckle. Everyone had them. Some were just better at camouflaging them than others. The seven deadly sins were right up there at the top of the list—basic stuff like greed, pride, jealously, etc. In a moment of weakness, if properly tempted, most men would sell their soul to the devil himself and then spend the rest of their lives regretting it. Mitch had long since identified President Maxwell's weakness. Lacking in basic character and moral fiber, the President was first and foremost a politician. Principles were only as good as the mileage one could gain expounding them on any given occasion. As such, he was driven by public opinion polls and concern over his legacy. When confronted with what he perceived to be a threat to his popularity or his place in the history books, President Maxwell went limp, instant "milk toast," immediately rendering himself susceptible to manipulation. On these occasions, he could be played like a cheap accordion. All you had to know was which button to push and when.

You had to know the rules to get ahead in this business. Mitch knew the rules and played by them—his rules. Right or wrong was not determined by ethics or morality, but rather was a matter of willpower and perseverance. The ends certainly could justify the means. If something needed to be done, there was rarely anything sacred enough to stand in the way of doing it. If you had a problem bringing someone around to your point of view, you put them in a corner, and then confronted them with two bad choices. Forced to choose the lesser of two evils, they were already well down the yellow brick road. When the smoke cleared and the mirrors were rolled away, chances were that most unsuspecting people would never realize that they were no longer in Kansas.

Mitch had never considered himself ruthless, but clearly understood the principle of getting ahead at someone else's expense. After all, wasn't that the payoff for all those long hours and hard work. You manufactured your own good luck. The harder you worked, the luckier you became. He was prepared when someone else stumbled. And now, he couldn't seem to believe his good fortune. Mitch returned his chair to its upright position on the floor, and reopened the file folder stamped both "top-secret and urgent," that lay on his desk. It contained an intelligence finding from the National Security Agency. Saddam Hussein, in spite of the UN's best efforts to the contrary, had apparently been able to resurrect his weapons of mass destruction capability, developing weapons that threatened Turkey, Israel, and Saudi Arabia. And, it got worse. He also had the means to deliver them.

"Well, well, what have we got here?," Mitch exclaimed out loud. "Look what our close friend and associate has been up to this time." A small smile began at the corner of his mouth and quickly spread across his face. He swivelled his chair around facing the wall behind his desk. Squarely in front of the NSA, placed there to remind him of precisely such an occasion as this, hung his favorite quotation. It read, "A bump in the road can be either an obstacle to stumble over or an opportunity to be exploited."

Mitch allowed himself another smile, closely followed by a snicker. Who better to serve as the fall guy than the world's number one "Bad Boy," Saddam himself? Just look at the possibilities, he kept repeating over and over to himself. His mind raced ahead a mile a minute, identifying and examining various scenarios, and how, he as the President's National Security Advisor, could exploit the situation to get the maximum mileage out of the key role that he was prepared to play.

There is an old adage which says, "he who controls policy, controls the organization." As the National Security Advisor, Mitch was the President's chief visionary on the nation's foreign policy. Foreign policy was staffed and created by the office of the NSA. The Secretary of State and Assistant Secretaries had responsibility for implementation and oversight. He had a laundry list of world class foreign policy initiatives, but those pukes over in the State Department didn't have the competence to implement them. They had contracted out the nation's foreign policy to the United Nations. The wimps in the Defense Department weren't much better. Our foreign policy was largely ineffective because the U.S. was perceived around the world as a "paper tiger." There was nothing behind our policy and threats, and, therefore, no respect. What was really lacking, was presidential leadership. While the country had enjoyed a long run of economic prosperity at home, our foreign policy was devoid of purpose and direction. We had won the Cold War. The East-West superpower standoff with the Soviet Union was history. However, with the collapse of Communism, and unprecedented opportunities for U.S. foreign policy triumphs around the world, the U.S. had not stepped in to fill the vacuum. Consequently, regional conflicts abounded, and terrorists threatened Americans abroad.

As a student of history, President Maxwell was well aware of the major military engagements that the U.S. had committed itself to over the years in the cause of freedom. However, never having served in the armed forces himself, his perception of war had been assimilated from the pages of a text book. Committing Americans to combat and placing them in harm's way was something he was not comfortable with and would only consider as a last option. The thought of asking America's youth to do something that he had never had to face, didn't set well with him. That wasn't the worst character flaw in the world. Unfortunately, our enemies abroad had long ago picked up on this weakness and had taken full advantage of it. Consequently, when confronted with a crisis, the U.S. reacted tentatively, allowing itself to be pushed around by third-class world powers until military force was the only course of action left. However, by that time, we were frequently backed in a corner by the international community, and forced to fight our way out with one hand tied behind our backs. It was a loser's game, and Mitch shuttered every time he thought of it. Threats needed to be backed up with action. It was not enough to project military power around the globe. It had to be exercised. Successful foreign policy was based on respect. Respect is not awarded by the world community of nations based on good intentions. It has to be earned through good deeds. On occasion, these good deeds have to be written in the blood of our military personnel.

The NSA had political ambitions of his own for elected office and his present job was an ideal jumping off point. However, for the time being, his future was very much tied to that of the President. He must be perceived as politically correct, and properly motivated with no personal agenda of his own. That meant, loyal to a fault. He needed to reign-in his aggressiveness, being careful not to get out in front of the boss on foreign policy issues. Finding yourself out on a limb, only to have it sawed off behind you, was a sure way to bring a promising career to a screeching stop. But perhaps above all, Mitch needed to be a workaholic. Chances are, even as bright as he was, there was someone out there somewhere whom he might come up against someday, who was even brighter. That was something he had no control over. However, there was no excuse for being outworked.

Mitch closed the file and allowed a flicker of a smile to cross his face before returning it to his desk. He intended to make the most of this opportunity that Saddam had unwittingly dumped in his lap. Wouldn't it be ironic if his intentions at division and destruction, turned out to be the catalyst that would bring the squabbling parties together? A peace agreement in the Middle East ensuring the President's foreign policy legacy would also be a feather in Mitch's cap and a springboard to the presidency. He was determined to handle this just right, orchestrating it like a world-class conductor with his prize baton. He planned to bring in the strings, or pull all the right strings, just at the right time.

# CHAPTER THREE

## BEHOLD A PALE HORSE

*The National Security Advisor has a private audience with* President Maxwell in the Oval Office and briefs him on the intelligence finding from the National Security Agency. The Commander in Chief reacts with anger. Fists clinched and nostrils flared, a sea of crimson washes up the back of his neck, spills over his collar and splashes up against a set of tightly locked jaws.

"Just when we were beginning to make some progress on the Middle East peace talks and appeared to have a real opportunity for success—'Up pops the Devil.' He's doing this to torment me."

"Calm down, Mr. President. You're talking as if this thing between you and Saddam is personal. You can't let it become personal. It's business and you've got to keep it professional."

"I've invested all this time in the Middle East peace process to get the negotiations back on track and now he comes along and threatens to derail it once again. This is the proverbial straw that broke the camel's back. He has embarrassed and humiliated me for the last time. I will not allow Saddam to come between me and my rightful place in history. So help me, I'll turn Baghdad into one big parking lot." President Maxwell's face smolders with fury and malice as he bears the very depths of his emotional soul on this issue to his National Security Advisor.

"Don't overreact Mr. President. You need to take some time and think this through."

"Let's see if I've got this straight. Saddam is about to bomb the entire Middle East back into the stone age, and you're suggesting that I may be over reacting! I'm going to order the Crisis Task Force activated and I want you to give me a national security briefing on the situation as soon as possible."

***

One by one, the members of the National Security Council file in and take their customary positions around the massive executive conference table in the Situation Room located in the West Wing of the White House. A memo stamped "urgent," circulated yesterday afternoon over the signature of the National Security Advisor, had advised them of today's special session of the Council. While the unclassified memo did not specifically state the purpose of the meeting, they had all heard the whispers in the halls of the White House. As those who worked in this Administration knew, there were very few true secrets in government. What good was knowing a secret if you couldn't pass it on to someone? The best secrets were made to be shared with one or two close friends and possibly a stranger if a "quid pro quo" was in order. After all, it was still a secret. The only thing that had changed was that more people knew about it.

The rather ordinary clock on the wall, complements of the General Services Administration, which was also responsible for the nondescript carpet on the floor and the imitation executive office furniture that filled the room, read one minute before the hour of 10.00 A.M. President Maxwell's hallmark with his staff was punctuality. He was fastidiously punctual to a fault and insisted upon the same standard from his staff. No one was ever late to a meeting a second time. The public dressing down and personal humiliation received by an offender on the first occasion stood as a constant reminder that the only excuse for not being on-time was to be deceased. And, that only counted if you had three properly certified documents attesting to your demise.

To ensure that he was never late for a meeting, President Maxwell had a lower grade enlisted man assigned to the White House as a military aid. His sole responsibility was to carry around a copy of the President's daily schedule, constantly reminding him of where he was suppose to be, and what time he was supposed to be there. At precisely 10:00 A.M., as attested to by the sweep of the second hand across the large Roman numeral 'XII' on the face of the clock, the door swung open and the members of the National Security Council collectively sprang to their feet as the President of the United States of America briskly strode into the room. NSA members exchanged a wink of the eye as he entered, knowing full well that the office pool they put together last year, and contributed to each succeeding week was still alive and well. Would this be the first office pool in government history that would go uncollected due to perfect punctuality on the part of a government employee?

President Maxwell was well aware that he was a better politician and a vote-getter than he was a leader of the free world. With that realization came the key to his success. When appointing the members of his Cabinet and Administration, he had been determined to ensure the selection process was based strictly on merit as opposed to returning political favors or naming personal friends. After weeks of agonizing over hundreds of resumes and referrals, and personally interviewing dozens of highly qualified candidates, he had belatedly named his staff. Those involved in the process jokingly suggested that by the time the selections were complete, constitutional term limits would kick in and he wouldn't need a staff after all. Conspicuously absent from his selections were Ivy leaguers, Yuppies, and good-ole down-home boys. Judgment was still out on how well he had done. However, in his own mind, and that was most important, he was firmly convinced that he had put together the greatest gaggle of bureaucrats ever assembled under one roof. Seated at the head of the table surveying his staff this morning, President Maxwell couldn't help but feel a surge of old fashion American pride in knowing that his will was their will. Moreover, they were all bound by an oath of allegiance to serve the country that had entrusted them with this enormous responsibility, to the best of their ability.

On his right was Hal Justin, his trusted Chief of Staff. Some previous Presidents had not included their Chief of Staff in meetings of the NSC. However, President Maxwell didn't attend a meeting without him at his side. After all, how was he going to successfully direct traffic around the White House, and in and out of the Oval Office, without a complete knowledge of everything that went on around the President? Seated on his immediate left was the Vice President, Tim Staley. He had been located in that seat of prominence in close proximity to the President after a considerable amount of thought. The positions of Secretary of State and Secretary of Defense seemed to create a natural rivalry in the Cabinet. They were always jostling to see who could curry the President's favor. It was well known in government that proximity to the seat of power was an outward sign of power itself. Therefore, to avoid the appearance of favoritism or preferential treatment to either of his Secretaries, he had placed the Vice President in that chair. His Secretary of State, Peter Whittenburg, and his Secretary of Defense, Grant Sherman, occupied the next positions, seated across the table from each other. The next tier of personnel, including the Director of the Central Intelligence Agency, Jeff Hendricks, and the Chairman of the Joint Chiefs of Staff, General Broughton, were seated further down the table. Mitch Richman, the National Security Advisor, and assistant to the President for national security affairs, headed the National Security Council's staff. He was the individual who customarily gave the preponderance of the briefings and steered the discussion of the Council's business while the President presided over the meeting. As such, he was seated at the "secondary" head of the table at the far end. In this position, he could access his briefing charts and maps, and also be easily seen by everyone else.

Mitch Richman, looks up from his notes and begins to summarize. "The UN weapon's inspectors have been off the job since mid-December 1997, opening the way for Saddam to resurrect his chemical and biological weapons program. U.S. economic sanctions remain in place, and we continue to enforce the 'no-fly' zones over northern and southern Iraq, leaving him little rattle room to re-establish his military capabilities to the level prior to Desert Heat and Desert Storm. However, Israeli intelligence reports indicate that Iraq has reconstructed facilities associated with its weapons of mass destruction program, and is continuing the covert weapons development effort. The missile production facility at Ibn al-Haythem has physical facilities large enough to produce longer-range missiles than the SCUDs fired at Saudi Arabia and Israel during the Gulf War. In spite of our best efforts to the contrary, Saddam has still been able to pursue the development of chemical, biological, and nuclear weapons as well as the missiles to deliver them on his neighbors in Turkey, Israel, and Saudi Arabia.

"Those," declared the NSA, "are the known facts, gentlemen. Our intelligence agencies have spent a great deal of time verifying the Israeli findings and cross-checking various sources. All indications are that Saddam possesses a credible threat."

"I don't want to rule out anything at this juncture," interjects President Maxwell, eager to crown his checkered presidency with the legacy of a major foreign policy achievement. "I want to review a full range of options with spirited debate, uninhibited by preconceived notions of what is or what is not permissible." The President had made an agreement between Israel and the Arabs his top foreign policy priority. The country had enjoyed a remarkable period of economic prosperity at home, but he still felt that he needed a standout foreign policy achievement to cement his place in history.

"There, literally is nothing that I would not be willing to do if I thought that it would promote a lasting peace in the Middle East. We have an opportunity within the reasonable near future for a peace agreement between Israel and its neighbors. However, like all opportunities in life, it is fleeting. We cannot freeze the moment. We are either going to move forward or slip backward. Success will require both hard choices and hard work within an abbreviated period of time. The region could still reverse course. The enemies of peace, extremists, and terrorists are also hard at work. Saddam is the major stumbling block to achieving our objective. As long as he prevails, a threat to peace in the region remains. One way of viewing this whole situation, is that the road to a lasting Middle East peace leads through Baghdad, Iraq.

"There's nothing like a good old fashion surprise. Right, Mr. Director? Why wasn't the CIA on top of this?" The President's blood pressure had just gone right off the scale. He was shaking uncontrollably and veins were bulging out on his neck. Being one-upped by Saddam, had been his worst nightmare. This madman seemed determined to come between the President and his legacy.

Jeff Hendricks, longtime Director of the CIA, glances around the table at the ear-to-ear grins on the faces of his contemporaries. Today is apparently his day in the barrel. He is from the old school, having risen through the ranks of the organization on the spy agency's campus at McLean, Virginia. The majority of his time as a field agent had been spent down in the trenches engaged in a battle of "I Spy" with the Soviet Union. The big East-West thaw in the Cold War had brought with it the demise of the KGB, a singular event that had ironically been the blow which literally brought the CIA to its knees. With the competition for world domination eliminated, the agency's budget and thus, staffing had been cut to the bone. When the reductions were fully implemented, the CIA would be a mere shadow of its former self. Although Director Hendricks was still resisting the inevitable downsizing the agency was going through, it was a losing battle. His reluctance or inability to read the handwriting on the wall only brought further scorn upon the agency and its reputation. Had there really been "one" hiding behind every tree all these years, or had it merely been a figment of the imagination of a government agency dedicated to its own preservation in the finest tradition of J. Edgar Hoover?

Director Hendricks clears his throat, straightens his tie, and weighs in forcefully. He is not about to let his agency become the scapegoat for this fiasco. If those U.N. weapons inspectors had done their job, we wouldn't be in this mess today, he mummers to himself. "As you are aware, Mr. President, Carter dismantled the

CIA's network of spies due to the agency's role in overthrowing governments in Viet Nam and Latin America. We have been attempting to rebuild the network and place our people in critical areas in the field ever since. It takes years to place a mole in close proximity to the principal, just as it takes a worm time to reach the core of an apple. Long periods of proven patriotism and loyalty are required before you are trusted in a foreign culture. Once an agent goes in, he is basically on his own. Contact and communication with the outside world are few and far between to minimize the risk of detection. The life of a successful mole is similar to that of a cockroach—friendless and in constant fear of being discovered. The ultimate success of a mole is dependent upon commitment. In terms of priority, there is nothing in second place. Anything and everything else must be placed far behind commitment to cause, even to the point that you must be prepared to swallow the cyanide pill if you are compromised, captured, or tortured.

"In all fairness, Mr. President, we have not been soft on Saddam. Baghdad's military move against their Kurdish population in 1996, broke up a CIA covert operation designed to generate indigenous opposition to Saddam, and, perhaps, spark a coup. It will be months before our agents can be inserted back into Iraq to supply the detailed intelligence and on the ground assistance that may be the difference between failure and success, humiliation and pride, and between losing lives and saving them. In addition, Iraqi troops blanket the streets of Baghdad, making it very difficult for U.S. agents to obtain intelligence.

"Perhaps this is just supposition, another one of Saddam's idle threats. It isn't the first time he has threatened to use weapons of mass destructions. During the Gulf War, the Iraqis broadcast a 72-hour warning for all loyal Muslims living in Riyadh, Saudi Arabia, to evacuate the city as it was going to be destroyed on January 27, 1991. Saddam was quoted in that broadcast as stating that after the attack, there would not be so much as a bird alive in the air, a fish in the sea, or any living creature on the ground. The implication was that some form of a chemical, biological, or nuclear weapon was going to be used. To add credibility to his threat, Saddam had been publicly announcing in advance some aspects of his military operation. On these occasions, the predicted events occurred right on schedule. This threat understandably bothered many people. Consequently, as the deadline approached, many Riyadh residents evacuated the city and sought temporary refuge in the desert. The capital city became a virtual 'ghost town.' However, the appointed 'doomsday' came and went without incident. One day later, on January 28, 1991, a Voice of America broadcast quoted Saddam Hussein as saying that Iraq SCUD missiles were capable of carrying nuclear, chemical, and biological warheads, but he was praying his country would not have to use them."

Mitch Richman, sensing that the Director had made a conscious effort to divert attention away from the seriousness of the problem at hand, jumps back in with both feet. "I understand where you're coming from Mr. Director, but this time is different for two important reasons. First of all, on the occasion you referenced, he used a verbal threat. We have found that as long as Saddam is talking, he is fairly predictable. It's when we don't hear from him that we get worried, as we don't know what he's up to. And, in this case, he fully expected that his sinister plot would remain a deep dark secret and never see the light of day. Secondly, we have never previously been able to confirm that Iraq possessed weapons of mass destruction and the ability to deliver them. That fact has now been confirmed. So, this is an entirely different scenario."

"May I remind you gentlemen that Iraq has an incoherent command & control decision-making system. Saddam is the National Command Authority. However, as we have learned from past experience, he is very unpredictable. There is no way to determine what that volatile dictator will do next. With his finger on the button, we cannot anticipate what will happen in a crisis." All heads at the table quickly swivel in the direction of the speaker. The comment came from a distinguished gentlemen with short, iron-gray hair, wearing the uniform of a four-star Army general. Although no one would admit that the primary selection criteria for the

Chairman of the JCS was physical presence, recent history seemed to bear that out. General Broughton was a full load and a half, who it appeared, would be just as comfortable playing the "incredible hulk" on a movie set. His enormous chest was more than large enough to accommodate the jumbo bowl of fruit salad that he wore. Rumor had it, that the primary reason the U.S. Army introduced the Abrams' M-1 Main Battle Tank, was because he had outgrown the M-60. They took the general's measurements and passed them on as military specifications to the defense contractor to size the new tank.

General Broughton was a graduate of the U.S. Military Academy at West Point. That's Hudson High, as the other inter-service Academy rivals located at Annapolis and Colorado Springs refer to it, because of the school's location on the bank of the Hudson River. He rose to national prominence as the Commanding General of the lst Infantry Division, "The Big Red One," stationed at Fort Riley, Kansas. General Broughton conducted the initial allied ground attack during the Gulf War, penetrating Iraqi's defensive position. That was followed up by a night attack against elements of Saddam's elite Iraqi Republican Guard, thereby, dispelling the aura of their invincibility. For an encore, he led the allied force's advance into Kuwait which cut off the Iraqi's escape route. Successful execution of this "hammer and anvil" military maneuver led to the resulting annihilation of the retreating Iraqi Army on the "Highway of Death." General Broughton was accustomed to letting his size, rank, and ribbons speak for him. That was more than enough to intimidate most people. However, here with the rest of the elephants, no quarter was expected and none given. He was just another one of many heavyweights.

"Perhaps there's an opportunity to snatch Saddam or have him assassinated." Although everyone in the room recognized General Broughton as a hawk, they were nevertheless taken back by the abruptness of his suggestion to personalize this situation and have a go at Saddam. While heads along both sides of the conference table nodded up and down like a tree full of owls, it was just a spontaneous outward display of wishful thinking that no one other than the

General himself took seriously.

Director Hendricks ponders General Broughton's remarks, waiting for the undercurrent of murmurs moving around the table to subside, and then responds. "This wasn't our first attempt to topple Saddam. During the Gulf War, U.S. military strike planners intentionally targeted headquarters, command bunkers, and palaces in hopes of killing Saddam. At one point, analysts discovered through review of TV footage that Saddam appeared to be moving about the country in a mobile home. For the next few weeks, our warplanes then conducted a hunt for a Winnebago."

President Maxwell had been leaning back in his chair, quietly listening to the give and take among his staff. However, he couldn't pass up the opportunity to chuck another spear in the direction of his CIA Director. Man, how he hated surprises. Especially when they led to national, or even worse, international embarrassment. "Since you are always so well informed, perhaps you can enlighten the rest of us?" He spat the words out like a rifle shot fired with intent to inflict deadly harm.

The CIA Director winced as he took a direct hit. He was now on his bicycle, pedaling furiously as if climbing a hill on the last lap of the "Tour de France." Tiny beads of perspiration suddenly appeared on his forehead. He reached into his pocket and removed a neatly folded silk-monogrammed handkerchief boldly displaying the letters "JH" which he used to carefully wipe them away. Avoiding eye contact with the president and carefully choosing his words, Jeff Hendricks, responds. "Saddam is under the most intense surveillance that we can bring to bear. We're using satellite photos, electronic eavesdropping, and informants to track his movements closer than ever. However, we can't remove him by force. He is so well protected that it would be a blood bath. Saddam is constantly surrounded by a small army of personal bodyguards. When he's on the move, he's escorted by military personnel armed with assault rifles, and trucks carrying surface-to-air missiles, rocket-propelled grenades, and a mounted multiple-rocket launcher."

General Broughton nodded his head in agreement. "We're

dealing with a mad man. Saddam is a dictator, and the quality of life under his regime is unacceptable. He has a long track record of terror, including gas attacks on his own people, the summary execution of subordinates who lost favor with him, the killing of his own relatives, and an apparent assassination plot on a former U.S. President. There are periodic purges of those in trusted positions. People lie awake in their beds hoping against hope that they don't receive a knock on their door in the middle of the night, only to disappear and never be heard from again. Saddam blames the U.N. sanctions for the critical shortages which exist in his country. However, he continues to spend millions on military weapons, his palaces, and his propaganda war with the U.S., while his people go without medical supplies and food.

"Add to all of that, Saddam's 'scorched earth' policy when his forces withdrew from Kuwait, destroying everything in sight and leaving the oil fields ablaze. And, Mr. President, let us not also forget that, first and foremost, Saddam is a terrorist. His finger print is on terrorists acts around the world. It is a well-known fact that Iraq encourages, supports, and funds several terrorists' organizations. We need to stop treating him like a King, and start treating him like a terrorist. We need to take the gloves off, Mr. President. Although, it certainly was not his intention, Saddam has unwittingly handed us a golden opportunity. He thought his sinister plot would never see the light of day. I see it as a 'carte blanche' ticket for us to react with relative impunity. This latest threat to world peace will justify our actions. We should take advantage of the situation and make him pay dearly. We need to complete what we didn't finish last time. Let's go for the jugular," the general declares emphatically, banging his West Point Academy ring on the table for emphasis.

Secretary of State Peter Whittenburg had hunkered down in the deep weeds as long as possible. If he didn't surface soon, they would send the bloodhounds in after him. The Secretary was a career diplomat having served in several important postings abroad, including Ambassador to France. However, he had never experienced political infighting this brutal before. As Secretary of

State, he occupied what was considered the most challenging of all Cabinet positions. He was the designated fall guy for international diplomacy. When the ball was rolling downhill, the President or the NSA took most of the credit. However, when things went south, he was road-kill. There were hundreds of countries in the world. On any given day, chances were that at least one of them was having a bad hair day. When that happened, stuff hit the proverbial fan, most of which got blown in his direction. Like smell on a skunk, it was his job to pick up the pieces and run with them. Then, there were the usual trouble spots like North Korea, China, and Iraq which were always a pain in the backside.

The Secretary played a lot of dodge ball. Unfortunately, most of it was three on one, with the Secretary of Defense, Chairman of the JCS, and National Security Advisor, all ganging up on him. As isolated as he was on major foreign policy issues, the Secretary felt like the Lone Ranger on many occasions. The only thing missing was a few lines from "The William Tell Overture." He wasn't on Saddam's side, but even an individual as disliked as Saddam needed to be viewed in the proper perspective. It was easy to get emotional about the unfortunate plight of the Iraqi people, but major foreign policy decisions should not be driven by emotion. As much as his esteemed colleagues didn't want to hear it, they apparently needed to listen to this message once again. "Gentlemen, it appears that we need to refresh our memories as to why President Bush pulled the plug on the Gulf War just as it appeared that we were getting up a good head of steam and had the Iraqi military on the run in what must have been 'the mother of all retreats.'

"In the first place, the U.N. resolution which authorized the Allied military action in the region was couched to 'free Kuwait,' not topple Saddam. Secondly, there was a well-founded concern that if Allied Forces pursued the fleeing Iraqi military into Iraq, the fragile Arab coalition might come unglued. Thirdly, as previously alluded to, the whereabouts of Saddam was unknown. Finding him would have been like looking for a needle in a haystack. We would have had to conduct a house-to-house search throughout the entire nation of Iraq. Worse case would have been that we stumbled onto him. With all the personal security which surrounds Saddam, it would have most surely been a blood bath. And last, but perhaps most important, let us not forget that the nation of Iraq is composed of essentially three separate mini-states. We've got the Kurds in the north, the Sunni Muslims of central Iraq, and Shi'ite Muslims in the south. None of these groups is strong enough to survive as a separate entity. Without Saddam's strong-armed dictatorship at the top, the country would undoubtedly fragment. Turkey, Syria, and Iran would all most certainly move swiftly to take advantage of the situation. For years, Iraq and Iran have balanced each other off in the power struggle in the Middle East. With Iraq fragmented, Iran would be left as both the dominant economic and military power in the Gulf. That scenario would be our worst nightmare come true, and something that none of us seated here today would ever want to see. Therefore, any efforts to topple Saddam would not have been in the national interests of the United States and its Western allies."

CIA Director Hendricks had taken so many hits that he was as jumpy as a long-tailed cat in a room full of rocking chairs. However, he was most appreciative of some late hour, but nevertheless much needed support from the Secretary of State. "The system is our enemy, Mr. President. It's the system that's broke and at fault. It's not us. We inherited it and we're stuck with it. There will be no assassination attempt. May I remind all of you that it is a violation of both U.S. and international law. We are a nation of laws underwritten by the most noble of human principles. We play by the rules, only coloring outside the lines from time to time as we can justify or rationalize it. In the meantime, Saddam lives in a world and plays the game as if there are no rules and no boundaries. His pictures have no borders on them. He is literally getting away with murder with relative impunity. However, in spite of how lopsided the playing field may appear to be gentlemen, we can't afford to take the lid off Pandora's box on this one. If it became known that the U.S. was behind an assassination attempt on Saddam, Mr. President, you would immediately become the target of every terrorist organization

in the world. We might as well paint a large bull's eye in the middle
of your back. There would be no way that the Secret Service could
protect you when you ventured outside the White House. We would
have to erect a barricade around the entire White House, and you
would become a virtual prisoner in your own home."

Secretary of State Whittenburg takes a calculated gamble,
attempting to pile it on higher and deeper without some of it falling
off the wagon on him. "We're spending $2 billion a year on a policy
of containment of Iraq. This policy is not working and the American
public is becoming less and less enamored with it, each passing day.
In addition, it is obvious that the economic sanctions have failed.
Saddam defies us at every turn and has rebuilt his weapons of mass
destruction program. Even the 'no-fly' zone policy we established to
provide a measure of protection for the Kurds of northern Iraq and
the Shi'ite Muslims of southern Iraq who rebelled against Saddam in
the aftermath of the Gulf War, has been short of a rousing success.
Iraq continues to fire on our pilots patrolling the 'no-fly' zones. In
addition, their pilots continue to violate the 'no-fly' zones at will.
And, to add insult to injury, Saddam has offered a reward of $14,000
to any Iraqi who shoots down a U.S. warplane. In the mean time,
the 'flimflam' man continues to jerk us around, and it is the Iraqi
people who bear the brunt of his intransigence. Our critics are now
suggesting that the Administration lacks a coherent foreign policy
approach in the Middle East. We are being accused by foreign policy
experts as pursuing short-term gains at the cost of lasting solutions.
I'm afraid at this point, Mr. President, I'm also confused. What is our
foreign policy in regard to Saddam Hussein's Iraq? Is it containment
or removal?"

President Maxwell appears as agitated as a honey bee in an
empty fruit jar, clearly not appreciating Secretary Whittenburg's
comment one bit. He shoots a multi-daggered look in the direction
of his Secretary of State that very distinctly says, "we'll discuss this
issue later, just you and I, out behind the woodshed."

"What about our program of training Iraqi opposition to
overthrow the Saddam regime?" Vice President Tim Staley had

just spoken up for the first time. Not unlike small children, Vice Presidents are supposed to be seen and not heard. Tim fit that stereotype perfectly, preferring to remain on the sidelines rather than mix it up with the elephants. He had ended up in the second spot on the ticket as the result of a major political compromise forged at the party's national convention in Chicago. President Maxwell had polled well in the northeast, midwest, and western states. However, he was seen as vulnerable at the ballot box across the south. Tim Staley, the favorite son and Governor of Texas, had suddenly appeared out of nowhere as the perfect running mate. He was popular and well respected in the south, and his selection guaranteed that Maxwell carried the state of Texas with its important electoral votes.

Mitch Richman surveys the room to see if there were any takers. The topic the VP has just surfaced is a hot potato that no one is eager to grab hold of. He decides it is up to him to fill the vacuum. Temporarily discarding his long held principle that "discretion is the better part of valor," he takes a deep breath and reviews the bidding on the issue of training Saudi dissidents, essentially rehashing the earlier position which had been laid out by the Secretary of State. "In response to the President's call for an end to the Saddam regime, Congress approved $97 million to fund Iraqi opposition groups under the Iraq Liberation Act of 1998. However, as you may recall gentlemen, the U.S. military commander in the Persian Gulf did not buy-in to our strategy for dumping Saddam. He stated that the Iraqi opposition groups are not strong enough to topple Saddam, and arming them could splinter the country and further destabilize the region. These groups are fragmented and their ability to cooperate is questionable. As bad as the current problem is, it is possible to create a situation that could be even worse. In addition, two of the seven groups that we certified as eligible to receive U.S. support have said they do not want the assistance. I'm afraid that I don't hold out much hope for success in this area. The record on insurgencies is clear. Most of them fail, and innocent bystanders are killed along with rebels."

Arming and training people to defend themselves was a topic

near and dear to Secretary of Defense Grant Sherman's heart. Having spent the better part of his life as a senior executive in the defense industry, he knew which side his bread was buttered on. After years of marketing and smoozing senior defense department officials in an effort to peddle arms, he was now sitting on the other side of the table. However, this political thing was only temporary. One day, he would walk back through that revolving door into the real world. When he did, he didn't want to have to mend any fences with his future employers. As a former Secretary of Defense, his political clout in a CEO position with a major defense contractor, or as a lobbyist on Capitol Hill peddling influence would be invaluable. This little patriotic stint as a public servant would more than pay for itself in a few short years.

The Sec Def usually let General Broughton act as his point man, slashing and burning the loyal opposition as was customary for a military man of his reputation. However, this was an issue that needed name identity— Grant Sherman's name. He needed to be on record in support of the Congressional plan. It wasn't often Congress could be counted on to support issues such as this. Now that it had spoken, the National Security Council needed to give them the benefit of the doubt. However, their legislation which sounded good in theory, didn't pass muster when it came to practical application. "While we don't see Iraqi opposition groups as a short-term solution to Saddam's regime, we plan to continue to work closely with them in an effort to promote change within Iraq. The first three Iraqi opponents of Saddam Hussein recently completed a two-week course in non-lethal training called 'Civil-Military Strategy for Internal Development,' at Hurlburt Field, Florida. Obviously, two weeks training of three individuals is not going to produce a finely honed fighting machine. It will, however, serve as a pre-screening whereby U.S. instructors and observers can get an up close and personal opportunity to observe potential future leaders of the resistance movement. Those possessing the prerequisite qualities, including stability, commitment, and trustworthiness, can then be earmarked for more specialized in-depth training at a future date."

A rare moment is about to occur in the deliberations of the National Security Council where the NSA, Sec Def, and Sec State were all lined up on the same side of an issue. Secretary of State Whittenburg adds his concerns to those espoused by his contemporaries.

"Aren't we going way out on a limb here? This could all come back to haunt us big time. Once you train these individuals, how do you know that they won't turn on you? What guarantee do you have of good citizenship? How can you be sure they don't become a double agent, working for the other side, passing on information which will compromise our operational plan and endanger the lives of the participants? The last thing this world needs is the good taxpayers of the United States creating additional terrorists through the training of extremists and fanatics. In this regard, I am reminded of the fable of the fox and the scorpion. A scorpion approaches a fox at the edge of a stream and requests transportation to the other side. The fox, weary of the undependable and deadly poisonous insect, replies that he cannot trust the scorpion to ride across on his back. The scorpion attempts to alleviate the fox's fears by reminding him that if he stings him in midstream they will both perish in the water. Accepting the scorpion's logic, the fox invites him to hop on and jumps into the swift current of the stream. Midway across, the scorpion stings the fox. As he feels the deadly poison overtaking him and sapping his remaining strength, the fox inquires, 'Why did you sting me? As you indicated, now we will both die.' The scorpion responds, 'yes, I know. But I couldn't help myself, it's my nature.'"

Mitch, appreciative of support from both the Sec Def and Sec State on this one, now saw an opportunity to put the cork back in the bottle. "The bottom line, Mr. President, is that while it makes for good hypothetical discussion, the stark reality of the situation is, dependence upon opposition groups to overthrow Saddam isn't a viable option that we can consider within the narrow window of opportunity that we are faced with in neutralizing the current threat. And, as hard as it is to stomach, gentlemen, up to this point, Saddam has proven far better at hatching conspiracies and at stopping them, than we have been at planning them."

"We've eliminated a lot of things that weren't good ideas, but we still have no workable solution." President Maxwell was now feeling they had made a complete 360 degree circle on this issue, with the only thing gained in the process being a case of the dizzies. This whole discussion was going nowhere. In total frustration, he slams his fist on the table. "Someone, please, say something that makes some sense!"

There is complete silence in the room. President Maxwell gazes into the faces of his NSC members seated around the conference table, pausing as necessary to ensure that he makes one-on-one eye contact with each individual in the room. All eyes are focused on him. He now has everyone's complete and undivided attention. Carefully measuring each world, he brings down the hammer. "I've taken great pains to surround myself with what I believe to be the best foreign policy and military minds in the country. Tell me that I wasn't wrong when I made those selections. People, for crying out loud, I've seen better problem-solving sessions than this in World Wrestling Federation matches. What is going on here? Has everyone suddenly gone brain dead? Speak to me!"

The president pushes back from the table and begins to pace around the room. While it gives him an opportunity to contemplate, it makes his staff feel even more uneasy. Everyone in the room is firmly convinced that Saddam's threat is real, and needs to be addressed in the near term. However, they cannot collectively agree as a group on what specific course of action is appropriate. Talking about issues at the macro level within a committee is always easier than working them at the micro level. As is usually the case, "the devil is in the details."

"We'll use the missionary approach—build on common ground. Fashion a consensus, first at home here with congressional leaders, and then abroad with our allies. That's the 'how,' then there's the 'what' and there's the 'when.'" The members of the NSC share a look. No one needed to be reminded that it was Mitch Richman speaking. How far could the NSA ride this missionary thing? He'd gained more notoriety from that statement than Moses had by parting the Red Sea. No one was exactly sure what it meant, especially the part at the end about the "what" and the "when."However, at this point, no one really cared. If it would satisfy the President and get them off the hot seat, it had to be one heck of a great idea.

President Maxwell took the cue. He had enjoyed about all this that he could stand. It was time to bring this discussion to a close and get on with the task at hand. He stopped pacing and reclaimed his seat at the head of the table. "Enough already," he exclaims, extending his arms with palms down in a conciliatory gesture. "General, I want you to put together an operational plan to neutralize the threat. Put your best people on it. As you are aware, there's an awful lot riding on this. We've got to do it and we've got to do it right the first time. There won't be an opportunity for a second chance. And, it's not too soon to start identifying the primary operatives with the right stuff to pull this off. You have a large number of good people to choose from. I'm counting on you to make the right selection."

The National Security Advisor had carefully steered the discussion to the point that the table was set. Now, it was time for the main course of meat and potatoes to be served. "You know, Mr. President, I was just thinking. This situation appears to be very grim, and I do not mean to imply that it isn't. However, on occasion, fate is not without a sense of irony. Wouldn't it be the ultimate in irony, if a premeditated act of terrorism by Saddam precipitated a response from us, that proved to be the lynch pin in a lasting peace in the Middle East?"

"Do I detect a note of optimism from my National Security Advisor? While I appreciate any ray of hope at this point in time, I'm not sure that I follow you. How in the world could Saddam's latest efforts at destroying civilization be possibly viewed as him doing us a big favor? Would you mind sharing your little secret with the rest of us, Mitch?" President Maxwell's tone straddled the fence between sarcasm and cynicism. As confident as he was in the judgement of his NSA, it appeared that he had completely lost his mind.

The main course was being devoured. Now was the time for

Mitch to trot out the flaming cherry's jubilee. "Saddam's threat to the region, could conceivably not only facilitate the bringing of the parties to the peace process together, but be the adhesive that binds them in a common effort to foil Saddam. The resulting commitments, goodwill, and trust that ensue, could then become the fabric from which a final peace agreement is cut and stitched."

"President Maxwell nods his head in understanding. His National Security Advisor's point appears to be a far stretch from the likely reality of the matter, but any small grain of hope is a boulder on the beach at this point. Well, we'll give you a capital 'H' for 'Hope' at this point, Mitch. In the meantime, we need to move on. We want to be politically correct as well as morally right on this one. As such, we're going to do this by the book to comply with the law and to ensure bipartisan support. The last thing we need is second guessing from Congressional leaders of the loyal opposition. Mitch, I want you to prepare a 'Presidential National Security Finding' for my signature, showing that the possession of weapons of mass destruction by Iraq and apparent intent to deliver them on their neighbors in Turkey, Saudi Arabia, and Israel, presents a clear and present danger to the stability of the Middle East and lives of American citizens. In addition, state that I have authorized the preparation of an operational plan and subsequent execution of a covert military mission against Iraq to neutralize the threat. Also, indicate that we will inform the chairman and ranking minority member of both the House and Senate Intelligence Committees of the intended action prior to its execution.

"This is a time sensitive issue, gentlemen. The gun is loaded, cocked, and pointed, and the clock is ticking. No one knows, what might set it off, or when it might go off. We need to act with expediency. I want to move forward along parallel tracks on all three fronts, the devising of a strategy and appropriate tactical military response to neutralize the threat; identification, selection, and training of key participants; and collation building of necessary support here at home within the Congress and abroad with our allies.

"Thank you for your input, gentlemen. That will be all for now." With a collective sigh of relief, the members of the NSC push back from the table and head for the door. Those who have taken hits are particularly anxious to improve both their scenery and company. However, before they can clear the room, the pensive sound of President Maxwell calling out, stops them in their tracks.

"I was just wondering," mused the President, "is anyone here besides me reminded of a quotation from the New Testament Book of Revelation, Chapter 6, Verse 8? 'And I looked, and behold a pale horse: and his name that sat on him was Death, and Hell followed with him . . . ' Can we contain this madman? Can we stop a war? Can we prevent an Armageddon?"

# CHAPTER FOUR

## LIFE IS A TEAM SPORT

*"Good morning gentlemen. Welcome to the Pentagon. My name* is Colonel Rampkin and I will be your host. I'm from the office of the Air Force Directorate of Plans. We are assigned the responsibility for oversight of this planning effort. I trust that you found the quarters, food, and amenities to your liking, and hope that everybody got a good night's sleep.

"As I understand, everyone in attendance has received a preliminary briefing on the intelligence finding. Our purpose in gathering here today is to participate in an intensive top-down review of the overall situation, including such major aspects as national security policy, threat analysis, and operational contingency planning. We have a distinguished group of speakers who will walk us through each major area of consideration over the next few days. When we complete this review, individually and collectively, we will be up-to-speed on what we're up against, the guidelines within which we are to proceed, and the objectives of the operational plan that has been conceived to neutralize the threat.

"Before we proceed any further, I need to remind each of you that this and every other session that you will participate in here at the Pentagon contain 'Top Secret' information. Therefore, it is imperative that you do not discuss any aspect of what you hear outside this room, even with each other. This area is considered a 'vault' for security purposes, and is, therefore, secured 24 hours a day. Your working papers must stay in this room, however, it is not necessary to put them away each and every time that you depart the area. Communications security is also of the utmost importance. The telephones in this room are not, I repeat, not secure. Do not discuss classified information over them. If it becomes necessary to discuss some aspect of your work with an individual who has been properly cleared, please see me. I will arrange for you to access a secure telephone. The element of surprise will be a very critical factor in determining the success of this mission. Remember, 'loose lips, sink ships.'

"Seated in the front row with us this morning are two very special guests. These are the gentlemen who have been selected to be the primary operatives in the ground and air phases of our mission, based on the qualifications, background, and experience that they each bring to the table. As such, they have responsibility for its successful implementation. I would like to make it clear at this time that while both of these individuals were hand-picked, they subsequently volunteered without any hesitation, whatsoever. Thus, they are here of their own volition, wholly committed to the success of this mission. They are the first team with the 'right stuff.'

"I would like to introduce them to you at this time. Gentlemen, please stand as your name is called. To my right, we have, Mr. Donovan. I understand your friends call you 'Pounder.' Mr. Donovan will be the team chief and primary operative in charge of activity on the ground in Iraq. On my left is Mr. Packard, or 'Slash,' as he prefers to be called. Slash, and a few of his friends, will be flying the air strikes against the designated targets in Iraq. I understand that Pounder and Slash's paths crossed while serving with the 'Wolf Pack,' the 8th Tactical fighter Wing in Kunsan, Korea. Slash's reputation proceeds him. This guy is a top notch, 'hair on fire' fighter pilot who honed his flying skills as the Squadron Commander of the 'Juvats,' the USAF's premier fighter squadron. He is a multi-talented individual, who also found time to be the lead singer in a distinguished musical group known as the 'Kunsan Boy's Choir.' This group is a legend in their own time, or perhaps in their own mind. While Slash was roaming the skies over Korea, striking fear into the hearts of the North Koreans, Pounder was busy providing the logistics support necessary to keep the fighter jocks airborne.

"While they are quite impressive, I will not read the bios of these individuals at this time. They are available for you to review on your own. However, what we hope will happen and encourage for reasons that you will soon learn, is for you to get to know each other on a first-name basis. Contrary to what they preach to the officer core about 'familiarity breeding contempt,' this is a horse of an entirely different color. Intimate familiarity with the mission planning details, each other, and every other aspect of this operation is not only encouraged, but absolutely essential. Intricate coordination of activities, based on split-second timing, will be the watchword of this mission, and the key to its ultimate success.

"As you are aware, inviting you to participate in the planning review phase of the mission is somewhat of a departure from standard operating procedure. Individuals selected for mission implementation are not normally involved up-front. They are brought on-board after the fact, given a copy of the plan, and an assignment to get up to speed in a hurry. However, in addition to the obvious bonus of being able to take advantage of your expertise during the planning review phase, we believe there are at least two additional major benefits associated with this approach. First of all, management studies support the fact that involving employees in the goal-setting process within an organization results in greater commitment to achievement of those goals. Second, feedback from lessons learned from previous missions, points to the fact that lack of familiarity between participants and insufficient opportunity for integrated training are the biggest contributors to mission failure. Individuals can be the best and the brightest, but they must train together long enough to ensure that they can achieve success with all the intricacies of interaction required of a team effort. It's the old adage, 'Tell me and I forget; Teach me and I remember; Involve me and I learn.' The bottom line is, that you can put together the world's greatest plan based on superior intelligence and the latest in hi-tech equipment. However, if all the players are not acting in complete unison like a well oiled machine, chances are that a hick-up may occur, impacting mission success. Let's face it gentlemen, 'Life Is a Team Sport!'

"The approach we will be using in the planning of this mission will employ the maxim of 'Murphy's Law.' As such, the first planning assumption will be 'what can go wrong will go wrong.' This concept reflects the reality of everyday life. However, with the mission that we will undertake, the consequences of failure could be much greater, even grave. Individually and collectively, we cannot possibly conceive, even in our wildest imagination, all the possible unanticipated glitches, and their implications and ramifications which can suddenly materialize in the fog of war. Once the balloon goes up, it's frequently wall-to-wall chaos. In this business, good intentions only count in helping old ladies cross a busy street, and close only counts in horseshoes and hand grenades. One mistake, one small miscue, can cost a life and put the entire mission in jeopardy.

"The second planning assumption, closely associated with the first, will be 'there are no givens.' Consequently, we will not take anything for granted. Nothing is set in concrete beyond the mission tasking order that we received from the Secretary of Defense. We will question everything, not once, but over and over again until we are convinced, not beyond a reasonable doubt as in the court room, but beyond any shadow of a doubt that we have it right. In addition, a review of lessons learned from previous efforts will be a good investment of our time. That will provide us with the opportunity to refresh our memories on the wide range of factors and concerns that should be taken into consideration in planning a mission of this nature. After careful study and consideration of all pertinent data, we will then begin to distill it down to a basic residue that we can get our arms around.

"During this process, I must ask each of you to keep an open mind, leaving behind at the door any preconceived notions that you may have or inherent prejudices you may harbor. This is bigger than any of us individually, but not all of us collectively. That is, if we work as a team. There will be no pride of authorship, and all of us will remain open to constructive criticism. For us to succeed, gentlemen, we are going to have to put aside any and all personal parochialism and petty professional jealousies, and be one in mind and purpose. I visualize you as a matched set of Siamese septuplets, joined at the hip—all singing off the same sheet of music and marching in lockstep precision to the same drummer at exactly the same cadence. When you complete your training, you are going to have all the harmonious moves of the women's USA Olympic gold medal synchronized swimming team, with the same split second precision.

"And finally, gentlemen, for the foreseeable future, we own your body, mind, and soul, 24 hours-a-day, seven days-a-week. If you've ever been sequestered while on jury duty, you may have some idea of what this is going to be like. This means no distractions, which means no dependents. If any of you have been considering a divorce, this might be a good time to see how you function without the wife and children around. That's a bad joke and a poor attempt on my part to impart a little humor. However, what you will be engaged in here is very serious. The fact of the matter is that we need your undivided attention, completely, and totally focused on the task at hand. Although the rest of the world doesn't know it, they are heavily dependent upon you. What the future will hold for them and their offspring will be dependent upon your success. Have I made myself perfectly clear? If anyone has any reservations about any aspect of their commitment to this mission, now is the time to speak up, or forever hold your peace. Are there any 'Nay-Sayers?' Ah yes, the sound of silence, music to my ears.

"We'll take a short break in just a minute or two. If any of you need any administrative assistance, please see the secretary in the back of the room. Her name is Margaret. You will find that she is extremely efficient in handling any official requirements that you may have. However, the rules of engagement are as follows. She doesn't phone wives with messages and she doesn't do coffee. OK, gentlemen, lets take five, relieve yourselves, and warm up your coffee. When you return at the top of the hour, we're going to kick the tires, light the fires, and get this show on the road."

***

"Shoot low sheriff, they're riding Shetlands."

"I always wondered what it would take to get you to the Pentagon, Slash."

"Well, as you're probably aware, Pounder, I'm not here by choice. I spent my entire career avoiding this place. No one in their right mind would give up flying an airplane to be a desk jockey."

"You're looking good for as much milage as you've got."

"Not too shabby for an old washed up Air Force toad. I can't sustain the level of effort that I once could, but I can still rise to the occasion."

"Listening to you, Slash, reminds me of a sales pitch a used car salesmen gave me a while back. He's pointing at the biggest clunker on the lot and pumping me full of it, like there's no tomorrow. According to him, this bucket of nuts and bolts was owned by a little old gray haired lady who only drove it back and forth to Church on Sundays. And, then after a brief pause, he added, and she was an atheist."

"We're a long way from Kunsan, Korea, good buddy."

"Isn't that the truth. Man, I never thought the time would come when I would long for the taste of a big bowl of kimshe down in Kunsan city. But, I do believe that day has definitely arrived. Any excuse to get out of here would be worth its weight in gold."

"The Pentagon has been unfairly maligned over the years. It can grow on you, if you give it a chance."

"Yea, just like a tumor. I take it, this isn't your first time to the Pentagon, Pounder."

"No, I was stationed here for three years just prior to my retirement from the Air Force."

"That bad, huh?"

"That wasn't the reason I retired. I had just come up on my 20 years, and received an offer from a defense contractor that I couldn't refuse."

"What is your view of the Pentagon?"

"Well, most of the people that work here insist that there is only one good view of the Pentagon. That's in the rear view mirror of your car as you are driving away. However, I didn't think that it was all that bad. The Pentagon is a unique place. It's the world's largest office building. But, more important, it's an impregnable fortress, the primer symbol of America's global military superiority.

"My work here was challenging, but not overwhelming. One of the toughest decisions an action officer has to make each day is where to eat lunch. The problem is, there are too many good places to choose from. The Metro-rail station under the Pentagon can zip you to the Crystal City Underground, to Roslynn, or to any number of other stops with excellent restaurants. If you got stuck and can't leave the building, there are several cafeterias to choose from, plus the Executive Dining Room. Or, if you're into physical fitness, you can workout at The Pentagon Officers Athletic Club. We refer to it as the POAC. During the summer, I used to brown-bag it a lot, eating my lunch in the courtyard. This area was a favorite with many of the secretaries that worked at the Pentagon, and an excellent place to meet someone or just enjoy the view."

"How many people work in this building?"

"I'd guess about one-third. The rest have positions with fancy titles, not jobs.

"Our real mission at the Pentagon was to move paper. We generated more paper than you could shake a stick at. And, this isn't just your ordinary, everyday, run-of-the mill paper. This paper is very special."

"What's special about it?"

"It's special because all of this paper becomes part of every action officer's own personal 'baby.'"

"You mean you had babies?"

"Not the human kind, but just as important to us. Our baby, was a 'package,' and here's how it worked. Our job was to assemble pertinent information pertaining to a particular issue in the form of a 'package,' complete with a staff summary sheet. The package contained background information on the issue, with a proposed plan of action for resolution, along with supporting documentation. As indicated by its name, the staff summary sheet provided the reader with a short summary of the issue addressed in the package, and required action to be taken. And, equally important, it identified the office symbols of all of the functional organizations which needed to coordinate the package, to ensure that it was completed staff work.

"Now, just to ensure that you understand what was really going on, I need to explain a few terms. In the Pentagon, the worker-bees are referred to as 'action officers.' They don't receive an assignment, they receive a 'tasking,' and they don't address problems, they address 'issues.' And, just as important, these 'issues' don't just come up, they 'surface.' Oh, and one other important matter. Action officers at the Pentagon never make mistakes. Whenever a SNAFU (situation normal, all fouled up) occurs, it is referred to as 'an inadvertent administrative oversight.'

"Let me give you an example. One day, I was reading an after-action report on the results of the latest deployment of the U.S. Air Force to Egypt where we had participated in an operation 'Bright Star' Exercise. One of the 'issues' that 'surfaced' in this report was the need to develop a desert camouflage fatigue uniform for Air Force personnel. Our people were still wearing their forest green camouflage fatigue uniforms that were designed for the jungles of Southeast Asia. It was pointed out that it is most difficult to find a tree to hide behind in the deserts of the Middle East. Consequently, our troops felt quite conspicuous by their presence, all decked out in a forest green camouflaged fatigue uniform against a background of light brown Middle East desert sand. It was also mentioned that the U.S. Army already had their personnel outfitted with a desert camouflaged fatigue uniform. The question put to the Pentagon Air Staff was: 'When was the USAF going to get with the program?'

"Consequently, I received a 'tasking' to work the 'issue.' I completed all the necessary pick-and-shovel research work, and came up with a proposed solution. Then, it was off to the races to 'run' the package around the Pentagon without getting lost, and obtain all the necessary coordination. That meant keeping track of all the floors, rings, and corridors, which was a major job in itself. This process was known as 'floating,' the package. The action officer starts the process by obtaining the coordination of the lowest organizational level in each affected functional area. That was generally the 'Branch,' which had a five-digit office symbol. Once, all of the required functional branch coordination had been obtained, it was time to start the process all over again by 'floating' it up to the next organizational level. This was the four-digit office symbol, or the 'Division.' Then to the three-digit, or 'Directorate' level, and finally onto the two-digit, or 'Deputy Chief of Staff.' This whole 'float' process was explained to me my first day on the job in the following manner. Just think of it as adding water to a bath tub. First, you put just a little water in the tub, representing the Branch. Then you add successive additional amounts of water to the tub as you complete each level of coordination. Thus, in this manner, your package literally 'floats' from the bottom of the tub as you start the process, to the top of the tub, as you complete the coordination cycle. Makes great sense, doesn't it?

"On one occasion, I was about my official business of 'floating' a package around the hallowed corridors of the Pentagon to obtain the required coordination, when I noted that I had a few pages out of sequence. Not wanting to retrace my steps all the way back to my office, I looked for a place that I could exchange the pages. The only usable thing in view was a large round trash barrel which was used for waste paper. Carefully balancing the package on the edge of the barrel, I located the pages that were out of sequence. It occurred to me at that time that carefully exchanging the pages in my package was somewhat akin to tenderly changing the diaper on a real baby. I just hoped that the work that I had done on my package didn't stink up the place like the job done by a real baby in theirs.

"I was close. I was just about there. I had all of the offending pages out and just about back together again in proper sequence. Then, it happened! At that critical moment, the package slipped off the edge and fell in its entirety into the trash barrel. My heart sank. I had spent hours putting this package together, and was under a short suspense to complete the coordination, get it into the General for signature, and distribute it to the field. I surveyed the situation with extreme anxiety. This was it. There was no other alternative. I tipped the trash barrel over on its side, crawled in and retrieved the mess of papers which I believed to have been my package. Faced with a situation like this, it's better to have too much rather than too little. Not entirely certain which papers were mine and which were just trash, I snagged everything I could get my hands on to ensure I didn't leave any of my package behind. I could sort it all out later after I got back to the office, and dispose of any extra papers.

"Just at that moment, I sensed that someone was behind me, observing what was going on. I turned and looked up nervously to meet the eyes of a General Officer. Before I could offer up any explanation as to what in the world I was doing in what must have appeared to be a rather ridiculous position, he spoke. I will never forget his words. 'I knew that if I stayed around this place long enough that I would see the inexplicable—an Action Officer putting together a package out of waste paper he retrieved from a trash barrel in the corridors of the Pentagon. I always wondered how you guys put those packages together. My suspicions have now been confirmed.'"

***

"Please take your seats gentlemen. I would like to reintroduce Mr. Donovan. As you recall, he will be the primary operative on the ground in Iraq. I have asked him to take a few minutes at this time and brief you on his visit to an air show in Baghdad in 1989. I think that you will find it both interesting and informative. His insights were the earliest indication of Iraq's sinister intentions which came to fruition during the Gulf War. They provide a rare look inside the previously secret realm of Saddam's world, and an appropriate backdrop as a point of departure for our planning effort. Mr. Donovan, the time is yours."

"Thank you, Colonel Rampkin, and good morning gentlemen.

"Defense equipment exhibitions frequently provide a first look at the emerging equipment and capabilities of sponsoring and participating countries. Attendance at these exhibitions provides the opportunity to assess the current and future capabilities of both allies and potential adversaries.

"Just 15 months prior to Iraq's invasion of Kuwait, we got a sneak preview of Saddam's military production capabilities. The 'First Baghdad International Exhibition for Military Production' was held in Baghdad, Iraq, from April 28, 1989, to May 2, 1989. As it turned out, gentlemen, it appears that it was not only the first 'Exhibition for Military Production' to be held by Iraq, but undoubtedly also the last ." Pounder's comment draws loud laughter from the audience.

"The exhibition was inaugurated by Mr. Mohiuddin Mauruf, the Deputy President of the Democratic Republic of Iraq. It attracted 200 exhibitors from 28 countries, with France having the largest display. Three hundred different categories of arms, equipment, military systems, ammunition, and explosives were displayed at the show, with Iraq producing some 200 categories of items. At that time, it was planned that Iraq would host the exhibition on alternate years in conjunction with Egypt.

"During the course of their eight year protracted war with Iran, Iraq faced difficulties in obtaining Western technologies. Most Western and European countries, with the notable exception of France, had official embargoes on selling military arms to Iraq. This did not, however, prevent Iraq from procuring and producing a wide range of defense equipment. No longer content to acquire technology through covert or semi-official channels, Iraq set an ambitious goal of establishing a major, full fledged, national defense industry.

"Upon witnessing the Iraqi products, it became quite apparent that Iraq had come a long way in arms production and had achieved considerable expertise. It appeared that the Iraqis had advanced in two parallel ways.

"They had modified their stocks of old weapons, such as missiles, artillery guns, and other items captured from the Iranians, to meet their current operational commitments. Their skill and technical expertise in this area had resulted in large economic savings.

"In addition, they were knocking at the gate of modern military technology. Although these efforts were still limited, the Iraqis had made a good start, especially in the areas of airframe, armament, and electronics.

"A French industry official at the Exhibition, observed, if they wanted to continue selling military arms to Iraq, they would have to accept the condition of industrial cooperation. Substantial technical assistance from several Western and Soviet Bloc countries had already enabled Iraq to acquire the ability to manufacture and, in some cases, develop complete weapon systems of unexpected size and capability.

"Iraq's ambitious entry into the military manufacturing market shows how ineffective arms embargoes are and how they can seemingly promote the growth of the embargoed countries industry. Once Iraq's internal requirements are satisfied, the next logical step for a new arms producing country is to offer its products on the international market place.

"In the interest of time, gentlemen, I will just highlight a few of the more impressive exhibits that Iraq had on display at the exhibition to give you some idea of the extent of the progress they have made in the development of their military production capabilities. I have prepared handouts for each of you that provide details on many of the other items of arms and equipment that I observed. You can review them at your leisure.

"One of the areas of special interest at the Exhibition was the Iraqi integrated air defense system. Our evaluation was that it appeared to be long on equipment and apparent capability, but very short on real capability. Iraq's problem was not with lack of quality equipment, as the country had large numbers of surface-to-air missiles, fighter aircraft, and an early warning aircraft. Iraq's problem was in the areas of command, control, communications, and intelligence , and training in the effective use of an air defense system. Probably the best known failure of Iraqi air defense was the Israeli raid on their nuclear reactor. Even after the raid, Iraqi air defense was unable to intercept Israeli strike aircraft on their way out of the country. The limitations of the Iraqi air defense system were also brought out during their war with Iran. Iran successfully launched air raids against Baghdad and other key areas well inside Iraq. Despite a significant advantage in equipment and air superiority, Iraq was unable to effectively stop these raids. As you are aware, these deficiencies were reconfirmed during the Gulf War with the UN coalition's air forces ability to neutralize the Iraqi's air defense system with apparent ease as a prelude to establishing air superiority over the battle field.

"Some of the more interesting weapon systems on display by Iraq at the exhibition were three types of locally manufactured SCUD 1B medium-range surface-to-surface missiles . They were known as the Hussein, Abbas, and Al-Waleed. The SCUD missile system was a Soviet developed surface-to-surface mobile battle field tactical artillery missile. It was propelled by a single stage liquid rocket motor, and carried a conventional high explosive 800 kilogram or 1,764 pound warhead. The missile followed a calculated ballistic course to target at a speed of about 3,200 MPH. Minor in-route course corrections were possible through the use of a simple inertial guidance system, and jet vanes. The earliest model of the SCUD missile was first seen in 1957, and became fully deployed in the early 1960s. Later models incorporated improvements in both performance and utility. Upon arrival at the site, the launch crew would establish the winds at altitude through radiosonde techniques, and survey in the site, if it had not been previously surveyed. The missile was then elevated for launch on the mobile transporter erector, and the target position input. After launch, the crew immediately moved to an alternate site to reload, refuel, and avoid destruction from a retaliatory coalition air strike. The missile's range was in excess of 400 miles, which allowed it to threaten the capital city of Riyadh, Saudi Arabia, and areas in Israel.

"Because of the SCUD's dated technology and primitive guidance system, it was unlikely that the missiles would come close, let alone score a direct hit on their target. Therefore, the U.S. military declared that the SCUD was not an effective military weapon. It was, however, a terror weapon when used against heavily populated civilian areas, like the capital city of Riyadh, Saudi Arabia.

"The first SCUD attack on the city of Riyadh, Saudi Arabia, occurred early in the morning of January 21, 1991. We were awakened shortly before 1 A.M. by a tremendous reverberating explosion. The force of the detonation, literally snatched us from our dreams, and launched us out of our beds back to reality. It was obvious that we were under attack, but at the time I wasn't sure from what. It seemed to go on forever, explosion after explosion. We lived in a villa with concrete walls that were at least a foot thick. They were shaking so much, that it appeared the house was in danger of structurally collapsing around us. Because of the duration of the attack, I began to think that it wasn't the dreaded SCUD missiles, but an air raid by manned aircraft, dropping bombs on the city. In any case, it really didn't matter. The bottom line was that someone was trying to kill us, and our lives were in danger. Later that day, the U.S. Central Command in Riyadh, held an emergency briefing. At that time, they reported a total of 10 SCUD missiles had been launched by Iraq into Saudi Arabia in the past 24 hours."

"The number of SCUD attacks on Riyadh was substantially diminished after counter-SCUD operations were initiated by the allied forces. SCUD hunting by coalition air forces did not eliminate the threat, but they did affect Iraq's ability to accurately launch them. Each time a SCUD was launched, the mobile transporter erector was in near immediate danger of being hunted down, attacked, and destroyed by an air strike with cluster bombs. Therefore, as the war continued, SCUD launches were less frequent and less accurate.

"The Gulf War ended on February 28, 1991. Counting from the day Iraq invaded Kuwait, on August 2, 1990, it had lasted 210 days.

From my best count, gentlemen, a total of 47 SCUD Missiles had been launched against Saudi Arabia during this time, with 18 of those targeted at the capital city of Riyadh.

"Gentlemen, that concludes the formal portion of my briefing. However, we still have some time before we break for lunch. Therefore, I would be happy to entertain any questions that you may have for the next 15-20 minutes."

"Did you observe any evidence of offensive capabilities?"

"Yes, I did. The most obvious example was the SCUD missile which we have already talked about in some detail. However, there were others, most notable, a large production bomb weighing 9,000 kilograms (19,800 pounds), and containing 4,000 kilograms (8,800 pounds) of explosives. Carried by the Tupolev TU-16 Bomber and fitted with impact, proximity, or air burst fuzes, the bomb was developed to neutralize enemy rear echelon forces. Heat and television-guided aircraft bombs as well as deep sea mines demonstrated the Iraqi technical ability in producing weapons."

"What about evidence of Iraqi cooperation with the Soviet Union?"

"Yes, on that count, also. Two examples come to mind immediately. The first, a locally manufactured variant of the Soviet T-72Ml main battle tank or Assad Babyl, equipped with a 125mm gun. Iraq also displayed a Soviet X29L laser-guided missile which they modified to double its effective range to 12-15 kilometers (7-9 NM), and further adapted it to a Thompson-CSF Atlas laser designation pod for use on Iraq's Mirage F-l Fighters."

"I'm curious regarding evidence of any cooperation with other Arab countries?"

"In addition to working to reach its own industrial goals, Iraq appeared to be working closely with Egypt's 'Arab Organization for Industrialization' to avoid duplication of efforts and to standardize military equipment to simplify training and logistics. This cooperation was expected to be formalized through the 'Arab Cooperative Council,' which includes Egypt, Iraq, Jordan, and Yemen.

"Gentlemen, I see that our time is up. Thank you for your kind attention. I believe Colonel Rampkin has an administrative announcement for us before we break for lunch."

"Thank you Mr. Donovan. We appreciate the briefing. That was good background information and will provide an excellent point of departure for the work we have ahead of us. However, that was then and this is now. We need to spin you up-to-speed on what has happened since, with more recent developments. As you all are aware, any planning effort, and consequently, subsequent mission success, is only as good as the intelligence on which it is based. If you don't know where you're going, any road will get you there.

"Let's break for lunch now, gentlemen. When you return at 1300 hours, we will hear from our Intel people. They will provide us with the latest update based on CIA information which defined the threat, and became the basis for our planning effort to neutralize it. By the way, with the agenda that we have laid-on this afternoon and the full plates you will subsequently have, I recommend that we eat in, today. My favorite watering hole is the Executive Dining Room. It is located in room 3C1063. For you green beans that are new to the Pentagon, that's the Third floor, C Ring, and Corridor 10. Today's special is New England corned beef and cabbage with all the trimmings. I highly recommend it, with just a dash of horse radish to give it a little extra pizzaz. In the unlikely event that anyone should get lost, just turn yourself into the nearest General Services Administration security guard and ask him to phone us with your location. We will send someone to get you. However, getting lost will not be an acceptable excuse for being late for a meeting."

# CHAPTER FIVE

# WHAT GOES AROUND, COMES AROUND

*"Welcome back gentlemen. I appreciate your returning on time.*
From the looks of things, it doesn't appear that anyone went hungry.
How about that horseradish!

"Please take your seats so we can get started. We have a lot
of important ground to cover. The briefer this afternoon is Agent
Quibar of the Central Intelligence Agency. His assignment is to
define the nature of the threat which is responsible for bringing
us together. As I emphasized earlier, good intelligence is absolutely
critical. You must have good intel to have a good air campaign, or
any other combat mission for that matter. The Air Force's inability
to rapidly destroy Iraq's mobile SCUD launchers during the Gulf
War was not so much a failure of airpower as it was a failure of
human intelligence to compensate for the inherent limitations
in sensors. While satellite capabilities continue to grow, they are
not the complete answer to either strategic or tactical intelligence
collection. Stationing mobile missile launchers in residential areas
or employing low-technology modes of communication immune
to electronic jamming or interception, continue to pose serious
targeting challenges. You can't hit what you can't find. However, the
flip side of that coin, may be even worse. Poor Intel may result in
inadvertent strikes on facilities that should not be on the target list.
As you recall, the attack on the Chinese Embassy in Kosovo was an

intelligence failure which resulted in irreparable damage to U.S.-Sino relations.

"What you are about to hear, gentlemen, is extremely important. Therefore, please give Agent Quibar your undivided attention. When I look out in the audience, I expect to see everyone alert, attentive, and leaning forward in their foxholes, breathlessly anticipating the next word out of his mouth. Sir, the podium is yours."

"Good afternoon, gentlemen. I thought the introduction was going pretty well, until Colonel Rampkin dropped that little tidbit regarding the CIA intelligence failure in Kosovo. In spite of the Chinese government's media accounts of the incident stating that the bombing was intentional, I am here to tell you that it was an accident. We just flat out messed up. Several CIA officers at various levels of responsibility failed to confirm that the intended bombing target had been properly identified and accurately located before we passed the target nomination package on to the U.S. military. I sincerely hope that the Chinese can find it in their hearts to forgive us. If they will, perhaps we can look the other way a bit in regard to all the nuclear secrets they have been stealing from us, and even forgive a few of their less flagrant human rights violations.

"All right, now that we have kissed and made up with the Chinese, let's see if we can jerk Saddam's chain a time or two. I think that as each of us is aware, no intelligence briefing is going to end up as a best seller or a major motion picture. They are unfortunately, inherently dry in nature, due to the purpose they serve. As Joe Friday of 'Dragnet' used to say, 'Just the facts Ma'am, just the facts.' My job for the past six months has been to collect, assemble, analyze, and report all available data on the threat. In the time I have today, I will boil it all down to the key succinct elements.

"By way of background, the Central Intelligence Agency was established in 1947. It is an independent agency in the Executive Branch at the Cabinet level. CIA Headquarters is located on a sprawling 258-acre campus in McLean, Virginia. Among the many missions of the agency are support of those who make America's foreign policy, and ensuring the success of our armed forces in whatever mission they are engaged in, wherever they are deployed. The Department of Defense frequently relies on specialized intelligence support from the CIA in such important areas as peacekeeping and hostage rescue.

"While much has been made of the CIA being a super cloak and dagger 'spy agency,' its mission is to coordinate the country's intelligence activities and to correlate, evaluate, and disseminate intelligence relating to national security. Consequently, a good deal of the agency's time is devoted to the collection, analysis, interpretation, and distribution of information obtained from open sources. It is surprising, how much useful information of importance to national defense is available out there in the public domain. Then again, in this enlightened age of investigative reporters, and mass communications, it may come as no surprise to those of you assembled here today. Do you realize how hard it is to keep a secret anymore?

"The initial portion of my briefing was obtained from overt open sources, and consequently, is unclassified. A little background on related events might be in order to put things in a proper perspective and serve as a point of departure.

"Saddam's limiting of access to his palaces triggered a three-week crisis between the United Nations and Iraq, resulting in the expulsion of the American members of the U.N. inspection team from the country on November 13, 1997. One day later, the U.N. withdrew the rest of its inspectors as a show of protest in support of its American team members. A total of seventy-five inspectors, including four Americans, returned to Iraq on November 19, 1997, in return for Russia's support for lifting the U.S. sanctions. When U.N. inspections resumed, weapons experts visited only factories, warehouses, and other suspected weapons areas. They did not try to enter any of Saddam's scores of palaces and other sensitive sites where it was believed that Iraq was hiding documents, weapons, and chemicals. While it is not known precisely how many residences Saddam has, U.S. officials say between 43 and 50 have been constructed since the end of the 1991 Gulf War. Some members of the Administration believe that total may be as high as 78.

"In the absence of U.N. inspectors, Iraq has reconstructed some U.S.-bombed buildings associated with its weapons of mass destruction program. While the Pentagon says the intelligence picture of Iraq is fuzzy, many foreign policy analysts believe Iraqi President Saddam Hussein has used the inspections respite since December to push a covert weapons program. Analysts believe Iraq is pursuing chemical, biological, and nuclear weapons as well as the missiles to deliver them.

"Jane's Intelligence Review reported that Iraq still has the scientific talent and industrial base to build nuclear weapons, and there is some evidence it has hidden a good deal of bomb-making material. The report suggested that Iraqi President Saddam Hussein had come close to building a bomb before the 1991 Gulf War, and concluded that Iraq still has nuclear ambitions. Information obtained from Iraqi defectors and sources close to the International Atomic Energy Agency indicated that the Iraqis still possess an active nuclear weapons program. The magazine also reported that the scientific and industrial infrastructure required to build a bomb are in place, and hundreds of government-supported employees of the nuclear establishment remain on permanent standby. While a great deal of the material necessary for building a nuclear weapon has been discovered or destroyed, evidence indicates that much still remains hidden..

"Iraq retains the technology it acquired before the war, and evidence clearly indicates an ongoing research and development effort on missiles. Photographs by U.S. spy satellites show Iraq has rebuilt its al-Kindi facility for conducting research on ballistic missiles. Iraq is also expanding its missile production facility at Ibn Al-Haytham, which has two new buildings large enough to manufacture longer-range missiles than the SCUDS that Iraq fired in the Gulf War. Missile development is particularly important, because any chemical or biological agents that Iraq already has, in violation of the U.N. commitments it made at the end of the Gulf War, are of little military value without a means of delivering them across its own borders.

"For those of us who thought the end of the Cold War and the East-West thaw eliminated the threat of nuclear war, these findings are somewhat unsettling. While the possibility of an American-Soviet confrontation seems to have abated, the proliferation of developing threats among smaller rogue nations seems to be the order of the day. In addition, while we are still obviously concerned about nuclear weapons, there is a growing concern over the use of other weapons of mass destruction by terrorist groups. Let's spend a few minutes examining the nature of the threat of these type weapons.

"Considered to be 'The Poor Man's Nukes,' two types of mass destruction, chemical and biological agents, have become the center of attention. Many experts believe that these arms, which can wipe out entire military units or populations, pose the greatest threat that the world may face in the coming years. One example of this threat is Anthrax, a lethal biological agent. Bacterial organisms may enter the body through skin wounds, be inhaled, or ingested. The incubation period for inhaled Anthrax is one to six days. Fever, malaise, fatigue, cough, and chest discomfort are rapidly followed by severe respiratory distress. If untreated, shock and death normally occur within 24 to 36 hours after the onset of severe symptoms.

"In a November 27, 1997, news article, Defense Secretary William Cohen declared that Iraq may possess from 20 to 200 tons of the lethal nerve agent VX, as well as 6,000 gallons of Anthrax. Cohen also said that 200 tons of VX would be theoretically enough to kill every man, woman, and child on the entire earth. Concerned about the threat of germ and gas warfare and the need to protect troops at home and abroad, the Pentagon ordered 1.4 million active duty personnel and one million reservists and civilians to be vaccinated against Anthrax.

"We are now at that portion of the briefings where we get down to the nitty-gritty. This is where the rubber meets the road. Before we start, I feel the need to remind you of the extreme sensitivity of the information we are about to cover. It is classified 'top secret' for reasons you will soon discover. Unauthorized leakage or rumors regarding any aspect of this material would be devastating to our relationship with Israel, as well as having grave implications for our national security. Therefore, I would request that there be no note-taking during this portion of the briefing.

"During the 1991 Persian Gulf War, Iraqi President Saddam Hussein fired a total of 39 SCUD missiles at Israel in hopes of breaking up the Arab coalition arrayed against him. Under intense U.S. pressure, Israel did not retaliate, exercising what to them was agonizing patience. Because of concern that Saddam might use chemical weapons, Israelis were issued gas masks as a precautionary measure. However, to the best of our knowledge, all SCUDS launched both at Israel and Saudi Arabia, contained conventional warheads. No evidence has ever been found to the contrary.

"After enduring Iraqi SCUD attacks throughout the war, Israel went on record that it would not be so restrained with any Iraqi military strikes in the future. Vowing 'never again,' Israel promised to meet force with force. The government also authorized the creation of a secret planning cell. Their objective was to intensify surveillance of Iraq's military capabilities and operations. It became a top priority of the 'Mossad,' the Israeli foreign intelligence agency. If a weapon was being developed that could threaten their security, they were determined to know about it before it was deployed. With this knowledge, military action could be initiated to neutralize it. Saddam would be held responsible and accountable for any sinister plot against the State of Israel. There was already a precedent in this regard. Israeli aircraft attacked and destroyed an Iraqi nuclear reactor under construction outside Baghdad in 1981.

"If anyone here is not familiar with or convinced of the nature of the commitment by Israel to this type of cause, let me refresh your memories for a moment. They don't just get mad. They get even! Does everyone recall the Munich summer Olympics in 1972, when 11 Israeli athletes were attacked and killed by a PLO affiliate group known as 'Black September?' The Israelis got their revenge, hunting down and killing each and every perpetrator of that tragic event. Like the 'avenging angel,' driven by the Old Testament Mosaic Law of 'an eye for an eye and a tooth for a tooth,' they extracted their pound of flesh to avenge the cruel and cowardly deaths of their countrymen who had been engaged in that most noble of nationalistic endeavors–participating in the Olympic games.

"Israel's efforts to keep tabs on Saddam paid off in spades. The Mossad fortuitously stumbled upon access to top-secret Iraq communications, broke the code through the help of dissidents who had defected, and pieced together many pieces of the puzzle. They could not believe their good fortune. God must have been watching over and smiling down on them.

"Gentlemen, the bottom line is, Israeli Intelligence has gathered information indicating that Iraq has developed weapons of mass destruction with the ability to deliver them on Tel Aviv, Israel, the U.S. airbase located at Incirlik, Turkey, and Prince Sultan Airbase in Saudi Arabia. The U.S. Government has spent a great deal of time and money conducting an independent verification of the Israeli findings and cross-checking various sources. All indications are that it is a creditable report, and thus, a creditable threat. Therefore, we must treat it as serious. Now that we know the nature of the threat, the real challenge emerges. We must act with expediency and resolve to neutralize it.

"The Western allies set up 'no-fly' zones to give a measure of protection to the Kurds of northern Iraq and the Shiite Muslims of southern Iraq who had rebelled in the aftermath of the 1991 Gulf War. Baghdad regards these as impositions that were not authorized by the U.N. Security Council, and considers our flights to be a violation of Iraqi sovereignty. Saddam has threatened both Turkey and Saudi Arabia with retaliation for allowing their airbases to be used as sanctuaries by the United States. USAF jets based at Incirlik, in southern Turkey, have struck Iraqi air defense sites after being targeted by Iraqi defenses while patrolling the 'no-fly' zone over northern Iraq. Similarly, USAF jets stationed at Prince Sultan Airbase, located south of the capital city of Riyadh, patrol the 'no-fly' zone over southern Iraq. Therefore, Saddam's targeting priorities come as no surprise to those who have continued to monitor events in the Middle East following the Gulf War.

"Saddam has met with his military chiefs on numerous occasions to discuss ways of upgrading air defense capabilities in Iraq to confront what he considers as continuing American and British aggression. An executive of the ruling Baath Party has vowed that Iraq would continue to fire on U.S. and British planes patrolling the 'no-fly' zones over northern and southern Iraq. In addition, Saddam has offered a reward of $14,000 to any Iraqi who shoots down an enemy plane.

"Well, there it is gentlemen. I've laid it out to you as we see it from an intelligence standpoint. We've addressed all three aspects of Saddam's premeditated plot to commit a horrendous international crime: means, opportunity, and motive. The ball is now in our court. It's up to us to act before he takes advantage of the opportunity to implement his plan.

"In the remaining time we have this afternoon, I would like to open the floor up to questions. Is there any aspect of the briefing that you would like to discuss further?"

"Yes, I have a question. Why hasn't your agency been more active in efforts to destabilize Saddam? Has the CIA been sitting in the back pew of the church on their hands all this time?"

"No, there have been several reported U.S. attempts to topple the Iraqi leader. A CIA covert operation in Iraq intended to generate indigenous opposition to Saddam in hopes of sparking a coup, was broken up when Saddam's military moved against his Kurdish population in 1996. Also, according to one Air Force account, U.S. strike planners intentionally targeted command bunkers, headquarters, and royal palaces where they suspected Saddam may have been residing, hoping to kill him. In addition, at one time during the Gulf War, U.S. warplanes were on the lookout for a Winnebago, after analysts reported through review of TV footage that Saddam was moving about the country in a mobile home."

"With our superior technology, fire power, tactical execution, and the element of surprise, shouldn't this mission be basically a piece of cake?"

"Easy for you to say, sitting here in the safety of the Pentagon. Never underestimate your enemy. Consider this: We ride in there like the Midnight Cowboy and take our best shot. However, through bad intelligence, a miscalculation, or for any number of reasons, we don't neutralize or destroy the threat. Saddam reacts like a bumblebee you have just taken a swat at and inadvertently knocked down the back of your shirt. The bee stings, and you jump up in pain. Saddam in a 'knee-jerk' reaction pushes the button, and Tel Aviv, Israel; Prince Sultan Air Base in Saudi Arabia; and the U.S. airbase at Incirlik, Turkey, become an asterisk in a history book. The stakes are obviously very high here. In addition to the unthinkable destruction and loss of life in Tel Aviv, thousands of American servicemen's lives are at risk at our air bases in Turkey and Saudi Arabia."

"OK, let's assume Saddam gets lucky and is able to launch one or more of his missiles. Can't we deal with it? From everything we saw on CNN and read in the newspapers, the Patriot Missiles were quite effective against Saddam's SCUD attacks on Israel and Saudi Arabia during the Gulf War. Why don't we just deploy more Patriot Batteries to the area to neutralize the threat?"

"Before I answer your specific question, a little background information may be in order. The Patriot missile system was developed by Raytheon. It was originally designed as a high altitude surface-to-air, site-defense system. It is propelled by a single stage solid propellant rocket motor with approximately a 23-second burn, which provides a range of 65 miles. The missile is truck-mounted and uses a guidance system which allows data processing on the ground in conjunction with the missile's homing radar system to acquire the target. After launch, the missile proceeds to the vicinity of the target. The missile's radar data is then transmitted to the ground station which calculates the best course for the missile to intercept the air-borne threat. The Tactical Control Officer usually engages the missile when it is about 50 miles from the control station. At this point, the SCUD is approximately 40 seconds from impact. Two Patriot missiles are launched in quick succession. The first to intercept the SCUD, and the other as back-up in case the first misses.

The missiles, about 17 feet long, break the sound barrier before their tails have cleared the launcher tubes and soon reach Mach 2, twice the speed of sound. They are designed to explode in close proximity to the SCUD, with the fragments of the explosion destroying the SCUD and detonating its warhead. The entire intercept process must be timed to a split second or the incoming and outgoing missiles will fly past each other in a failed attempt. The cost of the Patriots was about one million dollars per copy.

"Now, back to your question regarding the effectiveness of the Patriot Missiles during the Gulf War. That's a good question, one that certainly generated a lot of controversy and debate after the war was over. The military view of their effectiveness was understandably closely guarded during the war. However, the view of one senior U.S. commander involved in the conflict, stated later that it didn't really matter if the Patriot's intercepted any SCUD Missiles. Armed with conventional warheads and no internal guidance system, the SCUDs were not considered a military threat. Therefore, since the Patriot Missiles were being used as an anti-terror weapon to defend a civilian population, if the individuals being protected perceived that it was effective against the threat, then it was effective. In actuality, there were mixed emotions within the expatriate community regarding the Patriot's effectiveness. However, in retrospect, I would tend to agree with the opinion offered above. Most people viewed the Patriot's as a kind of security blanket. You know, like our old friend Linus in the comics. That old dirty tattered blanket that he drug around with him all the time, really didn't do him any good. However, he believed that it worked for him, and therefore, it did. And, gentlemen, as you know, that's the bottom line. Reality is as it is perceived to be in the minds of the individual, regardless of what the rest of the world may think.

"Each time Patriot Missiles were launched to intercept an incoming SCUD over Riyadh, three possible things could happen. First of all, the intercept could be successful, the missile destroyed and the warhead detonated. At that point, red-hot debris, including some sizable pieces, would shower down on the city below. A lot of the damage done in Riyadh was the result of falling debris. A second possible scenario was that the explosion of the Patriot would dislodge the missile from the warhead without detonating it. The live warhead would then fall onto the city below and detonate upon impact. That leaves us with the obvious third alternative, which was a miss. Yes, misses did occur. Did you notice, that each of the three scenarios which I described, all had a 'down side,' even the one with a successful intercept?

"So, once again, beauty is in the eye of the beholder. Even though the Patriot Missile was perhaps not as effective as all the worldwide publicity made it out to be during the war, it was a winner in the eyes of nearly everyone in Riyadh, Saudi Arabia. If someone had proposed that the Patriot's be removed during the course of the war because of their ineffectiveness, there would have been a public outcry that would have been heard clear back in Washington, D.C. It would have been such a deafening roar that it would have drowned out the sounds of all the warheads that detonated throughout the remainder of the war. And, in all fairness to the Patriot, let's give it the benefit of the doubt. As I noted earlier, it was originally designed as a surface-to-air, site-defense system. Riyadh, Saudi Arabia, is a big city, covering a very large geographical population area. It could hardly be defined as a 'site.' This missile was not designed to protect a target of this nature. Remember, it only had a range of approximately 65 miles. It just didn't have the 'legs' to get out and intercept the SCUDs before they were over the city. However, those who were in Riyadh during the war were most appreciative of both the missile, and the soldiers of the U.S. Army crews who manned the Patriot anti-missile batteries around Riyadh. As a matter of interest, I believe that the Patriot missile has subsequently been modified to counter the tactical ballistic missile threat."

"I understand that the 1998 Iraq Liberation Act funded nearly $100 million in support of equipment and training for opposition groups. Is it not also true that the President designated seven organizations as eligible to receive the approved U.S. military aid? If this is the case, is it necessary to put together yet another group and spend more of the taxpayers' money to deal with Saddam? Why not turn this task over to one of the organizations already certified?"

"That's an excellent question. Let me respond. Since the 1991 Gulf War, the main goal of U.S. foreign policy toward Iraq has been to contain Saddam, not remove him. However, President Maxwell signaled a change in that policy, pledging support for the Iraqi opposition and a renewed effort to bring a new government to power there. In October 1998, Congress passed the Iraq Liberation Act, funding $97 million for military equipment and training to unspecified opposition groups. The President apparently is ready to spend the money. One likely recipient is Ahmad Chalabi, who heads the Iraqi National Congress, a London-based umbrella group. He has enlisted an all-star team of former American officials to assist him in his efforts.

"The INC's proposed first step for covert military action against Saddam would be to train the trainers. As many as 200 to 300 Iraqi exiles would be trained by the CIA, Army Special Forces, or perhaps a trusted foreign country, to serve as trainers themselves. Russian-made weapons, rather than American rifles would be used in training to facilitate eventual infiltration into Iraqi military units. The trainers would then build-up a 'liberation army' of 3,000 to 5,000 soldiers, establishing units specializing in commando operations, anti-tank warfare, and propaganda. Obviously, a force of this size could not compete with the Iraqi Army in conventional combat. Their objective would be to establish 'liberation zones' in the regions north, west, and south of Iraq. Political and military leaders would then be encouraged to defect to these zones, joining up with the opposition to Saddam.

"Having said all of that, let's examine the downside for a moment. Some experts question whether Chalabi can deliver trained military units capable of challenging Saddam. In addition, many military analysts believe that for any destabilization plan to have a chance of success, outside protection, including American airpower and logistics staging areas in neighboring countries, would be required. When one reviews the record on the success of insurgencies, it is apparent that most fail, with significant loss of innocent lives, as well as the rebels. In any case, gentlemen, it appears that it will be some time before both a credible plan and a credible force can be put together, if ever. Needless to say, the powder keg that we're sitting on has too short a fuse to roll the dice on the INC with those long odds. We are going to have to deal with this threat ourselves in our own way."

"Assuming that Saddam has the weapons and the delivery capability, does he have the will to use them? As I recall, he claimed to have weapons of mass destruction during the war and threatened to use them, but never did. Was he bluffing then?"

"We assumed that he was bluffing because he had his back to the wall and was expected to pull out all the stops. If he had an ace up his sleeve, that certainly would have been the time to play it. Mr. Donovan, what can you tell us about that?"

"On August 8, 1990, 'Expats International,' a group headquartered in London, England, and claiming to be the world's largest service organization for expatriates, released correspondence addressing the threat of an Iraqi chemical attack which was widely read and distributed throughout the expatriate community in Saudi Arabia. The first paragraph of that article read as follows, 'We sent out a large number of telexes and faxes earlier today appraising expats of the Gulf crisis because we were fearful of an Iraqi attack. We knew through our own sources that chemical weapons were on the move by truck in Iraq. The situation changes from hour to hour and we are now less fearful of an attack on other Middle East countries by Iraq.' The fourth paragraph of that same communication, provided detailed information on what everyone should know and do in the event of chemical attack."

"Mr. Donovan, what was your own feeling regarding Iraq's possible use of chemical weapons during the Gulf War?"

"I have two personal experiences to relate. However, I am not sure of what significance, if any, to attach to them.

"Since it was sometimes difficult to hear the Civil Defense air raid siren in the housing area where we resided, we implemented our own pyramid alert system. As soon as one person became aware of an alert, they would phone the two people on their list, who would phone two additional people, etc., until everyone working for the company was notified. All of this had to happen very quickly, because there wasn't more than a few minutes possible warning from the time a SCUD missile launch in Iraq was detected, and its arrival over Riyadh.

"One day, I was visiting a friend of mine who worked nights at King Abul Aziz International Airport, located north of Riyadh. Many of the KC-135 Aircraft that provided in-air refueling to other USAF aircraft were stationed there. He informed me he carried a hand-held radio so he could constantly be in touch with operational activities at the airport. Consequently, he would usually receive warning of a SCUD missile attack prior to the activation of the civil defense air raid siren. At my request, he agreed to inform me as soon as he received notification over his radio. He had phoned on several previous occasions to this evening, and always without a doubt, shortly after his call, the civil defense siren outside our compound was activated.

"On this particular evening, he initially phoned in his usual manner and informed me that there was a 'red alert.' I understood this to mean that there was a confirmed launch of a SCUD missile at Saudi Arabia. I thanked him, and quickly called the two people on my list to notify them. Shortly thereafter, my phone rang again. I was surprised to learn it was my friend once again. Thinking perhaps he mis-dialed, I reminded him that he had already called. He replied that the threat had been upgraded to a 'black alert.' Since I had never heard this term before, I asked him what it meant. He informed me that 'a black alert' was the U.S. military warning for a 'probable chemical attack.' We came under SCUD missile attack on that occasion, but to the best of my knowledge, there was no evidence of the use of chemical weapons. However, answers are still being pursued as to the origin or cause of illness, termed 'Gulf War Syndrome,' from which many Gulf War veterans suffer.

"A second concern occurred on January 27, 1991. This was a date of particular significance. The Iraqis had previously broadcast a 72-hour warning for all loyal Muslims living in Riyadh, to evacuate the city. As I understood the warning, the city was going to be completely destroyed, with the accompanying implication that some form of a 'dirty' weapon, either chemical, biological, nuclear, was to be used. Saddam was quoted to the effect that after the attack, 'there would not be so much as a bird alive in the air, a fish alive in the sea, or any living creature on the ground.' This broadcast understandably frightened many people. Consequently, as the deadline approached, most residents of Riyadh evacuated the city and sought temporary refuge in the desert. To add credibility to his threat, Saddam had been publicly announcing in advance some aspects of his military operation. On these occasions, the predicted events had occurred pretty much right on schedule. Therefore, it was a serious threat and needed serious consideration. At this point in the war, Saddam, was beginning to see the handwriting on the wall. The possibility that the 'mother of all wars,' just might turn out to be the 'mother of all defeats.' Consequently, he was becoming desperate. As you know, desperate people often resort to desperate measures, and Saddam had already proven that he was capable of just about anything.

"As the day of the deadline wore on, the implied danger of the threat was constantly in the back of my mind. As much as I tried to dismiss it as just another scare tactic, it wouldn't go away. However, I was determined not to give in to Saddam's threats. I had come this far, and there was no turning back now. Fortunately, the day passed uneventfully. The following day, the morning sun came up as usual on Riyadh. The dreaded 72 hour deadline had come and gone without incident. After all the concern, it was another beautiful day in the 'Magic Kingdom.' According to a Voice of America broadcast on January 28, 1991, Saddam Hussein was quoted as saying that 'Iraq's SCUD missiles are capable of carrying nuclear, chemical, and biological warheads, but prays his country will not have to use them.'"

"How did the residents of Riyadh respond to the threat of a chemical attack?"

"Many of the Saudis living in Riyadh who held non-essential

positions evacuated to cities such as Jeddah and Taif, located in
the western part of the country. This area was considered to be a
safe-haven, as it was outside the range of the Iraqi SCUD missiles.
Most of those who stayed, temporarily relocated their families to
these same locations, so that they were removed from the threat,
and out of danger. Those who remained in the capital city handled
the missile attacks on their homes and families very well. There was
no sense of panic. They responded to the situation with a calmness
which exceeded that of many of the expats who resided there. It was
certainly a character building opportunity, and all the Saudis whom
I knew came through with flying colors. On several occasions, after
an early morning SCUD missile attack, I would receive a phone call
from one of my Royal Saudi Air Force counterparts, inquiring as to
the well being of my family. Their appreciation for our commitment,
presence, and efforts to assist on their behalf, was evident in the
concern they expressed for us and in the manner in which we were
treated."

"Were gas masks available?"

"Representatives of the U.S. Central Command in Saudi
Arabia repeatedly told the U.S. civilian community that Iraq did
not have the capability to deliver chemical weapons on Riyadh.
Therefore, the U.S. Embassy did not issue gas masks to American
citizen civilians. Nevertheless, it appeared that all American military
personnel stationed in Riyadh, had been issued a complete set of
protective gear, including a mask, suit, gloves, and a needle to self-
inject the antidote, Atropine, in case nerve gas was used. Some U.S.
civilians were not comfortable with this arrangement, believing that
it appeared to imply that there were two classes of Americans in
Saudi Arabia—those working for the U.S. Government and those
who weren't. However, others recognized that military personnel
were subject to redeployment at a moment's notice to anywhere
within the theater of operations and, therefore, needed to have all
their protective gear with them at all times."

"OK, gentlemen, it's the time of day that dedicated civil ser-
vants wash out their coffee cups and ride off into the sunset. Let's

call it a day. Our thanks to Agent Quibar for the intel run-down on Iraq, and to Mr. Donovan for his insights on Saddam's chemical weapons program. Have a nice evening, and we'll see you back here bright and early tomorrow morning."

# CHAPTER SIX

## CHECKMATE

*"Gentlemen, I've got a special treat for you today. I spoke to* Colonel Spice and he agreed to show us around his operation for a few minutes this morning. He runs a secret Air Force planning cell code-named 'Checkmate,' here in the Pentagon. I'll fill you in on a bit of background on the way down to their hangout. We need to be on our way. He's expecting us at 0900 hours.

"The people that you are going to meet are a special bunch of guys. They are a select hand-picked group of planners and operations research specialists working under the direction of the Deputy Chief of Staff for Plans & Operations. They are on-tap to respond to taskings from the Chief of Staff and other top-level urgent operational requirements that may surface. Their weapons of war are their planning expertise and ability to create various algorithms representing potential real world scenarios, and then use the latest computer modeling and simulation techniques to evaluate the feasibility of proposed operational contingency plans to counter the threat. This is the same group that was the brainchild of the 'parallel-war' theory adopted in Kosovo. Their strategy called for an air campaign that simultaneously targeted Serb air defenses, communications, supply lines, and logistics bases, in an attempt to neutralize Serbian air defenses and minimize allied casualties as a precursor to degrading Milosevic's Army.

"Well, here we are, Room 5D423, home of office symbol XOOIR, and some of the sharpest guys in the Pentagon. Hit that buzzer for me, Slash."

"Good afternoon gentlemen and welcome to 'Checkmate.' I'm Colonel Spice and I'll be showing you around our 'think-tank.' "First of all, let me introduce my staff. These are the gentlemen who have been involved in the planning phase of the mission on which you are about to embark.

"As you are aware, early management gurus defined the four basic functions of management as planning, organizing, directing, and controlling. It was not an accident that they placed planning at the top of the list. As such, it is the most important aspect of any activity, and therefore, the foremost responsibility of leadership. It sets the stage for everything else that follows. Consequently, the adequacy of the planning performed by the organization largely determines the ultimate success or failure of the endeavor. It is certainly a truism today that 'if you fail to plan, you plan to fail.'

"We take our work very seriously here in 'Checkmate,' and are very proud of the role we play. My people can make an important 'value added' contribution to just about anything that comes along. The size and nature of conflicts have changed, often requiring an untraditional response. This new special warfare–which can run the gamut from providing humanitarian assistance, to chasing down missing nuclear weapons, or rescuing hostages halfway around the world–still requires the application of airpower. Our job here in 'Checkmate' is to examine a problem or threat, come up with alternatives to neutralize it, and systematically evaluate them. We look at problems from the perspective of what analysts refer to as a 'model.' This is a representation or simulation of a real world situation which can be used to express and test ideas and concepts against prescribed criteria to determine effectiveness and measure risk. From here, a strategic approach and tactical plan can be formulated to accomplish mission objectives.

"This is the information age and my staff is at the cutting edge of computer information technology, knocking on the door of the practical use of artificial intelligence to further enhance our simulating and modeling capabilities. They possess skills that are in a real premium in the marketplace today. With the training and experience they possess, many of them are snapped up by the Rand Corporation immediately after they retire.

"There are three levels of planning factors that must be considered in operational contingency planning. First, there are the 'known-knowns.' These are things that we can anticipate and forecast with relative certainty. In essence, in this category, there should be no surprises. Next, there are the 'known-unknowns.' These are things that we can anticipate with some certainty that will take place, however, we are unsure of the outcome. And, finally, there are the 'unknown-unknowns.' This category frightens even the most gifted and talented of planners. It encompasses all those unexpected challenges that we cannot anticipate. They are hidden somewhere out there in the darkness waiting to leap out of the shadows and ambush us when we least expect it. It's our job to somehow ferret them out and make allowances for them so they don't endanger mission success. In this regard, we are in the business of mitigating risk.

"Before we get into the nitty gritty details, let's take a peak at the big perspective. One of the first points I want to make is that we do not work in a vacuum. We are believers in the old school which subscribes to the philosophy that all new knowledge is derived from existing knowledge. Consequently, we begin every new planning effort by a thorough research and review of 'lessons learned' from previous operations. There is frequently no time to 'reinvent the wheel.' In addition, an examination of previous efforts enables us to identify and steer clear of known mistakes and problem areas. While our goal is perfection, we understand that the perfect plan is yet to be written. What works well in a sterile laboratory environment does not always adapt well in the real world. However, we attempt to duplicate the actual environment through computer modeling and simulation, as closely as possible. A review of previous operations enables us to introduce many factors and elements into the equation which would otherwise be unknown to planners, thereby, creating a realism, otherwise not possible.

"Two of the many operations we looked at in the planning of Operation Desert Heat, were the 'Mayaguez Incident,' and 'Desert One.'

"The final battle of the Viet Nam War occurred on May 15, 1975. This brought an official end to the involvement of the United States in the Southeast Asia conflict. Oddly enough, the final chapter of this war was played out on the beaches of a small island off the coast of Cambodia, named 'Koh Tang.' It came to be known as the Mayaguez Incident. The SS Mayaguez was a merchant vessel carrying large containers of goods and merchandise destined for the Post Exchange in Bangkok, Thailand. Three days earlier, on May 12, l975, it was plowing through international waters off the coast of Cambodia, when it was attacked by naval fores of the Khmer Rouge. Over the next three days, Washington negotiated with Phnom Penh for the release of the crew of 40 merchant marine seamen captured at the time of the hijacking. During this three-day period, word of the crisis made headlines around the world.

"Although the Mayaguez incident became an international crisis, the real focus of attention was in the capital city of Bangkok, Thailand. The Thai Government was understandably concerned about possible repercussions from their new Communist neighbors if the U.S. used military units based on Thai soil to assist in the rescue operations. It was reported in the Bangkok Post, that the U.S. Government understood the concerns of their Thai allies and had promised not to involve Thai-based forces. When negotiations failed, President Ford approved a rescue effort to free the Mayaguez crew.

"On the morning of May 15, 1975, the rescue operation was launched. It included a ship-seizure team from the destroyer escort ship, the USS Harold E. Holt, which assaulted and boarded the Mayaguez. However, the crew had already been removed. Also involved in the rescue effort, according to Thai Government officials, were several Sikorsky HH-53 Helicopters carrying air-sea rescue teams based in Nakhon Phanom Air Base, Thailand. They were known as the 'Jolly Green Giants.' Their mission during the Viet Nam War was search and rescue, attempting to locate and rescue downed aircrew members from the jungles of North Viet Nam, and the waters offshore in the Gulf of Tonkin. During the attack on the eastern beach of Koh Tang, three of the HH-53 Helicopters were shot down and nine others received severe damage. At the completion of the mission, only one was still air worthy. In the darkness of the night, a total of 231 airmen, marines, and naval personnel were extracted from the island. However, this heroic rescue effort was not without a heavy price, as eighteen men were unaccounted for, and presumed lost. While U.S. newspapers hailed the rescue effort as successful, Thai newspapers condemned the operation as a flagrant violation of a sacred promise and solemn oath given by a friend.

"In the evening of April 24, 1980, an elite U.S. military force launched a bold attempt to rescue 53 American citizens held hostage in the U.S. Embassy in Tehran, Iran. The effort ended in failure at a remote location in Iran now known as 'Desert One.' Five United States Air Force personnel and three marines lost their lives in that fiery disaster. Eight aircraft were also destroyed.

"Two weeks after the Shah of Iran was allowed to enter the U.S. for medical care, 3,000 Iranian students took 66 Americans hostage in the U.S. Embassy. The majority of the hostages were held for 14 months while the students demanded the Shah be returned to Iran for trial.

"The Chairman of the Joint Chiefs of Staff, at the request of the National Security Advisor, established a small, secretive planning group termed 'Rice Bowl,' to study military options for a rescue effort. However, it quickly became apparent that this would be a most difficult undertaking, fraught with obstacles. The capitol city of Tehran was isolated, surrounded by more than 700 miles of desert and mountains in every direction. This negated any opportunity for the employment of U.S. air or naval forces. In addition, the U.S. Embassy was located in the heart of a city populated by more than four million people.

"U.S. Special Operations Forces had taken a beating during the draw-down after the withdrawal from Vietnam. The cutbacks which occurred greatly reduced both the size and quality of elite forces available to counter the danger of international terror. A recently formed unit of soldiers dubbed 'Delta Force,' was, therefore, selected for the mission.

"The final rescue plan was staggering in its scope and complexity. It called for the bringing together of scores of aircraft and thousands of men from all four Armed Services extracted from military units literally scattered around the world, and tasking them with performing a highly complex mission. All this was to be accomplished in a five-month period of planning, organizing, training, and a series of intricate exercises. Lack of necessary detailed intelligence on the facilities in Tehran, and difficulty in achieving a coherent team effort, contributed to mission failure. In addition, a commission investigating the reasons for the tragedy, suggested that apparent weaknesses in the chain of command, and emphasis on excessive security also hindered the effectiveness of the operation.

\*\*\*

"Keep in mind gentlemen that what we're going to see today is a computer simulation. As in any other computer operation where data is input and manipulated, the statement 'garbage in, garbage out,' or simply 'GIGO,' is equally applicable here. Simulating the details of a real world operational mission to successfully neutralize Saddam's missile capability on a computer, is somewhat akin to 'catching lightning in a bottle.' We are attempting to create a microcosm of real world conditions right here in the office. Our ability to predict mission success is only as accurate as the algorithm that we construct mirrors reality, and the data elements that are utilized to portray the variables, reflect actual real-world conditions.

"When conducting operational contingency planning in the military, we generally examine at least three alternative scenarios: best possible case, worst possible case, and most probable case. With this range of data, it allows us to pretty much see the entire playing field and evaluate options and alternatives. Think of it as the offensive coordinator calling the plays from his vantage point high-up in the stadium. Based on his assessment of the game situation, he is scanning his play book for something that will catch the defense off-guard. However, as you are aware, every play-call does not result in a touchdown. The opponent is not under the grandstands napping. The defensive coordinator is calling defensive signals, anticipating the offense's next move. Similarly, no military operation is risk free. There is an element of danger associated with crossing the street.

"First of all, we establish some basic ground rules by way of definitions to guide us in simulating our mission. Definition number one is that of 'Mission Success.' As we successfully exit each phase of the operation, we enter the next succeeding phase. Mission success is defined as achieving success in each of the four individual operational phases of the missions.

"Definition number two is that of 'Mission failure.' Mission Failure is defined as lack of mission success in any one of the four individual phases of the operation. If any individual phase of the mission is a failure, then the entire mission is aborted at that point. All subsequent phases of the operation are scrubbed, and we move immediately to phase four of the mission–extraction. The probability of mission success at this point is defined as zero.

"For illustration purposes, we have divided the mission into four operational phases, including insertion, missile system control center neutralization, air strikes, and extraction. Each operational phase of the mission is then assigned a probability of success based on the accessed opportunity for successful execution. Let's assume that we are examining the 'most probable' case, and have assigned the probabilities of success, as reflected on this overhead viewgraph, to each of the operational phases."

## DETERMINING THE PROBABILITY OF MISSION SUCCESS

| Operational Phase: | INSER-TION | NEUTRALIZA-TION | AIR-STRIKES | EXTRAC-TION |
|---|---|---|---|---|
| Probability of Success: | (.98) | (.75) | (.90) | (.95) |

| Mission Success: P(P1) | x | P(P2) | x | P(P3) | x | P(P4) |
|---|---|---|---|---|---|---|
| Mission Success: (.98) | x | (.75) | x | (.90) | x | (.95) |

"When we do the math, we find that the overall probability of mission success in this example is .63, or 63 percent. We are also conducting some sensitivity testing on such critical elements of the mission as time, to determine how slight variations in execution of each operational phase impact the overall mission. Any unanticipated delay that disrupts the timing of any phase of the operation, has the potential for grave potential consequences on the successful execution of the following phases. Each second is extremely critical with human lives hanging in the balance. To ensure successful extraction, all elements of the ground teams must be safely withdrawn to the collection point prior to the discovery of our evacuation aircraft standing by in the staging area by elements of Saddam's security or military forces.

"Please remember, that this is a grossly oversimplified example of how the model works. In actuality, the simulation is far more complex. We are still fine-tuning and tweaking the algorithm. It takes into consideration scores of variables representing all the various elements which have to be considered in a complex mission planning effort such as this.

"Results from the preliminary runs are pretty much as expected. Examination of the output indicates, for the most part, things tend to run pretty smoothly through the early stages of the mission. It's during the later stages where execution starts to get a little ragged, and the wheels threaten to come off the operation. This comes as no big surprise. At this point, the ground elements have been successfully inserted, Saddam's missile launch control system neutralized, and air strikes on the missile silos executed. Needless to say, our gig is no longer just our little secret. It's probably fast breaking news around the world, pre-empting the TV coverage of your favorite sports team at the most critical juncture of the game. That's when the network switchboards are flooded with complaints from irrate fans. The average 'Joe,' your basic couch potato, is far more interested in berating the officials one minute for a 'bad' call that might cost his team the game, and his wife the next minute for not hustling another cold brew over to her man, than he is over what he thinks are some lunatics attempting to pull Saddam's chain in Iraq."

"Thanks a lot for mentioning that, Colonel. It helps me put this whole idiotic plan in some kind of a proper prospective. This is a recipe for disaster. It's a plan designed to incur casualties, a suicide mission. Undoubtedly, those probabilities of mission success you showed us earlier, already have losses factored in as a cost of doing business."

"Hey, you know what they say, Slash. If you don't have a passion for what you're doing, you shouldn't be doing it."

"Yea, that's what I keep telling myself. Unfortunately, somebody else keeps answering for me."

"So what's the problem? You got a mouse in your pocket, or something?"

"Close, but no cigar. It's more like a rat, and it's not in my pocket. If it were that simple, I'd deal with it."

"Oh, by the way, Colonel Spice, we appreciate the fact that you world-class 'air heads' or 'whizz kids, 'or whatever it is you call yourselves, were involved in the planning of this mission. However, we're the guys committed to its execution. If you have any doubt as to the degree of difference, consider this next time you sit down to a breakfast of ham and eggs: 'The chicken was involved, but the pig was committed.' So, with all due respect, Colonel, you can take that 63 percent probability of mission success and stick it somewhere it will never again see the light of day."

"What's with this guy, Colonel Rampkin? He handles like a used car, totally out of control. I'd put him in the garage for a front end alignment for starters, and then slap on some new brake pads to curb that attitude of his."

"It's a long story, Spice. You know, when you're not the lead dog, the scenery never changes. When we have more time someday, I'll tell you about it."

***

"Can you believe those guys, Pounder? You buy 'em books and send them to school, and they sit in the corner and chew on the backs. I'm not saying our old buddy Spice is incompetent, but I've heard tell that he couldn't stand on the beach and spit in the ocean.

"Take it easy, Slash. You know what they say, 'Never wrestle with pigs. They enjoy it and all you get is dirty.'"

"Yea I know, but it just eats my lunch to think that the taxpayer is picking up the bill for all that bologna. And, it's so nice to know that they all have such nice cushy jobs waiting for them when they retire. That gives me such a warm, fuzzy feeling when I think about it that I could almost puke. Whatever happed to the Air Force motto, 'Our mission is to fly and fight and don't you ever forget it?' It used to be so easy in the old days. You packed up your warrior's mentality, strapped on your big silver jet, kicked the tires, lit the fires, and off you went full afterburner into the wild blue yonder. This new high-tech Air Force has gone overboard. In their headlong rush into the world of the latest and greatest bells and whistles mode, they've left behind an important part of their tradition. Man, I'm glad that I did my time while we were still a first class outfit."

"I agree that our 'think-tank' friends have a bit of an attitude, Slash. However, based on your comments, it appears that you've led somewhat of a sheltered life in your Air Force career. You were a line pilot during your time in the Service. You had a specific mission that you went out and flew every day. Now I don't want to bust your bubble or anything like that, but you were operating in your own little world. Out there with your head in the clouds everyday, flying around in the wild blue yonder, you were oblivious to that 'other' world. I'm speaking of the world of the headquarters staffer. Many people think that headquarters staffers only exist to provide top-level support to the primary mission. That is, their job is to take care of all of the overhead type functions. They manage tasks like administration, budgeting, and so forth, so you fighter jocks can spend your time doing what you're trained to do without having to worry about all the little 'nit-noys' that go along with running an air force. Ah, but that's the great fallacy of military life.

"While you war heroes were out fighting Communism and making the world safe for Democracy, the headquarters staffers pulled off the greatest military coup of all times. And, the amazing thing was, they did it without firing a single shot. In an absolutely bloodless coup, they wrestled control of the military away from the guys with the primary mission. In their eyes, they are now the primary mission, and line pilots like you, only exist to do their bidding. In their minds, you need them more than they need you. You exist only as an adjunct of their being. In other words, all you base level operators could dry up and blow away, and the headquarters staffers would still continue doing their thing, uninterrupted. They would still make plans, policy, or whatever, even though there wasn't anyone outside their office cubicle to execute them anymore. And furthermore, they would still go home at night with an over-inflated feeling of self-importance. Headquarters staffers have taken on a life and importance of their own that is now bigger and more important than the Air Force mission itself. The 'warrior' mentality of the 'old' Air Force has been replaced with the 'administrative management' mentality of the 'new' Air Force. Guys like you are relics. You're out of step and out of touch with today's Air Force. The fact of the matter is, we don't need pilots in the Air Force anymore. The Air Force's motto now days is, "Give me enough staffers, enough computers, and enough hi-tech equipment, and I'll bring the enemy to his knees."

# CHAPTER SEVEN

# JOGGING MEMORIES IN D.C.

*"Hey Slash, we've got an extended lunch break. I don't know about* you, but I need some fresh air to clear my mind from all that hot air we were exposed to this morning. How about a little physical exercise? Let's head down to the Pentagon Officers Athletic Club, change into our sweats, and take in the tourist sites with a run down to the Capitol Mall."

"Wow! I didn't know that you guys had your own private athletic club. This is one heck of a good deal."

"Well, you know what they say, Slash, RHIP—'Rank Has Its Privileges.' After all, we are 'Officers and Gentlemen by Act of Congress.' Therefore, we should be afforded all the comforts and pleasures commensurate with our exalted station in life."

"Yea, sure. You're going to have to take the time someday to sit down and explain to me what I've obviously been missing–that part about our exalted station in life."

Pounder and Slash take their leave of the Pentagon, crossing the Potomac River into Washington, D.C. The Jefferson Memorial soon comes into view. A number of small rental paddle boats dot the Tidal Basin, formed by the backwaters of the Potomac. Completely surrounded by cherry trees, a gift of the Japanese Government, this area is the eighth wonder of the world for a few days in early Spring. The trees burst forth with an abundance of blossoms creating an incomparable display of radiant pink color that would make a flamingo proud. With spirits soaring from the temporary escape of the dullness of the Pentagon into the magnificence of the scenery they are witnessing, Pounder and Slash continue north in the direction of the Mall. Many locals and a number of tourists to the Nation's Capitol are relaxing on the lush green grass, soaking in both the grandeur of the view and the warm rays of the afternoon sun.

It is a beautiful Fall day in the nation's Capital. There is just a nip of coolness in the air, reminding Pounder and Slash that old man Winter is waiting in the wings ready to burst through the door with all the furry of a woman scorned, and intrude upon the world's stage at the first opportunity. The trees are breathtaking, all decked out in their Autumn leaves of gold, brown, red, and every shade in between. Mother Nature is at her very best in New England as she extends her personal easel to the entire area, splashing dazzling colors across the canvas and countryside that make a mockery of Claude Monet's great masterpiece "Water-Lily Pond with Bridge." The vivid splendor of the colors leap off her canvas, permeate every pore in the skin, are instantaneously absorbed in the blood stream, and rushed to the extremities of the human body. There, they illuminate the mind and radiate the soul with a warmth unmatched by the rays of the sun on the finest of summer days.

Drinking in the peerless beauty of the scenery with an unquenchable thirst, Pounder and Slash are seemingly suspended in time, overcome with feelings of inner peace, calm, and tranquillity that can be found in no other way or place in this momentous world in which they dwell. As they ponder their future and fate, they find temporary escape and sanctuary from the waves of anxiety that continually sweep over them like the breeze through a field of wheat, bending them in one direction and then another with swirling currents of air. They are reminded that some say we are never as alive as when we come face to face with the end of our own human existence. Perhaps, they think, this is but a prelude to the ultimate peace that each of us is promised after our escape from the trials and torment of this world.

Arriving at the Mall, Pounder and Slash make a left turn heading west away from the U.S. Capitol in the direction of the Washington Monument. They marvel at the majesty of the Monument reaching up toward the heavens, its angelic appearance scarred by the extended scaffolding put in place for a much needed facelift. Up ahead, they see the Reflecting Pool with a full length image of the Washington Monument shimmering on its surface. It is strategically placed in an East-West direction, stretching between the Washington Monument on the East and the Lincoln Memorial on the West. They jog past the breathtaking Constitution Gardens in the direction of the Vietnam Veterans Memorial located in the shadow of the stately Lincoln Memorial.

The Vietnam War Memorial was built in Washington, D.C. in 1982. Designed by American sculptor and architect Maya Ying Lin, it is a large sloping, V-shaped, black granite wall. Inscribed on it are the names of more than 58,000 Americans killed or missing in the Vietnam War. Erected nearby in 1984, are sculptures of three soldiers by Frederick E. Hart. Sculptures of a wounded soldier and three nurses by Glenna Goodacre, were also put in place in 1993. As they drew close, memories of its dedication flood Pounder's mind. They had been running silently up to that time, side by side, and stride for stride, however, each very much alone with his own personal thoughts. As they near the striking black marble of the Memorial, Pounder feels the sudden need for a sounding board, someone to listen to what has been bottled up inside for a very long time.

"You know, Slash," Pounder said, breaking the silence and startling his companion who appeared to be mentally a few hundred-thousand light years away, "I was here on November 13, 1982, the day they dedicated the Memorial."

"You were?" Slash responded. "I'll bet it was a very special occasion with a lot of lingering memories." They slow to a walk and select a park bench in the shade of a tree with a view of the Memorial. Although unplanned, it was a great place to catch their breath and reminisce about their Viet Nam War experiences.

"Unfortunately, it did not turn out to be the memorable event that it should have been. I was in the audience that day to pay tribute to our comrades in arms who had fallen in battle or were reported missing in action during the Viet Nam War. However, as I was soon to find out, while many were there to dedicate and commemorate, a few were there to desecrate. Shortly after the ceremony began and the TV cameras went live, an individual standing directly behind me in the packed crowd began shouting anti-Vietnam War slogans in an effort to disrupt the dedication. He was joined by a few others dispersed throughout the crowd. I remember thinking to myself, what a truly sad occasion this was. The military members whose names were engraved on the Memorial died defending the rights and freedoms of the very protesters who were now disrupting the dedication ceremony. Unfortunately, Slash, it sometimes appears that the greatest strength of a democracy, the classic freedoms we enjoy, are used and abused by people with no thought of the sacrifices that were made to put them in place and to ensure their continuance."

"Well, good buddy, as you know, you're preaching to the choir. If you're expecting a rebuttal from me, you're going to be very disappointed. I couldn't agree more. However, the draft has been scrapped along with the requirement for mandatory military service. Therefore, the vast majority of Americans will never know, or for that matter, understand the personal sacrifices required of members of the military serving their country in uniform. Being an American with all of the attendant freedoms we enjoy is the greatest privilege in the world, as long as someone else has the responsibility of fighting for the preservation of those freedoms."

"The worst part, Slash, is that this is beginning to sound more and more like an instant reply. It appears that we're being set up to do some dirty work for which someone else is going to receive the credit."

"And that surprises you?"

"No, I've been around too long to be surprised much anymore. Seldom surprised, but frequently disappointed. However, I am still a little confused from the last time around."

"What last time was that?"

"One day, I'm stationed at a radar squadron on a mountain top just outside the capital city of Charleston, West Virginia. The next day I'm on my way to Southeast Asia to fight a war."

"Well I hope that you didn't feel like the Lone Ranger. You were in good company."

"Yes, I was. Some of the finest people you would ever want to meet. Of course, just as in other aspects of life, it takes all kinds. We were a diverse group bound together with a common mission."

"What stands out in your mind about your contemporaries?"

"As you know, it is never safe to generalize, Slash. However, for the sake of this war story, I need to take a little literary license."

"You've got my permission, Pounder."

"It appeared to me, Slash, that there were three types of people involved in the war effort. First of all, there were the 'real macho types' who enjoyed talking tough and flexing their muscles. They seemed to really be into and take pleasure in what they were doing. You know, kind of like, 'just stand back and give me some room, and I'm going to take care of this thing.' Chances are, when their time was up they would volunteer to extend their assignment and continue on in the theater. Then, there were 'the adventurous types.' They were most likely there to escape their meaningless lives and be relieved of the boredom back home. They considered themselves to be better lovers than fighters. As such, they were in no particular hurry to get back home, as long as their lives were in no immediate danger. Finally, there were 'the true, blue, all American boys,' who were there because it was the patriotic thing to do. They did not get any enjoyment out of what they were doing, but understood that it was a job that had to be done. Their spare time was spent thinking of their families and loved ones, and counting the days until they could return home.

"Music has always played a big part in the lives of Americans. We love our music, and we all have our own favorites whether it is pop, rock, heavy metal, jazz, rock and roll, country western, rap, the blues, or what have you. And, as you might expect, when Americans pack their bags, and go to war, they take their music with them. It's never left behind. After all, what would life be without music, war or no war? So, it was in Southeast Asia during the Viet Nam War. Every GI bar had its jukebox loaded with popular American music. I don't know how they managed to do it, but they always had all of the latest tunes. Regardless of where you went, you could always find a jukebox to drop a quarter in and listen to your favorite song."

"What were the most played songs, Pounder?"

"I'm sure they never took an official survey to determine what the most played song was during the Viet Nam War, but I had my own opinion, Slash. At the time, I was so sure that I would have been willing to put a day's wages on it. It was a toss-up among 'The Green Beret,' 'Love Potion Number Nine,' and 'The Green, Green, Grass of Home.'

"As you know, Slash, the mood of a person is often reflected in the music they listen to. By observing an individual and listening to the song they play, you can possibly gain some insight into what they are thinking at the time. Here's how I had it figured. If an individual walked up to the jukebox and played the song, 'The Green Beret,' he placed himself in the first category that I described. He was there to make a statement. Anyone playing the song, 'Love Potion Number Nine,' was definitely in the second group looking for a little adventure. Even the war in SEA was better than joining the French Foreign Legion. And, last, but not least, Slash, the people who voted with their quarter for the song, 'The Green, Green, Grass of Home,' were the all American boys in my third category."

"Was there ever any time that you questioned the war effort or your participation in it?"

"No, not at the time. We were too caught up in the day-to-day work to step back and question the big picture. We had a job to do and we did it well. However, there was one occasion, when our involvement in the war was called into question."

"What was that, Pounder?"

"One evening, after another 12-hour day on the flight line, I was sitting on the steps of my hooch with a group of fellow lieutenants from the 355th Tactical Fighter Wing at Takhli Royal Thai Air Force

Base in Thailand. One of them had purchased a new short wave radio from the base exchange and was trying it out to see what they could pick-up. At first, all we heard were a lot of loud buzzing and static. It was like the radio signal was being jammed. Then all of a sudden, there it was, loud, clear, and distinct. It was the voice of 'Hanoi Hanna.'"

"Hanoi Hanna?"

"I assume you've heard of 'Tokyo Rose,' and 'Peking Polly?'"

"Yes, I believe that I have."

"Well, Slash, Hanoi Hanna was North Viet Nam's answer to the other two aforementioned ladies. It was the voice of the North Viet Nam's propaganda machine at its very best. And, then the most remarkable thing happened. Just as we tuned her in, she was referring to the 355th TFW. She was talking directly to us, or as she so eloquently put it with just the slightest of an accent, 'the airman stationed at the large American Air Base located at Takhli, Thailand.' At first, I thought it was amusing. But, as I continued to listen, I got a cold shiver up my back, and my breathing became shallow as I hung on every word."

"What did she say?"

"For the most part, the typical propaganda message. She was attempting to plant seeds of doubt in our minds as to the legitimacy of the U.S. war effort. Of course, it was all packaged in a masterful way. She wasn't blaming us for the war. We were all just innocent victims, as were the North Vietnamese people. This unjust war was being waged by the U.S. Government with the assistance, support, and encouragement of the U.S. defense industry. We were killing hundreds of innocent civilians each day with our reckless acts of war, destroying entire villages with our bombs, maiming and injuring thousands more. When would all the senseless killing stop? How much longer were we going to stand by and be a party to the atrocities that were taking place? Wouldn't we all be happier if we were back home with our families and loved ones, instead of participating in this genocide against the peace-loving Vietnamese people?

"At the end of the broadcast, she alluded to the fact that

another American airman from the 355th TFW had been taken captive that day after his airplane had been downed over North Viet Nam. I believe that she even mentioned him by name. We were never sure whether that information was accurate or not, as we did not receive daily updates on aircraft and aircrew losses over the North. Understandably, this information was kept close-hold on a need-to-know basis, while rescue efforts were still underway. At the time, we all took it for what we assumed it was, a cleverly disguised propaganda effort with the intent of affecting our morale. However, to this day, her words still echo loud and clear in my memory.

"With 20/20 hindsight, a lot of people questioned our involvement in the war. However, the one that caused the most stir was the then Secretary of Defense, Robert McNamara.

"John Kennedy, in putting together his Cabinet after the presidential election of 1960, selected Robert McNamara as his Secretary of Defense. He was a highly successful businessman who at the time was President of Ford Motor Corporation. Robert McNamara served as U.S. Secretary of Defense from 1961 to 1968. During this period, he modernized management techniques within the Department of Defense, and de-emphasized nuclear weapons. During the early stages of the Viet Nam War, McNamara's hawkish approach to the conflict was attributed as the key to Washington's military involvement.

"However, the former Defense Secretary under Presidents Kennedy and Johnson, later said that the war was a grave error. He sent a memorandum to President Johnson on May 19, 1967, that stated, 'There may be a limit beyond which many Americans and much of the world will not permit the United States to go. The picture of the world's greatest superpower killing or seriously injuring 1,000 noncombatants a week, while trying to pound a tiny backward nation into submission on an issue whose merits are hotly disputed, is not a pretty one. It could conceivably produce a costly distortion in the American national consciousness and in the world image of the United States—especially if the damage to North Vietnam is complete enough to be successful.'

"Robert McNamara's doubts about the Vietnam War led him to resign from the Cabinet in 1968. He later served as president of the World Bank from 1968 to 1981. His memoirs, published in 1995, contended that U.S. forces—at that point only military advisors—should have been pulled out of Vietnam as early as 1963, when American casualties stood at only 78. 'Although we sought to do the right thing—and believed we were doing the right thing—in my judgment, hindsight proves us wrong,' he wrote. Veterans have denounced McNamara for his belated confession, saying he had been wrong to keep sending soldiers to die in a war he considered unwinnable.

"So, many years later, and at a cost of 58,000 American, and more than three million Vietnamese lives, the Vietnam War was officially declared a mistake by the same gentlemen who sent me and hundreds of thousands of other Americans to Southeast Asia. As I said earlier, Slash, I'm still a little confused about all this."

"Ponder no more my good friend, Pounder. Perhaps I can enlighten you a bit and help clear up your confusion. You've obviously never completed the basic course entitled 'The Economics of War 101.'

"Did you ever notice that GI bars never close in a war? That would be disastrous for at least a couple of reasons. First of all, war is not just an eight hours a day operation. You don't just grab your old lunch pail, head for the barn, and take the rest of the day off at five o'clock in the afternoon. Unfortunately, war is a 24 hours a day, seven days a week affair. There are no time outs to take a nap, or any other luxuries like that. There is always someone who is just getting off duty, who is looking for a watering hole, and a place to let off a little anxiety and frustration. The last thing they want to hear at that point in the day, is 'the bar is closed.'

"Secondly, and perhaps most important, look at the economic impact of closing just one bar for one day in a war, let alone every bar in the entire theater. Think of all the money that would be lost. Most of the communities located near U.S. military bases overseas are heavily dependent on the income generated from GI bars.

Remember back when you studied Economics 101. Do you remember the term, 'trickle down' effect? When one dollar is spent for an item of goods or for some service, it doesn't stop there. That same dollar gets recirculated several times through the local economy as people pay their bills and purchase the things they need. Therefore, many people on down the food chain benefit economically both directly and indirectly, apart from the business that initially generated the expenditure. The GIs probably didn't stop to think about it, but every time they dropped a dollar on the local economy, that dollar filled many rice bowls. Hey, Pounder, The Office of Management and Budget in the nation's capital in Washington, D.C., has got an entire room full of so called 'experts' in this area. Their entire purpose in life is sitting around attempting to forecast the economic fallout of the Government's spending of each dollar of the taxpayer's money, in terms of the stimulating effect it will have on the U.S. economy. And, an important part of that calculation, is taking into consideration the 'trickle down effect,' of the initial expenditure on the economy as a whole. As they say, 'it's a tough job, but somebody has to do it.'

"We're getting a bit off the track here, Pounder. However, your confusion strikes right at what many feel is the heart of the war issue. Specifically, what role does economics play, if any, in the decision to engage in a war? When President Eisenhower warned us against the acquisition of unwarranted influence by the military-industrial complex in his farewell address to the nation in January 1961, was it just fortuitous? Norman Cousins once stated, 'The possibility of war increases in direct proportion to the effectiveness of the instruments of war.' Who can forget all those hi-tech 'smart weapons,' that we used in the Gulf War? They were most definitely the difference. We 'liked Ike,' but should we take his warning seriously? How effective are defense contractors and special interest groups in influencing political decisions regarding the expenditures of tax dollars for research & development of new weapon systems? And of course, that begs the question, of what need are new state-of-the art weapons of war if there is no longer a threat of war? It all gets a bit dicey at this point, Pounder, well beyond my pay grade. But one thing is for sure, and you can take it to the bank: 'money may not sing and dance, and it can't walk, but it sure talks—loud and clear!' And, when big business and big money talk, politicians whose future depends on the expenditure of that money, listen. They listen very carefully.

"The Communist experiment has failed and the Soviet Union, our once feared adversary, the 'great red bear,' has been housebroken. The phrase 'Better Dead Than Red,' was well put. After all, the best definition I ever heard of a Communist was, 'A person who had nothing and wanted to share it with you.' That opportunity wouldn't turn many people on, no matter how desperate a situation they found themselves in. The U.S. had been engaged in a relentless war against the great red scourge. This cause consumed a good share of the nation's attention, time, and resources, including many of her finest sons and daughters. The Communist threat had been the central focus as a rallying point to unify Americans over an extended period of time. However, the long sought after victory was finally achieved. All of the great enemies of the people have been defeated and the flag waving is now over. NATO has expanded its membership to include several former members of the WARSAW Pact. As a result, the once perceived threat of an East vs. West nuclear, or even conventional war is greatly diminished. Many American citizens expect to see a downsizing in the U.S. military, and a corresponding decrease in the defense budget. People are talking about the possibility of a 'peace dividend.' Is there such a thing, and if so, when and where will it manifest itself?

"The U.S. defense industry as a whole is in trouble. There used to be dozens of prime defense contractors waiting with bated breath to participate in the next DOD competitive procurement for hi tech state-of-the-art weapons of war, whether it were aircraft, tanks, or ships. Now, with a greatly reduced defense budget, such procurements are few and far between. There just isn't enough business to go around, Pounder. Consequently, defense contractors are scrambling to survive. The defense industry has undergone consolidation, the likes of which have never been seen before. We are now down to two or three industry giants who have swallowed up everyone else.

"Can the U.S. survive without a McDonnell Douglas Corporation? If they were a plant or an animal, perhaps they could have gotten themselves on the 'endangered species' list. However, it is not a laughing matter for those who depend on the defense industry for their livelihoods. Many people are out of work because of the consolidations, downsizing, and shutdowns, without usable job skills to land employment in other industries. A substantial investment in training programs is required to relocate these individuals to areas that have a shortfall in technical skills, such as information technology.

"My advice, Pounder. Call your broker and sell your defense stocks. Invest in biotech, medical, and healthcare stocks. Perhaps there will be a 'peace dividend,' after all. Hopefully, sufficient tax dollars will now be available to properly fund the required research necessary to find cures for cancer, AIDS, arthritis, Alzheimer, and the many other dreadful diseases that inflict pain, suffering, and loss of life on the human race. In my humble opinion, we've taken enough lives. It's now time to save some. Hopefully, we can start with our own. Having said that, let's head on back to the Pentagon. We've got bigger fish to fry right now, attempting to come up with a plan to keep Saddam from making complete chaos out of world order."

# CHAPTER EIGHT

## OPERATION DESERT HEAT

*"Well gentlemen, aside from D-day itself, this is perhaps the* most important day that we will spend together. Today, we're going to go over the operational mission briefing. So, make yourselves comfortable. During the next few hours, the briefer will walk us through the planning scenario that we have laid-on at this time. It's an excellent opportunity for everyone involved to get a first-hand look at what is coming down the pike and how we plan for it to go down. If we can talk our way through all of it and it makes sense to everyone here, with a lot of classroom training and integrated field exercises, chances are we'll be able to pull it off at game time."

"Thank you, and good afternoon, gentlemen. I'm Lt. Colonel Smith. Let's get right to it. We're going to begin today's briefing with an overview of the mission. The big picture, if you will. As such, on the first pass through, I'm just going to hit the hot buttons. With the skeleton in place, we'll then have a framework against which to flesh out the details. Hopefully, approaching it in this manner, will provide each of you with a clear picture of what we plan to do and how we expect to execute our plan. From time to time, I will refer to the maps and charts on the wall behind me, which highlight the locations of major points of interest and principal data used in planning the operational mission.

"The Task Force will be composed of the two major components, the aircrews and the ground crews. The ground crews will be made-up of the assault team and the seizure team. The assault team will be responsible for neutralizing Iraqi security, and the seizure team for neutralizing the Missile System Control Center. The composition of the aircrews will be driven by the weapon systems selected to accomplish the airlift and air strike portions of the mission. The composition of the ground crew will be based on the different specialists required to carry out the assault and seizure portions of the mission. The final numbers will be determined during the training phase, prior to the last dress rehearsal.

"Intelligence predicts minimum Iraqi resistance at the MSC2, assuming we can successfully penetrate their outer security without detection. The rule of thumb generally used to size an assault force, is to have a three to one advantage in manpower. In combat, the technique of reconnoiter by fire is frequently used. However, this being a covert mission against a facility guarded by security forces, we won't be using that tactic and, therefore, won't require those odds. Our primary weapon on this mission is the element of surprise, and our primary fear, the possibility of being detected. Therefore, the fewer people involved, the less equipment required, with less risk of detection.

"With a parachute drop ruled out due to lack of jump-qualification of some of the seizure team, helicopters became the best option for insertion of the Task Force into Iraq. They will be airlifted From King Abul Aziz Air base in Eastern Saudi Arabia to a secure location in the desert where they will rendezvous with members of an Iraqi opposition force's group.

"After refueling, the helicopter aircrews will return to the staging area in Saudi Arabia, and standby for orders to extract the Task Force. Members of the Task Force will then be driven to the vicinity of the MSC2 in vehicles obtained by the Iraqi agents.

"After successful neutralization of the MSC2, the aircrews will be given the green light to proceed. The timing and coordination between the ground and air elements of the Task Force will be critical. The senior operative on the ground will be responsible for providing the coordinates and calling in the air strikes. Because of its super stealth qualities, the F-117A Nighthawk is the weapon system the aircrews will fly the planned air strikes against the MSC2, and the three 'hot' missile silos containing the weapons of mass destruction. The chopper will then return to extract the Task Force and fly them back to the staging area at King Abdul Aziz Air Base in Saudi Arabia.

"A three-ship flight of F-15s will be airborne during the entire operation under the control of an E-3 Airborne Warning and Control System aircraft. They will remain outside of Iraqi airspace to avoid being detected by Saddam's integrated air defense system, and alerting the Iraqis to the mission. If unexpected resistance from Saddam's air force is encountered by either the helicopters airlifting the Task Force into Iraq, or the F-117A aircraft enroute to their targets, the F-15s will be on the scene in a matter of minutes. They will also provide cover for the E-3C while in orbit, be available to defend the rescue force from any Iraqi counter attacks during extraction, and to escort the Nighthawks back to their recovery bases in Saudi Arabia.

"An AWACS aircraft will oversee the entire mission, maintaining a surveillance orbit at a safe stand-off distance from the designated area of operations for surveillance, communications, and command & control purposes. The surveillance crew will be alert for any Iraqi aircraft that may be airborne at the time of the operation and pose a threat to the mission.

"Well, those are essentially all the big pieces, gentlemen. And, I know exactly what you're all thinking at this point: Easy for him to say. Right? Please holster those weapons and hold your fire. Remember. I'm just the messenger. A little cog in a very big wheel.

"All right, now that you've all got a view from topside, let's ratchet it down a few indentures and sneak a peak at some of the details.

"The ride in will be strictly first class, compliments of the 20th Special Operations Squadron, the largest of four special operations helicopter squadrons in the active Air Force. They are a unit of the

Air Force Special Operations Command which is globally committed to delivering special operations personnel and combat power in the form of Navy SEALs, Army Special Operations Forces, and Air Force Special Tactics personnel. Headquartered at Hurlburt Field, Florida, since 1990, their motto proclaims, 'Anytime, Anyplace.'

"Flying what is acknowledged to be the most sophisticated, technologically advanced helicopter in the world today, the MH-53J, or upgraded M model, Pace Low III, the 20th SOS has been involved in many critical missions, some of which are now public. Choppers from the 20th opened the Gulf War when they led Army Apache helicopters into Iraq at night to destroy air defense systems and create an open corridor for the air campaign. More recently, two MH-53 Pace Lows and one MH Pave Hawk rescued an F-117 pilot whose plane crashed March 27, 1999, during a bombing mission near Belgrade, Yugoslavia. The helicopters flew out of Tuzia Air Base in Bosnia, and transported the downed pilot to Aviano Air Base, Italy, after the rescue.

"However, the role of the 20th in special operations missions is far more than simply moving personnel and their equipment from point A to point B. The MG-53J Pave Low crews can be counted on to provide round-trip transportation, even if things should get hectic on a covert mission. To counter the hazard of a hot landing zone, the requirement to administer first aid, or to assist in combat search-and-rescue operations, the Air Force has fielded its own version of special forces. Known as the Special Tactics Group, this elite cadre is made up of superbly trained, physically fit combat controllers and pararescuemen. These fast-reacting fully deployable teams can be inserted forward, into non-permissive environments on short notice to effectively deal with the most challenging of missions. Personnel of the Special Tactics Group are trained in the same tactical insertion methods–scuba, military free-fall parachuting, and overland infiltration, as the SEALs and Special Forces units they frequently support. Through necessity, as a result of the multi-service support they provide, their skills encompass the core specialties of both sister services, and the specialty missions on the Air Force side of the house, including forward air control, close-air support, medical air evacuation, and combat weathermen.

"The MG-53 carries a standard crew complement of six and can haul up to 38 passengers. It is capable of flying at a speed of 164 miles per hour and up to a maximum range of 630 miles without aerial refueling. For logistics purposes, we will require only one chopper to transport the team in and out of Iraq. However, as dependable as this weapon system is, a second aircraft with a full crew complement will be standing by as backup. Once again, gentlemen, an example of our basic mission planning philosophy for this operation–worst case scenario, redundancy in essential mission equipment, and jointness as the underpinning of everything we do. We're going to have one crack, and one crack only at this. There's far too much riding on the outcome to leave anything to chance. 'For want of a nail a shoe was lost, for want of a shoe a horse was lost,' etc. Anyone here ever hear that sad tale of woe?

"Saddam's missiles are housed in missile silos that we believe to be strikingly similar in structural design to those used by the USAF to shelter our Minute Man & the Peacekeeper ICBMs. Assuming this is not just a fluke of nature, it appears that Iraq's spies have been just as busy as ours over the past few years in gathering intelligence data on their adversary's military weapons and capabilities. However, our good friends in Baghdad, have even taken it one step further. In a somewhat successful effort to conceal their weapons of mass destruction in the face of curious U.N. weapon's inspectors poking around every nook and cranny in the country, they just happen to be located inside a privileged class of buildings which fall under the general umbrella of Saddam's palaces. However, as every royal family member knows, there are palaces, and then there are palaces. You won't find any of Cinderella's slippers in these palaces. They are the biggest forgery since the U.S. treasury's failed effort to foist the Susan B. Anthony coin off on an unsuspecting public as genuine currency. The exterior facade appears to be that of a palace, but within the outer walls and beneath a specially constructed retractable composite roof designed to conceal it from the prying eyes of orbiting U.S. satellites, the interior is a military complex. Hidden four stories beneath the surface of the desert is the Missile System Control Center, and several missile silos capable of launching weapons of mass destruction.

"Our first challenge in deactivating the MSC2 is to breach the outer perimeter security of the palace itself. Then, we must neutralize the security forces co-located with the launch crews inside the missile silo. Defeating Saddam's security forces will be the mission of our assault team. Like the other teams supporting this mission, they will receive a combination of classroom and field training. Their field training will be conducted on a replica of a palace, constructed as close-to-scale as possible.

"Once inside the MSC2, the Task Force will have two primary areas of concern . One is the missile launch control system, and the other is the shell game whereby the missiles are periodically and randomly shuttled between launch areas.

"The missiles equipped with the warheads containing weapons of mass destruction move from one missile silo to another under program control. A random number generator is used to select both the time of movement and the new location of each missile. Therefore, we have to determine the physical location of the missiles, and then neutralize both the launch and movement capability until our air strikes destroy them on the ground in their silos. While the entire missile system is interconnected as a network, each individual missile launch site is also capable of independent and self-sustaining operation in case of network failure. In other words, if one missile launch site goes down for any reason, the others will continue to function.

"Needless to say, we are confronted with many challenges which will have to be successfully met to achieve mission success. Saddam has definitely thrown down the gauntlet to anyone brave or foolish enough to attempt to infiltrate and disable his missile system. A variety of factors might make it difficult or even impossible to find, much less to destroy, all of the weapons which constitute the threat. Stationing mobile missile launchers in residential areas or employing low-technology modes of communication immune to electronic jamming or interception, continue to pose serious targeting challenges. Good intelligence is absolutely critical. You can't hit what you don't know or can't find. The Air Force's inability to rapidly destroy Iraq's mobile SCUD launchers was not so much a failure of air power as it was a failure of human intelligence to compensate for the inherent limitations in sensors. Satellite intelligence or overflights with spy planes are not going to cut it on this mission. We must confirm the exact location of the missiles at a point in time. And, since these birds are nested in underground silos, 'humint,' or feet on the ground intelligence is necessary to pinpoint their location.

"The missiles are located four stories underground in missile silos. The silos are hardened with untold cubic yards of reinforced concrete. The launch control center is a box about the size of a tour bus that is mounted on springs for shock absorption. It acts as a built-in industrial strength suspension system to cushion the shock of a near miss without detonating the warhead, damaging the missile, or disrupting launch capability. The entire concrete egg could rock around the missile crew and they would remain steady, assuming they had their seat belts fastened. Therefore, anything less than a direct hit on the target will not suffice. Unless we strike it with surgical precision, chances are, the missile will survive to fight another day.

"Iraqi missile crews pull a 24-hour alert duty about eight times a month. They live in nearby camps and are driven back and forth to work by security patrols. All missile launch locations are manned seven days a week, 24 hours a day regardless of whether the missile is in the silo. Each new crew coming on duty receives a 30 minute status briefing which includes information on maintenance schedules, weather forecasts, and an intelligence report. The launch crews are not told the location of the missiles for security reasons. Rooms to sleep and cook with security are provided on-site. Paired off in two-person crews, the Iraqis employ the 'Buddy' system. Neither crew member is ever out of sight of the other at any time. The combat crew commander and his deputy sit on chairs mounted on rails. Each crew member monitors two display screens, one for the missiles, and a second for communications traffic.

"If ordered to launch their missiles, both crew members working in tandem must concur and act within milliseconds of each other, following an extensive checklist requiring several security codes and computer keystrokes. In addition, all launches must be authorized by the National Command Authority, none other than Saddam himself. However, I'm sure that comes as no surprise to anyone in this room. It appeared that he called most, if not all, of the shots in the Gulf War. Even his most senior field commanders, lacked authority to act without first checking-in with him for approval. Please remember, this is the same Saddam Hussein who required all typewriters to be registered with the Iraqi Government prior to the Gulf War.

"Once again, much to our chagrin, the entire system bears a striking resemblance to a plan given serious consideration by the USAF in the late 1970s to provide an element of enhanced survivability to our ICBM fleet. We envisioned a railroad system operated by Uncle Sam to shuttle missiles between various possible launch locations, designed to ensure a retaliatory strike capability if the Soviets launched a pre-emptive first strike on the Continental United States. The USAF's concept of the 'shell game' included about 50-60 shelters in a cluster, dispersed over a large geographical area far from centers of population. However, only 10-15 missiles would actually be located within the cluster. Specially constructed railroad cars with covered containers would constantly move between the various shelters within the cluster. Thus, the missiles could be shuffled in secret between shelters at random. Assuming that we had 15 missiles spread out between 60 possible shelters in a cluster, an enemy's chance of scoring a successful hit on a missile with a single weapon would be one in four, or 25 percent. If that same enemy wanted to improve his odds, the investment cost penalty would be significant. To ensure single weapon coverage on one entire weapons cluster would require 60 missiles, plus associated launch sites, and missile crews. Saddam's version of the shell game is essentially a microcosm of what ours would have entailed, similar in concept, but significantly smaller in numbers. However, he shuttles his missiles between shelters in large container trucks in lieu of a rail system.

"The threat of 'if you kill us first, we'll still be able to kill you back,' didn't make a whole lot of sense to most rational people. However, somehow we managed to avert a catastrophic nuclear confrontation over several decades known as the 'Cold War.' You may remember this whole nightmare as the strategic doctrine of 'Massive Retaliation,' which marked our national security policy for more than 40 years."

"Before we leave this area and move on, I want to be completely honest with you gentlemen. The long pole in the tent in planning this operation was intel. We have not been able to obtain all the detailed information on the physical layout and technical inter-workings of the MSC2, and the numbers and locations of the Iraqi security forces, that we would like to have. Saddam's military move against his Kurdish population in 1996, broke up a CIA covert operation designed to generate indigenous opposition to Saddam, and, perhaps, spark a coup. It will be months before agents can be inserted back into Iraq to supply the detailed intelligence and on the ground assistance that may be the difference between failure and success, humiliation and pride, and between losing lives and saving them. In addition, Iraqi troops blanket the streets of Baghdad, making it very difficult for the U.S. to obtain intelligence. This was one of the biggest problems that the planners of this operation faced.

"However, as you are all now aware, we do not have the luxury of waiting until all the 'nice to have' information is available. We have a time bomb ticking and it may be on a very short fuse. Without detailed intelligence data, the Task Force will have to proceed with extreme caution, possibly improvising along the way. This is where the integrated nature of the training will become invaluable. The Task Force members, including the assault forces, seizure team, helicopter crews, and the tactical fighter strike crews will painstakingly rehearse several possible scenarios to develop the flexibility, coordination, and trust which are essential to high-stress, complex combat missions. If this mission is to fail, it will not be because of the disjointed nature of Task Force training, which has plagued similar missions in the past.

"While we won't have all the detailed intelligence data that we would ideally like to have, we will have two important things working for us. The first is the element of surprise. We will be initiating the action, and they will be forced to react. Obviously, we will know in advance what our plan of attack is, and they won't. Secondly, but of equal importance, we will have a big cultural advantage. The enemy that you will be up against is well meaning and to the best of our knowledge, composed of loyal Iraqis. However, within their armed forces, the exercise of personal initiative is not only discouraged, it can be fatal to one's health. They work within a very structured system. Literally no one makes a decision without consulting higher authority for direction and permission. Therefore, when confronted with a situation which exposes them to the elements of surprise and confusion, they will most likely follow their innate human reactions, and panic. Consequently, their actions may appear to be both unexpected and irrational from the perspective of a Western mind. Do not, therefore, mistake or assume their behavior for either acts of cowardice or bravery. Take it for what it is–the spontaneous reactions of individuals confronted with a situation for which no previous military training has ever prepared them.

"Once the guards on the sentry posts are taken out by the assault team's sharp shooters, we plan to blow the steel blast door which covers the access ladder extending from ground level to several hundred feet down into the operational area of the silo. The missile crew and accompanying security forces inside the facility will then be neutralized with 'flash-bang' explosives thrown down the shaft. This will render them helpless for a period long enough to allow the assault team to rappel down the shaft and neutralize them. The stunning effect of the flash-bangs and subsequent disorientation will give us approximately five seconds of total incapacitation of the enemy, and an additional 20 seconds of sub-par performance. That means we've got less than 25 seconds to descend the four stories to the floor of the control room in full Kevlar body armor packing our weapon, and get the drop on the bad guys. Obviously, we aren't going in the gentlemen's way, one step at a time down that long ladder. By the time we reached the floor of the control room, we would have lost the temporary advantage that we gained. We can save valuable seconds by rappelling down the passage, and landing feet first on the floor with weapons in the ready position authorized to 'free-fire' as necessary to neutralize anyone who may pose a threat. The Iraqi security guards will be equipped with Soviet AK-47s and sidearms.

"The entire building will then be searched to ensure it is secure before giving the all-clear signal. As soon as the assault team confirms that everyone is accounted for and all resistance eliminated, they will call out 'all clear' three times. Upon hearing this signal, the seizure team will descend the steps to the control room floor with their equipment. Only then, can they begin the task of disabling the MSC2.

"Once inside the MSC2, the seizure team will do their thing. This will be accomplished by severing the systems head containing the brain from the torso and its appendages. They will break the entry code, access the missile control system program, and shut down the system, rendering it inoperable. At this time, the three missiles with warheads containing weapons of mass destruction will be rendered ineffective. They can neither be launched nor moved to another location.

"Computers have tremendous power and capacity. However, that same ability to process billions of bits of information in nanoseconds is also an inherent Achilles-heel. When your computer 'crashes' and the network system goes down, the failure can be catastrophic. It's a bit like a businessman getting down on all fours and crawling back into the darkness of the cave his ancestors crawled out of millions of years ago. Oh yes, there are manual work-arounds, but it's like operating back in the stone age. Once we cut off the missile system control center's head, leaving it braindead, the rest of the missile system will be struck dysfunctional, atrophying like the wings on a chicken. There will be no chickens flying out of the henhouse at that point.

"Remember gentlemen. Time is our enemy. Each additional

second that we lose in the timely execution of this mission has the potential to add up to disaster.

"I see a hand. Is there a question?"

"Yes, is every second really that critical?"

"Probably the best way to answer that question is to ask you to try thinking of it this way. No individual rain drop ever takes responsibility for a flood, and no individual snowflake takes responsibility for an avalanche. Nevertheless, these disasters occur, and it was the addition of one more individual particle of matter which spelled the difference in each case.

"Once the missile launch control system is neutralized, and the locations of the launch sites of the three missiles of mass destruction are confirmed, air strikes can be called in to destroy the missiles. Pounder, you will act as the Forward Air Controller for Slash and his friends. As soon as your seizure crew wraps-up business in the MSC2 and is well clear of the facility, you are authorized to break radio silence and contact Slash with the location of the three 'hot' missile silos with warheads.

"Slash, once you receive the radio transmission from Pounder, you and your friends have the green light to proceed with the air strikes. We will take out the MSC2 first, and then the three missile silos in order of their proximity to the MSC2.

"Perhaps some of you are asking yourselves at this point, why don't we just drive in with enough air power and destructive weaponry to turn the entire area into one big parking lot? That would certainly be much easier, eliminate the threat, and expose the participants to far less personal risk. I've got to admit, it sounds good to me. However, gentlemen, as you probably suspect by this time, our friends in Congress have expressed some well-taken concerns regarding this operation which resulted in some very definitive top-down operational planning guidance. As big a menace as Saddam is, and as serious a threat as this presents, we still need to minimize the fall out on the Iraqi people. As I think everyone recognizes, they have suffered greatly under Saddam's leadership. In addition, there are two other 'drivers' here. First and foremost is public opinion.

Regardless of how good our people are at painting the best possible 'PR' face on this operation, after the fact of course, there will still be those critics who accuse us of overreacting and using excessive force. And secondly, if the world is ultimately to succeed in the removal of Saddam from power, it's the Iraqi people who are going to have to get the job done. Obviously, we aren't going to make any friends and win over the man on the street if a great number of them become civilian casualties of this operation. Therefore, we must do everything possible, consistent with our mission objectives, to mitigate the potential collateral battle damage from the force of the blast, secondary explosions, and the effects of the chemical and biological agents which are unleashed into the air.

"The weapon's delivery platform will be the Lockheed F-117A fighter, the most sophisticated stealth warplane ever built. The 'Nighthawk' is a single-seat fighter with a combat radius of 750 miles, unrefueled. Deployed to Saudi Arabia by the USAF, for service in the Gulf War in 1991, it was the only coalition aircraft able to operate with complete freedom over Baghdad's sophisticated air defenses. Roaming the night skies over Iraq, it struck the most heavily defended Iraqi targets with stunning effect. The F-117s unusual shape and advanced radar-absorbent material from which the skin of the aircraft is manufactured make the Stealth fighter all but invisible to radar. The effective range of the radar image is so short that it can operate in the vicinity of radar warning sites with relative impunity. The F-117s radar cross-section is about one one-hundredth of a square yard–approximately the same as your basic seagull. By flying at night, the black jet also goes undetected to the naked eye.

"The 40 F-117s deployed to the Gulf flew more than 1,270 missions, dropping 30 percent of all precision-guided munitions. They used laser-guided weapons to destroy Iraqi military installations and concrete bunkers housing their fighter aircraft. The F-117 weapon system is deadly accurate, capable of hitting a target one yard square. Principal weapons carried by the aircraft are BLU-109 low-level or GBU 10/GBU 27 medium-level laser-guided bombs. It also has provision for two AIM-9L air-to-air missiles. The

Nighthawk has a load capacity of 5,500 pounds of weapons which are carried internally.

"As I mentioned earlier, the F-117A has a combat radius of 750 miles unrefueled. The distance from Prince Sultan Air Base, Saudi Arabia, located south of the capital city of Riyadh, to the target area outside Baghdad, is approximately 800 miles. To ensure that we don't have any fuel problems, the F-117s will hit the tanker on the way in, just outside Iraqi air space. The tankers will also be available to refuel on the way out if required. We're planning on the conservative side to allow for the extra fuel required by the fully loaded aircraft and desert heat.

"The publicized maximum speed of the F-117A is Mach 1. However, we won't be going supersonic. Our cruising speed will be approximately 550 miles per hour. Our en route flying time from launch at Prince Sultan Air Base in Saudi Arabia to target engagement in Iraq will be approximately one and a-half hours.

"Putting the weapons on the targets will not be a problem with precision-guided munitions, and the sophisticated state-of-the art fire control systems employed by the F-117A. The F-117A pilots will launch their weapons at maximum range and medium altitude. This weapons delivery profile will expose the aircraft and aircrews to less risk of detection by Iraqi radar, provide the pilots with more room to maneuver if they do encounter SAMs or AAA, and consume less fuel. We aren't going to take any chances here, gentlemen. As you may recall, we lost an F-117A in Serbia during Operation Allied Force, that was apparently downed by an enemy missile. At the time of the incident, our pilots were restricted to a 15,000 foot flight ceiling to minimize losses.

"The GBU-15 class of munitions weigh approximately 2,500 pounds. Each F-117A Nighthawk can carry two bombs. As you are aware, gentlemen, we have a total of four targets. Therefore, we will require a total of four F-117As, two armed with penetration weapons, and two armed with our new fall-out suppression bomb. Each aircraft will be assigned two targets to provide the required coverage. But remember, gentlemen, these targets are not your normal run-of-the mill facilities. Saddam's missile silos are below ground and hardened with enough concrete to construct a four-lane interstate around the equator. I'm sure you all recall Saddam's hardened aircraft dispersal shelters where he ordered his air force pilots to hibernate during the Gulf War. This was a tactic successfully employed by some Arab air forces in the 1973 Yom Kipper War against Israel. What probably seemed like a perfectly good idea at the time, turned out to be one of Saddam's biggest miscalculations of the entire war. Those Iraqi aircraft which were not destroyed on the ground began flushing and flying into what they believed to be was the sanctuary of Iranian airspace. Once on the ground, they were not allowed to depart. Consequently, his air force posed no threat to the allies establishing air superiority over the skies of Baghdad.

"The laser-guided BLU-109/B bomb is the weapon of choice to soften up the target areas. It is made from hardened steel and shaped like your basic VICKS inhaler. With a penetrating warhead, it is capable of boring through layers of earth, armor plating, and concrete before detonating. These are the same 'smart' bombs that destroyed Saddam's hardened aircraft dispersal shelters in 1991 during the Gulf War.

"After the can opener has opened the can, we've got another little surprise in store for Saddam. Perchance, did anyone here do a close read of the September 9, 1998, issue of the Commerce Business Daily? Nobody? How do you gentlemen spend your free time after you get through reading the sports page and the comics? If you had read the CBD on that date, you might have run across an interesting notice. I just happen to have a copy of it right here. What a coincidence!

"Let's see what this 'puppy' says. 'The Air Force plans to spend $16 million over nearly four years to develop a conventional warhead tailored to destroy chemical and biological warfare production facilities. The program could eventually lead to the production of 10 weapons for operational use. Air Force officials said that they want the new warhead to be compatible with a wide range of existing munitions from the AGM-130 stand-off weapon to the

GBU-24 bomb. It is intended to create widespread physical damage to factories, said the CBD notice, while limiting collateral damage from released agents. Neutralizing chemicals or high heat from incendiary blasts might be ways of reaching this goal, according to the Air Force, although several techniques may have to be combined before a satisfactory result is achieved.'

"Well, gentlemen, what do you suppose happened after the release of that notice? I know what you're thinking and you're absolutely correct. A $16 million dollar payday was apparently sufficient for more than one defense contractor to devote a little time and effort to developing such a weapon. It's just what the doctor ordered. If Saddam is experiencing flu symptoms, this certainly ought to act as a decongestant. Limited testing of the new weapon has been conducted and it has shown great promise. Upon conclusion of this mission, the final test results will be in.

"The entire operational mission will proceed under the watchful eye of an AWACS aircraft. The Boeing E-3C Sentry Airborne Warning and Control System is housed in the airframe of a Boeing 707/VC-137 aircraft. It is the complete package, providing us with radar surveillance coverage, secure communications, and an air battle control staff. The E-3C carries a flight deck crew of four and a mission crew of 13-18 personnel, including weapons controllers, technicians, and supervisors in the main cabin. The radome which appears as a large flying saucer atop the fuselage, houses the APY-2 radar antenna capable of sweeping and painting an area of from two to three hundred miles. Four Pratt & Whitney JT3D/TF-33 turbofan engines, power the E-3C with a top speed of nearly 600 miles per hour. It cruises on operational missions at an altitude of 29,000 feet, and has an unrefueled endurance in excess of eleven hours. The USAF has 34 of these aircraft in their inventory. The Royal Saudi Air Force also purchased several of these aircraft and re-engineered them with the more fuel efficient and powerful SNECMA CFM-56 turbofan engines. This upgrade provided them with increased power, improved fuel efficiency, and shorter take-off capability, which is important in the operational environment of the heat of the desert.

"Should we encounter unexpected resistance from Saddam's air force at any time during the mission, we will be ready. As I mentioned earlier, a three-ship flight of F-15s will be airborne just outside Iraqi airspace ready to respond at a moment's notice. The requirement for the F-15 Eagle was born out of necessity in 1967, to counter the threat of the Soviet MIG-25. The Soviet Foxbat had set the standard for all-important measures of a fighter plane's performance in combat, including speed, altitude, rate-of-climb, and time to altitude. Our F-4 Phantom, having seen its glory days in the skies over Viet Nam, was no match for this flying mammal, which literally flew like a 'bat out of hell.' The first of the F-15 fledgling eagles flew out of its nest on June 26, 1972. Designed by McDonnell Douglas to be an air-superiority aircraft, it is powered by two Pratt & Whitney F-100 engines. Operating in full afterburner, the engine generates 25,000 pounds of thrust, or eight times its own body weight. Outfitted with all of the latest state-of-the-art avionics and armament packages, the Eagle has been all that was advertised. She has carried the U.S. flag, establishing air superiority over enemy skies for the past 28 years defeating MIG-21s, MIG-25s, and the French Mirage F-lQs. F-15s have been credited with nearly 100 air-to-air enemy kills without a single combat defeat, a truly remarkable record.

"When the balloon goes up and we pull the chocks, kick the tires, and light the fires, it's going to be complete chaos. 'The fog of war' will envelope everything like a wet blanket. Everyone will be running around with their hair on fire with no time to 'check-six.' We'll only have a small window of opportunity to successfully execute. Each second will be critical. There will be no time or opportunity for original thought. Consequently, we will have to plan each detail of this operation down to a gnat's eyelash, and then rehearse it until we can execute it in our sleep.

"And, finally, gentlemen, just a brief word on the rules of engagement. They are concise, clear, and unambiguous. Any perceived threat to the success of the operational mission will justify the use of deadly force. All Iraqis in the immediate vicinity of the MSC2 facility will be assumed to be armed and dangerous. All airborne Iraqi aircraft will be treated as hostile. And, of course, the right of self-defense against armed attack is never denied. As always, consistent with mission objectives, we will do our best to minimize collateral damage to civilians and religious sites.

"In summary, gentlemen, what we envision are surgical strikes with the precision of a brain surgeon. In and out with the speed of heat. If everything goes as planned, it will be over before our Iraqi friends in Baghdad are aware it has begun. We're talking the 'mother of all surprises.' Saddam's first indication of a problem will be the receipt of an 'after-action' report detailing the extent of the damage. That is, if anyone is brave or foolish enough to stick around and complete one. Mission success will be defined as 'slaying the beast in its lair.'

"Well, that concludes this portion of the briefing, gentlemen. Are there any questions?"

"Yes, I have both a comment and a question. From everything I've heard here today and from what we were briefed during our visit to the Checkmate planning cell, it appears that this mission is a high-risk operation. We're definitely pushing the envelope. You are tasking the participants and the equipment with performing at the upper limits of human capacity and equipment capability. In addition, there is little, if any, margin built into this plan to compensate for unknowns, mistakes, or just plain old bad luck."

"Thank you for that shrewd observation, Slash. Consider it 'noted.' And, what pray tell, is your question?"

"What happens if things go South? What is Plan 'B,' if the wheels come off this operation?"

"Perhaps it's an appropriate time to invoke the old adage, don't ask the question if you can't stand the answer. In this business, you fly where you're told to fly and drop what you're told to drop. Leave the politics to the powers that be in Washington. They're paid to make the big decisions. We're all adults here. You know the drill–name, rank, service number, and date of birth. I think that at this time, it will suffice to say that if you are captured, most assuredly, there won't be any Christmas visits from Bob Hope or a USO troop.

"Gentlemen, on that happy note, let me just say it's been a long day and an even longer week. The good news is that it's Friday. And, I've got even more good news. We've worked hard and made a lot of progress the past few days. If we were a multinational corporation working a major contract, I guess you could say that we're ahead of schedule and under cost. So, let's cut ourselves a little slack for good behavior. There are a lot of things to see and do here in the D.C. area, much of which is free. Take advantage of the opportunity. Get out and see how your tax dollars are being spent.

"Oh, did I mention, the Dallas Cowboys are in town Sunday to play a little game of 'drop the handkerchief' with the Redskins? Appropriately, the most requested song on the radio this week was 'Mama, Don't Let Your Babies Grow Up to be Cowboys.' If you have access to the U.S. Treasury vault at Fort Knox and happen to get lucky, you just might be able to pick up a ticket from a scalper between now and game time.

"Once a year, this singular event of human civility unites the good citizens of the Nation's Capital, otherwise torn asunder with the partisan politics of division, contention, and destruction. But, this child's game played with celebrated enthusiasm by grown men, is far more than a red herring. It is not merely a diversionary tactic concocted in the deep creases of cerebral gray matter of some shrink's mind in a convoluted attempt to keep the residents of Washington, D.C. from going over the edge from the sheer weight of the realization they are residing in a city, which among other things, just happens to have the highest crime rate of any nation's capital in the entire world.

"To Redskins fans, this is reality, what they live and die for. Each bone crunching tackle by the home team is wildly cheered, while each success, no matter how small, by the enemies of the Redskins, is a curse which the fans loathe with every fiber of their body, and will resist acknowledging as superior play with their last gasp of breath here on this earth. Everything else in this city is but a ruse, just a necessary distraction to be overcome until Sunday afternoon rolls around once again. Victory, will perpetuate the dream, assuring them of another seven days of escape from the daily flitter-flatter of life in the city. Defeat, will send them reeling back to the reality of who they are and where they are, praying for the swift passage of time and an opportunity for redemption the following Sunday. Thank the good Lord for football. Hail to the Redskins!

"We'll see you all back here bright and early at 0730 hours Monday. By the way, don't anyone get any ideas about going AWOL over the weekend. You'll most definitely find yourself in 'deep Kimshe.' Punishment is an all expense-paid trip to Iraq."

\*\*\*

Pounder and Slash leave the Pentagon with the post-briefing blahs. They have just had one big heap of "stuff" piled on their plate. Without sideboards, much of it will eventually end up on the floor before they can digest it all. Staggering under the weight of the load they have been asked to carry, they turn to each other looking for relief.

"Looks as if we're going to be doing some time together," Slash.

"Yea, Hard time, like in a maximum security prison. Lucky me, teamed up with a pounder. And, I used to complain about the Weapons System Officer following me around. The good news was that if he ever got out of line, I could always punch the ejection button for the back seat."

"Just think of us as un-indicted co-conspirators. How did you get sucked into this operation, Slash?"

"Don't even ask! I won't go into the gory details, however, I assume you're familiar with the term 'coercion?' The short version is that I exercised a little too much personal initiative in target acquisition on a mission in a restricted area that nearly escalated into an international incident. Needless to say, the Pentagon brass was up in arms. You've worked with those guys. No sense of humor at all. With my career hanging by a thread, they had me between the proverbial rock and a hard spot. I'm still working off the time–doing odd jobs for Uncle Sam, here and there. Black hole stuff, cloaked in a thick blanket of secrecy. I've kind of thought of myself as an ambassador at large, spreading goodwill and cheer around the world on behalf of the U.S. Government to some of America's nearest and dearest friends. Special people like Muamar Khadaffi in Libya, and Osama bin Laden in Afghanistan. An air strike here, a little napalm there.

"In addition, I give the Pentagon deniability if things go south. My records have been expunged. There's no evidence of any such person as me working for the U.S. Government. They've constructed a maze so complex, a bionic rat with the blueprint could not successfully navigate it. There is so much segmentation and departmentalization that the right hand doesn't even know what the left hand is doing. A lot of middle level players have pieces of the puzzle, but only a select few at the top levels of government are cleared with the big picture. Everyone else is running around without so much as a clue. Once they get their claws into you, they never let go. To hear them talk, I will always be beholding to them for everything they're doing for me. From my perspective, it appears that I cut a deal with the devil himself."

"You know, Slash, sometimes I lay awake at night wondering if we were engaged in a just cause, or just being used. It seemed all right at the time, but we were caught up in the esprit de corps, excitement, and emotion of the moment. However, we must be cautious. Sometimes our passion may be so intense that it blinds us to the truth. Therefore, if we are not careful, it can be used against us. The truth is out there somewhere, but so are the lies. The clever ones understand that the best place to hide a lie is to carefully conceal it between two truths. I've spent years tracking down and sorting through insidious lies and half truths. I wanted so badly to believe, just accept the obvious and walk away. It was time to move on, to something else, somewhere else. Looking back on all of it, I can put most of it to rest. However, there are still some questions that I don't have answers for, and pangs of guilt that just won't seem to go away."

"Like what for example, Pounder? Give me a specific."

"After I returned stateside from the Middle East, I did something I had always wanted to do. I tried some teaching. Since

I didn't have a teaching certificate, I signed up to be a substitute teacher. I had always enjoyed teaching, and thought that perhaps the kids could use a good role model. It was a real eye opener. There's been a lot of water under the bridge since I sat in the classroom in one of those chairs. Today's kids are bright and straightforward. They don't just sit back and wait to be ordered around. They want answers and they expect straight talk. When they became aware of my military background, I was frequently asked if I had ever killed anyone. At first, it stopped me in my tracks. I didn't have an answer. I knew that I had never pointed a gun at anyone and pulled the trigger. However, like every other God-fearing, law abiding, and taxpaying citizen of the United States, I was part of Uncle Sam's big war machine. A portion of every tax dollar is earmarked for national defense. Those funds are spent for airplanes, tanks, bombs, and bullets, and all of the other accouterments of war required to support and sustain the U.S. Armed Forces.

"Thus, in our own way, we all contribute to the death and destruction that takes place in war. We, in the miliary, are the point of the spear. The taxpayers are the shaft , or get the shaft, and the politicians provide the thrust. We are all in it together, Slash. The blood which is shed on both sides is on all of our hands. The only difference is a matter of degree in the roles that we play and the risk assumed. We assume the physical risk of loss of life and limb by confronting the enemy on the field of battle, the taxpayers the added burden of financing the war, and the politicians the moral dilemma of deciding whether the cause is of sufficient national interest to commit the nation, our economic resources, and their youth to the battle. But, it isn't our job to decide when and where we fight. It is our job to carry out the orders of our superiors, and do what we were trained to do, to the best of our ability. We are just one spoke in one of the many wheels on which the success of the war machine rests."

"Tell me about it, Pounder. Everyone that served in Nam knew it was a bad war, but we didn't complain too loudly because it was the only one we had at the time. There's nothing worse than being a peacetime soldier. Lack of military conflict means declining military appropriations and smaller Service budgets. We were asked to do more with less for so long, that eventually we were expected to do everything with nothing. The worse part of it is that it all runs downhill, finally dumping on the poor individual soldier in the foxhole. The bottom line is less training, older equipment, more deployments, all adding up to higher risk, and lower morale. We're definitely not appreciated for the dangers we are exposed to, and the sacrifices we are required to make. It's like, I know that you risked your life for your country yesterday, but what have you done for me today? The American public has short memories."

"Yea, like a nanosecond, Slash. The peacetime soldier is the poster boy for a 'scapegoat.' And, perhaps the worst part is that eventually, all the frustration and hostility is internalized within the organization and spills over into the work area. Reduced funding also means cutbacks in authorized manpower ceilings. This, in-turn, translates into fewer promotions and more pass-overs. Yesterday's valuable soldier becomes tomorrow's casualty of the peacetime Army, being forced out because of the numbers game. It then becomes a case of 'the enemy within.' To survive, you spend more time 'checking-six' to see who is about to stab you in the back, than you do taking care of business. In combat, you're promoted based on merit—'No guts, no air medals.' However, in the peacetime Army, it's the number of your contemporaries bodies that you're able to climb over that's important. Forget the camaraderie. It's dog eat dog, and every man for himself.

"We've got a real dilemma here, Slash. We chose military service as a career, a profession, and a way of life. But, you can't have it both ways. The peacetime soldier gets no respect, and the wartime soldier looks forward to coming home in a body-bag. It's your basic ' Catch 22' situation. What are we going to do about it?"

"Beats my hole card," Pounder. "Besides that, it's way above my pay grade. Perhaps some secrets are meant to remain secrets because they are truths which are not yet ready to be revealed. They say whatever doesn't kill you makes you stronger. However, even a great white shark, as intimidating and formidable as he appears in the water, is vulnerable. If he stops swimming, he will perish. In our circumstance, we can either live with it, or die with it, as the case may be. Personally, I believe that the greatest threat to democracy is not Saddam Hussein. It's the unbridled power that government has over its subjects. However, at the moment, it appears that we have no choice, but to keep on paddling."

# CHAPTER NINE

## FIGHTER PILOT

*"I'm getting the feeling that our time here in the land of the 'Big* BX' is quickly coming to an end, Slash. This may be our last weekend in the city. I know just the place to clear our minds and celebrate a bit. Let's head on over to the Bolling AFB Officer's Club this evening."

They drive down King Street in Old Town, Alexandria, taking in the sights. At this time of year, it's almost a mirror image of Georgetown. The sidewalks are crowded with young people ecstatic to have another work week behind them, looking for a place to celebrate this TGIF occasion. King Street ends abruptly at the Potomac River near the location of the historic Torpedo Factory which now houses arts and craft shops. Pounder is tempted to stop at the Fish Market for a stuffed crab sandwich. However, "happy hour" beckons. They continue, crossing the Woodrow Wilson Bridge that separates Alexandria, Virginia, from Maryland. Pounder informs Slash that they are passing over "Jones Point," and nods in the direction of "Hunting Towers," situated on the edge of the Potomac on their right. He also feels the need to tell Slash a bit of trivia that he picked up while living in the area. As declared by their respected residents, "Virginia is for lovers," and "Maryland is for crabs." Memories from Pounders three years at the Pentagon flood his mind as they move along in the evening traffic. However, like all other good things, it was bound to come to an end. The sound of Slash's voice, rudely intrudes, snatching him back to the world of reality.

"I didn't know that there was an active duty Air Force Base here in the D.C. area."

"You know about Andrews Air Force Base in Camp Springs, Maryland. It's the home of the Presidential Wing and Air Force One. Then, there's Bolling AFB. However, it's more of a metamorphosis than an air force base. It has no runway, and the only aircraft is a static display. It exists to provide administrative support for military personnel assigned within the D.C. area, and to provide general officer housing for the many senior officers working at the Pentagon. However, they do have a first class officer's club with a great happy hour on Friday night. Drinks are half price and we can 'pig out' on the free hors d'oeuvres. There's no better place to swap a few war stories than over the bar, and if you're up for it, we can even take a shot at the karaoke machine."

"I'm good to go, Pounder. However, I am a little leery regarding your reference to the 'free' hors d'oeuvres. As I recall from my graduate studies at the Air Force Institute of Technology, there's no such thing as a 'free lunch.' Remember, there's 'free' cheese in a mouse trap."

***

Slash and Pounder are seated in the Bolling AFB, Officer's Club. It's Friday night and there is a festive mood in the club. A Waitress approaches their table.

"Good evening gentlemen. How are we doing tonight?"

Slash and Pounder sing out in unison, "everything's shaken but the bacon, and that's taken."

"All right. I appreciate you sharing that little insight with me. I expect that's a closely-held state secret. What can I get you two?"

Slash responds, "I'll have a Harvey Wall banger, with a beer chaser."

"Spoken like a true fighter pilot. And, how about you sir?"

"Pounder replies, "I'm the designated driver, I'll have a virgin Margarita."

"Something tells me that you're not one of those guys who wears a 'goatskin' to work every day."

"You got that straight, Mam. I'm a 'ground pounder.' It's nice to know that there are still a few discriminating women out there who can distinguish between a true officer and a gentleman and the riffraff."

"To tell the truth, sir, I seriously doubt that even an act of Congress could make either one of you, an officer and a gentleman."

"Man, shot down again. Spinning, crashing, and burning, before I even had the wheels retracted. It must be the company I keep."

"Here you are gentlemen. I'll run a tab for your drinks. You can pay on the way out."

Slash decides it is time to inquire as to the rules of engagement. "Hey, I've got a question for you sweetheart. Is this bar cleared for 'carrier landings?'"

"Only if you want to spend the rest of your evening bunked up with the military police? But, hey, I've got a question of my own. What are a couple of war heroes like you doing in a nice place like this?"

"We could tell you, but then we'd have to kill you."

"Oh, I get it. You two are super sleuths operating deep undercover, disguised as a washed-up fly boy and his trusty ground-pounder sidekick."

"You're getting warm, Mam. Real warm! Before you run off, how about joining us in a toast?"

"Sure, why not. So, what's the occasion? Whom are we going to toast?"

"We propose a toast 'To Absent Friends.'"

In the finest of military tradition, they collectively raise their glasses in a toast "To Absent Friends."

The waitress quickly discerns that Slash and Pounder are not just two of the regular patrons who frequent the officer's club. "I'm not liking the sound of this. There's too much gloom and doom hanging over you two. Are you guys going to be all right?"

Slash is a bit taken back by the fact that he and Pounder are apparently radiating pessimism and despair on an occasion they intended to be festive. While he is sworn to silence as to the nature of their mission, his flippant response drops a hint as to the importance of their involvement in something big. "At the moment, we've not sure. Check the headline news in a couple of weeks for an update."

As soon as the words pass his lips, Slash realizes that this conversation is obviously headed in the wrong direction and quickly changes the subject. "By the way, Pounder, it's your turn to buy."

"What do you mean, my turn, Slash? I picked the tab up last night at dinner. You were so cheap, you didn't even leave a tip. You've got the deepest pockets of anyone I've ever known."

" Close, but no cigar, good buddy. These aren't deep pockets. They're empty pockets."

"You've probably still got the first buck that you ever earned. If you opened your wallet, moths would fly out of it."

"Well, just to clear the air on that subject, the fact of the matter is that I donate all of my money to charity."

"Yea, and I'm the Easter Bunny, except every other Friday when I'm the Tooth Fairy. Yes, I recognize you now. I thought that we'd met before. You're the one that sold me the Brooklyn Bridge."

"OK, you've got me cold turkey. But, you've got to admit, you got it at one heck of a price. At the time, it was worth two or three times that much."

Slash and Pounder ask for a dice cup and roll the dice to determine who will pay for the first round. Determined to shed the air of melancholy that has settled over them, they move the conversation in a direction that allows the fantasy of their imagination to temporarily force the hard reality of their predicament to the back of their minds.

"You know. You really ought to buy, Slash?"

"Oh yea, how's that?

"When I was young, I was so poor, I couldn't afford to pay attention."

"Sounds like you were pretty well off compared to me. I was

just a poor country boy from Oregon. When I was young, my parents were so poor, they couldn't make a down payment on a free lunch."

" I'm thinking that's mighty poor, my friend. However, that being the case, I'm still not moved to tears. And, furthermore, I'm light-years away from any thoughts about ponying up."

"Slash, if there is, but an ounce of compassion in that sea of enmity awash here in the club masquerading as a fighter pilot, consider this: When I was born, I had less than a dollar's worth of change in my blue jeans. Can you imagine that? Here I am, a newborn baby about to embark on the journey of life, and no pocket money! Sometimes life can be so cruel."

"Pounder, you old spear-chucker. You got me with that one. My heart bleeds for you. However, better a bleeding heart than a bleeding wallet. I'm thirsty. Quit stalling and roll the ivories.

No guts, no air medals."

"Well, I'm down to my last roll of the dice, so here goes. But, just for a little luck, I'm going to lay one more on you. Try this on for size. When I was young, they had to pay most kids to be good, but my old man said that 'I was good for nothing.' Hey look at this! Read 'em and weep, Slash. A roll that would make Boxcar Willy proud–sixes all around. I'm afraid you buy, my man."

"Yea I know, and it's breaking your heart. Let me just reach down in here and retrieve my money clip. The one with all the hundred dollar bills. Hello, what's this in the old pocket, a 'DEAD BUG!'" Chairs are overturned as both Slash and Pounder dive head first on the floor. However, due to the head start that Slash got, he was the clear winner.

"So sorry, my friend. It seems that even though you successfully cheated me on that dice roll, your reflexes aren't what they should be. As I recall from military tradition, since you were the last dude to hit the floor at the sound of the dreaded 'dead bug,' you buy after all!"

"You know, Slash, military tradition aside, that was absolutely and unequivocally the sorriest example of good sportsmanship that I have ever witnessed in my entire life. I'm beginning to think the stories I've heard about you are true. You would steal the combat boots off your own grandmother if you thought you could get away with it."

"Roger that! I considered it. However, she slept in them, and was an extremely light sleeper."

"Rumor has it, Slash, that you're a Zoomie—an Air Force Academy grad. Rumor also has it that there are three classes at the Academy–the 'upper class,' the 'lower class,' and the 'no class.' It's pretty evident at this point which class you were in."

"Negative tower! 'We do not lie, cheat, or steal, or tolerate among us those that do.' "

"If you live up to each and every word in that oath, Slash, you're in a very select group. On the other hand, if you don't, you're just another 'wannabe.'

"Is being a jet jockey all that it's cracked up to be, Slash? What's the story behind all the aura and mystique that surrounds a fighter pilot, and the glamour of being a 'Top Gun?' There are no more WWII biplanes with open cockpits, pilots wearing scarves flying in the wind, leather jackets and goggles, and the one-on-one dog fights. Snoopy and the Red Baron are a thing of the past, just a romantic memory. The new state-of-the-art, high tech aircraft that the USAF now flies have moved us light-years beyond those days. Isn't it time to bring the curtain down on that scene?"

"Not so fast, my fine-feathered friend. Just because both of your flat feet are nailed to terra firma, doesn't mean that the entire world is grounded. You've heard the old expression, ' it ain't over till it's over.' Once you've been up there and it's in your blood. It ain't ever over. You just exist between flights dreaming about the next time you can get back up there. As far as the romanticism having been taken out of it, beauty is in the eye of the beholder. Hey, 'a rose by any other name is still a bloody rose.' If they were going to ground me, Pounder, they might as well bury me. Life would be over, at least the very essence of life would be missing. We fly boys would just be mere shadows of our former selves, carted off to the unclaimed baggage area never to see the sunrise of another day.

"I fly jets, strafe, bomb, and a lot of other neat things like that.

You're as free as a bird up there, as you roam the skies, striking fear and terror in the hearts of all those unfortunate souls that you encounter. After all, I belonged to the world's largest flying club, the United States Air Force. And, I might add, the world's best."

"How would you describe the life of a fighter pilot, Slash?"

"There's only one way to describe the life of the fighter pilot. It's hours and hours of pure boredom, inter-dispersed with moments of sheer terror. You train, train, and train some more, until you can strap that big silver jet on and fly it in your sleep. Then, one day, as you are beginning to think that it's going to be just another routine, out and back, milk-run mission, it all happens at once—complete and total chaos. The 'fog' of war is upon you, and your world literally comes unglued right before you in the blink of an eye. The enemy has just thrown everything he has up against you—anti-aircraft fire, surface-to-air missiles, and MIGS. It's a triple threat, a deadly combination—more than enough to take out, all but the very best. Thank goodness for all that training, because you don't have time to think at that point, just react. You're on a wing and a prayer, and its gut-check time. One miscue and you're history. That's when you really earn those air medals and that flight pay.

"Being a fighter pilot is far more than just an eight to five-job. It's also much more than a profession. It requires complete commitment. You must be totally immersed, completely swallowed up, and fully consumed in this occupation. There is nothing else in second place. Fighter pilots must have nerves of steel, and ice water in their veins. That enables you to remain cool, calm, and collected regardless of the circumstances you find yourself in, or how hectic it gets. Fighter pilots must also have the hands of a brain surgeon. Those hands must be welded to the stick, so that man and machine are one in mind and one in purpose. A fighter pilot's reactions, must be honed to a razor's edge. Virtual reality: I see, I react. The hand-eye coordination is so quick that it would appear to a casual observer the in-between thought process has been bypassed. A fighter pilot must also have a mind that can create order out of pure bedlam, chaos, and mayhem. Or at least, attempt to understand it to the degree that you can deal with it—complete concentration, totally focused on the task at hand. And last, but perhaps most important—the mind-set, temperament, and mentality of a hired gun—an assassin, with one very big difference. Fighter pilots have a conscience. A conscience free and clear of all guilt, beyond any doubt, for any act of violence which they may have committed in the name of the United States of America. A conscience fueled by the belief that they were engaged in a righteous cause, and God was on their side. They were, after all, fighting Communism and keeping the world safe for democracy. A most lofty goal and noble endeavor, for which they received full and complete absolution.

"In the competition in this profession, there is no second place, and no loser's bracket. It's winner take all and then move onto the next round of elimination. The loser is dispatched swiftly and permanently—instant history. And when it's over—relief and jubilation. You taxi in and climb out of the cockpit. Your heart is beating so loudly in your chest that you can feel the pounding in your brain. Even though you're back on the ground, your head is still far up in the clouds in that rarified, thin air. Your legs are weak and appear to have such length that they seem to go on forever, just barely reaching the ground. You're on an adrenaline high, still feeling the exhilaration. Every fiber of your being is completely and totally alive, pulsing and pushing the absolute limit. You could get arrested in most states for being that high.

"You want to scream out from the bottom of your lungs. No, from the very depth of your very soul. A blood curdling, ear-piercing scream. All of the pent up emotion is rushing to get out at once. And as it does, it serves two very important purposes. First, to let the whole world know that you have been to the edge and back. But even more important, to return you to reality. The reality that you have come back from the point of no return, and have survived what could perhaps best be described as an 'out of body' experience. You have lived, for a brief time, in the twilight zone. That ever so small space or sphere which exists between mortality and immortality, literally eye to eye with death. You looked the angel of death in the face and stood your ground. And in the final analysis, it wasn't you that backed down. He knew that it wasn't your time. It was more what went unsaid than what was said. And what went unsaid was loud and clear. That steely, gray eye stare said it all: 'I've got you, and there's absolutely nothing you can do about it. I own you. You are mine.'

"The first time you engage an enemy aircraft and score a confirmed kill on a bandit will never be forgotten. It will be etched in your mind and memory forever. You are now 'one of them.' The consummate professional. A fighter pilot's, fighter pilot. And, as such, you will never be the same person again. A part of your being has been changed forever, and there's no going back. Because they now know, and better yet, you know what you accomplished and what it took to make it happen. Those few seconds were the culmination of an entire lifetime of preparation. This was the moment that you had dreamed about, and worked for, ever since you had decided as a young boy that some day you would be a fighter pilot, one of the world's best. You have confirmed what you have always known, that you have what it takes-'the right stuff.' You are a proven commodity. Your election and place in this elite profession and organization have been made sure. You have successfully completed your baptism under fine. You have taken it up to another level, and raised the bar to a new height. You have set the standard against which all other efforts will now be measured. You have been awarded, not merely the blue ribbon for first place, but the majestic purple of a grand champion. And, it is interwoven with threads of pure gold, fit for the royal robe of a king. Ascend your throne. You are now king of the mountain until someone can bring you down. Until someone better than you comes along. In your dreams. Not in my lifetime!"

"It's hard to imagine how anyone could survive an experience like that, Slash. How do you guys keep it all together?"

"It's like I have been trying to tell you, Pounder. You have to believe! From day one when we enter flight training as a cadet, every waking moment is spent instilling in us that we are the world's best trained, best equipped, and most highly motivated fighter pilots in the world—and that we can engage the enemy on the field of battle at any place, at any time, and come away victorious. With this type of belief, there isn't room for fear. Neither is there room for any self-doubt—not even a flicker. And, it has to go well beyond the point of just being self-confident. Most fighter pilots who fly for our adversaries are self-confident. You've got to have an edge. You have to feel it, be full of it, puffed up, and even cocky. You have to be able to walk the walk, and talk the talk—any time and all the time. You have to be willing to lay it all on the line with the belief that when the big shoot-out at high-noon is over, and the dust clears, you're going to be the last man standing. And, if you can't deal with all that, you don't belong with the world's best. Sooner or later you will put your own life in danger, or endanger the life of one of your fellow pilots. It's time to get out of the way and make room for someone else who can."

"Were you ever afraid, Slash?"

"There's a very thin line, but a very big difference, between knowing fear and being afraid. True bravery, is the ability to do your job in spite of your fear. You must learn to control fear, instead of allowing it to control you. Being anxious is healthy to the extent that your nervousness doesn't interfere with or affect your performance. It's an outward indication that you care about and are concerned with your performance. It's all right to have butterflies in your stomach, as long as you teach them to fly in formation."

"Was there ever a time when you thought you might not make it as a fighter pilot?"

"I remember my first instrument check ride at night with my instructor pilot at Williams Air Force Base. We were somewhere over the Arizona desert. Where, I hadn't the slightest clue. Unlike daylight flight with visual flight requirements, it was pitch black, and consequently, there were no landmarks for navigation purposes. About that time, my IP apparently deciding enough was enough, yelled into the intercom, 'Lt. Slash, you're way off course. Where do you think you're going?' I responded, 'beats the heck out of me Captain. The bad news is I'm lost. However, the good news is that we're making record time. Wherever we're going, we should be there very soon.'"

"What is your greatest concern as a fighter pilot, Slash?"

"Being a jet jockey has been described as 'flying around in a bucket of nuts and bolts, strapped to a jet engine.' The scary thing, is that I'm told that every one of those nuts and bolts in the aircraft was procured by the U.S. contractor who was the low bidder. When you stop and think about it, that isn't exactly the greatest confidence builder in the world."

"When did you get your nickname, Pounder?"

"Well, this isn't anything that you would want to send into the Readers Digest. They probably wouldn't print it."

"I'm not wired, Go ahead."

"I need to warm up a bit to get into the story-telling mood, Slash. Perhaps a line or two from one of my favorites: the 11th verse of the poem "The Walrus and the Carpenter," by Lewis Carol. 'The time has come the walrus said, to talk of many things, of shoes, ships, and sealing wax, and cabbages and kings. And why the sea is boiling hot and whether pigs have wings.'

"It occurred at an 8th Tactical Fighter Wing party we had at the Officer's Club at Kunsan Air Base in Korea. This was a special occasion. Our Wing Commander had completed his one year tour, and the wing was honoring him with a 'going away' party. As was customary, we were seated by squadron, all decked out in our party suits. They were attractive jump-suits, made by a Korean tailor in Kunsan City. Each squadron wore different distinctive colors. Our squadron colors were green and yellow.

"Just as everyone was being seated, we were honored with a surprise appearance by the Kunsan Boy's Choir. They were at their very best that evening, outdoing anything that I had ever seen before, except in the men's shower. As I recall, all the female officers made an early exit. A spontaneous food fight promptly followed their performance. Unfortunately for our squadron, we were strategically located right between the fighter squadrons. They caught us in the worst cross fire that I can ever remember."

"What happened?"

"After I took a few direct hits, I hit the floor and kept my head down until it was all over. You always knew when you had taken a direct hit."

"How's that?"

"The sour cream and butter on the baked potatoes, and the ketchup on the dinner rolls leave a big stain on your party suit."

"When did it end, Pounder?"

"When there wasn't anything left to throw. All the food was either on people, on the floor, or on the wall."

"What happened then?"

"Well, since there wasn't anything left to eat, we just passed up the meal, took a short break so the waiters could clean up some of the mess, and then went right into the awards presentation portion of the evening."

"How did that go?"

"It went great until it was my time to present. By that time, as a logistics officer, I was the only non-rated officer left in the club. As such, I knew that I was definitely in for a hard time. I walked up to the front of the room, stepped up to the mike, and started to deliver my prepared speech. However, no one could hear a word that I was saying."

"What happened, Pounder? Did they turn off the mike?"

"No, the mike was on. But, by this time all the squadron pilots had removed their shoes. Every time I opened my mouth to talk, they banged them on the table as loud as they could and yelled, 'ground-pounder,' 'ground-pounder,' 'ground-pounder.' This, of course, was a reference to my non-rated status."

"Did you ever get a chance to make your presentation?"

"Not a single word, Slash. Every time I stopped and attempted to start over, I was immediately drowned out all over again by the pounding and shouting. I finally got the message that I wasn't going to be allowed to talk, so I just handed my gift to the Wing Commander and returned to my chair."

"Were you upset about what happened, Pounder?"

"Not at all, Slash. After all, this was a fighter wing. And more than that, this was the 'Wolf Pack.' In their own way, the squadron pilots had actually honored me by acknowledging that even though I was a 'ground-pounder,' I was an important member of the Wolf Pack. As you are well aware, it was all part of the good-humored exchange that goes on between rated officers and non-rated officers in organizations all over the Air Force. As a matter of fact, it gave me even more incentive to work harder in supporting the mission. After all, we were all in this together. It was a wing effort. If we succeeded, we succeeded as a wing. And, if we failed, we failed as a wing. However, there was no way that we were going to fail. That's why we were selected to be members of the Air Force's number one fighter wing, the 'Wolf Pack.'

"The only thing missing at this point, Slash, is a little tribute to the Wolf Pack, compliments of Rudyard Kipling's poem. 'The Law of the Jungle.'"

> Now this is the law of the jungle
> as old and as true as the sky.
> And the wolf that may keep it shall prosper,
> but the wolf that shall break it must die.
>
> As the creeper that girdles the tree trunk
> the law runneth forward and back.
> For the strength of the pack is the wolf,
> and the strength of the wolf is the pack.

"Last call, gentlemen. Can I get you another round? How about one for the road?"

"No thanks," Slash responds. " I think the road has had enough. I'm cutting him off. You know how those roads are. Sometimes you just can't trust them. But, we would like to sing a little fighter pilot song for you to remember us by. In the best tradition of the Kunsan Boy's Choir, of course."

" As if I had a choice. Right? Here's the mike. Knock yourselves out boys."

> Living in the air we said,
> was going to make us free and lean.
> Now our skin is hard and rough,

the wings upon our chests to glean.

Fighting hard and flying low,
anywhere we're sure to go.
We don't think that we might die,
they say it's our foolish pride.

Yes, we are the Juvat's boys,
just as fast as polished steel.
War machines strapped to our backs,
for all the frigging world to fear.

Some have met their match you know,
bandits, flack, and SAMs too.
No one heard their dying words,
but that's the way it goes.

Some of us might one day say,
sitting there with you today.
We faced the MIG 21s unafraid,
and blood was shed that day.

Poets tell how the Phantom's flew,
105s and Linebacker too.
The jungles quiet, the wind is cold,
it carries the names of the fallen bold.

They don't need your prayers, it's true,
save some for me and you.
We will do what we have to do,
before we all go home.

Before we all go home. Juvats!

"Well done!" Says the waitress.
"Not too bad for two old washed up Air Force toads, if we do

say so ourselves."

"You guys take care and remember to 'check six.'"

"Thanks for the advice. See you around campus."

*** 

It's lights out and Slash and Pounder depart the club. In their vernacular, they 'flee the scene.' While the evening in the Officer's Club has been lighthearted and somewhat uplifting, the reality of the bleak situation in which they find themselves, begins to sink in once again. Consequently, the mood during their ride back to the motel is subdued.

"Slash, I remember when the going got tough in Kunsan, Korea, with the long hours and never-ending exercises. We would just shake it off with the expression, 'no sweat-e-da.' Then in Viet Nam, we attempted to dismiss all those annoyances by saying, it was just a 'nit-noy.' And then there was the Gulf War in the Middle East. In spite of incoming SCUD missiles compliments of Saddam, tomorrow morning would always usher in another beautiful day in the Magic Kingdom, Bukhra Inshallah,' God willing.

"However, I'm getting the feeling that this one is different from all the rest. I'm waking up in the middle of the night, staring at the ceiling with eyeballs as big as an owl's, and my imagination is running wild with all kinds of crazy things. Why do I get the impression that this whole gig is somehow like a house of cards? One misstep, and..."

Slash, anticipating where this conversation is heading, picks up on the prompt. "You mean it's curtains."

"Yea, either that or Venetian blinds. Like lambs being led to the slaughter."

"Thanks Mary, you took the words right out of my mouth."

"Realistically speaking, Slash, what do you make of our chances of getting in, getting the job done, and getting back out in one piece?"

"Realistically, Pounder. As I see it, we have two chances, slim and none."

"Well that's so comforting. You must have been a brain surgeon in your former life. You're so smart and you've got such a great bedside manner."

"Hey, maybe it's not as bad as it seems, Pounder. Try looking at it on the bright side. As you know, death always rides along as a silent partner on any dangerous mission. It's only when he speaks up that things start to get hairy."

"Remind me once again, Slash. Exactly why are we doing this?"

"I assume for the purposes of this conversation, that's a rhetorical question. We both know the answer in our heart of hearts. I guess it's because we're the kind of people we are, gluttons for punishment. Or worst yet, masochists. Somehow, we seem to get off on self-inflicted pain. Just think how good it feels when you take your hand out of a bucket of boiling water.

"Pardon me for drifting off for a moment there. Oh yes, it's all starting to come back to me now—duty, honor, and country. Derived from Pentagon doctrine, of course. The school solution, if you will. Let's see, as I recall, it goes something like this: 'The key to air power is flexibility, and the key to flexibility is indecision.' Or is it, 'we've been asked to do more with less for so long, that now we can do everything, with nothing.'"

"Slash, as a friend, I must warn you that you are treading on some very sacred ground here and it's approaching blasphemy. The 88th Article of the Uniform Code of Military Justice states that 'Any officer who uses contemptuous words against the President, Vice President, Congress, Secretary of Defense, or Secretary of a Department, a Governor of a legislature of any State, Territory, or another possession of the United States in which he is on duty or present shall be punished as a court-martial may direct.' Perhaps you should consider recanting that statement."

"Wow! You're absolutely right, Pounder. Whatever possessed me. What in the world was I thinking. No disrespect intended. I could get sent to Iraq if I'm not careful. The problem is I have been doing this so long, it seems at times that I'm programmed. After awhile, you can't tell whether you're in a rut or a groove. Sometimes there's a very fine line between the two. You know, my friend, even in the absence of widespread acute casualties from battle, war takes its toll on human health and well-being long after the shooting and bombing stops. When we were in Nam, you couldn't tell the good guys from the bad guys, the friendlies from the enemy. However, when we came home, we all thought things would be different. Somehow, I have the feeling that things haven't changed all that much."

"I agree Slash. This whole exercise is beginning to remind me more and more of the six phases of a project that every Action Officer in the Pentagon has posted on the wall near his desk to remind him of the certain disaster that lies ahead: (1) Enthusiasm; (2) Disillusionment; (3) Panic; (4) Search for the guilty; (5) Punishment of the innocent; (6) Praise and honors for the non-participants.

"Maybe I'm losing it, good buddy, but this is starting to remind me more and more of Nam. Will the last one out please turn off the lights and lock the door."

# CHAPTER TEN

## UP UP AND AWAY

*Mission planning for a flight on one of the VIP aircraft from* the Presidential Wing is done through the Office of the Vice Chief of Staff of the Air Force located in the Pentagon. When planning a travel itinerary to Saudi Arabia, there are several special considerations. For starters, there is an eight-hour time difference between Washington, D.C., and Saudi Arabia. Then, there is the trip duration, an exhaustive nonstop flight of 13 hours in the air. And finally, there is a difference in days of the week. The Saudi's celebrate their weekend on Thursday and Friday. Therefore, a businessman's best bet would be to schedule a departure from Andrews AFB, Maryland, at 10:00 A.M. on Friday. Accounting for the 21 hours of flight time and time difference, the traveler would arrive at King Abdul Aziz International Airport just north of the capital city of Riyadh, at approximately 7:00 A.M. on Saturday morning, which of course, is Monday in Saudi Arabia.

Having sorted all of this out, the National Security Advisor could now plan his routine and how to best utilize his time en route to Saudi. It all starts off with a cheap psych job on one's own mind. The secret to arriving at the destination as rested and relaxed as possible, is to disrupt your daily routine as little as possible. The approach that works best for Mitch is to surround himself with familiar items that remind him of home. He always takes his favorite pair of house slippers along to slip on as he relaxes before turning in at night. When he retires, he carefully places them under the bed so that they are the first thing he has contact with in the morning when he awakes. They have been with him through the good, the bad, and the ugly times in his life, and consequently, qualified as perhaps his most faithful friend. Then, there is his favorite tape, or CD, and a book. Stretching out on the bed with a good book and soft relaxing music playing in the background never fails him. It is prelude to the sandman's quick arrival and sound sleep. And finally, there is his usual nightcap. It consisted of a piping hot cup of caffeine free "Echinacea" herbal tea. The warmth of the liquid not only soothes his mind and soul, but also supports his body's defense system, helping fight stress and fatigue. Having to cope with jet lag, and trying to get a good night's sleep in a strange bed, are inherent challenges to all world travelers. Fighting a cold at the same time, is a traveler's worst nightmare.

The limo driver arrived promptly at 9:00 A.M. at Mitch's townhouse in Old Town Alexandria. He had packed the previous evening, laying out sufficient change of clothes to last him for two weeks. The NSA hoped he could wrap things up sooner and wouldn't be away that long. However, he realized there would be a lot of convincing to do, and the talks could hit a snag.

The driver pulls out into traffic on Highway 95/495, and is soon crossing the Woodrow Wilson Bridge over the Potomac River into Maryland on the way to Andrews AFB. Mitch stretches out, relaxing in the comfort of the spacious back seat of the limo. Many thoughts crowd into his mind at once, all demanding to be heard from first. The NSA has mixed emotions about this trip. This will be the ultimate test of his diplomatic negotiating skills. To be successful, it will require something for everyone. Mitch would need a "win-win" scenario for each stop, with the only looser being Saddam Hussein. He would call for compromise, telling the two sides "no one can get everything they want in an accord."

Mitch was motivated and eager to succeed. However, he was also well aware of the nature of Middle East negotiations, and the difficulties and pitfalls that most certainly lay ahead. This area was a graveyard for failed diplomacy. Many skilled diplomats had preceded him to this part of the world, armed with world-class diplomatic skills, the best of intentions, and the highest of hopes, only to spin, crash, and burn in the killing fields of diplomatic futility. The headstones scattered about, carried the names of the fallen dead. Some epitaphs attributed failure to miscalculation on the part of the negotiator. Others, blamed it on intractable disputes between the parties. Would the NSA be the latest to taste the bitterness, disappointment, and personal political suicide of failure? If he succeeded, he should be awarded not one, but two Nobel Peace prizes.

Mitch's itinerary called for his first stop in Saudi Arabia. The plan was to use Saudi soil to train the participants, and as a jumping-off point from which to launch the mission against Iraq. In addition, the U.S. was counting on the Saudi's for monetary support to help underwrite the cost of the operation. There was also the small matter of finding a suitable area to test the new fall-out suppression bomb that was to be used on the Iraqi missile sites.

If the Saudi's didn't buy in, the entire plan was a non-starter. Their support was the underpinning that would keep the whole ball of wax together. With them onboard, Mitch had an ace up his sleeve. It was one which he planned to use to his advantage in talks with the Palestinian Authority and Israel to overcome inertia, and nudge this big political football known as the Middle East peace process down the field. Once agreement was reached in Saudi Arabia, Mitch would proceed to Dubai in the United Arab Emirates, where he would meet with the Palestinian Authority. His final stop would be in Tel Aviv, for discussions with Israel.

The traffic on the capital beltway wasn't bad for this time of day. The majority of the rush-hour commuters had completed their daily morning journey through purgatory and were sipping their second or third cup of coffee in their government offices. His driver completed the 14-mile drive from Old Town Alexandria to Camp Springs, Maryland, in good time, taking the exit to Andrews AFB, home of the 89th Military Airlift Wing. This number "one" outfit in the USAF provides worldwide airlift services for the President, Vice President, cabinet members, congressmen, and other high-ranking dignitaries of the Untied States, and foreign governments.

The limo slows as they approach the front gate. Air Force security policemen are on the job, directing traffic and checking vehicles for proper access authorization. The driver stops briefly, lowers the window and displays some official credentials. The guard waves the vehicle ahead, giving the occupants a snappy military salute as it passes. Proceeding the few blocks to the flight line, they approach another security checkpoint. These security policemen are assigned to the Presidential Wing, and are expecting them. They instruct the driver to proceed slowly through the gate to the chain link security fence onto the tarmac and directly to the awaiting aircraft. As the aircraft comes into view with its tasteful baby blue and white paint scheme, and large American Flag on the tail, Mitch's heart beats with pride.

Eight aircraft have been officially designated as a presidential plane. The first official presidential plane was a C-54 named the "Sacred Cow," apparently because of the security and secrecy which surrounded the presidential aircraft at the time. The year was 1944, and the first President to enjoy the privilege was Franklin D. Roosevelt. Since that time, the presidential aircraft have consisted of the "Independence," "Columbines I and III," "tail number 3240," tail number 26000, and its sister VC 137 aircraft, "tail number 27000," which replaced it in 1972.

President George Bush took delivery of the current presidential aircraft on September 6, 1990, which the President continues to enjoy today. They consist of two identical Boeing 747-200B aircraft officially designated as Air Force VC-25s. In keeping with the sequencing of tail numbers on the Presidential aircraft, the tail number of the 747 which the President normally travels on is 28000. They come complete with state-of-the-art satellite communications equipment, in-flight refueling capability, and electronic countermeasures equipment. However, contrary to what makes for an exciting motion picture, the aircraft has no presidential parachutes or escape PODs. The aircraft has approximately 4,000 square feet of floor space, and the capacity to carry 26 crew members and 70 passengers. It is truly an airborne oval office, with all the luxury appointments one would expect in support of the most powerful man on the earth. All that, for a measly $300 million a copy.

The amenities that go inside the aircraft, dictated by presidential protocol and etiquette, provide the expected level of comfort and courtesy to the VIP passengers. They are the trappings of service that differentiate the decorum of the interior of Air Force One from your basic commercial airline accommodations. They consist of a wide variety of items from presidential dinnerware, including china, crystal, and silver, to conveniences such as playing cards, and match books, all of which carry the presidential seal.

From the time the President boards in the aircraft until the time he deplanes, the call sign of the aircraft is "Air Force One." The call sign for an aircraft carrying the Vice President is "Air Force Two." The NSA is scheduled to fly on back-up Air Force VC-25, the one on which the Vice President normally travels. The pilot has the engines running and has received clearance from the tower to begin immediate taxiing and take-off. They roar down the runway and leap into the air, lifting off precisely at 10:00 A.M., maintaining the Presidential Wings remarkable on-time worldwide departure reliability rate of 99.6%

Shortly after take-off, the voice of the aircraft commander over the intercom fills the cabin. "Good morning and welcome aboard. This is Lt. Colonel Frederick speaking to you from the flight deck. Our flight today will be approximately 13 hours. We will be flying at an altitude of 43,000 feet and traveling at a ground speed of 635 knots. Our estimated arrival at King Abdul Aziz International Airport in Riyadh, Saudi Arabia, will be 7:00 Monday morning, local time. The weather is expected to be good enroute and we are anticipating a smooth ride. Please make yourself comfortable and enjoy the flight."

A flight steward from the 89th Military Airlift Wing had phoned the NSA's secretary last week inquiring as to meal preference and amenities desired during the flight. No sooner had Mitch slipped into his seat than a cold glass of cran-raspberry juice was placed on his tray table. He took a drink, closed his eyes, inhaled a deep breath of air, opened his eyes once again, exhaled, and swallowed. An ear to ear grin consumed his face as he took in his surroundings and thought to himself, "I must have died and gone to heaven." His short fantasy was interrupted by the voice of the flight steward.

"Welcome aboard sir. My name is Jerry and I am the head flight steward. We plan to do everything humanly possible to make your flight as enjoyable and relaxing as possible. If there is anything you need at any time, please don't hesitate to let us know. What time would you like lunch served?"

"Let's see. It's just after 10:00 A.M. now. Why don't we plan to eat at about 11:30? I'm going to have a working lunch with my two staffers to go over some background papers. Could you make us up some sandwiches with Swiss cheese and pastrami on whole wheat hoagie buns? And, some more of that cran-raspberry juice would sure hit the spot."

"No problem sir. We'll have it ready for you at 11:30."

Mitch notifies his staffers that they will be taking lunch at 11:30, and requests they have their background papers on Saudi Arabia available for review and discussion. For the next hour, he decides to just relax and gather his thoughts. He is one lucky man. Good fortune had indeed smiled down and richly blessed him. He had all that he had ever dreamed of and more. This was one heck of a good deal and he wasn't about ready to let it slip through his fingers. Opportunities like this came along once in a lifetime. Mitch had been in the right place at the right time and had been prepared when it fell in his lap. He was in the driver's seat, and he wasn't at all ready to take-up his old place as a passenger in the back seat. Now that he had "arrived," he would allow nothing to stand in the way of his continued success and progression. Once you had been bitten by the big power bug in the sky, you were indeed addicted. And, you couldn't just get by on cruise control any more, you had to have your "fix," a couple of times a day to keep up the adrenalin-rush.

As Mitch enjoys his lunch, he reviews the background papers on Saudi Arabia.

The modern history of Saudi Arabia dates from 1932. It was then that King Abdul Aziz bin Abdul Rahman Al-Saud, succeeded in uniting the three major territories of the Arabian Peninsula, Al-Nejd, the Central Province; Al-Hassa, the Eastern Province; and Al Hizaj, the Western Province, and the new nation assumed its present name, Saudi Arabia.

The strategic location of the Arabian Peninsula is among the most important in the world. It controls or lies astride of major choke points in the Gulf and the Red Sea through which pass a large percentage of the world's petroleum exports. In addition, the peninsula contains a substantial portion of the world's oil reserve. Because of its oil wealth, its status as the homeland of Islam, and its strategic location, Saudi Arabia commands the attention of outside powers, both regional and global, that have substantial political, economic, and religious interests in the peninsula. Those who may not have been aware of the Kingdom of Saudi Arabia or its importance, got a crash course through the continuous CNN news coverage during the Gulf War. In less than a century, the citizens of Saudi Arabia have literally been snatched from their quiet, peaceful Bedouin lifestyle in the desert, and catapulted into a front and center position on the world stage.

Saudi Arabia occupies four-fifths of the Arabian Peninsula. Because several boundaries remain undefined, its precise geographical area is uncertain. However, government estimates put the Kingdom's size at approximately 864,900 square miles or approximately one-third the size of the United States. The vast majority of Saudi Arabia has a desert climate with very little annual rainfall. Temperatures in the summer often reach 130 degrees F. The population of the Kingdom is estimated to be in excess of 18 million, with approximately 1.8 million of whom reside in the capital city of Riyadh. Saudi Arabia has a large foreign population with as many as 4.5 million nonnatives residing within its boundaries. A large number of these are expatriates who come to the country to work.

It is estimated that the foreign workers outnumber the indigenous Saudi labor force by nearly two to one. Almost all of the native-born Saudis are Arabic speaking Muslims.

Islam means submission to the will of God. The "Shahada" testimony or creed, is the first Pillar and fundamental duty of every believer of Islam. It is "There is no god but God (Allah), and Mohammed is his Prophet." Mohammed, the Prophet of Islam, was born in A.D. 570. He is believed to be the last and greatest of God's messengers. About the year A.D. 610, when he was approaching forty, he secluded himself in a cave outside Mecca. There, one evening, he received the first in a series of divine revelations from the angel, Gabriel. He then began to preach, denouncing the polytheistic paganism of his fellow residents of Mecca. Mohammed eventually defeated his detractors and consolidated the temporal and spiritual leadership of Arabia in his person. Following Mohammed's death in A.D. 632, his followers compiled those of his words believed to have been revealed directly and literally from God into the Quran, the holy scripture of Islam. God is believed to have remained one and the same throughout all time. However, men have strayed from His true teachings until they were set right by Mohammed.

Prophets of the biblical tradition, such as Abraham, Moses, and Jesus, known in Arabic as Ibrahim, Musa, and Isa, respectively, are recognized as inspired messengers of God's will. Muslims recognize Jesus as a great prophet of God. They also revere him as Isa ibn Maryam, meaning Jesus, the son of Mary. The story of the virgin birth of Jesus is contained in the Quran, although not as God's son. Islam reveres as sacred only the message, rejecting Christianity's deification of Jesus. Allah is God, and Abraham is the founder of monotheism, and father of the Arabs through his son, Ishmael or Ismail. In Islamic belief, Abraham offered to sacrifice Ishmael, son of the servant woman Hagar, rather than Isaac, son of Sarah, as described in the Hebrew Bible or Old Testament.

Saudi Arabia is the guardian of Islam's two most holy and sacred shrines, located at Mecca and Medina. One of the five Pillars of Islam, requires every Moslem who is capable, to make a pilgrimage to Mecca at least once in his lifetime. This brings approximately two million visitors to Mecca each year during the Hijja holidays. Saddam has done his best to use this aspect of the Moslem faith to embarrass Saudi Arabia. Not long ago, during the Hijji holiday, Iraq loaded up 18,000 impoverished pilgrims onto vehicles without the necessary passports, warm clothing, food, or tents needed for the journey. The convoy, consisting of nearly 400 buses and trucks, and accompanied by senior Iraqi officials, crossed the Saudi border, driving through two checkpoints without stopping. Despite the incursion, King Fahd agreed to allow the illegal arrivals to remain in the Kingdom, and to pay for all the expenses of their religious pilgrimage. The Hajj holiday is Islam's most sacred religious ritual. As such, even the deep political divisions which still exist between Iraq and Saudi Arabia, must be overlooked. Saudi Arabia and Iraq have had no formal diplomatic relations since Iraq's 1990 invasion of Kuwait. However, returning the pilgrims back to Iraq might have appeared that the Saudis were putting national issues ahead of their sacred religious obligations and responsibilities.

The Kingdom of Saudi Arabia is governed by a Monarchy. Islamic law is based on the Holy Koran or Quran, which serves as the constitution. The King rules with support of the Royal Family which is estimated to include thousands of members. Senior Royal Princes hold most of the key positions in the government. Nearly every Saudi from the Bedouins in the desert, to royal family members in the city, belongs to a tribe. This association is an important method of identifying themselves both socially and culturally.

The Kingdom of Saudi Arabia was long considered one of the safest places in the entire world for U.S. military forces to serve. Internal security is strict and violators are dealt with swiftly, and severely, compared to Western standards. During the Gulf War, one of the primary security concerns of residents, apart from Saddam's daily SCUD missile threat, was that of possible terrorist's acts by third country nationals sympathetic to Iraq. However, during the entire war, there was only one reported terrorist incident. That occurred on February 4, 1991, in Jeddah, which is located on the

Western part of the Kingdom on the Red Sea. On that date, shots were fired from a vacant lot at a bus carrying five people, including an Egyptian driver, three American Servicemen, and a Saudi guard. The occupants sustained minor injuries from broken glass. Two days later, Saudi Government officials announced that they would "deal firmly" with anyone convicted of disorderly or subversive activities. The expatriate community interpreted this to mean that violators would be publicly executed, which is the custom for capital crimes in the Kingdom, including drug trafficking. In addition, residents were encouraged to pass on any information regarding suspected subversive activities, spurred on by the promise of generous financial rewards from the Government.

Subsequent events have shattered the terrorist proof image of the Kingdom, bringing the threat to Americans living and working there close to home. Security concern for the 40,000 Americans working in Saudi Arabia, in addition to an estimated 5,000 military personnel, has been of primary importance since two fatal attacks against U.S. personnel in the Kingdom. The quiet peace within Saudi Arabia was first shattered in November 13, 1995, in the capital city of Riyadh. A car bomb with the equivalent of 200 pounds of TNT, exploded in the parking lot adjacent to the building housing the Office of Program Management for the Saudi Arabian National Guard. A total of seven members of the OPM-SANG staff were killed, including five U.S. citizens. In addition, more than 30 others were seriously injured in the blast. Initially, it was thought that the perpetrators were terrorists. However, after some great detective work on the part of the Saudi officials, four young Saudi dissidents were arrested and charged with the crime. They were later beheaded.

A second tragedy of even greater magnitude followed on June 25, 1996. A truck bomb exploded outside a high-rise apartment in the Khobar Towers complex in the eastern city of Dhahran, throwing a force of 20,000 pounds of TNT against a building housing U.S. Airmen, killing 19 and injuring some 500 others. An analysis of the large crater by the Defense Special Weapons Agency determined that the bomb was the largest terrorist device ever directed against

Americans. It far exceeded the magnitude of the bomb that destroyed the Marine Corps compound in Beirut, Lebanon on October 23, 1983, which contained the equivalent explosive force of 12,000 pounds of TNT. The alleged co-conspirators included 13 Saudi's and one Lebanese. A grand jury later indicted them for conspiracy to commit murder and several related charges. The indictment implicates the Saudi Hezbollah, or Saudi Party of God. Many of its members were from the eastern province of Saudi Arabia and belonged to the Shi'ite branch of Islam.

Thus, in the summer of 1996, the American military personnel were relocated to Al Kharj, a desolate area 50 miles southeast of Riyadh. Known by military personnel as the 'Sandbox," American troops stationed there are protected by miles of desert fenced with razor wire, concrete barriers, motion sensors, and uniformed security forces. Prince Sultan Air Base, a 225 square-mile installation named after Prince Sultan, the Minister of Defense & Aviation, had been in the planning and construction phases for some ten years. It was initially envisioned as the main operating base for the Royal Saudi Arabia Air Force's Project Peace Sentinel KC-135s and AWACS aircraft, which for many years were housed at the interim operating base located adjacent to the capital city of Riyadh. The U.S. side of Al Kharj Airbase, houses 4,200 personnel, approximately 10 percent of which are security force. This facility, is in all probability, the most heavily guarded military installation housing U.S. forces in the entire world.

Mitch had planned to turn-in early and get a good night's sleep so that he would arrive fresh and rested and could hit the ground running in Saudi Arabia. At 9:00 P.M., he left instructions with the steward to give him a wake-up call, an hour and a half prior to arrival. That would provide him with sufficient time to shave, shower, dress, and enjoy a leisurely breakfast prior to arrival in Riyadh. He completed the ritual that he went through each evening as he prepared to retire for the night. All that remained was to turn off the bedside lamp, remove his slippers and carefully place them under the bed, lie back, close this eyes, and make believe that he was back home in his own bed.

***

The next sound Mitch heard was the soft tapping of the steward on his bedroom door. "Sir, it is 0530. We are an hour and one-half out of Riyadh."

The National Security Advisor arose, feeling rested from a good night's sleep. He shaves, showers, dresses, and moves to a sitting area where breakfast is served. A call from a crew member in the cockpit informs him that they have made good time and will be arriving a few minutes ahead of schedule. They also update him on the weather and local time. He then positions himself in a wide-bodied seat leisurely looking out the window at the barren desert below.

Mitch hadn't lost his appetite and is looking forward to breakfast. It was a sign that the night had passed uneventfully. He would soon begin his real journey, that of entering into conversation, negotiations, and most importantly, the minds of those he had come to convince. He savors each spoonful of his bowl of hot oatmeal, and munches on a cinnamon-raisin bagel, washing it all down with a large glass of freshly squeezed orange juice. All this, served to him on the finest china and crystal, bearing the seal of the President of the United States. If he allowed himself, he could quickly get accustomed to being pampered like this. It certainly beat the heck out of the eat on the run, routine that his bachelor life afforded him each morning back in the nation's capital.

The hum of the engines relaxes Mitch, lulling him into a semi-trance as he gazes out the window. The aircraft descends and the pilot skillfully brings it in on final approach to King Abdul Aziz International Airport. With the desert floor swiftly passing beneath him, his thoughts float away for a few seconds as he pictures in his mind's eye a scene that occurred many years earlier here in this same desert sand.

At the turn of the last century, the powerful Rashid family ruled the small town of Riyadh, Saudi Arabia. The Saud family, the traditional rulers, seethed in exile in Kuwait. In January 1902, 21year-old Abd al-Aziz ibn Abd al-Rahman Al Faisal Al Saud, led 40 of his followers on a bold crusade to regain the disputed capital. Under cover of darkness on a cold moonless night, they slipped unnoticed into an oasis on the outskirts of town. He and six of his men scrambled over Riyadh's high mud-brick walls, quietly opening the gates to the rest of his band. During the night, they passed the time in hiding by sleeping, praying, eating dates, and drinking coffee. The following morning, they surprised Emir Ajalan as he emerged from his fortress surrounded by bodyguards. The battle was fierce, but brief. On that day nearly 100 years ago, although out numbered two to one by the emir's guards, Abd al-Aziz was victorious. The house of Saud was reestablished in Riyadh.

# CHAPTER ELEVEN

## WELCOME TO THE MAGIC KINGDOM

*The screeching of the tires of the Air Force VC-25 aircraft* touching down on the runway followed by the roar of the jet engines as the pilot reversed thrust, bring Mitch back to reality with a jolt. He is on the ground in Saudi Arabia, the first leg of his Middle East trip. The adventure has officially begun.

The pilot taxis for a few minutes and pulls to a stop on the tarmac. The NSA and his party deplane. Not in the main terminal, but in the VIP area of the Royal Terminal normally reserved for members of the Royal Family. As Mitch collects his personal belongings and debarks the aircraft, he feels a sudden rush of anxiety. He has been to the Middle East previously, but each trip seems to be a whole new adventure in itself. Memories of his last trip to Riyadh, Saudi Arabia, flash through his mind. The impressive infrastructure with its super highways, telecommunications, schools, hospitals. A modern city, all decked out in fashionable architecture. The home of a conservative Moslem society.

Entering the Royal Terminal, Mitch is mesmerized by the regal splendor of his surroundings. There are no words to adequately describe the breath taking beauty that surrounds him–the lush carpets underfoot, the sparkling crystal chandeliers overhead, and the fine tapestry that adorns the walls. Suffice it to say, it is indeed fit for a king.

Soaking in the imposing magnificence of the room like the warm rays of sunshine on a summer day, the spell is broken as Mitch hears the sound of his own name.

"Mitch, Mitch, over here."

Mitch turns in the direction of the voice, and spots a friendly face. It is Chad Duncan, the American Deputy Chief of Mission at the U.S. Embassy.

"Hi, Mitch. Good to see you again. How was the trip?"

"Oh, you know how those commercial flights are Chad, especially when you have to fly 'cattle class.' Man, we were jammed up and jelly tight, wedged in there like a can of sardines. I had to stand in line to use the John, the air conditioner was broken, and the meal was Spam which I had to fix myself. I couldn't catch a break."

"Yeah, I saw the airplane and all of, what, maybe four people get off. You could have gotten lost in there for several weeks before anyone ran across you. Well, as they say, it's a tough job, but someone has to do it."

"You're right Chad, but you know me. I'm a glutton for punishment."

"The limo is parked out front. The driver will get your bags."

Chad and Mitch step out the front door of the terminal into the bright sunlight. It's only 7:30 in the morning. However, with the sudden blast of heat that greets them, it feels more like it must be somewhere between 12:00 and 2:00 in the afternoon. The Saudi desert is like a furnace in the summer. The hot air quickly fills Mitch's lungs, and his mouth goes instantly dry. Due to the extremely low humidity, one does not appear to be perspiring outdoors, even when engaged in heavy physical activity. However, a few minutes inside a room without air conditioning will open the flood gates, soaking your clothing in sweat.

Mitch slips into the welcome air conditioning of the long sleek black Cadillac limousine with the American flag flying from the left front fender. The driver arrives with the bags and deposits them in the trunk. A moment later, he is behind the wheel, pulling out from the terminal in a southern direction toward Riyadh. The highway ripples beneath the morning heat, acknowledging the unrelenting rays of an angry desert sun. Glancing over his shoulder, Mitch confirms that his two staffers are safely deposited in the car with the diplomatic license plates following closely behind.

"Welcome back to the Magic Kingdom, Mitch. It's been a while since you were out this way. We thought that perhaps you had forgotten about us," the DCM jokes.

"You can be absolutely sure, the feeling is mutual, Chad. All the way over the Atlantic," Mitch adds with a wry smile, "I'm thinking that it's you jokers in the U.S. Embassy in Riyadh that cooked this whole thing up, just looking for an excuse to get me back over here again and make me suffer along with you." Chad nods in mock agreement, and laughter follows.

"You're traveling a little light, aren't you, with just a couple of horse holders?"

"Yes, I am. I purposely brought along just two staffers so as not to attract the attention that a large party of traveling diplomats invariably gets. Then, people start to ask questions. Who's that, and what's he doing here? As you are aware, this is a low profile mission with a highly classified agenda."

"Well, you won't have to worry about the paparazzi here in the Magic Kingdom. The news people are on an extremely short leash. All news reporting is subject to government censorship. There will be no coverage of your visit either in the newspapers or on T.V. Of course, with an internationally famous face such as yours, there's no telling how many people might recognize you out on the street."

"You know," Mitch smiles, "I was concerned about precisely that possibility. Always being one to plan ahead, I brought a couple of dozen extra pens with me to sign autographs. Do you think that will be enough?"

"I don't honestly know. You can't trust those U.S. Government pens. Two or three signatures are about all you can count on before they run out of ink."

"So what's the game plan, Chad?"

"Ambassador Paul Robinson would like you to stop by the embassy for a couple of hours. After you freshen up, we'll get together in the conference room and give you a run down on the issues from the perspective of the Saudi Government and our 'feet on the ground position' here in the Magic Kindgom. We'll have some of your favorite Middle East hors d'oeuvres brought in to munch on, along with a big frosty pitcher of Saudi Champagne to wash it down with. You know we give our VIP visitors from Washington nothing, but first class treatment."

"All right, now you're talking. I knew there was a good reason I came all the way over here, but it had just about escaped me. Of course, hummus, pita bread, tabbouleh, kibbeh, and Saudi Champagne. A meal fit for a king, but refresh my memory on this Saudi Champagne. We're talking a pitcher of apple juice mixed with Perrier, right?"

"You've got that right, Mitch. That's the closest thing to the real stuff you're going to find here in the Magic Kingdom. By the way, we should have things wrapped up at the Embassy by mid afternoon. A vehicle and a driver have been assigned to you. The driver will drop you at the Ambassador's residence just a few blocks down the street in the Diplomatic Quarter. He has a great VIP guest room which I'm sure that you will enjoy. If you'd like, we can take in some of the sights of Riyadh, after you unpack and settle in. No one comes here without a shopping list of items from the gold or the rug souk. That will give us a chance to visit a little more and help you get acclimated to the climatic environment of your new home for the next day or two."

"Sounds good to me. Let's do it."

"I live on the other side of the tracks with the poor folks. You could put my entire home in the swimming pool area of the Ambassador's residence. But, I'm just the DCM, the number two guy, except when the Ambassador is out of town. When that happens, I am instantly translated from the DCM to the Charge d' Affaires. Then it's my turn in the barrel. Of course, if I get put on the spot with a tough decision while the Ambassador is away, I can always say,

'I'm not the regular crew chief. I need to touch base with the boss on this one.' But, being the number two guy has its advantages. Without the visibility of the Ambassador, I can slip around town pretty much undetected. Consequently, I have a lot more flexibility and freedom of movement."

Mitch and Chad soon arrive at the entrance to the Diplomatic Quarter which houses the embassies of the major countries of the world maintaining diplomatic relations with Saudi Arabia. The limo driver slows as he approaches the uniformed security guards, and then continues as they recognize the diplomatic plates and give him a wave of the hand to proceed. At the first round-about, they keep right, down a one-way street lined with palm trees on both sides.One of the first embassies they pass after they enter the DQ, catches Mitch's eye. The building appears to be deserted and the grounds inside the security fence are in desperate need of maintenance.

"Let me guess what that building used to be," offered Mitch.

"Right," countered Chad. "I'll give you three guesses and the first two don't count. It's the home of the old Iraqi Embassy that was vacated after Saudi Arabia severed diplomatic relations with Iraq on the occasion of their untimely invasion of Kuwait. It has remained empty ever since."

Continuing on deeper into the DQ, they pass embassy after embassy with their flag's proudly displayed. The lush green foliage of the trees, bushes, and flowers that surround them defy everything they have heard about the barrenness and harshness of the Saudi desert. Once a visitor gets over the utter amazement of what he is witnessing, the message comes through loud and clear. With sufficient water and a green enough thumb, the desert could become an oasis.

Suddenly up ahead on the right, the outline of a very large sand-colored building emerges like a mirage rising from the desert floor. This is the most impressive structure they have observed in the DQ. As they draw near, there can be no mistake. The stars and stripes waving gently, yet gallantly in a soft breeze tells all. They are home! Chad instructs the driver to proceed to the private rear entrance behind the Embassy to spare them the time and frustration of going through the normal security checks that visitors to the U.S. embassy must pass.

"We are understandably very security conscious," Chad says, stating the obvious. "In addition to the identification check outside the visitors gate, once inside there is a hand-held metal detector check and physical pat-down of all visitors by a security guard. Any objectionable items are withdrawn and kept for safekeeping until the visitor reclaims them on the way out. Inside the front door of the embassy, there is walk-through metal detector check that proceeds under the watch-full eye of a uniformed security guard, and a U.S. Marine behind bullet proof glass. Visitors are once again asked to produce their official identification, sign their name, organization, and purpose of visit into a log, before being issued a visitor's security badge. All entry into the embassy at that point is by personal escort."

Parking in the underground garage, they take the elevator to the Ambassador's office on the third floor. The use of a special key is required to access the elevator. Mitch is duly impressed with the security precautions that have been taken to safeguard the employees and property in the U.S. Embassy. They exit the elevator and enter the outer office of the U.S. Ambassador. A secretary greets them just inside the door. She informs Chad that the Ambassador is expecting them, and invites them to go right on in.

The Honorable Paul Robinson, U. S. Ambassador to Saudi Arabia, looks the part of a diplomat. In his mid forties, he appears just as fit as the day he graduated from Yale. Standing ram-rod straight, he carries just a touch of distinguished gray in his sideburns. Saudi Arabia obviously agrees with Paul Robinson. He wares a permanent deep tan that quickly assures visitors he is indeed at home here in the Magic Kingdom. The Ambassador manages to squeeze a set or two of tennis into his busy schedule each day, followed by a refreshing swim in his private pool to wash off the desert dust. His previous diplomatic service included stints as Consul General in two large cities in Europe. Immediately prior to his appointment as

Ambassador to Saudi Arabia, he served as Deputy Chief of Mission in Kuwait. Paul had been well prepared for this assignment. He was a student of Middle East history, and completed the Arabic language course at the Defense Language School in Monterey, California. When he was nominated for the posting, it came as no surprise. It was the fulfillment of his destiny as a professional foreign service officer. Saudi Arabia was a country on the move, and the most important Middle East Arab ally of the United States.

"Good morning, Mr. Ambassador. It's good to see you once again. I just wish that it could be under better circumstances."

Ambassador Robinson steps from behind his desk and crosses the room to welcome his visitor.

"Yes, I do too, Mitch. However, as long as this gentlemen up north is unleashed, I'm afraid we will be forced to continue to have these kind of meetings to discuss these kind of problems. It's too bad that we didn't finish the job we started during Desert Storm."

"I couldn't agree with you more Ambassador. However, as you are aware, we politicians somehow have a knack of snatching defeat from the jaws of victory. Gains achieved at the expense of the sacrifices of our armed forces personnel are frequently bartered away at the conference table, either due to the lack of our negotiating skills or out of the kindness of our hearts for our adversaries. I'm really not sure which one it is.

"You know why I'm here, Mr. Ambassador. We desperately need the Saudi's support to successfully pull this off.

"First of all, we need to temporarily occupy a small piece of that big sand box out there for training, testing our new weapon, and the staging of operations. Secondly, we hope to be able to utilize a small amount of what lies beneath that big sand box to underwrite some of the costs of the mission. Now, before you respond, let me say this. We are well aware of the sensitivity of the Saudi Government to supporting operations such as this. As such, we are prepared to operate entirely out of sight and, therefore, out of mind. We will be located in the Empty Quarter, far away from prying eyes and listening ears. I understand that it is nearly the size of Texas, and is the largest continuous body of sand in the world, with dunes rising to a height of 500 feet or more. Top secrecy is absolutely essential for obvious reasons."

The NSA pauses, looking for feedback, well aware that he has dumped a large truckload of baggage at the feet of the Ambassador. Only a moment passes, before he receives his response.

"Well, thank goodness, Mitch. I was beginning to think that you were going to show up on our door step in a basket wrapped up in a blue baby blanket with adoption papers. Now, I find that all you want are the sun, the moon, and the stars all served up at once!

"You know what it is I really love about you Washington types?" the Ambassador asks with a scowl on his face and malice in his voice. "It's all coming back to me now. We're out here in the field, down in the trenches with our counterparts, busting our backside day in and day out to accommodate all their idiosyncracies and maintain a close working relationship. This, of course, doesn't happen overnight. Sometimes it can be a real goat rope.

"In this part of the world, it takes months, even years, to establish the requisite trust on which successful diplomacy is built. Then, just when things are moving along at what might be considered a half-decent pace with a minimum of hick-ups, in roll the G-men with some hair-brained cockamamie scheme that will not only be considered a major imposition on our friends, but an affront to their dignity. And, who might the messenger be to deliver up this bucket of Washington slime to our Saudi friends? Rumor has it that Paul Revere's no longer available. And, even if he was, we'd have to come up with a whole new set of signals. The old 'one if by land and two if by sea' gig just won't cut it any more. And in case you've forgotten, in addition to playing Mr. Ambassador with the Saudis, I've got this little additional duty that concerns the personal safety and security of approximately 40,000 Americans working in Saudi Arabia, along with 5,000 military personnel serving here."

Mitch was at least partially prepared for the shock wave of the Ambassador's blast. He had been given a "heads-up" by a friend in the State Department who had previously served with Ambassador

Robinson. By reputation, he was a professional statesman and a savvy diplomat. However, he also enjoyed the dog and pony show that came with the turf. When you entered the big top, he was the one performing in the center ring, and the more savage wild animals and flaming sword swallowing freaks that surrounded him the better. Nevertheless, Mitch had jumped in his "mental" foxhole to keep from being totally blown away by the response. Now that the side show was over, they could get about the real business of engaging in an amicable discussion regarding how they were going to pull this whole thing off.

"Hey, don't forget, Mr. Ambassador, that the Saudis have a lot at stake here. They've got a missile with a warhead pointed at one of their major military installations just south of the capital."

"Yes, Mitch, I understand. However, the Soviet Union had dozens of missiles with nuclear warheads pointed at major U.S. population areas for years and we didn't launch any pre-emptive air strikes."

"That was different. It was all part of the ground rules of the sick little game that we were playing with the Soviet Union at that time. The old delusion, know as the 'balance of power' arrangement. Both sides had an agreed-on number of missiles and warheads pointed at each other, with the threat of retaliation by one side keeping the other side from launching a first strike. However, Iraq isn't supposed to have any weapons of mass destruction, and the Saudis don't have a weapon pointed at Baghdad. In addition, Saddam has already proven on many occasions, including his invasion of Kuwait, that he can't be trusted to just project military power. If he's got it, he's prone to flaunt it.

"Apart from the philosophical argument, our intelligent sources have confirmed that the threat exists, along with apparent intent. In short, Saddam has the means, opportunity, and motive. And, we have enough evidence to persuade a jury of his peers to convict him in a court of law. Unfortunately, international law is not selling too successfully in Iraq at this time. We have an entire group of unemployed and disgruntled weapons inspectors who can vouch for that. The real bottom line is, the great debate is over. We ran this whole thing up the flag poll to see who would salute it, and the National Security Council sang out in unison 'yes sir, yes sir, three bags full.' Consequently, the President has already signed off on a 'Presidential Finding,' and we are in the process of briefing key congressional leaders and recruiting the primary operatives for the mission. The fact of the matter is, this train is loaded, has left the station, and is rolling downhill gathering momentum as it goes. Anyone that gets in the way at this point is going to be 'road kill.' We need you onboard the train, Mr. Ambassador, not tied to the tracks as a political hostage."

"As you are aware, Mitch, we have enjoyed an excellent working relationship with our Saudi counterparts over the years. The embodiment of the maturation of that relationship came during the dark and precarious days of the Gulf War. Prior to my predecessor's reassignment, the Custodian of the Two Holy Mosques, King Fahd ibn Abd Al-Aziz, honored Ambassador Smith by conferring on him the Abd Al-Aziz medal, first class, the Kingdom's highest award. To the best of my knowledge, that honor had not previously been conferred on a non-Arab ambassador.

"At the conclusion of the Gulf War, with Saddam out of Kuwait, we had a reservoir of goodwill built up with the Saudis. However, that was then and this is now. You can draw water from one watering hole in an oasis in the desert only so many times before it dries up, and all that remains is the dust of the desert sand.

"Upon the Allied Commander, Gen. Hammond's departure from Saudi Arabia, in March 1991, he sent a message to the men and women of Desert Storm praising and thanking them for their dedicated service. In that message, he stated in part that they had written history in the desert sands that could never be blown away by the winds of time. There were undoubtedly a large number of footprints left in the sand from the thousands of Americans who served here during Desert Storm. However, if you were to spend a day in the desert with a good Bedouin guide today, you would have a great deal of difficulty locating them."

"So, what has changed?"

"One of the primary drivers is on-going efforts at Arab unity and solidarity. The Saudis are intent on mending fences and normalizing relations with some of their Arab neighbors that were strained during the Gulf War. The gulf allies want to avoid conflict with Iraq. A U.S. decision to strike Iraq without Iraqi provocation would be a hard decision for them to support. It is something they really fear and they don't want to see happen. In addition, it is in the Arab's best interest to work toward building regional security with a lesser dependence on the West. King Fahd is urging countries of the Gulf Cooperation Council to pursue a united military force and economic unity. That group includes Saudi Arabia, Kuwait, Bahrain, Qatar, Oman, and the United Arab Emirates. In addition, Saudi Arabia, Kuwait, and other Gulf States are increasingly being criticized by some of their own citizens and other Muslim nations for hosting U.S. military bases.

"During my discussions with Saudi Government representatives regarding Saddam's intransigence in allowing U.N. weapons inspectors to complete their U.S. mission in Iraq, a senior Saudi official informed me that Saudi Arabia would not allow its territory to be used as a launching pad to attack Iraq. At that time, he contended that not even U.N. Security Council approval of an attack would change their position. Informally, I was told that Saudi reluctance to allow strikes against Iraq, under any circumstances, from its soil or bases in Saudi Arabia, was due to the sensitivity of the issue in the Arab and Muslim world. A war on terrorism could create harmful 'secondary effects' in the Muslim world. He added that the United States has plenty of fighter jets and troops afloat in the Persian Gulf which could be utilized for this purpose.

"That discussion took place shortly after Baghdad had threatened to attack a base in southern Turkey used by U.S. warplanes, along with other bases in the region, to patrol the 'no-fly' zone over the north of the country. Threats were also made to attack bases in Saudi Arabia and Kuwait from where U.S. and British jets patrol the southern "no-fly' zone. Iraq's Vice President Taha Yassin

Ramadan was quoted as saying, 'If they do not retreat, they will soon pay dearly in relation to the properties and elements they use to launch aggression on the people of Iraq.'

"But, let's not kid ourselves, gentlemen. This doesn't read like a real dime store romance novel. The stark reality of the situation is, that there is very little love lost between Saddam's Iraq and the Saudis. A Saudi government spokesman has publicly stated that the Iraqi regime still insists on its old practices, and is unable to learn from the lessons of the painful paths it has followed in the past. The Emirates and Qatar have led the call to end the sanctions that were imposed after Baghdad's 1990 invasion of Kuwait. However, Saudi Arabia and Kuwait blame the Iraqi government for the suffering of its people and continue to insist that the sanctions must stay in place until Iraq has complied with all U.N. resolutions, including destroying their weapons of mass destruction, and returning Kuwaiti war prisoners.

"The U.S. presence remains a politically sensitive issue in the region, with gulf states anxious to avoid angering Baghdad or to appear to be siding with the United States against fellow Muslims. The Saudi Government is also facing increasing internal pressures from religious fundamentalists. In their eyes, regardless of how much good we have done, we in the West are infidels, and the U.S. is still the 'Great Satan.' As you are aware, five Americans and two Indian Nationals were killed in an attack on the Office of Program Management of the Saudi Arabian National Guard in Riyadh, on November 1995. The carnage was initially blamed on terrorists. However, after an extensive internal investigation, four young Saudi dissidents were arrested and charged with the crime. They were later beheaded.

"A second act of terrorism followed in June 1996. Nineteen American airmen died in the bombing of Khobar Towers, a U.S. military barracks in the eastern city of Dhahran. The perpetrators of that cowardly act have still not been brought to justice. However, they are suspected to be Muslim extremists. The Saudis have become increasingly uncomfortable with their close ties to Washington since that time. The fact of the matter is, that while the Saudis are generally concerned about the motives and intentions of their neighbors in Iran and Iraq, Israel is not viewed as a threat. All the rhetoric in denouncing Israel as the enemy is just public posturing and window dressing to maintain peace and tranquillity among their Arab brothers. Truth and justice are less important at this time than unity among brothers. Therefore, it is important that they maintain a united front, and that there be no public display of differences or disagreements between or among Arab nations.

"There is an old Arab saying that may help you understand their position. 'It's me and my brother against my cousin; and me, my brother, and my cousin, against the world.'

"I understand, Mr. Ambassador," however, it appears that the recent acts of terrorism perpetrated on Saudi soil must have gotten the Royal family's attention. They surely understand that they have much at stake by not fully cooperating with the U.S. in dealing with the threat. Perhaps the most well known symbol of global terror, Osama bin Laden, was grown right here on Saudi soil. That's hitting pretty close to home."

"Trust me on this one Mitch, that fact has not gone un-noticed by the Royal family It's an issue of considerable embarrassment and concern. The Bin Laden family originated in Yemen. However, Osama, the 17th of 54 children, and believed to be the only child of the union of Mohammed Awad bin Laden and a Syrian woman, was raised in Saudi Arabia. He was born into considerable wealth as the family owned a prominent construction conglomerate that built much of the Saudi infrastructure after the discovery of oil in the Eastern province. It was while studying business administration at King Abdul Aziz University in Jeddah, that he embraced the Islamic fundamentalist ideology. However, because of restrictions on his lifestyle in Saudi, Osama was largely a rebel without a cause. It was not until after the Soviet invasion of Afghanistan that bin Laden really took root, and began to cultivate his legacy. As a wealthy businessmen, he helped finance the military operations of the anti-Soviet Jihad, which eventually liberated Afghanistan from the great red bear. As a Soviet-hating 'freedom fighter,' he was applauded by the CIA, next door in Pakistan, which was also funding the effort to fight Soviet troops in Afghanistan.

"At the conclusion of the war, Osama returned home to Saudi Arabia with a folk hero's welcome, and enjoyed considerable popularity throughout the Middle East. However, the honeymoon was short lived. After Saddam Hussein's invasion of Kuwait in 1990, bin Laden argued the case of recruiting mercenary Afgan 'freedom fighters' to take on the Iraq military. When the Saudi Royal family oped to dial "911," and request American assistance instead, Osama went ballistic. After all, these were the same Western infidels who were corrupting and oppressing Muslims throughout the world that he had come to love to hate. The physical presence of large numbers of American military personnel on the same sacred ground with Islam's two most holy shrines at Mecca and Medina in Saudi Arabia, was unthinkable. Speaking out publicly against the royal family, bin Laden found himself in very hot water. Having worn out his welcome in the magic Kingdom, he fled to Sudan. Forced out by Saudi and U.S. political pressure on the government, he left the Sudan in 1996, and sought refuge as a guest of the Taliban militia in Afghanistan. Under their protection, he has continued to build his al-Qaeda terrorist network to recruit, train, and logistically support his 'freedom fighters,' around the globe. Obviously, this business of 'the enemy of my enemy is my friend,' can be a very sticky wicket. Without considerable foresight, one can end up with some strange bedfellows down the line."

"OK, Mr. Ambassador, I think I've got the message. What do you say, we proceed as follows? I'm a proponent of the old 'carrot and stick approach.' The carrot in this case would be a commitment from the U.S. that we are predisposed to looking favorably on requests for future weapons systems sales of legitimate self-defense needs. This offer has the President's support.

"The stick is rather self-evident. If they don't work with us on this, they could end up being the recipients of a weapon of mass destruction on one of their major military installations, compliments of Saddam Hussein."

"I see the rationale and wisdom in your basic bargaining approach, Mitch. However, if I may, I would like to suggest a little different wrinkle. Why don't we think of this as 'quid pro quo' instead of 'carrot and stick?' They give us something and get something in return of perceived equal value. Directness and confrontation are not successful bargaining techniques in Middle East negotiations. I make it a rule to never put my Saudi counterparts in a corner, always leaving them some wiggle room. And, under no circumstances, regardless of the gravity of the situation, ever place them in a position where they could experience a loss of face. In addition to bringing the negotiations to a screeching halt, you will have made a lifetime enemy. Sometimes, the best approach on extremely sensitive issues, is to have an intermediary carry the message to avoid the directness of a face to face meeting. In other words, negotiate through a second party.

"There's no way the Saudi Government is going to buy into this plan based on the military aspects. They have articulated their position clearly and publicly. Consequently, we can't approach Foreign Minister Prince Saud al-Faisal directly with this no matter how it is wrapped. He's in a box, he won't deal. Regardless of which direction we come at him, he will suspect that he's being manipulated. If we go in there and just drop this package on the table, they'll jerk us around like yesterday's dirty laundry. Everyone in the room will have a shot at us. And when it's time for the serious discussion, conversation will shift from channel one 'English' to channel two 'Arabic.' After a considerable length of time, we will be informed in somewhat unobtrusive terms that our proposition is unacceptable. However, there won't be any specific reason given for their response. What you take back from the meeting is one of two likelihoods. Either the proposal was truly unacceptable, or it has possibilities, but the pot needs to be sweetened. We're dealing with a time sensitive issue here, and don't have the luxury of playing this scenario out to its final ending.

"If we packaged our proposal as an economic or financial deal, as opposed to a military plan, perhaps that would sufficiently change the focus to get it reviewed and given some serious consideration. The key then becomes identifying the ideal person to deliver the message. We need an intermediary. Someone to carry the mail."

Mitch inquires, "Is there anyone that we could call on to assist us with this?"

"Yes, there is. His Royal Highness, Prince Khalid al Turki. We recently worked up a due-diligence on him. Prince Khalid is one of the world's wealthiest and most powerful investors. He has invested successfully in banks, real estate, hotel chains, department stores, and most recently, in the information technology industry. The prince is truly an accomplished international businessman with a far-flung empire of financial holdings in Europe, the Middle East, and the United States. And, he also just happens to be one of the most respected members of Saudi Arabia's ruling family. His uncle is the King. Prince Khalid is someone with both respect and clout who can carry the mail for us."

"Well, Mr. Ambassador, it seems that we have come to a conclusion and agree on an approach. Visit with Prince Khalid. Put the proposition to him and see if he is agreeable to carrying it to the King for consideration by the Council of Ministers. This, of course, implies that you share with him the basic information on the threat. You are also authorized to inform him that you are speaking on behalf of the President of the United States of America."

"This might be a good place to break for the day. According to my watch and my stomach, it's time for lunch. And we have a special surprise for you today, Mitch."

"Yes, I know, Mr. Ambassador. Chad let the cat out of the bag on the way in from the airport. I've spent the entire morning trying to come up with an appropriate toast to go along with our first glass of Saudi Champagne."

"No surprise is secure with him around. That was supposed to be a well kept state secret. This man leaks like a sieve."

\*\*\*

After lunch, Chad calls for a driver, and he and Mitch head down to the center of the old city of Riyadh to take in the sites.

"You know Mitch, when all is said and done, Ambassador Robinson deserves high marks. Saudi Arabia is one of the highest profile and most difficult postings in the diplomatic field. Paul is thought of very highly within the Maxwell administration, and throughout the State Department. He is a pro, and a credit to his profession. There is a big difference between a career foreign service officer and a political appointee. I've worked for both. It's like day and night. The political appointee is either posted at an embassy to enjoy the prestige of the position and take an extended vacation at the expense of the taxpayer, or to fill a square on a resume as a stepping stone to greater political ambitions. When he is in-country, he attends all the high visibility socials, does the glad handing, and greeting of VIP visitors. The DCM shoulders responsibility for all the day-in and day-out management of work at the embassy. Ambassador Robinson, on the other hand, actively participates in the management of the embassy. However, he involves his staff in the decision-making process, with the objective of developing a well-functioning country team capable of meeting the challenges of the diplomatic mission.

"Darn straight Chad. Ambassador Robinson has been a great role model and a superb tactician. He most definitely has his finger on the pulse of the Saudi Government. Unlike many American diplomats serving abroad, he is able to get inside his counterpart's minds and think and reason with them in terms they understand, instead of attempting to force-feed American ideals down their throats. I have nothing, but the highest respect and admiration for the man. It's just too bad there aren't more Ambassador Robinson's around today. If we could find a way to clone him, we'd be onto something, wouldn't we? I'd put a Paul Robinson in every capital city around the globe. Within six months to a year, 90 percent of all the school children in the world would know the pledge of allegiance.

"The way he was able to cut through all the smoke and mirrors was amazing. He has a memory like an elephant and a mind like a steel trap. His recommended approach to the Saudi Government was right on."

"Say, Chad. You mentioned earlier today about the possibility of me being recognized by people on the street. I thought that you were joking at the time. However, I've noticed that every time we stop at a traffic light, the driver of the vehicle behind us honks his horn. Is it possible that someone has recognized me?"

"Well, I hate to crush your male ego Mitch, but you couldn't be more off base. Let me explain what's going on here. It's a rare fluke of nature. To the best of my knowledge, this is the only place on the planet where the speed of sound is faster than the speed of light. You hear the driver behind you honk his horn, before you see the traffic light change color. If you've ever considered entering the Indianapolis 500, in between street lights is a good time to practice your start. It's strictly every man for himself and there are never any yellow caution flags. And, you'll notice when we do stop at the light, this two lane street sometimes becomes four or five lanes. Speaking in the British vernacular, our friends here haven't quite captured the concept of 'queuing' up. The Westerners jokingly say that the definition of a Saudi line is 'one deep and 200 abreast.'

"The road we are traveling on is referred to as 'old airport road.' It is so named because it passes by the site of the old airport, prior to its relocation to the new modern facility where you landed north of town. Just up ahead, at the location of the entrance to the old airport, is a round-a-bout which for years was known as 'tea-pot' circle. Until recently, a huge oversized replica of a brass Bedouin tea pot pouring cascading water into a tea cup stood at this location. It was a beautiful symbol of Saudi Heritage which spoke volumes to passers-by regarding the traditional hospitality extended to travelers in the desert of Saudi Arabia. As you can see, now standing in its place is a concrete fountain, functional, but of absolutely no symbolic significance. The Western community here in Riyadh was in a state of shock when they learned that the tea-pot at 'tea-pot' circle was being replaced by just what every big city needs, another large slab of concrete. The Saudi nation is so young, and so busy rushing to catch up with the rest of the world, that it has not yet come to a full appreciation of the rich heritage that it has enjoyed and needs to preserve for posterity.

"We are now passing through an area of town known as 'Sulimaniyah.' That large complex on our right is the Al-Akariyah mall. It is only one of many modern shopping centers that have sprung up in the city of Riyadh over the past few years. Under one roof, you can shop for anything that is permitted to be legally sold in Saudi Arabia. With the exception of the larger department stores, an item is seldom identified with a fixed price. When shopping in the suqs, everything is open to negotiation. The seller initially asks several times more for an item than he expects to get. The buyer, understanding this, automatically counter offers at about one-third of the asking price. From there, the negotiations continue, with the difference between the parties narrowing with each exchange, until they meet somewhere in the middle. At that point, the seller says, 'kalas,' meaning that the price is final and a verbal agreement has been reached. The buyer repeats the word 'kalas,' signaling his acceptance, and the transaction is concluded.

"However, one word of caution. First impressions can be deceiving. As modern as the city of Riyadh seems to be, you must not forget that you are in a conservative Islamic nation and need to be sensitive to the cultural distinctions. This was graphically brought home to me just the past weekend. My wife I were shopping in the mall and decided to indulge ourselves with a soft vanilla ice cream cone dipped in butterscotch topping. The Dairy Queen had the usual sign on the front door which read, 'women cannot be served or seated here.' Leaving my wife outside the door, I stepped inside and placed the order. Just as I was reaching for my wallet to pay for our treats, I heard the frantic sound of my wife's voice calling out my name. She had been confronted by a uniformed Saudi policeman and a very large Saudi gentleman dressed in the traditional attire of a "Mutawwah.'

"The Mutawwahs are religious police known as the 'Society for the Promotion of Virtue and the Suppression of Vice.' They regularly patrol shopping areas to exhort laggards to make their devotions during the five times a day that the call to prayer is given by Muezzins over the mosque loudspeakers, and to ensure that the shops are closed during prayer time. They were questioning her as to why she was not accompanied by her husband, and why her head was not covered. Although she was wearing a floor length black cloak called an 'abaya,' she did not have a black scarf covering her head. I attempted to come to her rescue by reciting the U.S. Embassy position on this issue. 'We are Americans and Christians, and as such, my wife is not required to cover her head.' The response was instantaneous and unequivocal. 'American or no American, Christian or no Christian, she is required to cover her head in public.' I was then asked to produce my 'Igama,' or work permit to prove that this woman was indeed my wife. Her picture and associated documentation are included inside. My wife removed a black scarf from her purse and covered her hair to the satisfaction of the Mutawwah, at which point we were allowed to depart the area.

"Under Shariah, or Islamic law, women in Saudi Arabia still face many restrictions. As such, they remain secluded in Saudi society. Their primary role is in the home with the proper raising of children. This is in keeping with the strong family orientation of the Islamic faith. A system of women's education was introduced in the mid-1960's which prepares women to participate in certain aspects of community life, including the fields of education, medicine, welfare, and banking. However, in these roles, women are sexually segregated so that their work does not bring them into contact with men. They cannot drive a car, and they need their husbands' permission to travel. Excluding limousine drivers, a woman is not allowed to ride alone in a car with any male other than her husband, son, or brother. Although mosques provide areas for women, most prefer to pray in their homes.

"Embracing and kissing on the cheek between Arab men is a normal friendly greeting in the Middle East, and walking hand-in-hand is acceptable social behavior. However, any public display of affection between members of the opposite sex is strictly forbidden.

When invited to a Saudi's home, you never know in advance whether you will meet the wife and family. I have been in the homes of senior members of the Saudi government where I was introduced to the wife and daughters. On other occasions, I have been told by Saudi government officials that it is against the Holy Quran for a women to speak to a member of the opposite sex outside the immediate family.

"Because the sexes are not permitted to mix socially, young men and women have no acquaintances among the opposite sex outside their immediate family. Consequently, parents arrange marriages for their children, attempting to find a suitable mate through their own social contacts. The preferred marriage partner on many occasions is a child of the father's brother. Such marriages between first cousins are fairly common. This arrangement offers advantages for both parties. One important reason is that the payment of a dowry demanded by the bride's family of the groom's family tends to be smaller and more affordable. In addition, both the bride and groom are known quantities, and the danger of an unsuitable marriage resulting from the match of two strangers is greatly reduced. The down side of this arrangement is the possibility of bringing children into the world that have birth defects as a result of the genetic inheritance of the close family intermarriage. Islam gives the husband far greater discretion and leeway in the marriage than the wife. He may take up to four wives at any one time, providing that he treats them equally. In addition, a man can divorce his wife by simply repeating, 'I divorce thee' three consecutive times before witnesses. A woman can only have one husband, and can initiate divorce only with extreme difficulty. In the case of divorce, any children from the marriage belong to the husband's family and stay with him.

"Having said all of that, Mitch, I don't want to leave you with the wrong impression. As I mentioned earlier, Islam promotes a strong family orientation. Husbands are not abusive of their wives and divorce is rare within Saudi society. In addition, the vast majority of Saudi men only take one wife. To the best of my knowledge, most Saudi women are both happy and comfortable with this arrangement, feeling that their rights are well protected by a combination of Shariah and continued family interest after marriage.

"Traffic is backed up a bit. There must have been a little fender bender up ahead. Doesn't look like anything serious. See the green police car parked over there, Mitch? Traffic police drive green cars and security police drive blue vehicles. Now the amazing thing is, that this whole incident will be resolved without any auto insurance, and without any phone calls to a lawyer. When involved in a traffic accident in Saudi Arabia, the law requires that you do not move your car and do not leave the scene of the accident until told to do so by a traffic policeman. Based upon their investigation of the accident scene and statements provided by the drivers, the policeman will make an on-the-spot determination as to blame. It could result in a finding of 100 percent fault on the part of one driver, or partial responsibility for the accident being assessed to both drivers. The two parties are then taken to traffic police headquarters where the paperwork is completed. After the individuals involved in the accident produce official documentation from their sponsoring company stating that they will assume responsibility for the individual and any costs incurred, they are normally released. The party who the police find was not at fault or negligent then obtains three estimates of repair costs. The lesser of these is accepted by the police as the cost to repair the vehicle. The party held responsible for the accident then comes to the police station and pays for the cost of the repairs. Generally, there are no fines assessed unless someone was driving in a reckless manner."

"You've got to be kidding, Chad? You mean to sit here and tell me that all of this can be sorted out and resolved without the need to purchase any car insurance and without the involvement of any lawyers? That's incredible. Just think of the millions of dollars a year in insurance premiums and legal fees that could be saved by adopting a system like that."

"Nice thought, Mitch. However, you're overlooking one simple fact. How do you think we got mired down in that incredibly costly system that we have now? The insurance companies control a good portion of the gross national product in the United States, and each and every one of them has a large gaggle of lawyers and lobbyists on their payrolls to ensure that it stays that way.

"We are now heading in the direction of the older part of the city where the Ba'atha Suq is located, just east of Ba'atha Street. The main suq area has a variety of goods for sale, most of which are imported. The primary attraction is a gold suq where many small shops sell gold jewelry. The Dira Suq, also known as the 'clock-tower' suq, because of its proximity to the clock tower, is located nearby. It spreads outward from the Palace of Justice Building on Dira Square. One of the most popular sections is the 'antique suq,' which contains copper and brass shops, rug dealers, sandal makers, and clothing stalls. This is also the part of town where the public executions take place. Referred to by expatriates as 'chop-chop' square, if you have the stomach for it, you can observe a public beheading. That is the punishment meted out for capital crimes such as murder, rape, and drug trafficking. Lesser crimes, such as grand theft, will only cost you a hand. And, before you ask, the answer is 'yes' on both counts. 'Yes,' by our western standards the punishment imposed does appear to be cruel and barbaric, and 'yes,' it certainly does deter crime. The crime rate is very low in Saudi Arabia, and the streets of Riyadh are safe to walk day or night without fear of being the object of a crime."

"Well Chad, isn't it reassuring that there is still at least one place in the 'civilized' world where its safe to walk the streets at night?"

"Yes, you're absolutely right, Mitch. Each morning I awake to another beautiful day in the magic Kingdom."

# CHAPTER TWELVE

## AT HOME IN THE DESERT

*A message from Ambassador Robinson is waiting for Mitch* upon his return from the city tour and shopping trip. It contains two important pieces of information. He has spoken to Prince Khalid who has agreed to act as an intermediary with the Saudi Government on their behalf. The Prince has also extended an invitation to Mitch and Chad to join him for dinner that evening.

"Welcome to the Kingdom of Saudi Arabia, gentlemen." Prince Khalid extends his right hand in friendship, first to Mitch and then to Chad, in respect to Mitch's senior position in the U.S. Government.

"I am pleased that you were able to join me away from the hustle and bustle of the city. Here, we can relax and talk without being interrupted. I find much peace and solitude in my retreat in the desert. Everything seems to take on a little different meaning when viewed from the perspective of one's roots. Although we have come far in the past few years, traveling a great distance in terms of technological advances, we are still close to our origins."

The scene in the Saudi desert appears almost biblical. Under a crescent moon, they sit on carpets around a huge log fire, sipping tea and cardamom-flavored coffee. The pungent fragrance of burning frankincense fills the air, sharpening the senses as it is inhaled. Nearby, camels and goats mill about in the dark. At 12:00 P.M., the desert is silent. The only audible sounds are the crackling of the fire and the ambiance of sound of a fiercely contested soccer match from a nearby T.V. The desert is the ultimate escape for the Saudis. A place where they can retreat back to the roots of their heritage, and find peace and solitude from the hustle and bustle of the modern age in which they now find themselves entangled. However, this was not your basic Bedouin camp. This is the weekend encampment of Prince Khalid al Turki, one of the Kingdom's wealthiest and most respected citizens.

Although he has left his office in the city, the prince has transported many of the trappings of his power and position with him to the sanctity of the desert. There are a number of satellite dishes capable of pulling down every conceivable signal emanating from the heavens above. He also has his own up-link to a communications satellite that enables him to instantaneously connect himself with any human on the planet, and check stock quotes and market news 24 hours-a-day, seven-days a week all over the world with a simple click of a mouse. Then there are the basic essentials for every desert traveler, a large water truck filled with potable water, and a bank of ground power generators capable of brightening the desert in its darkest hours to noon-day illumination. Prince Khalid has temporarily reclaimed the most barren of land from the sand, rocks, and scorpions that laid claim to it for decades, breathing a new life into it that is nearly beyond the realm of believability. The stark contrast between the old and the new is awesome, yet he has blended the two into a comfortable weekend office.

"You are most gracious in extending us an invitation to join you here, Your Royal Highness. I must complement you. You have retained what I am afraid we in the United States have lost sight of in our haste to keep pace with the hectic schedule of our Western lifestyle. Driven by the hands on a clock, we can't seem to find the time to enjoy the journey, believing that we will collect our reward when we reach the station. Sitting here with you in this surrounding does indeed give one pause for reflection. I have a proposition that I would like you to consider. Would you be willing to trade your desert retreat for my air conditioned office in the Pentagon for one or two weeks each year?" Mitch's attempt at humor, strikes an immediate cord with Prince Khalid. He breaks forth with a deep belly laugh, slapping himself on the leg. While he enjoys visiting with Westerners from time to time, he wouldn't trade his lifestyle for a penthouse anywhere else in the entire world.

"I have heard much about you, Your Royal Highness. It is indeed my pleasure to finally get the opportunity to meet you. This is an experience that I will always cherish." One cannot help but be caught up in the excitement of the moment in the presence of the prince. Everything about him telegraphs power, wealth, education, and the sophistication of a true gentlemen.

Prince Khalid is attired in the customary dress of the Saudi male. He cuts an impressive swath with his floor-length white "thoub," and red and white checkered "guthra" held in place on his head with the black "igaal." The prince is slender in build and clean shaven with the exception of a well-trimmed moustache. There are few Arabs without some form of facial hair as it has been worn as a sign of manhood throughout their history. Prince Khalid was educated in the U.S. at San Diego State University in Southern California. During the time he spent in the West, he adopted a blue-collar Protestant work ethic. It is his habit to work late into the evening, and arise early in the morning to accommodate a busy, but tightly organized schedule. He thrives on challenges and is able to summon from some hidden source, boundless energy and enthusiasm. He has one speed, and that is "overdrive," recalling from his graduate studies in business school that "time is money." He also understands that fortunes are frequently made and lost while the lazy and unmotivated are still lounging in bed. Supernatural drive and ambition catapulted him into the next century while most of the world was still waiting for the count down of the final minutes of 1999. This is an extraordinary man with exceptional abilities. There was virtually nothing that was outside his reach or grasp.

"Please help yourself to some more dates, gentlemen. You have never tasted dates as sweet as these. They are from my private stock, set aside especially for breaking the fast at sundown during the period of our holy month of Ramadan. The oranges and grapefruit are from my orchard. I trust that they compare favorably with your prized Florida citrus crops. With sufficient water to quench the thirst, there is very little that will not grow and thrive here in the desert."

Hospitality is truly a way of life for the Saudis. Dinner parties begin late in the evening, often around 10:00 p.m. Snacks are provided, but the meal is seldom served before midnight. After-dinner conversation is rare among Saudis. Therefore, an extended period of time is taken before the meal to talk and socialize. Dinner is served as a climax to the evening's entertainment and it is time to leave soon after tea and coffee have been offered following the meal. Dinner consists of 'kapsa,' which is sheep served over a bed of rice, with soup, salad, and a can of soda pop. There are several types of dessert, including sweets, apples, and oranges.

"Your Royal Highness, Chad took me on a tour of the city this afternoon. I was impressed by the development of your modern infrastructure, schools, and hospitals."

"Yes, I'm afraid the only image that most Westerners had of Saudi Arabia prior to the Gulf War was the mental image remaining from viewing the epic motion picture, 'Lawrence of Arabia.' And, of course, Hollywood put their own spin on his exploits in the film, adding excitement and high drama to sell tickets at the box office at the expense of the preservation of history. Many still think of us as a country of Bedouins riding our camels, and herding our sheep and goats in a nomadic lifestyle across the desert. However, that was nearly a century ago during World War I.

"An alliance between the British and an Arab power group against the Ottomans was formed in 1916, which ultimately led to the total conquest of Arabia by the House of Saud. The Turks were drawn into battle in Arabia, suffering crippling defeats by the forces led by Lawrence, destroying the Fourth Turkish Army and capturing the city of Damascus. In an effort to mold the fragmented Arab forces into a credible fighting force, he went native. Dressed in a flowing robe and headdress, this legendary figure dashed about the desert on the transportation of choice at that time–your basic camel.

"Under Lawrence's leadership, supply trains were attacked, cutting off the resupply of critical goods required to sustain the Turkish military forces. Preserved by the low humidity of the desert air, miles of railroad tracks and several overturned locomotives can still be seen in the desert near the city of Tabuk, which lies southeast of the Gulf of Aqaba. Rumor has it that if you hold a small cross section of the narrow gauge railroad track to your ear, you can hear the muffled voice of Lawrence calling his forces to battle, as the roar of the ocean echos within a large seashell."

During the course of the evening, Mitch makes several attempts to steer the conversation around to the topic they had been beckoned here to discuss. However, on each occasion, Prince Khalid, brushes aside the thinly veiled invitation without taking the bait. Chad smiles to himself as he observes the game of cat and mouse being played out before him. He has learned through long experience that you have to reign-in your sense of urgency when dealing with the Saudis. Meetings often extend past midnight. The King himself frequently works through the night until sunrise prayers. Matters that would require a fifteen minute discussion to reach a decision back home in Washington, D.C., could consume as many as two to three hours in Saudi Arabia. Directness is usually avoided within the Saudi culture. Therefore, it is often difficult to determine what your host is thinking. The most effective approach is to practice patience, tolerance, and understanding. When a Saudi is ready to tell you what is on his mind, that is the time you will hear it. Until that time, one must be willing to be a good listener. After the message has been conveyed and the point understood, it is time for some discrete give and take discussion, followed by compromise to reach an agreement.

Recognizing the impatience of the Western mind-set, Arabs often use it to their advantage. Westerners quickly become frustrated at what we perceive to be unnecessary delays and the interjection of unimportant issues in discussions. After a period of time, in the face of mounting pressure back home, we are often willing to make concessions beyond that probably required to conclude a deal just to break the stalemate, and wrap up the process. This shortcoming has not gone unnoticed by our Arab friends. Furthermore, they understand that anyone that makes the long trip all the way over to the Middle East to engage them in negotiations is carrying some extra baggage from back home–they are laboring under a timetable, complete with a set of expectations. Time is on their side. Consequently, it is not imperative that all business be concluded by sundown today. Tomorrow will always bring another beautiful day in the magic Kingdom. Bukhra Inshallah–Tomorrow, God willing.

"That was a very interesting and highly complementary article of you in Business Week, Your Royal Highness. If the business community was not previously aware of you before, they certainly are now. I was particularly struck by your investment strategy of targeting stocks with global brand names, sound management, and battered values. Perhaps that is where I have gone wrong in my approach to the market. In retrospect, it seems my philosophy has been to buy high and sell low."

Prince Khalid is quietly pleased with Mitch's reference to his recent notoriety as an astute international business man, and outwardly entertained by his tongue-in-cheek poke at his ineptness in investing in the stock market. The Prince smiles broadly and makes two or three attempts to restrain his laughter, prior to responding. "So you are the one I need to thank. As you know, it takes many investors like yourself before a contrarian like myself can profit." Both Mitch and Chad take a mental note that this comment by Prince Khalid clearly reveals the significant influence that the time spent in the U.S. on his education has had on his outlook on life and sense of humor.

All joking aside, both Chad and Mitch are aware of the Saudi's reputation as shrewd negotiators, continuing in the ways of their Bedouin fathers. The Arabs have been engaged in commerce since ancient times. The trading routes known as the Frankincense Trails were among the most heavily traveled roads of the old world. They begin at the coast of modern day Oman, Jordan, entering Saudi Arabia near the Gulf of Aqaba. From there, they meander in a southerly direction from ancient water hole to water hole along the Red Sea, about three-quarters of the length of the Arabian peninsula, turning eastward at Abha to Salalah on the Arabian Sea.

Prince Khalid and his guests sip tea, tell stories, and philosophize until a little after midnight. It has been a wonderful evening. Mitch and Chad have thoroughly enjoyed the prince's hospitality and company. He is a gracious host with the gift to put his guests immediately at ease. However, due to the lateness of the hour, Mitch's jet-lag began to take its toll. On several occasions, he finds himself covering his mouth with his hand to mask the yawn that he is no longer able to hold back. Prince Khalid notices that he is about to lose his visitor. He instructs his staff to serve the meal, and quickly brings the conversation around to the topic that has prompted this evening together in the Saudi desert.

Looking Mitch and Chad squarely in the eye, Prince Khalid makes an abrupt, but aseptic transition from his role as host to that of diplomat. The time for business was clearly at hand. "The proposal that you carried from your President has been considered by His Majesty The King. As you are aware, it is a very difficult proposition in that it puts us in a position of doing something that we formally publically stated we would never consider. However, we place a high value on our friendship with American, and would like to find some way to assist if certain arrangements could be agreed-on to justify the great risk that we are being asked to assume.

"For our part, we will agree to make an area in the Empty Quarter available for training. Your request to allow the staging of operations against Iraq from our country was most difficult. After much discussion, we have concluded that it can be justified by virtue of the threat Saddam poses to Prince Sultan Air Base. We are also willing to discuss some contribution to offset a portion of the cost of the operation. However, we will not allow the testing of this new weapon of yours on Saudi soil. As you are aware, our King is also 'The

Custodian of the Two Holy Mosques.' This is a most sacred honor and responsibility. As such, we cannot consider the development and testing of weapons of destruction on the same sacred ground that is concentrated to the highest purposes of preserving human life. You must find other means to accomplish this testing.

"In consideration for our support, we would ask the following in return. Future requests for weapons sales of arms to meet our legitimate self-defense needs, with most favored nation trade terms and financial conditions, will be guaranteed by your government. Our future national security will no longer be held hostage to congressional politics."

# CHAPTER THIRTEEN

# THE PALESTINIANS

*Mitch Richman is airborne on the second leg of his diplomatic* journey enroute to Dubai in the United Arab Emirates. Dubai had been selected as a neutral site to parlay with Ishmael Gatachek, the leader of the Palestinian Liberation Organization. A meeting between America's National Security Advisor and the Chairman of the PLO was sure to draw a great deal of public attention and excite more than a few extremists. Holding such a meeting in Israel or on the West Bank would have invited disaster. Here in Dubai, they were out of the limelight, with diplomatic ease of entry of both parties. So far, so good. One down and two to go. Mitch had an added feeling of comfort and confidence now that he had a tentative agreement with the Saudi Government in his hip pocket.

Dubai is the capital of the sheikhdom of Dubai, and a port on the Persian Gulf with a population of 55,000. It is one of seven kingdoms comprising the United Arab Emirates located on the eastern coast of the Arabian peninsula. The capital and largest of the seven city states in the UAE federation is Abu Dhabi. The native population of the UAE is composed largely of Arab descendants who follow Islam, the official religion. However, the UAE is far less conservative than Saudi Arabia in observing Islamic law. Women are allowed to drive cars and work. Another attraction that makes the UAE a popular visitor's destination is a large "free-trade zone," where there are no taxes or tariffs on anything purchased. The most popular shopping area in the UAE is located in the Emirate of Sharjah, just a short drive from Dubai. Their large suq features imported goods from Iran, including handmade Persian rugs.

The timing looked to be favorable for Mitch's meeting with Ishmael. In some matters, timing is not only important, it is everything. This seemed to be one of those occasions. A small window of opportunity appeared to be open at this time for peace in the Middle East. If there was one thing about this business that Mitch had learned, it was "when a window of opportunity presents itself, crawl through it before it slams down on you once again." He intended to strike while the iron was hot.

Palestinian leader Ishmael Gatachek was desperately trying to win U.S. support for a Palestinian state with part of Jerusalem as its capital. He was also seeking to gain the 60 percent of the West Bank that Israel still controlled. Furthermore, the PLO leader had inferred that he would declare a state in the West Bank and Gaza Strip after the five-year period of Palestinian autonomy established in the Oslo Peace Agreement with Israel expired in May 1999. That was when the transitional phase of Palestinian limited self-rule was to be completed. As that date rapidly approached, he was under pressure from President Maxwell's administration to postpone a unilateral declaration of statehood.

The Palestinian leader had recently met with the Secretary of State at his Georgetown residence in Washington, D.C. On that occasion, the Secretary broached concerns over the expected announcement of statehood, and Ishmael was assured that the United States would work to get the stalled peace process moving again. However, what the Chairman was clearly seeking were international guarantees that he could present to his people, evidence that there would be a payoff for a postponement. This might include pledges to accept a future Palestinian state, promises of more financial assistance, or limited, but immediate recognition of Palestinian sovereignty by international institutions that lend money and mediate trade disputes. Mitch was now in the enviable position of being able to deliver on some of these issues in exchange for a Palestinian commitment to postpone a unilateral declaration of statehood at this time and continue good faith negotiations with Israel.

When Mitch first began working in the office of the NSA, he was both uncomplimentary and unsympathetic of the Palestinian's plight. Being what he considered a consummate professional that moved like a well oiled machine, he had little time for their fumbling, bumbling diplomatic style. They appeared to be their own worst enemy, often shooting themselves in the foot. Each time a little momentum seemed to be gathering in the delicate ME peace talks, a stupid act of violence would interrupt the process. On the majority of these occasions, some faction of the PLO would take credit for the despicable act against humanity. Then, there was Ishmael himself, an unlikely public figure. When he appeared on TV with his keffiyeh, he came across to the average American citizen more like a fugitive from the law than a head of state. Perhaps, partly because he didn't have any state to head up. He was an inspiring head of state without portfolio. In a business where you are required to put your best face forward in convincing people that your side is the good guys, image is everything. This gentleman needed to hire a good Manhattan public relations firm and pay them a bundle of money to come up with a facelift, a complete make-over of the image of the Palestinian cause. One, which would shed the image of a gang of terrorists that had been hung on them by their detractors and political enemies.

However, Mitch's view of the Palestinian problem had been somewhat modified over the past few months. Last year, he hired a new staffer in the office who had extensive experience in the Middle East. Charles Davis brought a whole new perspective to the discussion of the Palestinian problem within the office of the National Security Advisor. During the working of an extremely difficult Middle East issue, Charles had sensed Mitch's frustration with the Palestinians. On that occasion, he shared a personal experience which provided both insight and enlightenment on the complex Palestinian issue. Consequently, the NSA could now empathize with the difficult task that Ishmael had strapped on.

The Palestinian problem is somewhat akin to the weather—
everyone talks about it, but no one seems to be able to do anything
about it. Problem definition isn't that complicated, but finding a
workable solution has been both difficult and elusive. The plain fact
of the matter is that a large group of people have no place to call
home. In New York City and Washington, D.C., there are people
referred to as "the homeless." However, in these two locations
someone occasionally recognizes them as U.S. citizens with some
inalienable human rights guaranteed under the Constitution, and
provides shelter and food for them.

Shortly after his arrival in the Middle East as a defense
contractor, Charles set up an administrative office and hired a small
group of individuals to staff it. Much later, he realized that fate had
parted the veil ever so slightly, providing him with a glimpse into the
Palestinian problem. He selected three Arabs to serve as translators
and interpreters in the office. Although he was unaware at the time,
all were Palestinians. Having been in the Kingdom of Saudi Arabia
for only a scant few days at the time, Charles viewed the entire
population in terms of generic Arabs. The first gentleman's name
was Ali Bakheer. He held a Syrian passport. The second individual
was Mahmoud Ayash. He had a Lebanese passport. The third
person hired was Ahmed Ali, and he carried a Jordanian passport.
All three of these individuals had been working in Saudi Arabia for
an extended period of time. Ali Bakheer and Ahmed Ali had their
families with them. Mahmoud's family had remained in Lebanon,
where he owned a small home.

At the time, Charles was a neophyte in matters of this part
of the world. It seemed perfectly logical to him that his three new
employees working closely together in the office would quickly bond
as brothers in arms. After all, they were united by their Palestinian
heritage, and common objective of securing a homeland of their own.
However, as time quickly proved, nothing could have been further
from the truth. Charles had made the mistake that so many before
him had made, and many who followed would repeat. Applying

Western logic, rationale, and mentality in the Middle East is a non-starter. What works back home, doesn't necessarily, and usually doesn't work there. The Arabs have hundreds of years of customs, courtesies, and beliefs that do not accommodate Western thinking. Fortunately, one of the Saudis with whom Charles worked did him a huge favor, undoubtedly saving him untold weeks of anguish, pain, and suffering. Sensing his frustration one day, he sat Charles down, and in a very direct manner, quite unusual for an Arab, informed him that he had not been hired to import Western solutions to Arab problems. His role, after a sufficiently ample period of time to familiarize himself with his new environment, was to assist the Saudis in identifying and evaluating acceptable Arab solutions to Arab problems.

It quickly became apparent by their behavior, that Charles' three new Palestinian employees could have just as easily been lifelong enemies. They wouldn't even condescend to speak to one another, much less work together. Much of their time was spent scheming and plotting as to how they could put a knife in one another's back when it was turned. The only thing they appeared to share was a common hatred of Israel. However, time soon resolved this dilemma. Fate stepped into the lives of all three of these men taking the blade out of their hands, and inserting it squarely between their shoulder blades. Ali's oldest son, who had been born and lived his entire life in Saudi Arabia, received a draft notice from Damascus, indicating that he was being inscripted into military service in the Syrian army. He was to report immediately, or the Syrian passports of the entire family were to be recanted. Soon after that, Mahmoud received an urgent telegram from his wife. A major in the Syrian army, posted in Southern Lebanon, had moved into his home and evicted his family. Mahmoud quit his job that day and rushed home in an effort to intercede. Charles never heard from him again. Ahmed had been working as a translator inside the Royal Saudi Air Force Headquarters building. Unfortunately for him, he held a Jordanian passport, and Jordan appeared to be supportive of Saddam Hussein's invasion of Kuwait during the Gulf War. This wasn't altogether surprising, as approximately 80% of the population of Jordan is made up of Palestinians. They apparently held out hope that Saddam had sufficient military clout to assist them in some small way in their struggle for a homeland. Needless to say, the Saudi Government took a rather dim view of all of this. Ahmed's security pass to enter the headquarters was immediately pulled and his home searched. Paperwork was found that resulted in his arrest and confinement. Sometime later, he was released and deported to Jordan.

What recourse did these three gentlemen have when confronted with problems that threatened their families and their lives? Absolutely none! They had no government to turn to, and no one to plead their case or intercede on their behalf. They had no rights as they held no citizenship. They existed only in their own minds, and beyond that, only to the extent that they didn't have anything that someone else had a need for at that particular moment.

What Charles had inadvertently created was a microcosm of the larger Palestinian problem—a small representative world which was more or less analogous to interaction in the real world, in much the same way as a town meeting is a microcosm of American democracy. Granted, he had but three Palestinians within the walls of his office. However, they displayed the full range of human emotions, couched in terms of their ethnic backgrounds. Therefore, Charles was exposed to their hopes, dreams, fears, and prejudices. As he struggled to manage this small group on a day-to-day basis, he often thought of the difficulties PLO Chairman Gatachek must experience attempting to negotiate on behalf of hundreds of thousands of Palestinians. Would it ever be possible to pitch a tent large enough in the sands of the Middle East that would prove sufficiently all encompassing to cover the aspirations and satisfy the needs of all Palestinians? At what distance into the far reaches of the desert must the tent pegs extend to achieve this objective? And, once in place, how long would it be before camels intent on entering, put their noses under the tent, or a sudden sand storm brought it crashing down on its occupants?

***

Palestinian leader Ishmael Gatachek had departed Gaza International Airport earlier in the day. It was located near Rafah in the southern Gaza Strip, close to the Egyptian border. He had made history earlier in the year by being on hand to greet the first arrival at the newly opened airport, a plane carrying Egyptian officials from Cairo. The airport's opening had been delayed for more than two years as a result of disputes between Israel and the Palestinian Authority over Israel's role in monitoring passengers and cargo. It provided a measure of freedom to the Palestinians living in Gaza, a small over-crowded area ringed by the Mediterranean on one side and by barbed wire on the other three. It enabled them to travel without going through the normal Israeli controls established for Palestinians at Ben Gurion International Airport.

The Chairman's departure had been amid extraordinary security precautions, including a last-minute plane switch and the use of decoy limousines. He left in an unmarked white Gulfstream after a carefully planned effort at deception. It appeared to onlookers that his party was going to board a large military aircraft. However, at the last minute they detoured around the aircraft and climbed on the Gulfstream hidden from view behind the C-141 cargo plane. The Gulfstream was then cleared for takeoff by the control tower, and lifted off without filing a flight plan. In addition, the pilot was not told of his flight destination until after he was airborne. Sometime later, a decoy white Gulfstream landed in Dubai, and taxied up to the arrival stand. To everyone's surprise, Ishmael was not on board. Approximately 15 minutes later, the aircraft carrying the Chairman touched down. Before it rolled to a stop at the far end of the runway, four armored black limousines raced into position to shield the Chairman from public view as he deplaned. All four vehicles then departed in opposite directions, each with a passenger dressed in a Kaffiyeh headdress seated between two armed body guards in the rear seat.

Ishmael Gatachek had arrived in Dubai a few days early to allow time to make the necessary security precautions that must be taken. He was now resting and awaiting the arrival of the National Security Advisor. Ishmael had become the Chairman of the Palestinian Liberation Organization in 1969. The PLO was a loose alliance of many Palestinian organizations that existed as a government-in-exile within the Arab world of the Middle East. Ishmael was born in Jerusalem on February 17, 1929. Educated at Cairo University in Egypt, he was elected President of the Union of Palestinian Students. When the state of Israel was established in 1948, an estimated 726,000 Palestinians were displaced. Since that time, Ishmael had devoted his life to gaining a permanent homeland for his people.

The Palestinian leader's recent trip to the United States had gone well, and The European Union had responded better than expected to his goodwill tour of Europe. For the first time in a long time, it appeared that all the pieces of the puzzle were in place to finally make a Palestinian homeland a reality. But, would his luck hold out? Could he control the radical elements within his own party, and could they work side-by-side with their avowed enemy to accomplish a lasting peace? Many unanswered questions remained. However, for perhaps the first time, there was a glimmer of hope for an agreement. It represented what perhaps was a once in a lifetime opportunity that may very well never present itself again. After considering it carefully, Ishmael decided that he had better grab it while the offer was still on the table, before the shifting winds of time blew it away with the swirling sands of the desert into obscurity. It may very well be the best, if not the last opportunity for peace that would present itself in his lifetime.

Ishmael was now an old man, long in the tooth. He walked slowly with a stoop, his body bent and broken from the weight of the world which he had shouldered throughout his life. Using a cane to steady himself, his steps were now as shaky and unsure as the prospects for a homeland in his lifetime. His trembling hands and quivering lips displayed the advanced signs of a degenerative neurological disease, such as Parkinson. Perhaps it was fitting, he thought, that they would die together–he and his lifelong dream of a

Palestinian State.

Early in his youth, Ishmael had caught the vision of a Palestinian homeland. As a young man seated with his family in council around a campfire in a temporary refugee camp in Baqaa, Jordan, he had been instructed and taught in the ways of his father. He had listened to the stories, retold over and over, until they had consumed his soul, giving purpose to an otherwise unchartered future. The glow of the flames had warmed his body against the chill of the desert night, igniting a fire which burned within him. Ishmael soon gained his own testimony of the truthfulness of these beliefs, enabling him to stand firmly on his own, unsustained by his parents. It was then that he had decided to devote his life to bringing about the fulfillment of his dream. Ishmael had not approached this commitment lightly. He had pledged his life and whatever possessions that he accumulated to the accomplishment of this cause, to the exclusion of everything else. To this end, Ishmael had been a faithful soldier, serving with unswerving loyalty, never shirking his duty in shouldering responsibility.

Ishmael had emerged a leader. From his earliest recollection, he had been selected by his peers as a team captain whenever sides were to be chosen for an athletic contest. At first, he attributed this to his physical abilities. He was tall for his age, easily identified even at a distance, by the several inches height advantage that he overshadowed his playmates. Driven by a competitive spirit, Ishmael would not settle for anything less than total victory. He had especially enjoyed foot races with his friends, and was recognized as the fastest young man in the camp. However, even with his physical prowess, it was in matters of organization and preparation that Ishmael had truly excelled. The plans he drew up were without equal, tactically sound, and carefully rehearsed with attention to details that most would leave to chance. As a student of the history of the Palestinian people, Ishmael understood that when one is engaged in a struggle for survival, no detail is so unimportant as to allow fate to influence the outcome.

Later in life, Ishmael had earned a reputation for being tough, but compassionate. He took a "no nonsense" approach to his leadership position. Expecting the most out of his followers, he led by example. When Ishmael was not satisfied with the progress of the training being conducted, he would call an immediate halt to the activities. On these occasions, he would lecture them with the now familiar words, "We are on borrowed time, possessing Jordanian passports, and living in a 'temporary' refugee camp. When we started on this journey, we made a commitment to undergo whatever sacrifices were required for our cause to succeed. Our willingness to do these things is dependent upon the intent of our hearts. If our hearts are set on doing the right things, we can expect to succeed. Even then, there will be times when we will falter. When this occurs, we will pick ourselves up, learn from our mistakes, and move on. If our hearts are set on anything short of the achievement of our ultimate goal, we are not being faithful to our cause. Our success requires that each of us seek nothing less than that which we are capable of achieving."

There had been progress and even some moderate success. The Palestinian refugee camp where Ishmael was raised in Baqaa, Jordan, on the outskirts of Amman, had undergone significant growth and quality of life improvements. The ghetto composed of muddy streets, tents, and scattered cinder block huts which once were the hallmarks of the camp, had given way to many conveniences, rivaling a medium sized city. American soft drinks were readily available, as well as shops selling music and videos, banks, and a doctor's clinic. Yes, a considerable amount of nation building had taken place, but not his nation. The thing that Ishmael had coveted the most, was the thing which still eluded him, his quest for a Palestinian homeland. He now understood that generational change might bring modern conveniences. But, it didn't necessarily bring peace, and it wouldn't guarantee more freedom, democracy, or self-rule, either. That was something that required more than the mere passage of time. Before Palestinian statehood could be achieved, there were sensitive regional issues that must be resolved, such as borders, water, security, and agreement on the final status of the West Bank and Jerusalem. The Middle East states must then be willing to sit together and participate in good faith negotiations, brokered by major world powers such as the United States.

Ishmael had been a moderate, advocating peaceful alternatives to achieve the Palestinian cause, as he had been taught by his father. Through his influence, he had successfully urged others to pursue a similar path to self rule. It made more sense to him than throwing rocks in the street, or engaging in individual acts of terror in an effort to break the resolve of those who had taken an oath that the radical notion held by a few extremists of an independent Palestinian State, would never see the light of day. Blunted at peaceful attempts to negotiate, and crushed in two brief attempts to exert force, Palestinian hopes and dreams had been dashed like a ship driven upon the rocks by the wind and fury of an ocean storm.

Tears welled up in Ishmael's eyes, and a lump formed in his throat. Now in the twilight of his years, the dream had faded. Hope had been replaced by despair, faith by cynicism, and rage had long since pushed aside the peace and tranquility that had once calmed an otherwise troubled soul. But, perhaps the most telling sign of the hopelessness that Ishmael now felt, was the fear that fully consumed him. Not fear for himself, but fear for his family and children. Resigned to accepting the finality of his fate, he could not bring himself to reconcile the final chapter of his life on this earth–departure from his family without being able to comfort them with the legacy that had been handed down to him from his father. The promise, that some day, things would be different for them and their children.

The lengthening shadows on the walls told Ishmael that it was late in the day–which day he was not sure. The past few years had not been kind to him. Even now, the tortured thoughts in his mind crowded out everything else, filling him with sorrow and regret. He was unwilling to bear any more today, even if it were only being relived in daydreams. He had endured enough. After all, he was now an old man. Why should he continue to suffer the mental torment brought on by the failure of others? Ishmael made a concerted effort to force it from his mind. Other thoughts must fill the void, lest it creep back ever so quickly to once again occupy his subconscious, and prey upon his tormented soul. As the lights dimmed, he could feel the pain once again overcoming any weak resistance that his frail body was capable of putting forth. Surely, a merciful God would soon set him free. Allah would hear his prayer.

***

The mammoth Boeing 747 aircraft tastefully detailed in blue, white, and silver, with the words "United States of America" boldly displayed across its fuselage and proud American flag adorning its tail, rolled to a stop at the airport in Dubai after the short flight from Riyadh. Mitch and his staff cleared immigration and claimed their bags in customs. They caught a limo to the Hilton Hotel where he was booked into a suite and they had adjoining rooms. Mitch had planned their flight to allow himself the better part of the afternoon to unpack, settle in, and hopefully get a good night's rest in his new bed before his scheduled meeting with Ishmael tomorrow afternoon. He had agreed to meet with the Chairman at the residence where he was staying, due to concerns over his personal security.

After checking in at the arrival desk, Mitch stopped in the gift shop in the lobby to purchase a newspaper. He hadn't been away from the puzzle palace that long, but in the fast paced world in which he lived, it didn't take but a day or two for world events to pass you by. In this business, information was not only power, but also critical to sound decision making. Picking up a copy of the International Herald Tribune, his attention was immediately drawn to the large block headlines which shouted, "Lockheed wins $6.4 Billion Contract From United Arab Emirates." Reading on, the lead paragraph of the article stated, "Lockheed Martin Corporation, the world's No. 1 defense contractor, has signed a contract worth $6.4 billion to sell 80 advanced F-16 fighter jets to the United Arab Emirates, the company announced today from Abu Dhabi, the UAE capital."

Mitch was aware that representatives of the Department of Defense and the United States Air Force had briefed the proposed sale up on Capitol Hill at least six times since 1998. While the sale was technically still subject to approval by the U.S. Congress during a 30-day review process required by law, the briefings had not met with any sustained political opposition. Skimming down further in the article, he took particular note of the fact that the commander of the UAE Air Force said the F-16 had been chosen over the F-15, the Euro 2000, the French Rafale, and the Russian Sukhol.

The UAE's choice of the F-16, came as no surprise to anyone that followed the fighter aircraft business. In terms of the number of aircraft produced, the F-16 "Fighting Falcon" had been the leader over the past 25 years. Also known as the "International Fighter," a large number of F-16s were sold to international security customers of the United States around the world. The aircraft's popularity could be traced back to a recognition by the leadership of the USAF in 1970, that DoD budgetary constraints would no longer support the expenditure of unlimited funds for military weapon systems. The F-16s successful fighter design was born out of practical reality—a compromise between cost and operational capability. A military budget could support the purchase of two F-16 aircraft, as opposed to one of the heavier fighter aircraft loaded up with all the latest frills.

One key aspect of the lighter and less expensive aircraft design concept, was the determination to go with one engine. Engine selection, was therefore, critical. A decision was made to utilize the same F-100 series Pratt & Whitney engine that was used in the F-15. This provided the aircraft with a proven engine design, and the USAF with savings based on the greater production base of the F-100 engine. A second important reason for the aircraft's success was its fly-by-wire flight control system. Under this concept, electro-mechanical force sensors and computer software translate the pilot's movement of the stick into precisely regulated electronic commands, replacing the mechanical linkages in the flight control system of older vintage aircraft. The aircraft is rendered aerodynamically stable as a result of continual adjustments to its attitude and trim by the flight system software, made possible through the speed of the computer.

Mitch hurried through the lobby with his bags to the elevator, anxious to unpack, freshen up, and catch a short combat nap before dinner. Punching the elevator button, he continued to browse the article on the F-16 sale for additional details. You never knew in this business when a question might come up on a major arms deal such as this. The light on the elevator button went out indicating that the elevator had arrived. Mitch folded his newspaper under his arm, and picked up his bags in anticipation of boarding. As the doors opened, several Americans' dressed in dark pinstriped business suits emerged. From their conversation, it was apparent that they were defense contractors and representatives of the Lockheed Martin Corporation. They had obviously chosen to avail themselves of the same Hilton hospitality as Mitch. They brushed past him into the lobby, still understandably excited about the multi billion-dollar business transaction they had just closed. They were living proof that arms merchants employed by multinational corporations were the basic adhesive of world commerce.

Although Mitch was tempted to congratulate them on their success, he quickly had second thoughts. The nature of the business he was on, dictated a low visibility diplomatic mission. It would be difficult for him to explain his presence in the Emirates when there had not been any mention of a trip by a senior Administration official to the Middle East in the news. Hopefully, upon his departure, he would also have good news to celebrate. However, there would be no public high fives or the popping of corks from champagne bottles.

***

As the National Security Advisor approached the designated meeting place, members of Ishmael's security detail stepped into the street and stopped his vehicle. Satisfying themselves that Mitch was whom he said he was, they directed the driver to park some distance from the villa. He was then escorted to the front door and ushered inside. The first order of business was a complete frisk job with accompanying pat-down to ensure he wasn't armed. He was then led to a room in the rear of the building where Ishmael's personal bodyguards met him, once again checking for weapons. At that point, Mitch was admitted to the room where he was warmly greeted by the Chairman. Although this was their first meeting, and he obviously knew whom he was expecting to meet, there was no mistaking this gentleman. Dressed in his traditional freedom fighter utility uniform and keffiyeh headdress, Ishmael appeared precisely as he did in his pictures and on T.V.

Pressing up against the Chairman to exchange the traditional Arabic greeting of a kiss to each side of the cheek, Mitch felt the telltale impression of a concealed hand gun on his hip. Ishmael's obsession with personal security was obviously something he shared with Saddam. However, it was certainly a legitimate concern. The Chairman of the Palestinian Liberation Organization occupied a high profile position, with challenges to his leadership by enemies who had publicly avowed to take him out the first opportunity that presented itself, even if it meant the self-sacrifice of a kamikaze mission. He was seemingly preoccupied and mesmerized by concern for personal security to the point that it far outweighed every other consideration, affecting him both mentally and emotionally. Threats on one's life from both inside and outside their organization would drive most normal people over the edge before too long.

One foolish act of carelessness could result in disaster, providing those lying in wait with an opportunity for ambush. Consequently, Ishmael was forced to live a life closely akin to that of a fugitive from the law. He seldom slept under the same roof or in the same bed more than one or two nights in a row. In addition, he was meticulously careful in his movements not to develop any pattern to his daily activity. When being chauffeured to his meetings, he religiously insists that his driver vary both the route and the time of day that they traveled. He owned a small fleet of vehicles, several of which he uses as decoys. When he departs his residence each day, there are several staff cars with drivers and motors running outside. No one, but Ishmael Gatachek himself, knows precisely which vehicle he will get into on any given day. He makes that decision at the very last minute as he approaches the cars. The other vehicles also depart the residence with the drivers heading in different directions. Each one with an occupant in the back seat dressed as a double for Chairman Gatachek, complete with a keffiyeh headdress.

PLO Chairman Gatachek's obsession with personal security was not without merit. There was plenty of historic precedent for concern. Egyptian President Anwar Sadat, visited Jerusalem in November 1977, addressing Israel's Parliament, the Knesset. Reaching out to his historic enemy with olive branch in hand, he proposed a peace plan. In his speech, Sadat acknowledged Israel's right to exist, but called for return of occupied land and a recognition of the rights of Palestinians. For this initiative and negotiations that followed, he and Menachem Begin received the Nobel Peace Prize in 1978. On March 26, 1979, Israel and Egypt signed a peace treaty ending a 30-year state of war, and establishing diplomatic relations between the two countries. However, everyone was not happy with Anwar's efforts to establish a lasting peace with Israel. President Sadat was assassinated by Muslim fundamentalists in Cairo on October 6, 1981. At the time of his assassination, he was reviewing a military parade that marked the eighth anniversary of Egypt's crossing of the Suez Canal. Ironically, this was the act that precipitated the Arab-Israeli war of October 1973.

Israeli Prime Minister Yitzhak Rabin was another pioneer in the peace process in the Middle East. He signed an accord of mutual recognition with the Palestinians on September 13, 1993. The Israel-Palestinian peace accord provided for Palestinian self-rule in the Gaza Strip and Jericho, with the mutual pledge to work for a permanent peace agreement and to extend Palestinian rule to most of the West Bank. Yitzhak Rabin, Simon Peres, and PLO leader Ismael Gatachek were awarded the 1994 Nobel Peace Prize for their accomplishment. However, it prompted a sharp backlash of violence and terror from Israeli hardliners and opponents of the peace process. Prime Minister Rabin was assassinated by a Jewish extremist on November 4, 1995, after attending a peace rally.

The Chairman of the Palestinian Liberation Organization

often wondered if it was destiny or fate which seemed to dictate that prominent Middle East leaders recognized by award of the Nobel Peace Prize were sentenced to die by assassins bullets?

At long last, the NSA now found himself in the same room face-to-face with the gentleman who had caused him considerable consternation in his job. Mitch wondered if he was going to be as difficult to deal with up close and personal as he seemed to be at a distance. The meeting began as expected with the customary offering of Arabic tea or chy. Mitch accepted a glass and settled back into his chair attempting to appear cool, calm, and collected. One of the cardinal rules of face-to-face diplomacy with an individual with whom you have an adversarial relationship is to appear as unruffled as humanly possibly. In the best case, you are so sedate that people confuse you with a potted plant. Mitch was not expecting a confrontation to develop in this meeting. But, he did recall the Chairman being quoted as saying "the State will be established with Jerusalem as its capital, whether Israel likes it or not. And, if they don't like it, they can drink from the waters of the Dead Sea." Mitch had heard of people being invited to drink from the waters of the Nile, and wondered how that would compare to drinking from the Dead Sea.

In spite of all the mind games Mitch played, and as hard as he tried, the mystique of the Chairman got to him. His breathing became shallow and sweat broke out on the palms of his hands. He even surprised himself. It was the first time in recent memory this had happened. In his position as the NSA, Mitch was accustomed to being in the presence of important people on a regular basis. That, included the most powerful man in the entire world, the President of the United States. With everything that he had to worry about and concern himself with, Ishmael should have been the one with a case of the nerves, not Mitch. Apparently sensing that his guest was somewhat uncomfortable, the Chairman spoke in an effort to put him at ease.

"You have traveled a long way, Mr. Richman. Thank you for coming. I have looked forward to meeting with you."

"Thank you Mr. Chairman, but the pleasure is mine. I have admired you from a distance for some time now. It has been my experience that face-to-face discussions tell you a lot about people that long distance relationships do not reveal. This meeting will be something that I will tell my grandchildren about someday."

"For sometime now, I have felt that the Palestinians have a friend in the White House. As you are aware, that has not always been the case. We have traditionally had great difficulty finding a sympathetic ear in either the United States Congress or Administration. It is comforting to know that the people with whom we are now dealing are doing their best to maintain a level playing field, whereby both parties to the peace process have an opportunity to participate in good faith. And, of course, may I call you Mitch, I am not unaware that your input, advice, and counsel carry a lot of weight with the President. Therefore, I am in your debt for the kindness displayed by your government to myself during my recent visit and to my people."

"You are very kind, Mr. Chairman. I appreciate your saying that. As I believe you are aware, my purpose in meeting with you here today is to follow-up on the discussions that you had with the Secretary of State and the President during your most recent visit to Washington, D.C. From everything I've been told, the visit went exceptionally well."

"From the perspective of your government, I am sure that was the feeling. However, from our side, we were disappointed, of course, that we did not receive the strong support and endorsement for statehood that we were seeking. As you are aware, we were asked not to announce declaration of a state in the West Bank and Gaza Strip when the five-year period of Palestinian autonomy set out in the Middle Ease peace agreement expires in May 1999.

"Each time we prepare to issue a proclamation of Palestinian statehood, Israel threatens to use helicopter gunships and tanks to quell any uprising in the West Bank and Gaza Strip. But, we cannot be threatened by tanks and planes," the Palestinian leader exclaims, his voice strong and steady, but his hands shaking violently. "I would remind anyone who has forgotten, we have sustained seven years of intefadeh, and are prepared to continue if necessary. We will establish a state with Jerusalem as its capital," Chairman Gatachek calls out in fiery rhetoric, "and those who do not like it, can drink from the Dead Sea. Palestine is ours, ours, ours," he declares, stabbing a finger in the air for emphasis. "We will reclaim our sacred capital city of Jerusalem with shouts of 'Allahu Akbar,' God is Great."

"Please listen carefully to me, Mitch! The responsibility that I have assumed for my people has not come without a great burden over the years. I am no longer a young man. I am 71 years of age, and quite frankly not in the best of health. This round of talks with the Israelis will undoubtedly be my last opportunity to secure a lasting peace. Even if my health permits, Palestinian extremist groups, such as Hamas and Hezbollah, will regard our failure to reach a lasting accord as my personal failure. The next time around, your government will be negotiating with someone else. And, I can assure you, Mitch, that you will not find them, nearly as patient and accommodating as I have tried to be over the years. In my humble estimation, a small window of both time and opportunity lies ahead that we must avail ourselves of, if we are to succeed." Chairman Gatachek pauses to stress the importance of what he is about to say, and continues. "If we should fail, I cannot be held responsible for what might follow, nor will I be in a position to do anything about it. Do you understand what I am saying?"

"Yes, Mr. Chairman, I believe that I do. Your message came through loud and clear."

"Now that we understand each other, Mitch, let me lay out our position for you. We have been asked to postpone a unilateral declaration of independence in forming a Palestinian State on the West Bank and Gaza Strip. If we agree to your request, here is what we expect in return. The European Union has already affirmed in writing that negotiations should lead to Palestinian statehood within one year. Your President didn't go quite that far. In a letter that I received last week, he stated that the Palestinians should be able to live as a free people on their own land. That is a great principle and ideal. However, it is open ended. I can no longer ask the Palestinian Central Council and my people to accept that possibly, someday, if they are patient enough and wait long enough, they will be able to live as free people on their own land. There must be an end in sight. Therefore, we will agree to postpone our declaration of statehood and extend peace talks with Israel for one additional year on the following condition. Your government will issue a statement of unequivocal support for Palestinian statehood after an additional year. In addition, we expect you to work within the peace process with ourselves and the Israelis to resolve the outstanding issues, including their withdrawal from the occupied areas, and resolution of the status of Jerusalem."

"Mr. Chairman, let me first say, I appreciate your candor. And, secondly, nothing I have heard you say today sounds unreasonable to me. You want the same things for your people that I do. No one can ignore the suffering of the Palestinian people in recent decades. Your torment has gone on too long. Palestinians have the God-given right to live in peace and tranquility in a homeland with the other peoples of this region. I give you my promise that I will deliver your message to the President himself and personally support your position."

***

The National Security Advisor returns to his hotel feeling very upbeat regarding the meeting he has just concluded with Chairman Gatachek. In addition to the commitment received from the Saudi Government, he now has an understanding with the PLO in his hip pocket, that there will not be any unilateral declaration of Palestinian statehood in the weeks ahead. Armed with this agreement, he now has the leverage which he feels is necessary to convince the Israelis to buy-in to the U.S. plan, withholding any pre-emptive military strike on Iraq, and to continue good faith peace negotiations with the Palestinians for an additional year.

Reaching his hotel room, the NSA calls his staffers together in his suite and informs them of the good news. There are high fives and congratulations all around. To celebrate the occasion and to fill the void he is feeling in his mid section, Mitch takes them out on the town to eat. After a brief drive through the crowded streets of Dubai, they pull into the parking lot of Pancho Villas. A very short man wearing a large Mexican sombrero greets them at the door as they enter. Pancho's not only serves excellent Mexican food, but also has a disco with live entertainment. What a marked difference in social customs a short flight can make in the Middle East. All the basic taboos that abound in Saudi Arabia are for the most part missing in the Emirates. They order and enjoy a well-deserved meal.

"Boss, while you were out hob-knobbing with the Chairman, we were locked up in our hotel rooms. So, we want to hear all about it. How is he up close and personal?"

"Gee, I thought that you guys would never ask. As you are aware, the Chairman has a PR problem with his image, and consequently, doesn't project well on T.V. Therefore, the first impression is not good. Unfortunately, you never get a second chance to make a first impression. Judging him by our standards, with his Arab dress, unshaven appearance, and bad press, many Westerners think of him as nothing more than a terrorist. However, up close and personal, one-on-one or in a small group, Ishmael comes across much differently. In a secure setting where he can relax, he is articulate and warm, even charismatic in his own way. He speaks with conviction, obviously understanding the enormous weight of responsibility that he carries for the hopes, aspirations, and dreams of the Palestinian people. When you look into his eyes, listen to his voice, and observe his body language, you come away with a different perception of the man. He has a message to tell and is willing to sit and visit with anyone who will take the time to listen. Hey, give Chairman Gatachek a shave and a haircut, put him in a new suit of clothes, and he could host a late night talk show on any TV network."

# CHAPTER FOURTEEN

## THE PROMISED LAND

*The NSA is two-thirds of the way home, with what he considered* the toughest part of his trip behind him. The last leg should be a dream come true. He is on a biblical pilgrimage to the promised land, Jerusalem, Bethlehem, and other sacred places in Israel. And, all of this, at taxpayer's expense as the world teeters on the brink of a new millennium. However, he is feeling a bit of anxiety as he prepares to meet with his friends in Israel. As much as he searches his mind, he can not pinpoint any particular thing that is causing the apprehension.

Mitch's mission was to apply pressure on Israel to exercise restraint as they did during the Gulf War. The Israelis were considering their own pre-emptive air strike against Iran. In the mean time, Israeli military forces had been placed on full alert, and were prepared to retaliate if attacked. A coordinated military response was required. If Israel did launch a pre-emptive air strike against Iraq, and was successful in eliminating the weapon aimed at Tel Aviv, the attack might trigger a knee-jerk reaction from Iraq resulting in the launch of missiles against Turkey and Saudi Arabia. This was an unannounced visit with no advance publicity. Neither side wanted to alert the attention of the media, and thus, stimulate any speculation as to the reason for the NSA's stop in Israel.

The region between the Jordan River and the Mediterranean

Sea was known as Palestine until May 1948. At that time, most of the territory became the State of Israel and a homeland for the Jewish people. A portion of land adjacent to and west of the river was acquired by Jordan. Historically, Palestine's significance has always been far greater than its size. Strategically located at the joining of Southwest Asia and Africa, its geopolitical and historical significance is linked to its position in the world's three major monotheistic religions–Judaism, Christianity, and Islam. The city of Jerusalem has special significance to all of these religions. All three, have a common belief in one God as creator and ruler of the universe.

Judaism is by far the oldest of the three, tracing its roots back more than 3,000 years to Abraham, the patriarch, who is considered the father of the Jewish faith. Ancient Israel dwelled in the land of Palestine in the Middle East, where the modern state of Israel was founded in 1948. The events of Israel's past are recounted in the Hebrew Bible, which the Christian Church calls the Old Testament. To Jews, Palestine is the site of the ancient Kingdom of Israel and the land traditionally promised to them by God. In the Book of Genesis, God promised Abraham, in what is known as the "Abrahamic Covenant," that he would be a father of many nations, his posterity would be blessed, and that they would receive certain choice promised lands as an eternal inheritance. Long after Abraham's time, an agricultural crisis forced the Israelites to move to Egypt. They were initially made welcome there, but later bound into Egyptian servitude for more than 400 years. Eventually freed under the leadership of Moses, they were led back once again to Palestine, or Canaan as it was called at that time. This event represented a return of the people to a homeland that had been under other domination for more than 20 centuries. Zealous settlers on the West Bank today, still view it as part of the Land of Israel that the Bible says God gave the Jews, and thus, is theirs by God's will. Jerusalem has had a Jewish majority for the last century. The Jewish population now makes up more than 70 percent of the estimated population of over half a million people.

Christians view Palestine as the site of the life and ministry of Jesus. To them, Jerusalem is holy as the place where Jesus was crucified, buried, and resurrected from the dead in glory to fulfill God's will. It is the city where the Last Supper was celebrated and where, at Pentecost, the church was born. It is also the place where Christ will return to judge the living and the dead.

Though of lesser religious importance than Mecca and Medina, in Saudi Arabia, certain locations in Palestine are also considered sacred by Muslims. Their prophet Muhammad, the first leader of Islam and the messenger of God, tethered his horse on the Temple Mount in Jerusalem on the night of his ascension to heaven. This confirmed the continuity between Muhammad and previous prophets in a lineage back to Adam. In addition, it established a divine connection between the Muslim holy site in Mecca and the city of Jerusalem.

The State of Israel is bordered by Jordan on the East, Syria on the northeast, Lebanon on the north, and Egypt on the southwest. Israel has attempted to build a nation composed of diverse Jewish immigrants from all over the world, while also attempting to integrate a large Arab minority. The Gaza Strip is an area of about 5 by 25 miles located at the extreme southeast shore of the Mediterranean between Israel and Egypt, named for the ancient town of Gaza. It was retaken by Israel in 1967, and has an estimated population of 500,000, mostly Muslim Palestinians. Some 170,000 Jews live in settlements dotting the West Bank and Gaza, home to more than three million Palestinians.

Military conflict has been Israel's consistent companion, with five wars taking place between 1948 and 1982. In order to preserve its religious and cultural traditions, and guarantee its continued existence, Israel has been forced to become a military power. Their continued dependence on U.S. military and economic aid serves mutual national strategic and ideological interests. The Israeli Defense Forces with their high-tech battle tested U.S. weapons, superior military tactics, and disciplined training, have the best equipped and strongest armed forces in the Middle East. In exchange for assistance, Israel has acted as a military surrogate for the U.S.

They are capable of swiftly reacting to regional crisis that effect their own and Western interests, keeping the U.S. from being drawn into military conflict in the area. The Gulf War was an exception. During the 1991 Persian Gulf War, Iraqi President Saddam Hussein fired a total of 39 Scud missiles at Israel in hopes of breaking up the Arab coalition arrayed against him. Under intense U.S. pressure, Israel did not retaliate.

Negotiators to the Middle East peace process had been haggling over proposed borders for a Palestinian state to be carved out of land occupied by Israel since the 1967 war. Their objective was to create two homelands out of one relatively small slice of terrain wedged between the Mediterranean Sea and the Jordan River. In the meantime, each side has taken from history that which it requires to justify its demands at the bargaining table.

***

The National Security Advisor's aircraft touched down at Tel Aviv's Ben-Gurion Airport. Israelis returning home from vacation and scores of visitors to the holy land pushed their baggage carts through the crowded arrival area. They were drawn like moths to a flame by the long awaited ushering in of the Millennium. Many had come in the belief that this was to be the thousand-year period of holiness prophesied in Revelation 20:1-5, during which Christ was to rule on earth. A hoped for period of joy, serenity, prosperity, and justice. Grim-faced Israeli riot police stood guard at strategic locations throughout the airport to ensure that any violence that did occur was an act of God and not precipitated by some zealot fulfilling their religious fantasy.

Mitch was met by an Israeli cabinet minister assigned as the official coordinator for his visit. Although there had been no advance publicity of his trip, members of the media were present at his arrival gate. Outside the airport, protestors milled about carrying signs and waving flags. They appeared to be equally divided between Jewish and Palestinian activists. Earlier in the day, several Palestinians had been arrested by Israeli policemen for hanging Palestinian flags from trees and power poles in east Jerusalem, the section claimed by the Palestinians as their future capital.

Surrounded by members of Israel's elite security agency, the Shin Bet, Mitch was whisked off to an awaiting helicopter to airlift him to the government's VIP visitors guest house. A mix of undercover officers, and paramilitary border police lined the way between the main terminal area and the helipad. In the back of everyone's mind was the security breakdown that occurred in 1995, when Prime Minister Yitzhak Rabin was shot by a Jewish ultra-nationalist following a rally in Tel Aviv. However, in spite of the preponderance of security forces that blanketed the area, vandals had been able to spray paint slogans on the tarmac and plaster posters of PLO Chairman Ishmael Gatachek on airport buildings.

*** 

Seated across the table from Mitch Richman is a distinguished looking gentleman who appeared to be in his early sixties. He was of short stocky build, with a full beard of gray hair. Oded Eran, is a seasoned Israeli diplomat and senior member of the Israeli Knesset in Tel Aviv. As the delegation chief stared intently at him over his spectacles, Mitch could almost hear the wheels turning in Eran's mind. He was wondering if this stranger he had never spoken to before, and was about to enter into negotiations affecting Israel's national security, could be trusted. In religion, you are required to proceed on faith. However, in matters of national security, you are taught to depend on the "arm of flesh." On previous occasions, the Israelis had proceeded on faith, only to have their hopes dashed by deceptive predators who had taken advantage of their trust.

Before joining the Knesset, Eran had earned his stripes as a seasoned Israeli diplomat. On many occasions, he had been called on to face the enemy down in the trenches of diplomacy. While it was not a call to arms, per se, it was only a short step back from actual combat. His ability to take the measure of and defeat a foe seated across a conference table was as important, if not more important, than the role of an infantryman carrying a rifle on the field of battle.

If the infantryman made a mistake, it might cost him his life or those of a few of his comrades. However, if Eran erred, it could result in the loss of many lives, or perhaps even jeopardize that for which it was sometimes necessary to sacrifice human life. He could cost his countrymen their long sought after, hard fought, and well-deserved freedom.

As Mitch removed the last of the position papers from his briefcase and carefully arranged them on the table before him, he looked up into the gaze of the Israeli. Their eyes locked momentarily. In that instant, Mitch felt a sense of kinship toward this individual, the source of which he could not immediately explain. Perhaps it was empathy for the persecution, pain, and suffering which the Jews had undergone over the years. Perhaps it was born out of respect for the bravery that the Israelis had demonstrated in defending their beloved homeland against seemingly insurmountable odds. One other possibility remained, but Mitch was somewhat reluctant to explore that avenue. He had been christened, "Mitchell Levi Richman." The middle name "Levi," had been handed down on his father's side, generation after generation. While to the best of his knowledge, he had no Jewish ancestors, Mitch often joked that he had been adopted into the lineage of Abraham. From a little research in the Old Testament book of Genesis, he had come to learn that "Levi" meant "joined or pledged," and that Levi was the third son of Jacob by Leah. Jacob was the younger of the twin sons of Isaac, born to Abraham and Sarah in their advanced age. Isaac had been the son of promise, and heir of the promises of the Abrahamic Covenant. While he and this stranger were light years apart in such matters as religious beliefs and social views, there existed a small thread of connectivity between them.

Stoic in his posture and bearing, Eran radiated power and authority by virtue of his mere physical presence. He had what the military referred to as "command presence." You recognized and respected him as a leader of men even though he was not in uniform. Seated there in Eran's company, in a room otherwise void of substance, Mitch suddenly felt as though he was close to being checkmated even though the first move had not yet been made. If self-confidence had been clothing at that moment, he was sure that he would have appeared naked to his counterpart. Perhaps it had been a mistake for him to come here to meet on the opponent's turf, where he had given up the home court advantage. Things would have been different had the meeting taken place aboard the presidential plane. There, the NSA, surrounded with the enormity of the 747 aircraft and the trappings of power of a head of state, would have felt much more at ease, facing the difficult discussion that was sure to follow.

Several minutes passed without a word exchanged between the two gladiators. They mentally circled around an imaginary ring, sizing each other up, and looking for an opening to seize an advantage. It was nearing the point of becoming awkward. Perhaps, thought Mitch, this was a negotiating ploy of the Israelis, designed to gain the upper hand by placing him under undue pressure. In any case, he could no longer withstand the deafening silence which consumed the room. Suddenly, several words slipped passed his lips with complete spontaneity.

"We have a plan to neutralize the threat, and we are convinced that we can pull it off!"

As the words rolled off his tongue, they were so thick with irony that they fell directly on the table, striking it like a brick dropped from the top of the building. Mitch gasped as he heard with his own ears that which he had subconsciously spit out. Well, so much for tacit diplomacy. He had just tiptoed on stage like an elephant in high-heeled sneakers. The crassness of Mitch's remark provided Eran the opening he had been looking for. The drivers now had the green flag and were off to the races.

"Easy for you to say," Eran responded with disdain, a scowl suddenly appearing on his face. "Those weapons are not pointed at Washington, D.C., and your national survival as a nation is not at stake. We have much at risk. If the Iraqis launch their weapon at Tel Aviv, do you think for one moment that the rest of the Arab world will sit idly by and mourn the occasion? They will react like a pack of sharks sensing blood in the water. We will be under attack from every direction before the smoke clears. An instant feeding frenzy.

"With all due respect, you are either very naive or misinformed, Mr. Richman," Eran suggests, peering intently at the pink-cheeked baby face of the youngster across the table. "We are discussing a topic with most grave consequences for the State of Israel. While we appreciate your position and your request, we have our own interests to consider. Dependence upon others for our national security is a luxury that we do not enjoy. Look at our history in just the last 52 years since the founding of Israel. Our enemies have come at us on five separate occasions, intent on taking away our homeland. That which untold millions have dreamed of, sacrificed, and died for over the years. We must act with expediency. Every day that Saddam possesses this capability is one day too many.

"We sat on the sidelines during the Gulf War and depended upon the United States to protect us from Saddam Hussein's SCUD missile attacks. Some 39 SCUD missiles later, plus the accompanying death and destruction, we were second guessing ourselves and our faith in the United States. You have seen fit to contract out the management of your foreign policy to the United Nations. However, we cannot afford to have our national security and very survival held hostage to the whims of others. While we are the chosen people, we also understand that 'God helps those who help themselves.'"

With each word, Eran's brawny body inched forward in his chair, closing the distance between he and his American counterpart. The air in the room was suddenly still, without movement, and seemed heavier with each passing second. Mitch's breath stalled in his throat, and he leaned back from the table to create some space for himself. He attempted to speak but his throat was so dry and parched, he only made the faint hissing sound of a lizard. Was this his worst nightmare come true? Had he misjudged his worthy opponent, and not properly prepared for this encounter? Would yet another tombstone bearing the name of "Mitch Richman," be added to the Middle East graveyard of failed diplomacy?"

"In the Arab mind," Eran continued, cutting his American peer no slack whatsoever, "we do not exist. Maps of the Middle East used in Arab classrooms contain no mention of the word 'Israel.' The area of the nation of Israel is labeled as Palestine. They have rewritten history to strengthen their claim on Jerusalem. Arab youth are taught that Jerusalem has always been an Arab city, ignoring historical and biblical evidence of Jewish association with the area which goes back some four thousand years. The Palestinians want full sovereignty in Arab East Jerusalem as the capital of the independent state they plan to declare. However, Jerusalem is our indivisible, eternal capital. We desire a lasting peace, but there can never be peace at any price. On three issues we cannot make concessions: security for Israel, the holiness of Israel, and the unity of the nation.

"The real truth of the matter, Mr. Richman, is that Islamic extremists do not hate the West because of Israel. They hate Israel because of the West. America was referred to as the 'Great Satan' long before modern Israel became a nation. As the only democratic country in the Middle East, we represent a threat to the Arab world. Can you imagine for even a moment, the effect that introducing the principles of democracy into the countries surrounding Israel, would have on the royal families, the dictators, the oil-rich sheiks, and the Islamic extremists? Why does the United States continue to pressure us to cave into the demands of those who are committed to our demise, when in the rest of the world, you support democratic countries fighting against oppression?"

Mitch had taken some pretty good shots, some of them well below the belt. Mesmerized by his opponent's fancy footwork and dazed by his lightning quick jabs, he realized that if he didn't start counterpunching soon, the three knock down rule would come into play and he would be counted out. With his head spinning as if on a swivel, he recalled an old diplomatic trick. He was resorting to tactics of desperation. However, desperate times call for desperate measures. When in doubt, hit them with some impressive technical data. While they are sorting through all the extraneous information, it provides an opportunity to catch your breath and regroup.

His eyes fixed on the paper in front of him, Mitch went on

the offensive. "A variety of factors might make it difficult or even impossible for Israel to find, much less to destroy, Saddam's missiles. Stationing mobile missile launchers in residential areas or employing low-technology modes of communication immune to electronic jamming or interception, continue to pose serious targeting challenges. Good intelligence is absolutely critical. You can't hit what you are unaware of, or can't find. Our air force's inability to rapidly destroy Iraq's mobile Scud launchers was not so much a failure of airpower as it was a failure of human intelligence to compensate for the inherent limitations in sensors. Good intel is essential for a good air campaign. Saddam has cleverly devised a system whereby his missiles are periodically shuttled between launch sites. We must neutralize the missile system control center, and determine the location of the live warheads, before we can call-in the air strikes to destroy them."

"Just how convinced are you that this plan of yours will succeed?" Eran questions, glaring cross the table. Is it enough for Israel to mortgage its future on the outcome? I wish I shared your confidence, Mr. Richman, however, I have reservations. As you are aware, we are pretty good at this business ourselves. Israeli F-15 aircraft escorted the flight of F-16s that attacked and destroyed an Iraqi nuclear reactor under construction at Daura outside Baghdad in June 1981."

Mitch responds without flinching, "In all fairness, we have always placed the national security of the state of Israel right up there on a level with our own, and have consistently delivered on our promises. During the Gulf War, our military placed a priority on attacking SCUD missile launchers that posed a threat to Israel. We also deployed the majority of our Patriot anti-missile batteries to Israel in defense of Iraq's SCUD attacks. In addition, gas masks were made available for Israeli civilians through your distribution centers.

"I also recall another occasion of our partnership in October 1973, when massive Egyptian and Syrian military attacks at the onset of the Yom Kippur War took Israel by surprise. The word came down from the highest levels of the U.S. Government in an ungarbled message. The short form was, 'give them whatever they want, whenever they want it, and do it with the highest possible priority.'

"I was an airman stationed at Hill Air Force Base, Utah, home of Ogden Air Material Area, at that time. We were the USAF's prime depot for both worldwide F-4 weapon systems and munitions support. As such, we were responsible for much of the critical logistics support the Israeli Air Force required during the war. An IAF liaison officer was assigned to the depot to coordinate requirements. His wish was our desire. All other work ground to a sudden stop. The entire depot workforce was clearly focused on one overriding objective, ensuring the IAF had all the aircraft spares, munitions, support equipment, and whatever else they needed to keep their fleet of F-4 Aircraft in the air 24 hours-a-day for as long as necessary. A special logistics readiness room was quickly set up with necessary communications and expediters who worked around the clock to receive and monitor IAF requirements. The minute a request was received, the item was pulled from storage, quickly moved to the designated marshaling area, and loaded into awaiting C-141 and C-5 Aircraft which were lined up in the ready position.

"It soon became crystal clear to all involved, that this wasn't just a test of the IAF's ability to fly and fight and defend their homeland. It was also a critical test of U.S. resolve, technology, weapon systems, tactics, logistics support systems, and airlift capabilities, against that of the Soviet Union who was supplying many of the Arab countries involved in the conflict. A loss in either case was absolutely unthinkable, and would have been devastating to both Israel and the United States. With our assistance, Israel quickly recovered from initially heavy loses to inflict a crushing defeat on both Egypt and Syria. We worked together and were successful then, and we can do it again."

"What about weapons system sales to our enemies? We understand that arms sales are a 'cash cow,'and an important aspect of your government's efforts in battling the foreign trade deficit which the United States continually faces. Nevertheless, we would expect a little more backbone when it comes to standing up to the 'arms lobbyist' pressuring the government to peddle weapons to our enemies."

"We have in the past, as a matter of policy, honored the legitimate self-defense security assistance needs of our friends in the area," softly responded the NSA, barely audible over the sound of his foot rapidly taping the floor.

"Oh, is that right?" asks Eran, his eyes widening and his mouth dropping open in bewilderment. What about those F-15E Strike Eagle aircraft that you recently sold to your friends in Saudi Arabia? Do you classify them as defensive weapon systems? From everything we are told by the manufacturer of the aircraft, it is touted as a world class fighter-bomber. One without equal."

"Surely, you don't consider Saudi Arabia an enemy of Israel?"

"We understand that they are a close ally of the United States," Eran acknowledges with a shrug of the shoulders. "But, perhaps even more important, they are far and away the largest foreign military sales customer you have in the entire world. We also understand that your sale, and their purchase of F-15E aircraft, enabled Mc Donnell Douglas to keep their production line open for future orders from the USAF. Two important spin offs from this were the ability to keep the skilled personnel within your defense industry employed, and spreading production costs over a larger number of units, thereby, reducing the cost that the U.S. Government paid for your USAF aircraft. I have also heard the old blackmail argument that if your government won't sell them arms, someone else will. When the Bush administration could not muster up the necessary support in the U.S. Congress to sell 72 additional F-15 aircraft to the Saudis in the early 1980s, they purchased Tornado Fighters from the United Kingdom. The estimated economic loss of that sale to the United States over the 20 years expected life cycle of the defense equipment was $100 billion.

"By the way, Mr. Richman, I guess I would be remiss if I did not add my congratulations to those of many others that I'm sure your Government has already received," suggests Eran, each word dripping with sarcasm. "I'm speaking, of course, of yesterday's headlines announcing the $6.4 billion sale of 80 advanced F-16 fighter jets to the United Arab Emirates. I understand that these aircraft will come equipped with a new electronic warfare system that is carried inside the aircraft instead of in a wing pod, and a new generation of radar more powerful and precise than that used by the USAF. In addition, it has been reported that $1.3 billion worth of munitions will also be provided. These weapons include Amraam air-to-air missiles, Maverick air-to-ground missiles, second-generation Harm radar-killing munitions, and GBU-series laser-guided bomb kits. According to documents released by the Pentagon, the UAE will be the first nation in the region to receive the new model of Harm munitions.

"It has also been suggested in the newspapers that this sale is expected to sail through your Congress with little or no opposition. My, how times have changed," Eran exclaims, crossing his arms in an outward show of displeasure. "I can remember the day when even the passing mention of a major arms sale to an Arab nation in the Middle East would have provoked bloodshed on the floor of the U.S. Congress. People would have literally come to blows. Now, instead of a spirited, highly emotionally charged debate on the merits of the issue, it gets an automatic 'rubber stamp' approval. However, I guess that it is a sign of the times. And, I might add, it speaks volumes to the Israeli people regarding how our American friends value the cherished nature of our long-standing relationship."

The National Security Advisor remained silent.

"You can only guess, how happy all of this makes us, Mr. Richman. We are, how do you say it, 'absolutely ecstatic!' Let me see if I can put it into words that you can understand,"offers Eran, tilting his head to the side and raising his thick eye brows, creating long wrinkles in his forehead. "This, isn't a 'zero-sum' game we're playing here, but let's do the math for just the past two years. The United States sold 50 F-16 fighters to Israel in 1999, as well as 24 to Egypt. The current sale of 80 F-16s to the UAE, plus the 24 to Egypt last year, comes to a total of 104 aircraft. Adjusting the total to make allowance for the 50 that you sold to us last year, leaves a difference of 54 aircraft. How am I doing so far? Do these numbers make sense to you? Correct me if I'm wrong, but it would appear to me that the balance sheet is somewhat out of whack? All this talk of a 'level playing field,' just doesn't seem to ring true anymore. However, I suppose there are those military analysts in the Pentagon who would suggest that a mere 54 F-16s equipped with radar and munitions superior to our Israeli aircraft, would have no impact in the balance of power here in the Middle East. Especially, in view of the sale of all those F-15E Strike Eagle aircraft to Saudi Arabia that I mentioned earlier!

"Money talks, and the economics of your relationship with the Arabs is not lost on us, Mr.Richman. However, we also understand that the Saudis and the kingdoms that make up the Emirates are first and foremost, Arabs and Muslims. As such, their Arab friends in the Middle East expect them to be dependable members of the brotherhood and properly align themselves on Arab issues. In our position, we cannot afford to trust anyone. Everyone who lives in our Middle East neighborhood must be considered a potential enemy," proclaims Eran, his speech slowing and his voice rising in volume with each succeeding word for added emphasis.

"As you are probably aware, the timing of your visit and this request is not the best. The United States' other close friend and associate in the area, the Palestinians, are threatening to unilaterally declare statehood in the near future. I'm not sure how much more good news we can stand at the moment. A Palestinian state on our border! Just think of the possibilities. A legal international entity that would be able to raise a large army, and use it without limitations. Not to mention, the ability to forge alliances with regimes that aim to destroy us, and serve as a base of increased terrorism against Israel to threaten our very existence. By the way, the next time you visit with your Palestinian friends, please inform them that Israel will never agree to giving up a portion of Jerusalem. And, furthermore, we must respectfully decline their most gracious invitation to 'drink from the Dead Sea.'" The tone of Eran's voice is laced with defiance, and he punctuates his final sentence with the release of air, forced around an exposed tongue, forming the sound of someone spitting.

Mitch had heard enough. He had clearly been outflanked and was perilously close to being surrounded. It was time to circle the wagons before he was completely overrun. He reached for the bargaining chip that he was carrying in his hip pocket. Perhaps, he thought, that's why they referred to this as "hip-pocket" diplomacy. Collecting his thoughts, he extends an olive branch.

"Suppose for a moment that we could convince the Palestinians not to announce statehood at the expiration of the agreement in May. And, furthermore, that they would agree to continue participating in peace talks for another year. Would that be something of interest to the Israeli Government? Of course, if we were able to convince them to cooperate on that matter, we would expect your cooperation in dealing with this latest Iraqi threat. Israel must exercise restraint as you did during the Gulf War and not launch a pre-emptive strike. We need to ensure that we execute a timely coordinated military response because weapons are also targeted at Turkey and Saudi Arabia."

Twenty minutes later, the two men conclude their discussion. Mitch gives Eran a generous handshake and thanks him profusely for the support he has pledged. Israel will not become involved in a military altercation with Iraq, leaving the dirty work to the United States. For its patience and understanding, Israel received a pledge from the United States that there will be no unilateral pronouncement of statehood by the Palestinians. Mitch takes several deep breaths as he closes the door of the ministry building behind him and steps out into the warm sunshine. His mind is still reeling at how close he came to blowing the biggest negotiating opportunity of his political career. He had come within a nat's eyelash of being sent packing with nothing more that a suitcase full of the remnants of his professional dreams. However, in the end, through apparent divine intervention, he prevailed, snatching victory from the jaws of defeat. The NSA owed Eran two huge debts of gratitude–one for the agreement, and one for the education. He had been taken to school, and given a lesson in international negotiating by an individual who possessed world-class diplomatic skills. This was one lesson that he would not soon forget!

***

As the big bird gracefully lifts off the runway and carefully tucks its feet under its soaring wings for the return flight to Washington, D.C., Mitch summons his staffers for a short meeting.

"Well gentlemen, it's mission accomplished and homeward bound. We got everything we came after and can just about put this one in the books. The tough part is over. However, as you are aware, the job is never finished until the paperwork is complete. You guys now get to earn your keep. You know the bureaucratic drill. Working from your notes of our discussions, put this in the standard format. I need a trip report for each leg of the journey. I also need a formal talking paper to brief the National Security Council on the results of our trip. While you're slaving away, I'm going to catch a few Zs. I want to be well rested and ready to hit the ground running when we land at Andrews. Somehow, I've got this feeling that a whole lot of people are going to want to hear from us as soon as possible."

# CHAPTER FIFTEEN

## ELEPHANT TANGO

*"Gentlemen, please take your seats so we can begin. You all know* why you are here. At the conclusion of the NSA's briefing, we will take a few minutes and review the status of the planning, recruiting, and training aspects of the mission. Mitch, the floor is yours."

"Thank you Mr. President." Mitch had risen early, going over the trip reports and familiarizing himself with his talking paper. He had reviewed it carefully, highlighting in yellow salient portions which he wanted to be sure to emphasize to the group. Thank goodness for staffers. Just like a good secretary, they were worth their weight in gold. This great republic, driven by the engine of free enterprise and governed by democratic government, was still bound-up and hamstrung by bureaucratic red tape. Figuring out the paperwork was at least half the battle. Turning his attention to the distinguished group surrounding the conference table, Mitch begins, speaking clearly and distinctly. This was his time to shine, and he was determined to capture the moment.

"Generally speaking, I was well received on each leg of the trip. My assessment of the talks is that they were serious, intensive, and productive. If the operational mission goes off as smoothly as the diplomatic mission, we'll be in pretty good shape. I had to lean on them a bit, and play some hardball at times—put it in language they could understand and relate to. There were a few concerns as expected, and some concessions were made. Each of you has on the table in front of you a detailed copy of my trip report for each stop. In the interest of time, I will limit my remarks to the core issues."

As Mitch reviews his Middle East trip, the members of the NSC listen attentively to every word, knowing full well that this day will not pass without each of them having their turn in the barrel. They had learned from past experience that on those solemn occasions, when the national security policy of the nation was being formulated, to do otherwise was suicidal. As the discussion progressed, each member of the NSC anticipated in their own mind what questions might surface, and what their response would be if called upon. When their time came to paddle, they could then dip their oar in the water without so much as a ripple.

"The Saudis were very helpful, providing the necessary underpinning for the remainder of the negotiations. On the recommendation of Ambassador Robinson, Prince Khalid Al Turki played the key role of intermediator on our behalf with his Government. We owe him a huge debt of gratitude. Basically, they bought into our plan with the exception of agreeing to test the new weapon on Saudi soil. We have their support in using Saudi air bases to launch missions against Iraq. They will also fund a portion of the expense of the operation, and allow us to use the Empty Quarter for training."

"What was their objection to testing the weapon in the Empty Quarter?" Although disappointed with the Saudi's reluctance to test his latest weapon in the empty quarter, the President understood that this was not a make or break issue for the mission.

"As you are aware, Mr. President, the King is also the Custodian of the Two Holy Mosques, Mecca and Medina. This is a most sacred honor and responsibility in the Islamic religion. As a matter of principle, the Saudis cannot consider the development and testing of weapons of mass destruction which are to be used on their Arab brothers on the same ground that is consecrated to the highest purposes of preserving human life."

"That's understandable," the President acknowledged. "What's the work-around, Plan B?"

The ball was now in Secretary of Defense Grant Sherman's court, and he was anxious to get in the game and make a play. Pushing his "granny" reading glasses down on the bridge of his nose and peering over them at his esteemed colleagues, he joined the fray. "The specifications for development of the weapon included a requirement for the contractor to conduct extensive laboratory testing in conjunction with computer modeling and simulation. They also call for a limited field testing of the weapon. We will evaluate the results of these tests to determine the need for further testing by the U.S. Government prior to employment of the weapon in Iraq. Worst case, we may have to go without a field test."

Accepting the Sec Def's explanation, President Maxwell then asks the expected. There was never a "free lunch," in this business. Reciprocity was the name of the game. You had to give up something to get something. "'What did we have to agree to in exchange for the Saudi's cooperation?"

"As we anticipated, they were interested in U.S. guarantees of future weapons sales to meet their legitimate self-defense needs. They also insisted on most favored nation trade terms and financial conditions, guaranteed by the U.S. Government."

"Not an unreasonable request under the circumstances," remarks the President, smiling broadly. "In addition, it binds our largest security assistance customer to us for the foreseeable future, which isn't all bad news. Score one for the 'good guys.' We may have to twist a few arms over in Congress, but we've got the necessary clout to make that happen. Good! Let's move on to the Palestinians. I'm interested in learning how your meeting with PLO Chairman Gatachek went."

"Let me begin by saying it was a most interesting experience. The Chairman was disappointed that he did not receive stronger support and endorsement for statehood from the U.S. at the expiration of the five-year period of Palestinian autonomy set out in the Middle East peace agreement in May 1999. He went to great lengths to impress upon me that with his advanced age and failing health, the next round of talks with the Israelis may be his last opportunity to secure a lasting peace and a homeland for the Palestinians. The flip side of that coin is that the militant movements within the PLO are waiting in the wings ready to seize control at the next sign of failure."

Across the table, the CIA Director, Jeff Hendricks, raises his finger as a signal to Mitch, that he was prepared to support his position on this critical point before he continued on. " If I may, let me quickly add, that from everything we have been able to learn, Chairman Gatachek isn't just blowing smoke with that statement. He is expressing what we consider to be a very legitimate concern. The PLO leader faces likely assassination if he drops his demand that the capital of the Palestinian state be located in eastern Jerusalem. We are all aware of the terrorist tactics of the Shi'ite Muslim guerrillas of the Hezbollah, an Islamic movement aimed at forcing Israel out of southern Lebanon. If there is a deadlock in the peace process, things may get out of control. Any response by one side will only bring a counter-response from the other side, with the potential to quickly escalate into a major war."

"That is a point well taken." Secretary of State, Peter Whittenburg, continued by asking, "What is the Chairman's position? Is what he is after, supportable?"

"In exchange for their agreement to postpone a unilateral declaration of independence in the form of a Palestinian state in the West Bank and Gaza strip, the PLO is looking for a statement of unequivocal support from the U.S. for Palestinian statehood after an additional year. They also expect us to work within the peace process with the Israelis to resolve the outstanding issues, including withdrawal from the occupied areas and the status of Jerusalem." While there were no new issues here, the gravity of what the NSA had said was cause for everyone seated at the table to swallow hard, just as they had on every previous occasion they came to grips with the reality of the situation.

Even President Maxwell, who went to bed each evening wrestling with the seemingly unsolvable gut issues of a lasting Middle East peace, blinked when once again confronted with the sheer enormity of the problem. "Well, that's certainly a very big order. I expect they understand that we have no problem with their request. However, we can't always get our Israeli friends to go along with what we think is reasonable. What did you tell him?"

"I told him what he was asking for sounded fair to me, and gave him my promise that I would personally deliver his request to the President."

"Thanks a lot, Mitch," responded the President as he tilted his head back and rolled his eyes in dismay. "With friends like you, who needs enemies? You know, gentlemen, I've been thinking seriously of taking that 'Buck Stops Here' sign off my desk in the oval office and placing it on Mitch's desk in his new office in the broom closet. Since he's the one making all these promises, perhaps he should also be the one responsible for making them come true." The President's comment evokes a round of laughter from the NSA members and serves as a necessary light-hearted moment to break the tension consuming the room. "Well, Mr. Secretary of State, it looks like we've got our work cut out for us, doesn't it? O.K., let's move on. What do you have to report from your meetings with our friends in Israel?"

Mitch checked his watch. The meeting was well into its second hour, and he was well aware that at the "seventh inning stretch," it was two down and one to go. He took a deep breath, slowly exhaled, and continued. "We had a positive and constructive exchange of views on the key issues. The Israelis, as usual, are preoccupied with concerns over security. As such, they were contemplating their own pre-emptive air strike against Iraq. In the meantime, they have placed their military forces on full alert. The one sure thing we can count on, is that if Israel is attacked, their counter attack will be massive with no holds barred. A response which in their eyes will be considered both justified and proportional." Mitch, pauses, for emphasis and continues. "However, our offer to deliver the Palestinians on postponing a declaration of statehood for one year and continuing the peace negotiations definitely got their attention. In addition, I stressed the absolute importance of executing a timely coordinated military response in view of the fact that Saddam also has weapons targeted at Turkey and Saudi Arabia. The initiation of any unilateral military action by Israel, could result in a 'knee-jerk' reaction on the part of Iraq resulting in the launch of missiles against these countries."

"So, what's the bottom line here?" the President asks curtly, the annoyance in his tone of voice underscoring his impatience. He had heard the rhetoric, but was looking for an unequivocal clear statement of fact.

Mitch read between the lines, and focused his attention on providing the President a succinct response. "The Israelis are uncomfortable with the idea of depending upon others to do what they believe they can accomplish themselves when it comes to their own national security. I took some pretty heavy incoming rounds regarding their remaining on the sidelines during the Gulf War. They were quick to remind me of the 39 SCUD missiles that Saddam Hussein launched into Israel while we were guaranteeing their security. In addition, I got the party line on what they think of having a legal Palestinian State on their border with the ability to raise a large army and use it without limitations. However, after some tough talk on both sides, they agreed to play ball with us on this one, as long as we have the Palestinians on a short leash for the next year. Having said that, I need to add that they obviously view Saddam's threat as extremely time sensitive. As such, they are not prepared to wait indefinitely for us to initiate action. We need to proceed with all possible expediency."

Secretary of State Whittenburg, suspecting that they were not yet playing with a full deck, was determined to get to the heart of the matter. "Did they voice any other concerns?"

Mitch glanced at his talking paper to make sure that he wasn't over-looking anything at this critical juncture of the discussion. Sharing a look with the Secretary of State, he responds. "Yes, as a matter of fact they did. I also got an earful regarding the sale of U.S. arms to our Arab friends in the region." The news release on the F-16 sale to the Emirates was untimely, to say the least. It hit the front page the day before my meeting with Oded Eran. He still had smoke coming out of his ears when I arrived. The outrage he obviously felt was only thinly veiled by heavy sarcasm. The short version is that the Israelis feel betrayed by our continued weapons sales to Arab countries in the Middle East. As the arms race continues to escalate in the area, their count has them falling further and further behind. In no uncertain terms, they let me know that they did not consider our actions in this regard, the actions of a friend."

While security assistance was an issue of interest and importance to both the Secretary of State and Secretary of Defense, previous arms sales fell under the purview of the Sec Def. It was an issue that he took very seriously. "From what I'm hearing, it sounds as if the Israelis have been following our security assistance sales in the region quite closely," offered Secretary of Defense Grant Sherman.

"You've got that right," Mitch shot back. "They've got it all accounted for down to the last thin dime. I had to do a lot of tap dancing on that topic to the tune of the 'Tennessee Waltz.' They reminded me that even though the U.S. enjoys a close relationship with Saudi Arabia and the Emirates, they are still Arabs. And, as such, their Arab friends in the Middle East expect them to be a dependable member of the brotherhood and properly align themselves on Arab issues. When it comes to issues of national security, the Israelis cannot afford to trust anyone. Everyone living in their Middle East neighborhood must be considered a potential enemy."

President Maxwell, who had been following the conversation closely, decided it was time to reminisce a bit about a subject which fascinated him, "Old Testament history." "The Israelis have good reason for concern. It is fed by the mentality of years of wars and rumors of war, to the point that it is almost inconceivable that a lasting peace can be achieved. Furthermore, we are mere men suggesting that we can guarantee peace in the region. But, what does God say? The Old Testament talks of an Armageddon, an area located 50 miles north of Jerusalem. It was the scene of many violent battles during Old Testament times. A great and final conflict, in which all nations are engaged, will take place in the same location at the Second Coming of the Lord. Since no one knows when that will happen, it behooves everyone to be armed to the teeth so they won't be caught short on judgment day."

While the Sec Def had no interest in Old Testament history, he did feel the need to protect an area which he considered to be his personal "rabbit patch." Flaring his wings like an old bantam hen protecting her chicks from the proverbial fox in the hen house, Secretary Sherman came out cackling. "I need to remind everyone, that the most recent major defense package sale to Saudi Arabia providing 72 F-15 fighters and other defense articles is expected over time to generate or sustain at least 783,062 man-years of employment for American workers. The export of U.S. goods and services to the Gulf Cooperative Council totaled approximately $20.5 billion in 1994, which translated into more than 500,000 man-years of employment in the United States. America's security exports alone to GCC countries have approximated $5 billion a year. In recent years, exports have been the most impressive engine of growth for America's economy. According to the Department of Commerce, nearly 40 percent of the growth of America's Gross Domestic Produce resulted from U.S. exports of goods and services. Commerce Department statistics also indicate that $1 billion in U.S. exports creates 19,000 man-years of direct domestic employment. Moreover, private sector research suggests that if induced or 'indirect' jobs generated as a result of 'direct' export jobs are included, these numbers double. These jobs and exports translate directly into a stronger U.S. economy and increased domestic tax revenues. Each American working in the Gulf generates an average of some $812,000 in U.S. exports, enough to support 15 jobs in the United States."

Secretary of State Whittenburg, who had been on the losing side of many of those heated arms sales debates, decided to interject some "stuff" in the game in an effort to rattle the Sec Def's cage. "Those opposed to additional arms sales to the Saudis, express the opinion that they cannot effectively operate and maintain the weapon systems that they currently have on hand due to a shortage of technically trained manpower. Consequently, they are heavily dependent upon expatriates to maintain these weapon systems. If the Saudis were ever threatened by their neighbors, they could not defend themselves, regardless of the weapon systems they had available. Consequently, they would just pick up the phone, and dial 1-800-USA-HELP."

Like the good soldier that he was, General Broughton quickly jumped on his white steed and came riding to the aid of his boss. "As a vehicle for U.S. foreign policy, security assistance enhances U.S. influence in the Middle East, facilitates the Gulf States' ability to defend themselves, and reduces the need for another major U.S. military build-up in the region. By providing security assistance to our GCC allies, the United States furthers its own national interests while also meeting the legitimate defense needs of our friends. These allies are upgrading their collective defense capabilities and have expressed a preference for U.S. equipment in large part because of its superior capabilities, follow-on logistics support program, and our long-standing political, economic, and security relationships with the GCC countries."

The Secretary of State gave a menacing glare in the direction of the Sec Def's knight in shining armor, and continued. "Peace in the Middle East could be a two-edged sword. Israel's obsession with national security has fed the spiraling arms race in the region. We sell modern hi-tech weapons systems to Israel, and then sell them to the Arab countries to maintain the balance of power. Economists say that if that cash cow ever dries up, the U.S. is in deep kimchee. Am I the only one that is feeling a sense of hypocrisy here? In the same breath we're talking serious prospects for peace, the key negotiating point with the participants is a U.S. commitment to continue to provide arms to Middle East countries. How do you balance economic prosperity on the one hand with peace on the other?"

National Security Advisor Richman clearly recognized the logic in Secretary Whittenburg's argument, but wasn't about to let it breathe long enough to have a life of its own. Rationale like that had no place in a National Security Council debate. It was not consistent with historical precedent, and furthermore, not in the best interests of the United States. "Don't confuse a peace agreement in the Middle East with the end of arms sales in the region. Our arms sales are more than incidental to our economic prosperity. We are the world's leading arms merchants and aren't about to give up that distinction. No one is willing to kill the goose that lays the golden eggs. Whoever said that you can't have your cake and eat it too, didn't understand the economics of arms sales."

"Will the public take notice of this apparent contradiction?" Vice President Tim Staley had decided that he needed to fill his participation square, and a question like this was probably as nondescript as you could expect in a national security debate. He most certainly didn't want to say anything that would indicate he was taking sides on this issue. Rule number one, was don't burn any bridges. When he made his own run for the Presidency in a few years, he wanted to be able to count on the support of everyone in the room. And, most certainly, he didn't want to create any enemies.

The Chief of Staff's job was to keep the President's approval rating up in his first term, and get him reelected to a second term. Hal Justin was born a politician. While the doctor was delivering him in the hospital, he was busy conducting a straw public opinion poll. The Chief of Staff was a one stop weather service, combination weather vane and barometer all rolled into one. He knew which way the political winds were blowing and steered the President accordingly. It was now time for him to tell it like it was. "With all due respect, Mr. Vice President, the public doesn't have a clue. A recent pollster asked typical citizens on the street what they thought was more prominent in today's society, ignorance or apathy. Many people responded that 'they didn't know and furthermore, they didn't care.' We are experiencing an extended period of economic prosperity combined with low unemployment. Just like the man said, 'it's the economy stupid.' Everything else is secondary. You just haven't gotten the message yet have you? We've got the American public eating out of our hand. Check the public opinion polls."

This was obviously a teaching opportunity, one that Mitch

couldn't pass up. How he loved to teach this lesson in Psychology 101, especially to this select group. "Is everybody here familiar with Maslow's Hierarchy of Needs? Do you remember a need for honesty, character, or morality being on the list? The average American believes that life is good if he has meat and potatoes on the table, a cold beer in the refrigerator, a ball game on the T.V., and enough money to pay this month's rent."

With the "I've been put-upon pout" on Vice President Staley's mug, and the NSA having polluted the science of psychology to the point Sigmund Freud was probably rolling over in his grave, President Maxwell decides to steer the discussion in another direction. "All right, we've touched all the bases with our allies in the region, where do we stand regarding the other major aspects of this mission?"

General Broughton had spent the past two days with his staff being spun up to speed on the status of ongoing preparations for Desert Heat. To say that he was loaded for bear would have been a gross understatement. It was time to get the women and children off the streets. "Mission planning is being accomplished by personnel from the Pentagon office of 'Checkmate' under the auspices of the USAF Deputy Chief of Staff for Plans & Operations. This is the same group that put forward the 'parallel-war' theory which proved successful in Kosovo. Their state-of-the-art computer modeling and simulation techniques will allow for a number of possible tactical approaches to be tested and evaluated under various 'what-if' scenarios, assessing both risk and the probability of mission success. In an effort to avail ourselves of the best minds available and to ensure cohesiveness among our task force, the primary operatives of the ground and air portions of the mission were also invited to participate in portions of the planning phase."

However, just as he was getting up a full head of steam, his boss, Secretary Sherman, stopped him cold in his tracks. "What about input from the other branches of our Armed Services? The U.S. Army's Delta Force has extensive training and experience in countering the danger of international terror. Did you consider a multi-service approach to this mission?"

It appeared momentarily as if the highly decorated war hero had taken a broadside. However, General Broughton quickly recovered, without the assistance of a MASH outfit. He was quite nimble on his feet for a man of his size, and it was rumored that he could roller skate in a buffalo herd. "Yes, sir. We looked into that possibility early-on, but based on lessons learned from similar missions we decided to proceed with essentially a single-service approach. First of all, the USAF possesses all the resources required for the mission, including both personnel and equipment. Secondly, the wider the circle of participants, the greater the degree of difficultly in bringing them all together into a cohesive team. One of the major findings that came out of the investigation into the failed 'Desert One' rescue of hostages in Iran, was that we went out and found bits and pieces, people, and equipment. Then, with very little opportunity for interface, we tasked them with performing a highly complex mission. The end result was that while all the individual parts performed well, they didn't function as a team. Anticipating that the preparation and training time for this mission were going to be abbreviated, we decided that our chances of putting together a cohesive team effort could be best achieved through a single service approach."

"Have we identified the key personnel to carry out the mission?" The President had just asked the $64,000 question that was on everyone's mind.

The Chairman was obviously prepared for this one. He responded immediately, with no hesitation whatsoever. "We have recruited the two primary operatives to head up the ground and air portions of the mission. They were selected as much for what they aren't as for what they are. Worse case, these men won't crack. Not only are they outstanding professional people, but they come with old school values and traditions, seldom found in today's society. They are the epitome of what General McArthur had in mind when he gave his 'Duty, Honor, Country' speech at West Point. They've got that 'Warrior' mentality. In accordance with Article VI of The Uniform Code of Military Conduct, 'I will never forget that I am an American fighting man, responsible for my actions, and dedicated to the principles which made my country free. I will trust in my God and in the United States of America.' It will be 'Name, Rank, Serial Number, and Date of Birth.' Period!"

The Secretary of Defense feeling the need to cover his "six o'clock position" on this one, picks the Chairman up and sits him down right down on the point of the tack. "Are we sure we've got the right guys?"

"You can take it to the bank, boss. These two will definitely lay it all on the line if it becomes necessary. If you want more personal information on them or would like to meet them, that can be arranged."

The Sec Def's question had almost boomeranged and struck him in the noggin. Sometimes it's in everybody's best interest to keep the human element at arms length in the event difficult decisions have to be made down the road. "No General, that won't be necessary. I've heard all I need to know. If you're satisfied, I'm satisfied."

President Maxwell looks nervously at his watch and says "Let's move one. What have we got on training?"

This was the Chairman's turf once again. He settled back in his chair and spoke with the authority of someone who had been there and done that. "As noted earlier, in our review of lessons learned from previous missions of this nature, we noted that lack of familiarity between participants and insufficient opportunity for integrated training are the biggest contributors to mission failure. Participants must train together long enough to ensure that they can achieve success with all the intricacies of interaction required of a team effort. Anticipating that we will be faced with a compressed time frame for training in preparation for this mission, we are proceeding as follows.

"Aircrew members will receive their initial mission orientation and training from the 58th SOW at Kirkland, AFB, New Mexico. With state-of-the-art simulators and virtual-reality environments, a faculty composed of former special operations personnel teaches approximately 75 courses that combine hands-on flying time with 'electronic classrooms.' This will prepare the flight personnel to make the transition from traditional USAF flight methodology to the extreme techniques and technologically enhanced aircraft that distinguishes special air operations missions. The school library at Kirkland maintains the largest integrated digital terrain database in the world, covering about four million square nautical miles. Our flight personnel will receive extensive simulator training utilizing a virtual-reality Iraqi desert environment obtained from our reconnaissance satellite photo terrain imaging and mapping program.

"Follow-on training for the aircrews will be conducted at the USAF Weapons and Tactics Center at Nellis AFB, Nevada. Aircrews will fly against deep strike targets simulating a missile launch site on ranges 71 and 76. Their performance will be monitored and evaluated by the Red Flag Measurement and Debrief System, which provides a complete read out of the results of all bombing runs on the target. The final phase of the aircrew training will be conducted in the Empty Quarter in Saudi Arabia, in conjunction with personnel of the ground element.

"The ground element of our task force will receive their preliminary training at the 1st SOW at Hurlburt Field, Florida. Emphasis in this phase of the training will be placed on sharpening basic skills, and reviewing tactical skills. The basic skill portion will be a combination of activities aimed at improving self-confidence, such as physical training, and honing marksmanship skills on the weapons range. During the tactical training, personnel will be instructed in a variety of special operations tactics, including overland infiltration, tactical air control procedures, and combat assault techniques.

"Follow-on training will be conducted in the desert environment of the Empty Quarter of the Saudi desert outside Prince Sultan Royal Saudi Air Base. A United States Air Force Red Horse Team, a civil engineering unit trained and equipped for rapid construction or repair of runways and airbase facilities, will be tasked with a temporary duty assignment of deploying to Saudi Arabia. They will construct physical mockups of Iraqi facilities including the missile system control center. This will interject the essential element of realism into the training–the ability to train in the desert environment on a facility constructed to approximate the actual Iraqi facilities as closely as possible. Accomplishing the construction in-house using active duty military personnel will expedite the process due to their immediate availability and ease of entry in and out of the Kingdom. It will also minimize the number of personnel with a knowledge of various aspects of the operation.

"During the final phases of the training, both the air and ground elements of the task force will be based at Prince Sultan Air Base. This will facilitate the critical joint familiarization and training of the ground and air elements of the mission task force that I mentioned earlier. It will also provide sufficient time for our people to overcome their jet lag, become acclimated to the climate, and familiarize themselves with the hostility of the desert environment."

Convinced that the Chairman obviously had a handle on the military preparations for the mission, the Secretary of Defense skillfully pouched the ball over the net into the CIA Director's court. "What about intelligence? Have we got everything we need in the way of good intel to make this mission successful?"

Director Hendricks winced not once, but twice. He was obviously embarrassed. However, he also had the presence of mind to own up to the agency's shortcomings rather than attempt to pull a rabbit out of a hat in a room with this select group. Smoke and mirrors didn't go over big in the NSC. The members would see through the slight of hand in a heartbeat. The best policy was to lay bear his soul. "It goes without saying that good intelligence is absolutely critical. You must have good intelligence to have a successful air campaign, or any other combat mission for that matter. As the Director of the CIA, I am chagrined to say, that intel may be the long pole in the tent on this mission."

"Have you taken steps to ensure that the Chinese Embassy in Belgrade is not on the target list?" President Maxwell had just made sarcastic reference to the inadvertent bombing in May which occurred during NATO's 78-day air war. Three Chinese had been killed in the attack and 20 others wounded. The intended target had been the Yugoslav Federal Directorate of Supply and Procurement headquarters.

"As you are aware, Mr. President, the employee responsible for that inadvertent administrative oversight was fired. Six others, including a senior official and four managers, received various forms of administrative punishment. We have taken the necessary measures to preclude tragic accidents such as that in the future."

"What seems to be the problem here?" The President was still smarting from the surprise that Saddam had perpetrated on him, and the CIA's inability to sniff it out. He wasn't about to let the Director off the hook easily.

"Mr. President, as you may recall from my earlier briefing, a CIA covert operation in Iraq intended to generate indigenous opposition to Saddam in hopes of sparking a coup, was broken up when Saddam's military moved against his Kurdish population in 1996. We haven't been able to insert the necessary agents back into Iraq to supply the detailed intelligence we would like to have for this mission. In addition, Iraqi troops blanket the streets of Baghdad as well as many other parts of the country, making it very difficult for feet on-the-ground agents to operate and collect intelligence in Iraq. I'm also concerned about the security on our side. Any leaks will have catastrophic consequences. We need to wrap this up in an air tight zip-lock plastic bag. Mission success is predicated to a large extent on the element of surprise."

The President deciding that his Director had swung slowly back and forth in the wind long enough, turned his attention elsewhere. "I'm counting on each of you in this room to make that happen. This is a 'top secret' covert mission against an enemy of the state, and it will be treated as such!

"So, we have the coordination, planning, recruiting, and training, all underway. We need to discuss a projected target date for implementation. I understand that some aspects of the operation can be conducted simultaneously while others must proceed consecutively. How long is this going to take, General? When can you be ready?"

"Best case, Mr. President, with everything we've done to compress the preparation period, the minimum time without cutting any corners which might compromise mission integrity, I'd say between 45 and 60 days."

This was the NSA's baby and the President wanted to make sure that Mich was comfortable with the General's response. "What do you think Mitch?"

The NSA had been quite content to let the conversation take its course up to this point, knowing full well that the President was completely in agreement with his assessment of the situation. Furthermore, he enjoyed observing the interaction of the elephant herd as they scrambled, or better yet stampeded for position. That is, as long as he didn't get trampled underfoot in the process. "With all due respect for the Chairman, I doubt that we can keep our Israeli friends in the bleachers on the sidelines that long. To them, this is a game of Russian roulette, with the chamber containing the live round due to come up under the hammer at any time. Meanwhile, their military is on full alert, with their civilian population wearing gas masks and living in fallout shelters. It's a bad accident in the making, looking for a place to happen."

"General, you've got 30 days max. I know that's going to squeeze you, but I'm confident with the proper commitment you can make it happen."

The President had spoken and that should have been the end of it. However, the Chairman was accustomed to having the last word. "But, Mr. President..." For the first time since the General had joined this select group comprising the NSC, he appeared "nervous in the service."

Cutting the General off in mid sentence, his Commander in Chief appeared irritated, having tired of the exchange. He had obviously reached a decision and was ready to move on without further discussion. "I know, General, we would all like more time to prepare. But, this is a time-sensitive issue. We need to get the show on the road. Gentlemen, I want you to give this your highest priority. There is a great deal at stake here with a huge upside and an even greater downside. We pull this off successfully, and we'll be sitting pretty. If the wheels come off this mission, there will be severe ramifications and repercussions. We won't just be back to square one. We'll be back in an unlit cave crawling around on all fours once again. You've got 30 days. Get your best people working on this around the clock. No excuses, ifs, ands, or buts. I don't want to hear any more about the labor pains. Just show me the baby!"

# CHAPTER SIXTEEN

# IN HARM'S WAY

*After three months of planing, organizing, training, and a* series of increasingly complex rehearsals, the ability to neutralize Saddam's Missile System Control Center and destroy his weapons of mass destruction that threatened Turkey, Saudi Arabia, Israel, and American lives, was a reality. However, the execution of Operation Desert Heat still required the President's express authorization.

Mitch Richman briefs the members of the National Security Council on the readiness of the Task Force to execute Operation Desert Heat. He concludes the briefing with the recommendation that the mission proceed immediately, without further delay. For a period of several seconds, no one spoke. Each was alone with his thoughts, as the reality they were about to send Americans into harm's way in Iraq settled in. As was customary in these circumstances, the President provides an opportunity for NSC members to voice any opposition or concerns. As he looks, one by one, into the face of each individual seated at the table, he concludes that there is no dissent. In accordance with the chain of command, the Commander in Chief directs the Secretary of Defense to proceed. Secretary Sherman, in-turn, instructs General Broughton to give the operational order to execute Operation Desert Heat. The Chairman of the JCS, lifts the telephone on the table in front of him off the receiver, and speaks clearly and distinctly into the mouthpiece. "This is General Broughton. The Commander in Chief has authorized the execution of Operation Desert Heat. Proceed immediately."

A few minutes later a telephone rings in the wing command post at Abdul Aziz Air Base in Saudi Arabia. Pounder draws a deep breath as he receives a coded message from the Pentagon. "The fox is in its lair," meaning "execute mission 'Desert Heat' as planned."

The Task Force is gathered at the staging area, the jumping off point at Abdul Aziz Air Base in eastern Saudi Arabia, awaiting authorization to proceed. Pounder addresses the Task Force. "All right Gentlemen, listen up. We have lift off. The Pentagon has just cleared us to execute Operation 'Desert Heat.' We're center-stage."

There is cheering and fists are jammed into the air in the thumbs-up position. This is an emotional high for everyone. The adrenaline is flowing and they are pumped. After months of preparation they are anxious to engage the enemy and prove what they all believe—they are the best trained, best equipped, and most highly motivated fighting force on the planet. It is time to depart to the rendezvous point in Iraq.

Picking up their flight gear, the aircrew members go straight to the chopper and crank up the engines. The Task Force members climb aboard, and they lift off into the night. To ensure complete mission secrecy, the taxi, runway, and aircraft lights remain off. The aircraft control tower is empty, the controllers having been relieved from duty earlier in the evening. Even the base commander is unaware of the nature of the covert operational mission that is being launched from his airbase. There will be complete radio silence enroute to the rendezvous point.

The sky is clear, with visibility as good as it gets deep in the desert after dark. A full moon is struggling to hold its own, vis-a-vis the dazzling radiance of hundreds of twinkling stars. Night time temperatures are mild and pleasant this time of year. The air is still, without so much as a hint of a breeze. The briefer had predicted near-perfect weather conditions, and for once, delivered on his promise. The all-weather capability of the MH-53 Pave Low helicopter that swallowed the Task Force up in Saudi only to spit them back out in

Iraq, gets a well-earned night-off on this mission. The pilot uses his night vision goggles and his global positioning system to navigate through the darkness. Flying across the desert at night without proper equipment and instrumentation is a certain prescription for becoming disoriented and lost.

There is only intermittent conversation en route as most of the occupants are alone with their thoughts. Someone occasionally offers a word or two of small talk to mask the inherent anxiety that continues to build with each passing moment. However, it is largely an effort in futility. At the very moment the utterance clears the dry, parched lips, it is swept away by the roar of the chopper's engines.

They are skimming along the desert floor, 50 feet off the ground at the speed of heat, a low-level flight regime that's referred to as "paving." The terrain-following and terrain-avoidance radar, forward-looking infrared sensors, and projected map displays, make the MH-53 ideal for low-level, long-range flights. The low level flight enables them to scoot along under Iraqi radar. However, it also makes for an extremely rough ride. It's your basic buckle up and hang-on trip. Pounder says to no one in particular, "isn't it remarkable the basic transportation capabilities you can get for a mere $40 million a copy?"

This was the worst part, the waiting and anticipation. Pounder is reminded of the big homecoming football game his senior year in high school, preforming in front of his family and friends. The accompanying pre-game jitters during the playing of the National Anthem were almost uncontrollable. He was shaken like a strip of bacon sizzling in a hot skillet over a roaring campfire. It seemed like an eternity passed before the opening whistle finally rang out in its shrill voice, calling the gladiators to combat. He couldn't wait to get out there and hit somebody, anybody, to rid himself of the butterflies. Once the game got underway, the goose-bumps were quickly replaced by perspiration. The team that executed their game plan and took care of the basic fundamentals of running, blocking, and tackling, usually came out on-top on the scoreboard. Champions work and practice like champions. The Task Force had worked like champions and now it was time for all that hard work to come to fruition. Saddam could not deny them their due. They would succeed in spite of his reservations as to the nobility of their cause.

A few minutes from their destination, the pilot tells his passengers to prepare themselves for landing. Pounder instructs the Task Force to get all their gear and equipment together, and check it twice to ensure they don't forget anything. The aircrew wants to "touch and go" to minimize the risk of being detected and possibly being brought down by a rocket-propelled grenade. Night desert landings pose special challenges to an aircrew. A plane is 3.5 times more likely to crash while attempting to land in darkness than during the day. The desert night offers no land marks or lights by which the pilot can measure the plane's height or distance. Thus, the aircrew can fall victim to the "black hole effect," and become disoriented.

The chopper settles down on the desert floor and the occupants scramble out into the swirling sands beaten about by the wildly gyrating blades. It's an instant dust storm that penetrates anything and everything. Aircrew members wish them "God Speed," and quickly lift off for the return flight to the safety of the staging area. As their umbilical cord and lifeline to civilization is quickly swallowed up by the enveloping darkness, a cold shiver traverses the entire length of Pounder's body leaving no appendage immune. Was it the unspoken emotional expression of the mental realization that they are now alone on the enemy's turf, and very much in harm's way?

*** 

The members of the Iraqi opposition force's group are at the rendezvous point at the Wadi, having arrived within the hour. They have taken rest and dined on dates and goats' milk for nourishment. As the Task Force approaches, the leader calls out "Ahlan wasahlan," welcome!

Pounder and the leader embrace, kissing on alternate cheeks in the customary Arab greeting of the Middle East. In spite of the fact that they are operating under a tight schedule, Pounder understands the importance of sitting with his new friends and availing himself of their Bedouin hospitality. To refuse, even under these conditions would be considered rude and offend their hosts. The Task Force is depending upon them with their lives, and a few minutes to cement the relationship will certainly be time well spent.

"Assalamu aleikum," Ahmed says, Peace be upon you.

"Wa' aleikum assalam," Pounder responds, And on you be peace.

"Kayf hallak," Ahmed inquires, How are you?

"Tayyib, Al Humdillillah," Pounder answers, Fine, Praise be to God.

"Ismi Ahmed," My name is Ahmed. "Shoo ismak," What is your name?

"Ismi, Mr. Donovan ," Pounder replied.

Ahmed then says, "Tafaddal," please come in, and extends a hand to lead Pounder into his tent. The touch of his rough calloused skin, tells its own story. These are the hands of a man who earns his living through the sweat of his brow. The rounded shoulders and stooped posture betray a life of deprivation and submissiveness. Bowed but not broken, Ahmed is a survivor. They take their places on rugs spread in a circle on the sand, sitting with their legs crossed in the tradition of American Indians around a camp fire.

Making himself as comfortable as possible, Pounder carefully studies his newfound friend. Ahmed is attired in the customary Arab dress of a white, loose-fitting, ankle length thoub. A red and white checkered guthra covers his head, the corners flipped back and resting comfortably on his shoulders. It is held in place with a black igaal looped in two rings. A dark brown tweed sport coat provides needed warmth from the eerie cold of the desert night. Peaking out beneath the thoub are two well-worn, but comfortable, open-toed black sandals that have long ago reached a truce and fused a lasting friendship with the dust of the desert sand.

Deeply tanned by the midday rays of an unrelenting desert sun, Ahmed's face reads like a buried treasure map. Character lines abound in his leathery skin, cascading randomly about his face like the furrows in the sand formed by the torrential waters of a desert cloudburst. The prominent feature on his face is an elongated hawk-like nose. It is flanked by dark penetrating eyes sheltered beneath dense shaggy eyebrows. Ahmed's mandatory Arab facial hair includes a full mustache, heavily sprinkled with gray, and a goat-tee, badly in need of a trim. Teeth stained by the red juice of a thousand beetle nuts are exposed behind dry, parched lips that appear to be crying out for water.

As Ahmed speaks, he carefully and systematically fondles the prayer beads gripped tightly in his hand. Perhaps from force of habit, perhaps in response to an unspoken prayer, surely and slowly, the beads systematically make their rounds, always in motion, never resting.

"Bithubb ghawa wa shaay," he asks, Do you like coffee or tea?

"Nam," Yes, Pounder responds.

Arab coffee, flavored with cardamom, is served in tiny cups. It has never been a favorite of Pounders,' because of the bitter taste. Three cups may be consumed, but it is improper-even if the bearer offers it-to take a fourth. Pounder is careful to receive the cup with his right hand. It is impolite to use the left hand when offering, passing, or receiving anything. Highly sweetened tea, served in piping-hot small glass mugs, follows. Pounders' favorite is that prepared from leaves of the mint plant. He is in luck tonight, and accepts his full quota. As he savors the nourishment of his third glass, he feels a surge of optimism rush through his body. Perhaps this is a good-luck omen for his journey and the dangerous mission that lies ahead.

"Hal tatakallam Ingleezi" Pounder asks, Do you speak English?

"La, atakallam lughatak jayyidam," Ahmed responds, I don't speak your language well.

Pounder is not surprised at Ahmed's response. He had observed during his long stay in the Middle East that many Arabs have at least a limited conversational command of the English Language. However, as they don't have the opportunity to use it often, they are understandably shy about speaking in English, finding it more comfortable to converse in their native Arabic. From what little

Pounder had been briefed, he deduced that a man in Ahmed's position was probably more comfortable speaking in English than he was in Arabic. He had no more than formulated the thoughts in his mind when Ahmed spoke once again.

"My apologies, Mr. Donovan. I am unable to offer you the beauty and serenity of the white sand beaches, blue water, and pine tress of Fort Walton Beach, Florida."

"Yes, Ahmed, I understand that you attended the two-week course on 'Civil-Military Strategy for Internal Development,' at Hurlburt Field. What did you think of the training?"

"The course of instruction was interesting and informative. However, the real educational value of the time spent in your country came outside the classroom. Observing the people moving about unrestricted, without concern for the basic needs of food, shelter, and medical care, spoke volumes. How blessed you Americans are. Living in a free society, you may not fully appreciate what you have.

"Perhaps you have been to the zoo, and observed the animals in their cages. Born into captivity, they are lifeless and without spirit. Although they can sense that freedom lies just beyond the wall, they would make no effort to escape if the door to their pen were left open. Their wills are broken. That is how it is with life in Iraq where we have been trodden down and our resolve suppressed for so long. Spoon-fed the daily diet of state propaganda, we no longer have a dream.

"However, outside the confines of the depravation of my country, I once again caught the vision of freedom. A well hidden, residual ember of spirit, which I though had long ago been extinguished, has been rekindled. In one miraculous moment, the outer shell of numbness that has clouded my mind and soul since childhood was rolled back. The world came alive and took on new meaning. For the first time since I can remember, I felt the warm rays of the sunshine on my face and the wetness of the ocean spray on my skin. The dream is once again alive inside me. There is something to strive for outside the restricted and suppressed narrow confines of the world of darkness inside Saddam Hussein's Iraq. I am back from the dead."

Pounder was both impressed and somewhat taken back by the clarity and directness of Ahmed's response. Therefore, he decided to put the question to him that had been rattling around in the back of his mind ever since he learned of the role Ahmed was prepared to play to assist in destroying Saddam's weapons of mass destruction.

"We must be on our way soon. The rays of the early morning sun will be chasing us across the desert if we tarry much longer. But, before we proceed, Ahmed, I must ask you one question."

"Aiwa," he says, yes?

"Why, are you doing this? Why are you willing to risk your life to assist us?"

Ahmed fondles his prayer beads while gathering his thoughts, clears his throat and looks Pounder squarely in the eye. Then, speaking in near perfect English with only a hint of an accent, he responds in slow, measured speech, hanging on each word before allowing it to roll off his tongue for Pounder's personal consumption. It was a difficult question, and Ahmed was intent on choosing precisely the right words to express his feelings.

"I lost my father and older brother in the Gulf War, Mr. Donovan. For what? They died for no purpose. The great victory that Saddam promised the people of Iraq was like a mirage in the desert. It vanished before our eyes. The mother of all wars, quickly became the mother of all defeats. Saddam was humiliated. The loss of face that he suffered was perhaps a greater personal loss than the battle itself. However, the good people of Iraq lost far more than face. We lost our loved ones. And now, ten years later, we are still suffering. He says that he is a peace-loving man. However, all we see are war and preparations for war. How much longer must it continue? When will it end? The answer to your question, Mr. Donovan, is embodied in an old Arab proverb. 'An enemy of my enemy, is a friend of mine.' The once great leader of the people of Iraq has become the great enemy of the people of Iraq."

*  *  *

Recalling the admonition that "time is our enemy," they break camp and prepare to travel. Their Arab friends are driving Hum-Vs which proved themselves a worthy adversary of the multitude of sins encountered in desert travel during the vicarious days of Desert Storm. The single lane road is only little more than a well-traveled camel trail. The desert is void of vegetation from the gravel and rocky composition of the soil, and a debilitating hot and dry climate. The general notion that a desert is a great sea of sand is not exactly accurate. Unlike the deserts of the southwest United States, the greater part of the Arabian Peninsula is made up of gravel or rocky plains. It is a seemingly endless stretch of barren terrain and blanched nondescript landscape. The desert is a place of extremes, free of running water, with extremely few or nonexistent trees. A visitor will find that the harshness of the desert environment will challenge their survival instincts even for the briefest of excursions. Summer temperatures average about 112 degrees Fahrenheit, with temperatures frequently reaching 125 degrees. The air cools off rapidly after sunset, except along the costal areas where the high humidity adds to the discomfort.

They are off with the speed of heat, proceeding cautiously through the darkness—relentlessly pursued by a companion cloud of dust which threatens to overtake and envelope them; thereby, claiming them as one of the desert's own. A collective silence settles over the occupants of the Hum-Vs. The task force members attempt to relax and catch a cat nap or two along the way. Thoughts of family fill their minds, as they offer up silent prayers that God will watch over them and return them safely to their loved ones. However, the realization of what lies ahead, periodically brings them back to the present with a jolt.

After several hours of uneventful travel, the driver slows.

"Fi mushkilla," Pounder asks, Is there a problem?

"Mafee mushkilla," Ahmed responds, No problem. Then, he explains that they will soon be arriving at a checkpoint on the road.

As they approach, an individual in military dress stationed in a guard post calls out to warn them that they are entering a restricted security area. They are instructed to stop and identify themselves. Ahmed responds in Arabic, indicating that they are lost and require assistance. The guard directs them to remain where they are, offering to send someone out to meet them and render aid.

The rules of the road in this part of the world are a bit different from back home. The short version is, you don't refuse assistance, aid, or hospitality to a traveler in need. This is an old custom and part of the heritage of the Bedouin tribes that have criss-crossed the deserts with their families, goats, and camels, generation after generation, carrying on the traditions of their fathers. All this, and no "Good Samaritan" Law. One more vote for the side that believes you can't legislate good citizenship. It must be taught by the parents to their children.

Unfortunately, on this occasion, the Task Force has to take advantage of the Iraqi's kind offer to assist. On Pounder's signal, the assault team cuts down the guards. They drop in their tracks. At that moment, he experiences a twinge of conscience, feeling badly about having to shoot them as they were just doing their job. However, their doing their job was interfering with him doing his. Something had to give, and they weren't about to turn themselves in and ask if they could collect the reward money. The military would justify the taking of this action as required by the "exigencies of the service." Our friends in the CIA would refer to the completion of this job, as being "eliminated without prejudice." Whatever clever language one chose to smooth it over, it all came back to the old phrase, "the ends justify the means." And, in this case, Pounder couldn't argue, knowing what acts of terror Saddam was prepared to unleash on some of his closest friends and neighbors.

After another hour's drive, Ahmed announces that they are no more than a mile or two from their destination. Slowing to a crawl to minimize the engine noise, they proceed with caution. After another quarter of a mile, they pull to a stop, realizing that it would not be wise to proceed any further by vehicle. Any small advantage that could be gained by attempting to sneak in closer in their Hum-Vs would be greatly offset by the risk of being detected. It is time to bail out and get up-close and personal with the Iraqi desert. They will have to hoof it the rest of the way in from here. As they part ways, Pounder and Ahmed once again embrace and say their farewells.

"Laazem nisaafer," Pounder says, We must travel. "Shukran sadik," he adds, Thank you friend.

"Ma'assalaama," Ahmed responds, Goodbye Mr. Donovan.

" We will meet again, Ahmed."

"Inshallah, sadik," Ahmed responds, God-willing, my friend.

*** 

The Task Force members hike another 20 minutes into the desert. Approaching the crest of an incline, they pick up the outline of the palace in their night-vision binoculars. It is time to huddle up and take stock of the situation. Pounder reviews the tactical approach they will use to neutralize the guards.

"O.K. gentlemen. Everyone move-in close and listen-up. We will deploy on-foot from here. This is going to go down exactly like we've practiced dozens of times. All we have to do at this point is execute. One watchtower is located at each corner of the palace. Shooters, you've all got your assignments. The sentry positions are about 100 feet off the ground. Each of you locate yourself 300 yards from your target, in a position with unobstructed visibility and a clear line of sight. Get your weapons zeroed in for range and elevation and check-in by radio when you are in-position, ready to fire. Questions?

"Time hack. Gentlemen, set your watches. The time is now 2000 hours local. It's game time. Let's get ready to rumble. It's time to take some names and kick some fanny. We're going to rock Saddam's world."

Although Pounder has been around long enough that he no longer needs motivational speeches, he recognizes that they inspire the younger troops. "All of you have proven yourselves through rigorous training and exercises. There are no excuses from here on in. Mistakes can cost lives. O.K., gentlemen, let's rock and roll. Strike force shooters, move out and take-up your positions."

All four shooters are dressed in standard GI issue desert

camouflage fatigues, carrying their rifles and a backpack containing the tools of their trade. On the order to move-out, they disperse in the direction of their assigned watchtower, and are quickly swallowed up in the emptiness of the desert.

Shrouded in the darkness of the desert night, Shooter One proceeds the last two hundred yards on his stomach wriggling across the desert floor, propelled forward by his forearms and elbows. Doing his best impersonation of a sidewinder slithering across Death Valley, it is similar to the confidence course in basic military training with the exception of the barbed wire and the live rounds of ammunition passing overhead. He makes good time, only occasionally pausing to rest and check the laser-rangefinder to gauge the distance remaining between himself and the target. The only audible sound is that of his own heavy breathing as his chest billows in and out with a rhythmic beat. While the desert is as quiet as the proverbial church mouse on Sunday, there appears to be the dull roar of background noise within his mind. Could this be the deafening silence spoken of in the oxymoron, he wonders?

Arriving at his designated 300-yard interval-to-target position, Shooter One pulls the night-vision binoculars from his backpack and scans the watchtower for the sentry. There he is, exactly where he is supposed to be, silhouetted on the skyline against the light sand colored background of the high palace wall. The elevated guard post certainly provides him a "cat bird seat" and an excellent observation point from which to scour the area. However, it also renders him vulnerable. This should be like shooting fish in a rain barrel, Shooter One thinks to himself, as snipers practice plummeting a target up to 800 yards. However, on this occasion, there is no margin for error. The success of the entire mission is predicated upon the element of surprise. If they are detected and a guard is able to sound an alarm, the ramifications could be catastrophic. The strike force must get in swiftly, complete the mission, and rapidly extract themselves to avoid being captured or killed by Iraqi security.

Shooter One unrolls his shooting mat and carefully spreads it on the ground. It provides a comfortable pad for his chest and elbows when he is in the shooting position. He slips the rifle out of its canvas sleeve, and carefully removes the plastic covers from the telescopic sight. Setting up his weapon on its bi-pod, he sprawls prone on the ground. He calculates for vertical drop, and clicks the elevation knob on the night-vision scope to adjust for range. Picking up his radio, the sharpshooter plugs in his ear piece and checks the volume.

"Shooter One to Pounder," he whispers into his mouth mike. "Do you read me?"

"This is Pounder. I read you loud and clear, Shooter One."

"Shooter One reporting. In position, and target acquired. Ready to commence firing on your order."

"Copy, Shooter One. Maintain your position. Stand-by for further instructions."

" Copy, Pounder. Wilco. Shooter One out."

Shooters Two, Three, and Four, all subsequently report into Pounder within the next few minutes. All are in position with the target acquired and awaiting instructions to proceed. The cross-hairs of their optic-green scopes are zeroed-in on the sentry's temple.

"Pounder to Shooters One, Two, Three, and Four, we are ready to proceed. Please reconfirm your status."

Shooter's One through Four, in-turn, all reconfirm, accordingly.

"O.K. Shooters. We'll do this by the numbers. Mark, by my count: one-thousand one, one-thousand two, one-thousand three. Fire."

Each shooter lets out a slow breath and gently squeezes the trigger. A belch of gas escapes from the silencer at the end of their rifle barrels, verifying that the bullets are outbound and on the way to the targets. The muffled sound of the discharge of the rifles passes unnoticed by the Iraqis far below inside the missile system control center. The thick reinforced design of the concrete walls constructed to withstand the impact of the near miss of an incoming missile, also acts as an excellent sound suppressor.

His face devoid of expression, Shooter One witnesses what the others also see as a mirror image. The impact of the projectile snaps the head of the sentry back like he has been cracked on the skull by a baseball bat. His knees buckle and he slumps to the floor. He never knew what hit him. It was lights out with no pain or suffering. Although only three hundred yards away, the shooters are detached from the events they have just set in motion.

"Shooters, this is Pounder. Report your results."

All four shooters, in-turn, quickly report, "target down."

"Good work, Shooters," Pounder responds. "Gather up your gear and report back to our rendezvous point on the double. We've got more work to do.

"Assault team in position. Remember the drill—preparation, belief, expectation, and execution. Once again, just like we rehearsed. Haven't we got some party favors for our friends down there?"

Lady luck is indeed smiling down on Pounder. While he is wondering what surprises await them, the following scene is unfolding far down below in the Missile System Control Center.

The MSC2 is a dingy and dreary, poorly lit room with all the amenities and creature comforts that adorn the cell of a condemned man awaiting execution on death-row. Stifling heat abounds. The air exchange handler has long since died with no hope of being resurrected due to the United Nations embargo on the shipment of spare parts to Iraq. The stench of tobacco smoke hangs in the air, locked in a life and death struggle with the odor of dried perspiration for the dominant fragrance of the day. Large posters depicting Saddam with a broad smile on his face, and his hand extended in a gesture of friendship adorn the walls surrounding the room.

Two men slouch in their chairs in a zombie like trance, staring straight ahead at the missile launch control panel which they face. Boredom has long since overtaken them. Well into their 20th hour of duty, the members of the missile control team have exhausted all the small talk they can muster up. The clock displaying the official State time, seems to be mocking them. The second hand is creeping so slowly across the Arabic numerals that motion is nearly imperceptible. Could it be possible that they still had another four hours left before their scheduled relief will appear for shift change?

Is this a day that will never end?

At that moment, the voice of the official Iraqi State Radio rudely interrupts the patriotic music piped into the control room. Read in a slow somber tone punctuated with intermittent static, the usual announcement follows informing them that it is time for the morale building speech that Saddam prepares daily for the freedom loving people of Iraq. It is required listening for all citizens six years of age and older.

"Ibrahim, it is time for President Saddam Hussein's message. Quick, go inform the guards to assemble here with us."

"I will get them, Hamad.

"Come quickly, Our President's message is about to begin."

"Ana Jaay," the guard responds, "I am coming."

The voice of Saddam Hussein suddenly fills the room. "The United States is the Great Satan. They are intent on infecting our youth with the abominable plague of their society, which includes drugs, alcohol, pornography, divorce, gays, promiscuity, spouse abuse, decadent music and films, the AIDS epidemic, crime, and lack of modesty in their dress. All of this, will contribute to, and result in their demise.

"The Iraqi people will stand united against injustice and the unjust, and against the invasion and the invaders. The armies of the United States and the armies of its allies remain in the land of our sanctuaries. The occupation and invasion of the Prophet's birthplace and tomb are an insult directed not only against the 200 million Arabs, but the one billion Moslems. They will join and pool all resources to resist this obscene act and defeat the oppressors.

"Every politician knows the United States has been manipulating the world and dictating its terms with no one standing up to confront them with the exception of the brave sons of Iraq. They continue this unjustified and cruel blockade which is depriving the people of Iraq of food and medicine, and cutting off the supply of milk from children who need it. Iraq is a peace-loving nation, but we desire peace which is based on justice.

"Those who attempt to drive a wedge between Arab brothers

should remember that the Arab nation is one nation. Even though it is split now, it is a fact that the majority of its sons, rulers, and peoples are honored to be part of this great nation and they are longing to be one political entity, regardless of the specific characteristics of this or that country. Furthermore, the attempts aimed at promoting the instability constitute a premeditated conspiracy against the Arab nation, at the head of which is lofty Iraq. The traitors, who encouraged those who have been deluded, are a small minority.

"This is an Islamic Jihad. A holy war. When the final battle has taken place, then the Iraqi people, whom God has chosen to be in the forefront, will triumph. The Great Satan will be defeated, his banners torn apart, and deafened by the shouts of Allahu Akhbar, 'God is great and damned be the infidels.'"

"What was that noise, Hamad? Did you hear something?"

"Just the wise words of our President, Ibrahim. You should attempt to focus your attention on his message, and not let your mind wander at an important time like this."

The demolition's expert wraps a triple layer of Primacord around the heavy steel blast door covering the entrance to the MSC2. As he does, he realizes that this must be similar to blowing the hatch on an enemy submarine docked in port. He then inserts the detonator and scrambles back out of the way. There is a thunderous roar, and the door flies back off its hinges exposing the entrance to the silo. They quickly toss in four flash-bang grenades. Pandemonium follows. The Iraqis are temporarily blinded by what seems to be the brightness of a thousand flashbulbs simultaneously exploding in their faces, and thrown against the wall by the deafening blast of two freight trains colliding head-on in their living room. There is shouting and screaming as panic and confusion sets in. Disoriented, one of the guards begins firing his automatic weapon at random.

The assault team goes in first, rappelling down the length of the extended cylinder that connects the surface with the operational area four stories below. Pumped with adrenaline, they complete the trip in near world-record time. Team members hit the floor with their feet spread in a semi-crouch and weapon in firing position, quickly scanning the area in front of him. Visibility is obscured by a residual cloud of magnesium smoke hanging in the air. Two of the missile crew members are curled up on the floor in a fetal position, writhing and babbling in terror. However, a third, who appears to be security, is stumbling across the room with his weapon. The assault team leader shouts, "la, la," meaning, "no, no," but the guard doesn't respond. Having no choice, he fires off a quick burst, instantly cutting the Iraqi down. The entire encounter is over in a matter of seconds.

The assault team rapidly searches the remaining area of the control room. Not finding anything or anyone else that will pose a threat, the situation is defused and the area secure. The "all clear" signal is sounded three times alerting the seizure team standing by up above that it is safe to begin the climb down into the MSC2.

The lead technician on the team has a doctorate in advanced computer system applications. He goes right to work, unpacking his gear from his backpack, assembling the various components, and then plugging in and snapping the connectors into place.

Watching with fascination, Pounder asks, "How do you keep all of that straight?"

"That's what I'm paid for, Pounder. Lucky for us, this is the information age. Recent advances in computers and communications have made possible the opening of doors and unlocking of mysteries that are absolutely mind boggling. Without computer assistance, we couldn't break these access codes in our lifetime. My close friend and associate here, making reference to a computer monitor mounted on a black box inundated with knobs and switches and connected to a keyboard, is one heck of a lot smarter and light-years faster than we are. And perhaps, just as important, mental fatigue is never a problem. She never needs a coffee break, and never makes a mistake. We're talking the closest thing to infallibility that's ever come down the pike. You hook her up properly, turn her on, initialize the 'Cyber Assault Hacker' program, and she does the rest, plugging in numbers sequentially and chugging through the algorithms like Sally Shopper going through the ladies lingerie department on the occasion of the year's greatest sales, the day after Thanksgiving. Check out this digital display. She's already got the first two numbers up. Only five more to go, and we've got the seven digit code that's the key to accessing the missile control system program. As soon as the rest of that field is filled in, we're in business."

Pounder continues to stare at the digital display, praying silently that the five numbers that stand between them and success will soon cooperate and reveal themselves. As he sweats out the next few minutes, it occurs to him that this is exactly what millions of people do all over America, as they anxiously await the selection of the power ball lottery numbers. His daydream is suddenly interrupted by a soft "pinging" noise, indicating that they indeed have a "Bingo." Their dance card is now full and it is time to "swing" into action.

"Doc," as he prefers to be called, is hovering over his keyboard entering the magic code that will allow him to access the software program that directs missile control operations.

"Come on, come to daddy. We're going to make some sweet music together. Come on, don't be shy. There are a lot of people here who have been just dying to meet you. Ah-hah, Gotcha. The hot missile silo locations are numbers one, six, and nine. Now it's just a matter of shutting down the launch capability and disabling the missile rotation feature."

A loud Bronx cheer goes up from the team members who have been urging Doc on in his efforts to successfully do what they could only dream about doing with a computer. It will only be a matter of minutes now before they will complete the dirty deed, flee the scene, and hightail it out of there on their way back to safety. They are all definitely pumped. There was no explaining how good it felt to be pulling Saddam's chain right under his nose, and getting away with it. And, not to mention, all the lives that they were taking out of harm's way.

"Oh, No, exclaimed Doc! Tell me it isn't happening. It can't be. It just can't be."

Pounder's heart stops. He is close to cardiac arrest. Had they been celebrating prematurely? Was it about to rain on their parade?

"What's up Doc? What is it?"

The sheen of perspiration on Doc's forehead and pensive expression on his face, betray his usual "everything is under control" demeanor. "Whoever wrote this program apparently foresaw the day when we would be here at this place doing what we are doing. It seems they built a little extra protection into their software to ward off any unauthorized access. Part way through execution of the patch, we triggered an intrusion detection alarm system releasing a computer virus that immediately infected the missile control program software. The bottom line is, we've shut down the missile launch capability, but the relocation feature is still alive and well. And, the really bad news is that we have no way of knowing when the next rotation of the missiles is scheduled to occur, or where they will end up."

"What you're telling me Doc, is that we're playing a game of Russian Roulette. We've got three bullets and we're spinning the chambers on the revolver not knowing when we'll have a hot round under the hammer. That, of course, is unacceptable. There's got to be something that we can do. Talk to me, Doc! Don't make me come over there."

# CHAPTER SEVENTEEN

## THE FOG OF WAR

*Slash and his fellow F-117 pilots had lifted off from Prince Sultan* Air Base in Saudi Arabia on schedule. As planned, they rendezvoused with KC 135 tankers well out of range of Iraqi radar coverage, topping off their tanks prior to heading north toward Baghdad. After a one and a half hour flight, they arrived at their designated holding point, precisely at the scheduled time over target. They were now in position to respond to Pounder's direction to proceed with the air strikes, and were to maintain orbit until called in.

The flight completed a 360, awaiting the expected radio contact. Each minute that passed seemed like an eternity to Slash. Something was wrong and there was absolutely nothing that he or his companions could do about it, but sweat it out. He had that sick feeling in the pit of his stomach telling him that the news was not going to be good. They did several more 360s, frequently checking the time. Each second was critical at this point, as the mission was falling further and further behind schedule. Slash's mind raced ahead a mile a minute, flooded with possibilities of what could have gone wrong far below in the MSC2. His worst nightmare was that somehow the mission had been compromised and Pounder and the Task Force members had fallen into Iraqi hands. Slash reached for the radio wanting desperately to contact Pounder and see if there was something they could do to assist. However, he reluctantly drew back at the last minute. Under the rules of engagement for this mission, he could not break radio silence until he received the initial transmission from the Task Force.

Suddenly, Slash's heart skipped a beat. It was the sound of Pounder's voice over the radio. He sighed a deep sigh of relief and mopped the perspiration from his brow.

"Task Force Lead to the Midnight Cowboy. Please acknowledge."

"Roger, Task Force Lead. I read you loud and clear. What's your location?"

"We're clear of the MSC2, and 'The fox is in its lair.' Your hot targets are locations one, six, and nine. Do you copy?"

"Roger that. Hot targets are locations one, six, and niner."

"Confirmed, Midnight Cowboy. You are cleared to proceed. Dispense the packages with our warmest regards."

Due to the unforseen problem encountered in the MSC2, Pounder had remained behind while ordering the rest of the Task Force members to evacuate. Receiving transmission of the authorized code words and unaware of Pounder's predicament, the F-117 drivers go to work. Number two armed with BLU-109/B penetration bombs is up first. Maintaining the maximum standoff range to stay as far as possible out of reach of SAM's and AAA, he releases his weapon at high altitude, 20 miles from the target. The laser-guided bomb packs a destructive force with such accuracy and power that it has destroyed the once held myth of invincibility of hardened targets. One of the great lessons to come out of the Gulf War was that hardened aircraft shelters do not ensure survivability. Identified by reconnaissance satellites, targeted, and destroyed by precision-guided penetrating bombs, they are a trap.

The penetrating warhead attacks the reinforced concrete hardened structure of the MSC2 like an industrial strength can opener mugging a 15-ounce can of pork and beans. It boroughs through the concrete, metal plating, and earth like a corkscrew, detonating on the other side of the buffer. A thundering explosion, reminiscent of a volcanic eruption, rips a large gapping hole in the upper structure of the MSC2, exposing the cylindrical shaft leading to the control center four stories below. Debris is spued skyward in a huge cloud of smoke and dust. An incredible feat for a conventional munition, accomplishing that which previously required the employment of tactical nuclear weapons.

Slash follows with his newly developed fall-out suppression weapon, skillfully guiding the smart bomb on a trajectory that delivers it precisely into the area of pulverized concrete and spaghetti-like steel reinforcement bars blown out by the tremendous force of number two's weapon. He scores a bulls eye, right down the hatch, and is immediately rewarded with a ball of fire, accompanied by a deafening explosion. Letting out a deep breath, Slash mutters to himself, "One down and one to go. So far, so good."

\*\*\*

The Airborne Warning and Control System aircraft was nearly 10 hours into orbit. The airspace inside Iraq under observation had been unusually quiet. No abnormal air activity had been observed. The surveillance crew monitoring air traffic over the area of operations had nothing to show for their effort, but a good case of eye strain and tired backsides. The flight had been uneventful, almost to the extent that the mission crew had been lulled into a false sense of security. They were cruising at an altitude of 29,000 feet, with a speed of 420 miles per hour. The aircrew of the E-3 was navigating a wide oval orbit, while maintaining a level heading. Sharp banking turns could interfere with the normal sweep of the radar's beam.

Just about the time the mission crew had reconciled themselves into believing this might be just another milk-run, a small blip appears on the radar screen, immediately followed by a second. The surveillance crew member sits erect in his chair and stares intently at the small track that takes shape. He immediately makes note of the fact that it originated at the coordinates of one of Iraq's major airbases located at Najaf, south of Baghdad.

In the adjoining mission crew section, a weapon controller seated at his multipurpose console picks up the track on his screen and begins the process of attempting to identify the contact. While it appears intuitively obvious to even the most casual observer, based on the data displayed on the screen, that he has two Iraqi military aircraft airborne, you don't proceed on intuition in this business. The contact is officially unidentified at this point. The E-3C's APX-103 IFF/Tactical Digital Data Link System is quickly brought into play. This sophisticated "Identification Friend or Foe" can interrogate the transponder of nearly any aircraft in the world within a range of 200 miles. It is used to separate the good guys from the bad guys and preclude shooting down friendly aircraft. If the expected coded reply is received from the aircraft being interrogated, it is officially identified as friendly. If the proper response is not received, the aircraft's identification remains unknown. However, in this case, the crew member is about 99.9 percent certain that the blips he is observing are two hostile Iraqi miliary aircraft. After tracking them for a few minutes to determine their course heading and speed, it is clear they could pose a threat to the mission. These two aircraft were heading into airspace that would be dangerously close to that occupied by Slash and his friends. They were definitely "Bandits," exhibiting aggressive behavior.

It is time to alert the F-117 drivers of the intruders, and bring the flight of F-15C Eagles on board. The E-3 is equipped with both UHF and VHF communications, as well as a Joint Tactical Information Distribution System data link terminal which allows units with different computer systems to share critical operational data. Flight leader of the F-15Cs hears the duty AWACS weapons controller calling, assigning them the task of protecting the F-117s. "This is Peace Sentinel. We have two 'Bogeys' in sector four, at 'Bullseye'-120 degrees and 95 miles. They are cruising at Mach .82 at an altitude of 26,000 feet."

The voice of the senior weapons controller is clear and steady. He had proven himself in the skies over Iraq during the precarious days of Desert Storm. He has just informed the F-15 pilots of the location, speed, and altitude of the enemy aircraft. Their location has been described in reference to the capital city of Baghdad, referred to as "Bullseye." The coordinates are described in this manner, to avoid giving away the location of the F-15 flight, if the enemy happens to be eavesdropping on their radio frequency. Mach is the speed of sound at sea level, or 760 feet per second. Since sound travels faster in a denser medium, an aircraft's Mach number is dependent on altitude. "On their present heading, they will pose a threat to our F-117 air strikes. You are authorized to engage per Operation Desert Heat Contingency Plan B. Proceed under my command and control."

This was the moment that all fighter pilots dream of and live for their entire lives. They have the green light to engage the enemy. All those years of training and hard work are about to pay off in big dividends. While their hair isn't on fire yet, spontaneous combustion will occur within the next few minutes. Armed to the teeth with a maximum load of four AIM-120 and four AIM-9, air-to-air missiles, hunting season is officially open. The weapons controller is a master of air combat maneuvering, the art of getting an aircraft into position to shoot down the other guy, preferably from behind, before he gets a shot at you. He skillfully guides the F-15 jocks in to intercept the "Bandits," vectoring them on a heading and altitude that places them above and behind the two unsuspecting Iraqi pilots.

Staring off into space in bewilderment and disbelief at the huge ball of flame and accompanying black smoke billowing up in the distance that had once been Saddam's prized Iraqi Missile System Control Center, the Iraqi pilots exclaim, "Momkin," Is it possible? The majority of Iraqi pilot training had been conducted by the former Soviet Union. Emphasis was placed on rigid rules, strict command & control oversight, and standardized tactics. Consequently, while the Iraqi pilots could take off and land safely, they were grossly lacking in advanced air-to-air tactics. As such, they were no match for their Western trained counterparts.

With their attention temporarily distracted by the spectacular scene ahead, they are moments late in remembering the cardinal rule of aerial combat–"check-six." As a result, they find themselves in a "worst-case" scenario. The enemy is located above and behind them. They are two ducks on a pond, about to become duck soup.

The F-15s roll in on their prey, triggering their weapons at a range of seven nautical miles. The heat seeking AIM-9 Sidewinder missiles scream from their armament stations on the underwing pylons of the aircraft, rapidly closing the interval between the two adversaries. The only warning the Iraqi pilots receive is a short burst of flashing red light from an indicator in the cockpit. It is the last sight they would see. The missiles impact the rear fuselage of the two Mirage F-1 Aircraft near the engine exhaust port where they detonate. The aircraft instantaneously break in pieces amid a ball of fire. These guys are history. They tangled with the best and came in second place in a deadly game where second place doesn't finish.

A collective ear-bursting scream of emotion emanates from the cockpits of the F-15s, as the USAF pilots celebrate their victory. There are two confirmed enemy kills, which means that someone is well on his way to becoming an Ace. This is modern air warfare. No dog fight, just the optimum employment of a fighter plane. Reduced to its bare essentials, the sole function of a combat aircraft is to act as a platform from which ordnance is delivered on enemy targets. Although a lot of things about aerial combat have changed since the historic battles of "Snoopy and the Red Baron" in the skies over Germany, the adrenaline rush is still there and just as real.

Approaching the final target, Slash encounters unexpected opposition. The time lost as a result of the glitch in the MSC2 has placed the mission about twenty minutes behind schedule. Alerted by reports of unusual air activity, the Air Defense Commander has given the order to shut down the integrated Iraqi air defense network in his Sector. Conditioned by the dark days of the Gulf War and Operation Desert Storm, he is under the mistaken impression that Iraq has come under a saturated U.S. air attack. As such, leaving the net on the air would be tantamount to radioing the precise coordinates of his physical location to the attacking enemy aircraft.

With the air defense network down, the individual surface-to-air missile battery commanders are given the verbal order to "fire at will." Anything that moves within their airspace is fair game. The initial SAM streaks up from the ground, lighting up the sky for miles around in every direction. At first glance, it appears to Slash that he is witnessing a shuttle launch from the Florida Cape. There is no mistaking what is going on. Every Iraqi on duty that evening is clearly hopping to cash in on Saddam's promised $14,000 bounty for bagging an American aircraft. Several additional SAM launches quickly follow. Slash watches the smoke trails from the missiles angling up from the ground. There appear to be at least three SAM sites located within a few miles of the target area. This ballistic missile silo is as well defended as Hanoi was against the USAF air raids over North Viet Nam by Thailand-based F-105 Thunderchiefs in 1966. That is saying a mouthful. Hanoi had been a target more heavily defended than Berlin during the height of WW II.

Without guidance tracking radar, the SAM batteries are firing blindly at the nearly invisible Nighthawk. However, it was equally clear that with the number of SAM launches, the Iraqis are big game hunting with a shotgun, not a rifle. Quantity, not quality is the order of the day. The Iraqis are operating under the theory that if you throw enough Jell-O up against a wall, sooner or later some of it is going to stick. Slash is so preoccupied with flying and navigating through this munitions hailstorm that he can no longer keep an eye on all the launch sites. There appear to be three or four SAMs airborne at any one time, with missiles detonating all around him in lightening bright flashes. Combat is chaos and the line between control and mass confusion is sometimes indistinguishable. He continues to bump the stick forward attempting to nose the aircraft down lower on the deck to avoid the SAMs, only to find himself within range of the anti-aircraft artillery sites. The flak is so thick, he could cut it with a knife.

With the wall-to-wall violence that surrounds Slash, tension in the cockpit is now at a level of about 12.5 on a scale from one to ten. His face is pale and tense and his heart is pounding wildly. The site nearest him at his nine o'clock position, launches a missile that never seems to reach the horizon. Slash watches it rise and then almost immediately level off. As he looks back over his left shoulder attempting to locate it, the SAM suddenly appears out of nowhere.

Rapidly closing on his aircraft on a collision course, its rocket plume resembles the early morning sunrise. Breaking hard left, Slash narrowly averts a direct hit as the missile streaks by. However, before he can let out a sigh of relief, it explodes in a huge blinding flash. The Iraqis had apparently programmed the SAMs to self-detonate at either motor burn out or at a preset altitude.

Hundreds of jagged pieces of shrapnel are instantaneously flung in every direction, many finding a resting place in Slash's Nighthawk. The wounded bird is coming unglued around him, like a quail hit with a load of buck shot. The fuel tank has been penetrated, and JP-5 jet fuel is streaming from the aircraft. Ignited by its afterburner, the Nighthawk appears as a yellowish ball of fire streaking across the night sky. The instrument panel is lit up like a pinball machine, and warning indicators are sounding like a four-alarm fine. Although Slash is physically unharmed, the close proximity of the explosion rang his bell. With the rapid loss of fuel he is experiencing, he has no options available, but to continue on full afterburner, hoping that he remains airborne until reaching the target. The Nighthawk is still airworthy, but suddenly has a mind of its own. It is vibrating so violently, it appears on the verge of disintegration. Things are now so chaotic, that Slash is no longer in control, merely a reluctant passenger along for the ride. The deafening roar of aircraft engines and the pungent odor of jet fuel impinge on his senses, threatening to cast everything else aside. He is fully enveloped in the "fog of war," ten times worse that flying blindly through a cloud bank with no visibility and the resulting turbulence. With his flight suit soaked in sweat, and calling on all the divine powers in the universe for calm, Slash frantically reaches for his radio.

"This is 'The Midnight Cowboy.' I've taken a hit. May Day, May Day! I've got one turning and one burning. Last call before fall. Do you read me Task Force Lead?"

"Slash, this is Doc, and I copy. Pounder had some unfinished business with the Iraqis that he stayed behind to take care of. Give me your position and eject. I'll radio the rendezvous point for search and rescue. I repeat, get out of there before it's too late."

Slash's inborn will to live collides head on with his acquired sense of duty. However, the contest is short lived. His pilot training and resultant self-mastery quickly triumph. "Negative, tower. I also have a little unfinished business. I'm still airborne and I might just have enough left in this lead sled to get me over target number four before good old mother earth and I are flying at the same altitude. Nobody's going home until all the cows are in the barn."

Like an enormous wounded bird, the Night Hawk struggles to remain airborne as a blazing stream of flame and black smoke bellow out behind. As Slash approaches his target, Iraqi security personnel guarding the missile silo hear the roar of aircraft engines.

"Look! There at three o'clock, it's on-fire and headed right toward us. "Jawiah Tayyaarah Muskila Kabir." An air force aircraft in distress. They quickly utter the "Shahada," or death prayer, which Muslims must recite under these circumstances. "There is no God but Allah, and Mohammed is His Prophet."

Slash's aircraft becomes a manned ballistic missile as he buys a Nighthawk. He slams into the missile silo, reminiscent of Japanese Kamikaze pilot attacks on American ships in the Pacific during WW II. There is a deafening roar and resultant blast of heat as the impact detonates his remaining weapon which simultaneously explodes the missile's warhead.

Slash's last thoughts in that nanosecond before impact were of his father pinning those silver wings on his chest on graduation day from flight school, and then popping him a snappy salute. His dad's face had been lit up like a roman candle on the 4th of July, with his chest about to burst from the pride that swelled up in him over his son's success. However, as they had embraced, he had seen a single teardrop escape from the corner of his father's eye and slowly cascade down the furrows of his weathered face. For years, Slash had relived that moment, frozen in time, unable to fully comprehend what had prompted that sentiment on such a festive occasion, and from a man who had been absolutely rock-solid in charge of his emotions. Fighting communism and keeping the world safe for democracy was a tough job, but someone had to do it!

***

The remaining members of the Task Force reach the rendezvous point and join up with the extraction team that is to fly them back to the safety of the staging area outside Iraq. The stress was beginning to dissipate. It would be followed by elation, and then by an all-consuming fatigue.

"How did it go, Doc?"

"Well, let's put it this way. I'm not going back for a curtain call. I don't think they fully appreciated our performance. What's wrong with those people? We rehearse for weeks to put on a really big show and what do we get?"

"Everybody on board. We need to exit, 'stage left,' before they get a chance to give us what they think we truly deserve. Are we all present and accounted for?"

"All except Pounder, sir."

"What happened to him?"

"We successfully disabled the launch control capability in the MSC2, but with the compressed time frame we were working with, we couldn't be completely sure the missile exchange system was permanently inoperative. It is activated under program control through a random number generator. There appeared to be an emergency manual override, but it worked somewhat like a 'deadman's' switch. Someone had to be physically present to trigger it and keep it depressed. As soon as it was released, the system was reactivated.

"We were able to determine the physical location of the three missiles with the warheads, and radio the information to Slash. However, they were subject to move at any time. With the short interval of time that was expected to lapse between our extraction from the control room and execution of the air strike on the facility, we were pretty sure that all of the missiles would stay put. However, Pounder said, 'pretty sure' wasn't good enough, not even for Government work in this case. There was too much at stake. We had to be absolutely certain those missiles didn't get legs. This was a one-time good deal and we weren't going to get another crack at it. We were running out of time, and the operation had to move forward. Pounder stayed behind and ordered us out of the control room. We met up with our Arab friends and they took us back to the rendezvous point.

"Oh yes, he did give me these before we left. He said, he wanted his wife to have them."

"What are they?"

"They're his dog tags, sir."

"His dog tags! What in the world was he doing with his dog tags? He's been out of the military for several years."

"What can I say, sir? All I know is that he was wearing them at the time."

# EPILOGUE

## TO ABSENT FRIENDS

*President Maxwell strides into the room. He is fastidiously* punctual as usual. Dark shadows beneath his eyes betray a lack of sleep. He had tossed and turned the entire night, unable to dismiss operation "Desert Heat" from his mind. The sheer weight of the responsibility of acting as Commander in Chief when ordering Americans in harm's way, was simply overwhelming. " O.K. people, please take your seats. We need to begin so that we can get through this as quickly as possible."

Looking down the table at his National Security Advisor, he inquires, "Do we have a battle damage assessment?"

"Well sir, we have a preliminary report. Details are very sketchy at this point. Our people are out of Iraq, and it appears that the mission went pretty much as planned. All major objectives were met. Saddam's missile system control center was destroyed, as well as all three missile silos that housed the threatening weapons of mass destruction."

"Good, outstanding! What about casualties?"

Doing his best to keep his voice steady and speech normal, Mitch Richman responds, almost casually. "We have two dead, Mr. President. No report on the Iraqis."

Although in his own mind, he did not so much as flinch at hearing the response, the grimace on the face of the President of the United States was readily apparent to everyone else in the room. "Who did we lose?"

"Two Viet Nam vets, Sir. The primary operative on the ground who went by the nickname 'Pounder,' and an airplane driver, known as 'Slash.'"

"Bodies, remains?"

Looking up from his notes, Mitch elects to address the question with the old "good news, bad news" response in an effort to not make it sound any worse than it already was. " I guess you could say that there is both good news and bad news on that score, Mr. President. The bad news is that there are none. Pounder became trapped in the MSC2 at the time of the air strike and was not able to evacuate. Slash took some unexpected ground fire en route to the final target and was apparently unable to eject. He augered in with his aircraft."

President Maxwell does not react well to the information. His normal ruddy complexion, having lost much of its color, appears ashen, and his breathing becomes shallow. Feeling faint, he steadies himself, and reaches for the glass on the table in front of him. Giving the tall water glass the "bottoms-up" treatment, he empties its contents with a single swallow. Pausing for a brief moment to allow the reviving effects of the liquid refreshment to set in, he inquires further. "That's ironic. I guess you could chalk it up to bad luck that one of them was unable to get out, but how do you account for both of them experiencing the same problem? Was our training adequate?"

Sensing that his boss was hurting, the NSA decides to make "fate" the scapegoat. Fate has broad shoulders and is always an acceptable alternative to the assumption of personal responsibility in difficult matters. "Perhaps it was fate, Mr. President. Sometimes, you just can't explain these things."

President Maxwell, anxious to exonerate himself and his conscience from any lingering guilt, is appreciative of the avenue of escape offered up by his National Security Advisor. "You're probably right, Mitch. And, the good news?"

"There are no bodies, Mr. President. Both individuals were

essentially cremated and their ashes distributed throughout Iraq by the extreme heat and force of the blasts created by the explosions. Therefore, Saddam has no hostages to parade through the streets of Baghdad in an attempt to embarrass the U.S. and claim a propaganda victory. And, we don't have to get down on our hands and knees and beg for the return of their remains. The only evidence that anyone has been there is four large craters in the ground that just happened to appear overnight in precisely the same locations as Saddam's MSC2 complex and the three missile silos that housed his weapons of mass destruction."

Staring off into space and sighing a deep sigh of relief, President Maxwell accepts the reality of the situation. They now need to move ahead and tie up the loose ends. "So, it's over, but how do we bring it to closure? How much do we tell the American people, and when and what do we tell them? What do we say about the loss of the two participants?"

Mitch discerns that the President is gaining strength, but is not out the woods quite yet. He needs a good positive push in the right direction to clear the last hurdle. " Remember, Mr. President, this whole operation was classified 'top secret.' Therefore, we can justify the non-release of details for national security reasons. It's a privilege to serve your country. What's more, they understood the risks. We've got to put our best face forward on this."

Secretary of Defense Grant Sherman could not help himself. While he chose to remain a silent bystander, he swallowed hard as his mind fully absorbed the words spoken by the National Security Advisor. "What's more, 'they' understood the risks." These two brave gentlemen whom he had declined to meet, and who, within the last few hours had died for their country, no longer had names. They were now being referred to as "they." What's more, "they" would never be recognized for what "they" did. A major threat to world peace had been removed, and the two gentlemen primarily responsible, had not only given up their lives, but also their personal identity. There would be no internment at Arlington National Cemetery, no flag draped casket, no twenty-one gun salute, and no flag presented to the next of kin on behalf of a grateful nation.

Unaware of the burdensome thoughts of his Secretary of Defense, President Maxwell sensed it was time for some political "spin control." Looking in the direction of Hal Justin, his Chief of Staff, he asks. "What do the damage control people recommend?"

"We've got to go public and fast, Mr. President. Straight talk to the American people on national television. Get the best version of the story we can out there, before the investigative reporters have a chance to come up with their own. Address it as an issue of freedom. That's something that every American relates to and sympathizes with. Roll it up in the flag–red, white, and blue. Then, declare victory and move on."

President Maxwell is suddenly revitalized. The positive reassurance of his staff has displaced the compunction that he had felt a few minutes earlier. "That's the attitude I like! Hey, don't forget, we're the good guys. And, we need to start acting like it. We didn't kill them. Saddam did. Wasn't it General McArthur who once said, 'There's no substitute for victory, but you've got to expect losses?' Two lives! Some would say, a small price to pay for what we achieved."

The words were music to Mitch Richman's ears. Recognizing that his boss had fully absorbed the "stick" and turned the corner, it was time to hang a "carrot" out there to positively reinforce his response. "We acted with courage and restraint, Mr. President, the way a superpower is suppose to behave. Our response was proportional, reasonable, and responsible. In addition, we placed a high premium on civility in doing everything possible to minimize civilian casualties. And, perhaps most important, we have commitments from Israel and the Palestinian Authority that bring us to the brink of a lasting peace agreement in the Middle East. With this magnificent foreign policy achievement, your legacy as one of the great Presidents of all time, is all but assured."

Seizing the moment and fully regaining control of the meeting, President Maxwell turns to his Press Secretary. "Alert the networks. They'll need to pre-empt their regular programming. Tell them to make 30 minutes available exactly one hour from now for a national security address by the President of the United States. We'll take the high ground, make our case, and slam the door on anyone foolish enough to question our actions in view of the grave national security implications. And, put an airtight lid on this subject until that time. I don't want any details leaking out before I go live to the American public. If the press gets wind of it, they'll have a feeding frenzy. Stonewall if necessary–'we've heard the reports and we're looking into it. It's White House policy that we don't comment on unconfirmed news stories.' I want to stop the bleeding before it starts. This operation is going into the books as a success. We will release a sanitized version of what took place in Iraq to the public at a later date."

Pointing to his Chief of Staff, National Security Advisor, and his Press Secretary, President Maxwell exclaims, "let's get started! We've got less that an hour to put the finishing touches on this."

The National Security Advisor attempts to offer a bit of advice regarding the opening of the speech to get the President off on the right foot with the American public. "Mr. President, I would recommend that you broach this topic with the American public very gingerly. I would approach it as follows..." He is cut off in mid-sentence by the President who scowls his displeasure in Mitch's direction.

"Dog gone it, Mitch! Give me a little credit. I've been around long enough to know how to get on and off the stage. Just fill in the middle part for me. I'll take it from there."

***

A hastily arranged news conference is convened. As President Maxwell enters the packed room, the press secretary announces, "The President of the United States," and the press corps springs to its feet. He slips behind the podium bearing the Seal of the President of the United States of America, and carefully places his notes on the Rosewood lectern. The President is wearing a lightly starched, freshly pressed white shirt, and his favorite sincere navy-blue pin-striped business suit, garnished with a wine colored "power" necktie. The

White House make-up people have worked their magic, successfully hiding the dark circles under his eyes. On a somber occasion such as this, it is of utmost importance that he look and act "Presidential." He must appear to the entire world to be the man at the top of the nation's government, fully in charge and completely under control. Any indication of fatigue or anxiety on his part might betray this image, causing the public to doubt the sincerity or conviction of the important national security message he is about to deliver. Looking straight into the TV cameras with what he hoped was total self-assurance, and praying silently for the strength to do his duty to the best of his ability, President Maxwell clears his throat one last time and begins to speak.

"Good evening, my fellow Americans. Several hours ago, I authorized a pre-emptive air strike on Iraq to neutralize and remove a threat to our national security.

"Intelligence sources gathered information indicating that Iraq had developed three weapons of mass destruction with both the ability and apparent intent to deliver them on Tel Aviv, Israel, the U.S. airbase located at Incirlik, Turkey, and Prince Sultan Airbase in Saudi Arabia. We subsequently undertook an exhaustive cross-checking of various sources to validate the data. Our findings verified that it was a credible report, and thus, a credible threat. Therefore, we had to treat it as serious, and act with expediency and resolve to neutralize it.

"Just before we went live on the air, I received a preliminary battle damage assessment. I am happy to report that the mission was a success. The threat has been removed. Saddam has once again relearned the powerful lesson that America will not stand idly by while he threatens the peace and security of his neighbors, and the lives of U.S. citizens.

"There are no hard choices when it comes to issues of freedom. We simply cannot compromise that which we hold so dear and sacred. It is the very fabric of American life—who we are, and what we stand for. Without it, we would cease to exist as a nation. But, it is not enough just to talk about freedom. When it is threatened, we must act. Freedom has never been free. And, sometimes it comes with a very heavy price. The freedoms that we enjoy today are those which our courageous forefathers fought for and often died to acquire and preserve. The legacy of our generation can be no less. We must choose freedom over fear.

"Our heartfelt prayers and thanks go out to all of those brave men and women who have stepped forward without hesitation to serve their nation so valiantly in its time of need. These are the qualities that heroes are made of. They are the same qualities that made and have kept America great and free ever since our founding fathers landed at Plymouth Rock, dedicating their lives to raising up a great Republic that would forever be a beacon of freedom to the entire world. The world will sleep more securely tonight and awake a better place to raise our children in the morn, by what we have accomplished this day. Good night, and God bless America."

As the President departs the podium, a White House Reporter calls out after him. "Mr. President, Mr. President! Can you tell us who was involved in this operation and if there were any casualties?"

President Maxwell draws a deep breath and responds. "I'm sorry, but because of the obvious nature of the sensitivity and security of a covert military operation against Iraq such as this, that information must remain classified at this time. Please, no further questions."

## THE END

# ABOUT THE AUTHOR

Robert L. Jones, a graduate of the Air War College and the Air Force Institute of Technology's M.S. program, is a former Air Force Lt. Colonel with 20 years service. In addition to the three and one-half years he spent in Southeast Asia during the Vietnam War, he served with the Presidential Wing at Andrews AFB, Maryland, was a Squadron Commander with the 8th Tactical Fighter Wing in Kunsan, Korea, and worked as a Military Planner at the Pentagon. He was awarded 18 military medals, citations, and ribbons, including the Joint Service Commendation Medal, the Vietnam Gallantry Cross with Palm, and the Bronze Star. Following his military service, he accepted employment with a defense contractor in the Middle East. As Vice President of their Saudi Arabian operations, he was responsible for training the Saudi Arabian Armed Forces in the operation of their latest high-tech weapon systems acquired from the United States. Defying his CEO's direction to evacuate during Saddam's daily SCUD missile attacks on the capital city of Riyadh, he stayed on through the end of the Gulf War. Departing Saudi Arabia after a thirteen year stay, he told his many Arab friends, "I felt like I was leaving home, rather than returning home."

# ABOUT GREATUNPUBLISHED.COM

greatunpublished.com is a website that exists to serve writers and readers, and remove some of the commercial barriers between them. When you purchase a greatunpublished.com title, whether you receive it in electronic form or in a paperback volume or as a signed copy of the author's manuscript, you can be assured that the author is receiving a majority of the post-production revenue. Writers who join greatunpublished.com support the site and its marketing efforts with a per-title fee, and a portion of the site's share of profits are channeled into literacy programs.

So by purchasing this title from greatunpublished.com, you are helping to revolutionize the publishing industry for the benefit of writers and readers.
And for this we thank you.